D0587055

Available from Michael Kurland and Titan Books

THE PROFESSOR MORIARTY NOVELS

The Infernal Device
Death By Gaslight
The Great Game
The Empress of India
Who Thinks Evil

A PROFESSOR
MORIARTY
NOVEL

THE
EMPRESS
OF
INDIA

MICHAEL KURLAND

TITAN BOOKS

THE EMPRESS OF INDIA
Print edition ISBN: 9781783293322
E-book edition ISBN: 9781783293339

Published by Titan Books
A division of Titan Publishing Group Ltd
144 Southwark Street, London SE1 0UP

First edition: September 2014
1 2 3 4 5 6 7 8 9 10

A CIP catalogue record for this title is available from the British Library.

Printed and bound in Great Britain by CPI Group Ltd.

Did you enjoy this book? We love to hear from our readers.
Please email us at: readerfeedback@titanemail.com

To receive advance information, news, competitions, and exclusive offers online, please sign up for the Titan newsletter on our website:
TITANBOOKS.COM

For Linda—
Let me count the ways...

PROLOGUE

All the world's a stage,
And all the men and women merely players:
They have their exits and their entrances;
And one man in his time plays many parts...
WILLIAM SHAKESPEARE

FROM THE UNPUBLISHED JOURNAL OF JOHN H. WATSON, M.D.
It is with a heavy heart and much trepidation that I set down on
these pages the incidents surrounding the sudden and mysterious
disappearance of Sherlock Holmes. I shall record the few things that
I now know, as they happened, and can only hope that later entries in
this journal will reveal a satisfactory explanation, and indeed will record
the return of Holmes to his familiar surroundings alive and unharmed.

It was precisely one week ago, Tuesday, the fourth of February
1890, that saw the beginning of the incidents that I am about to
relate. My wife had gone to Bristol for the fortnight, visiting an
aged and infirm distant relation (indeed, she is not yet returned),
and so I found myself at loose ends that afternoon after completing
my hospital rounds and seeing two or three private patients at their
homes. I decided to brave the chill winds a bit longer and knock up
my old friend and companion to see if he was free to share a bite of
dinner with me.

"Ah, Watson," Holmes said, turning around to peer at me as I entered the old, familiar sitting room, "quite recovered, I see."

"Why, yes, thank you," I said, hanging my overcoat and scarf on the brass hook by the door. "I won't bother asking you how you know I have been ill; you probably deduced it from a little spot of grease on my waistcoat."

"Actually, from that second handkerchief peeping out of your back pocket," Holmes told me, "as well as the fact that you're wearing your Windsor hat, which I know even the coldest weather would not cause you to put on unless you were in the grip of the, ah, grippe, or something of the sort."

"And that I'm recovered?" I asked, pulling off the hat in question.

"Well, look at you," Holmes said. "Despite the precautions you felt it necessary to take when you left the house this morning, the spare handkerchief seems to be unused, and you seem quite like your sprightly usual self."

"Quite so," I agreed. "Quite so. And I've come up to invite you to dine with me at the Croydon, if you've nothing else on."

"But I have, Watson," Holmes exclaimed. "And you shall join me. Your timing is excellent." He jumped to his feet and strode to the door, clapping me on the back as he passed. "Just give me a moment to throw on my overcoat and we'll be on our way to a better, or at least more interesting, dinner than the Croydon could supply."

"What is it, Holmes?" I asked, pulling my own overcoat back on.

Holmes grabbed his cane and bowler from the rack by the door, wrapped a long silk scarf around his neck, and started down the stairs. "Come along, Watson," he said over his shoulder, "and dine with me at the Bank of England!"

"Really, Holmes," I said, hurrying after him. "I'm delighted to be of assistance, as always, but what is to be our agenda? Is this to be an evening of hiding in the cellar waiting for criminals to tunnel up into the vaults? Are we to bring sandwiches and revolvers, and perhaps a jug of hot tea?"

"Not at all, old friend," Holmes reassured me. "The dinner will be in the private dining room of the Honorable Eustace Bergarot, the governor of the bank, and the meal and the wine will be of the finest his personal kitchen has to offer. In return, I believe, I will be expected to offer advice on some trifling problem of bank security over our post-prandial snifter of brandy and several of the governor's excellent cigars."

"But, Holmes," I protested, "you can't just bring me along, uninvited—"

"Nonsense!" Holmes expostulated, winding a long scarf around his neck against the damp chill of the February evening. "Besides, the Honorable Bergarot mentioned that he enjoyed those little pieces you write about my cases, and warned me that if you joined us our conversation over dinner was to be regarded as confidential, sub-rosa as it were, and you were not to put it in one of your little stories. His phrase, 'little stories,' not mine, old chap. So, you see, you have explicitly been invited."

Holmes raised his arm to hail a passing hansom cab, and we were on our way to visit that ancient institution that has become known as the Old Lady of Threadneedle Street.

* * *

The dining room in the private chambers in the Bank of England was small, furnished with comfortable leather-covered chairs around an oval cherrywood table, rather like a private room at one of the better clubs. Its walls were covered with framed mementos from two centuries of private banking with clients that included dukes, earls, and archbishops, as well as sultans, emirs, aghas, kings, and queens. The Honorable Eustace Bergarot, a short, heavy man with muttonchop whiskers and a totally bald head, put us at our ease immediately with his informal manner and his humorous attitude toward the perils of banking and life. I should say put me at my ease, since Holmes has long since ceased to be impressed by any man or woman, or surprised by any circumstance that I am aware of.

We, in our turn, entertained the Honorable Bergarot with tales of Holmes's exploits. I told the tales, actually, and Holmes corrected me when I strayed too far from the truth, or drifted too far from the strict, almost scientific narrative into the romantic. Holmes still fails to understand that most people want to hear about the human aspects of his cases and not about what he deduced from two specks of green wool on a brown coverlet or a smear of liver sausage on the cheek of the portrait of a seventeenth-century baronet. I told Bergarot of a couple of cases I intend to write up someday that I believe show the human side of Holmes's work. In my notes I call them "The Case of the Alabaster Skull," and "The Case of the Myopic Magician."

After the dinner dishes were cleared away, Bergarot, as predicted, produced a decanter of brandy from the tantalus on the sideboard and a box of cigars from a drawer in the same sideboard, and reflected on the security aspects of running the world's most important bank. He told us, for example, of an incident in the 1830s when the directors of the bank received a letter from a man who offered to meet them in the bullion vaults at a time of their choosing. They didn't believe the letter, but took the anonymous author up on his challenge, assembling in the vault one night. At the appointed time there was a scraping sound, two of the floorboards were pushed aside, and a man in dirty white coveralls pulled himself up out of the hole thus revealed.

The man worked in the London sewers, and he had discovered, quite by accident, an ancient drain running directly under the bank and connecting to the vault. For his honesty in not making off with the millions of pounds' worth of bullion within easy grasp, the bank rewarded him £800. Which was a small fortune for a sewerman, but still one wonders how the figure was arrived at.

After perhaps half an hour of brandy, cigars, and stories, Bergarot leaned forward. "Now, if you have no objection," he said, "a brief spot of business." He put his hands flat on the table. "Mr. Holmes, on behalf of the Bank of England, I would like to employ you."

"So I surmised," Holmes said. "To do what?"

Bergarot considered. "I'm not sure how to put it," he confessed. "Perhaps it would be nearer to the mark to say that the bank would like to place you on retainer for the next few months. We would like you to, as the barristers say, hold a watching brief."

Holmes nodded. "And for what am I to be watching, burglars rising out of the drains?"

"Ah, yes, well, the answer to that is difficult. We don't know exactly. There is—now, this is strictly confidential, you understand—there is a large quantity of gold bullion even now being gathered in Calcutta for shipment to London, specifically for storage in our vaults. It is gold reserve that we are to hold for several Indian princes and maharajas and the like—people who rule over immensely wealthy provinces of India."

"I see," Holmes said. "The Raj is making sure that the underling princes behave by holding their wealth in protective custody."

"Even though it's a great aggregate of gold, it's only a small part of their collective wealth, Mr. Holmes," Bergarot said. "And, as many of these princes are now sending their children to public school or university here in England, I think we hold even more effective assurances of their good behavior. The gold is being sent by a group of the more, ah, progressive maharajas, who intend to use it to modernize their kingdoms and provide services for their subjects. Also part of the reserve is to be used to back a new paper currency that will be used throughout the subcontinent. Or such is my understanding. Besides, the Bank of England is a privately held company, and we do not make government policy."

"True," Holmes admitted. "But I don't know what you need my services for. I assume that this hoard will be adequately guarded. Surely you must take no chances with such a responsibility."

"It is precisely with the idea of taking no chances that we wish to hire you," Bergarot explained. "As you must know, shipments like this are best conducted in complete secrecy. Well, somehow word of this shipment has leaked out. Rumors have spread through the upper classes, and I must assume they have filtered down to the lower orders. Why, only last weekend at a dinner party the Duchess of Denver asked me whether we were going to have to enlarge our vaults to hold all this new gold."

"Ah!" Holmes said. "And are you?"

"No," Bergarot said. "Our vault space is adequate to the occasion.

But we are worried that, as word seems to have gotten out, criminal gangs might be planning to make an assault on the gold."

"They might indeed," Holmes agreed. "There is one man in particular—but that is merely surmise."

"We would like you to surmise, Mr. Holmes," Bergarot told him. "We would like you to use your knowledge of the criminal classes to tell us what we must guard against. Also we would like you to use your contacts in the criminal underworld to discover any plots against the shipment so that we can foil them before they have a chance to mature."

"How is the bullion being shipped?" Holmes asked.

"In the steamship *The Empress of India*. A special vault is even now being constructed in the cargo hold. The ship leaves for Calcutta at the end of the week. It will be used to take the currency to India, and to bring the gold back. The return journey should begin in about two months."

"Ah! The paper money is being printed here."

"Yes. The Tainsburn and Belaugh Mint here in London is printing the paper currency. We are not too concerned with protecting that on its way to Calcutta, as the currency is of a new design, and thus it is useless to anyone until after it has been introduced. We are concerned with safeguarding the gold on its journey from Calcutta to our vault."

Holmes shook his head. "That is not merely a watching brief you require of me, Mr. Bergarot; an assignment of that nature would occupy me full time until the shipment is secure in your vaults."

"Yes, of course," Bergarot agreed. "And we will pay you commensurately."

"I wasn't thinking of the money, sir," Holmes said. "I have other commitments at the moment."

"Surely none as important as this?"

"They are as important to the people involved," Holmes said. "But I'll see what I can do. I'll give you as much of my time as possible, and we'll have to hope that it will be enough. In the meantime, ask Scotland Yard to send along either Inspector Gregson or Inspector

Lestrade; I've found them to be the most alert and capable of the men of the detective division."

"I'll do that. Thank you, Mr. Holmes," Bergarot said, reaching over and shaking his hand.

* * *

When we arrived back at Baker Street, Holmes suggested that I stay the night. "You can have your old room," he said, "and leave for your hospital rounds tomorrow after breakfast."

"Gladly, and thank you," I told him. "And I have no rounds tomorrow."

"All the better. You can assist me in a little direct research. We'll let the Old Lady of Threadneedle Street pay your wages for the day."

"What do you have in mind?" I asked.

"Merely eliminating a few improbabilities," he told me. And, in his usual infuriatingly taciturn manner, he offered no further information.

Holmes stayed up long after I had retired, poring over ancient maps and charts of London that he took from his vast collection of such things, or so I surmised from the clutter of such documents on the table and the empty coffee urn on the sideboard when I arose the next morning. After Mrs. Hudson served up her usual overabundance of good, wholesome British food, we strode out into the chill fog in search of, so Holmes informed me, a specific manhole cover. "There are several possibilities according to the old maps," he told me. "We have to see which one still exists. If one man can come in through the drains, possibly another can follow where he led."

"But Holmes," I protested, "that was over fifty years ago. Surely that access has been thoroughly sealed by now."

"Probably," Holmes admitted, "but it's best to be sure."

It was close onto noon when Holmes found a suitable manhole in an alley by the side of an old brick office building on King William Street, so we paused for lunch at a nearby chophouse. By this I could tell that Holmes wasn't taking the current investigation too seriously. When he was truly on the scent of a criminal, or gathering information in a case, he would often forget meals entirely, sometimes for several days. It was this sort of single-mindedness, combined with his high intelligence and his great font of specialized knowledge, that made him the indefatigable crime-solver that he was.

After lunch we returned to King William Street and Holmes artfully removed the manhole cover with the aid of a small pry bar he had concealed under his inverness. My instructions were to wait on the sidewalk by the cover while Holmes dropped down into the sewer tunnel and investigated. "I don't really expect to run into a gang of desperate gold thieves down here," he told me, "but in case there is any trouble I leave it to you to give a few short blasts on your police whistle—you do have your police whistle with you?—and then come to my rescue with such reinforcements as you can gather."

"How will I know if you need me?" I asked him. "You'll be somewhere out of sight down there."

"True," Holmes said, reaching into his fob pocket and pulling out his own police whistle at the end of a short silver chain. "In those closed tunnels a blast on this should travel for quite a distance. I'll sound the alarm and you follow through."

"Right, Holmes," I agreed.

Holmes nodded and did up the belt on his inverness. "I shouldn't be too long," he said. He swung his feet over to the ladder on one side of the hole and clambered down. I watched him leave and followed his progress until he disappeared from view down the tunnel. For a while I could hear his footsteps on the brick walkway that ran along the side of the tunnel, and then they faded away.

I turned up my collar against the gusts of chill wind which blew down King William Street as I stood by the side of the manhole, stamping my feet for warmth, and waited. I occupied myself with reminiscing about my relationship with Holmes and our adventures together. If it wasn't for Holmes my life would have been—what?—an endless series of sore throats, upset stomachs, and broken bones, with the occasional incurable disease thrown in to remind me of how little we doctors actually know. My wife taught me to love, and Holmes gave me relief from boredom and tried to teach me how to think; it is not for me to say how well he succeeded. There is much I owe both of them.

Perhaps fifteen or twenty minutes after Holmes had disappeared down the hole, there was a rushing sound, and a torrent of water passed in the tunnel beneath me. It was only brief moments later when I heard the shrill blast of a police whistle reverberating below. Holmes was in trouble! I immediately blew on my own whistle and, when a constable came running up, explained the situation to him as best I could, urged him to get help, and plunged down into the tunnel below.

I was soon joined by several uniformed constables and then by Inspector Giles Lestrade of Scotland Yard and several of his men. We searched well into the night, but found nothing, no trace of Holmes's presence, no hint of what might have happened to him, except that after several hours one of the constables found, on a ledge some distance down a side tunnel, a police whistle attached to a short silver chain.

* * *

There has been no further sign of him, no word from him, and no hint of what might have happened to him until yesterday, when a constable noticed a beggar wearing an inverness coat several sizes too large for him. On inspection, it was shown to be Holmes's own coat, and the sack coat and trousers the man had on beneath the Inverness were those Holmes had been wearing when we left the house that day. The man claimed he had found the garments this past Saturday in a dustbin on Newgate Street, some considerable distance away from the spot where Holmes disappeared.

So Holmes did not drown in that underground torrent. Which is on one hand a relief, and on the other a great mystery. Why did he not return home? Who removed his clothes, and why? If one of his enemies caught up with him and did away with him, where is his body? If he is still alive, where is he being held, and again why?

I have been unable to sleep pondering these questions. It is now six in the morning of Monday, the tenth of February, and I am about to dress and await the arrival of Holmes's brother Mycroft, who sent me a message yesterday that he would come by this morning with two Scotland Yard detectives.

I try to be hopeful. I can only hope that time will provide an answer, and I can only pray that the time is brief.

ONE

CALCUTTA

A thousand tymes have I herd men telle
That ther ys joy in hevene and peyne in helle,
And I acorde wel that it ys so;
But, natheless, yet wot I wel also
That ther nis noon dwellyng in this contree,
That eyther hath in hevene or helle ybe...
GEOFFREY CHAUCER

E̲ast is East, strange and mysterious and slow to change, and West is most definitely West, and during the closing years of the nineteenth century there was little chance of their meeting. Bumping shoulders, crossing swords, shouting epithets, ruling and submitting, perhaps, but they made no pretense of understanding each other, and they seldom sat down anywhere as equals. Yet they mixed and mingled in almost unseemly intimacy throughout the vast, febrile reaches of the Indian subcontinent; mainly in the great cities, where the British Raj ruled, administered, taught, and imposed its will on Her Majesty's teeming multitude of Hindu, Muhammadan, Jainist, Christian, Buddhist, Parsi, Animist, Zoroastrian, and other assorted subjects. And the greatest of these cities was Calcutta. Some visitors found it the richest city they had ever seen, and wrote glowingly of its riches, its magnificence, and its multifarious wonders. Some found it the poorest place on earth, and wrote angrily of overcrowding, poverty, filth, and ignorance.

And both were right.

The capital of British India, and the terminus of the East Indian Railway, Calcutta had been an important outpost of British power since Job Charnock came to the Indian state of Bengal in 1690, and combined the adjoining villages of Sutanuti, Govindapur, and Kilikata to establish a trading post of the British East India Company. Some said that the name of the new city came from Kali, the Hindu goddess of murder and unspeakable crimes. Some, who should know, said that was not true, but they looked away nervously when they said it.

Over the next century Calcutta grew in importance, both as a major port and as a symbol of the East India Company's dominance. There were a few setbacks along the way: in 1756 the Nawab of Bengal died, and a power struggle arose between his widow, Ghasiti Begum, and his grandson, twenty-seven-year-old Siraj Ud Daulah. The Company sided with the widow, which proved to be a mistake. When Siraj became the new Nawab, his troops took Fort William, the British strongpoint in Calcutta, and occupied the city. They thrust over a hundred British prisoners into a small cell in the fort, and then promptly forgot about them. By the next day, when they remembered, many of the prisoners had died of heatstroke and dehydration—the temperature, even at night, was over a hundred degrees. This became known as the infamous "Black Hole of Calcutta" incident.

In 1757 Robert Clive and his army won the Battle of Plassey, retook the city, and ousted the Nawab. Calcutta was never again to suffer the embarrassment of being out of British hands. A grateful king ennobled Clive, and he became Baron Clive of Plassey. In 1855 political and military power was taken away from the East India Company, which had grown too big for anybody's britches, and Great Britain became the direct ruler of much of the Indian subcontinent, and the power behind the throne of most of the rest of it. In 1877 Victoria Regina, Queen of the United Kingdom of England, Ireland, Scotland, and Wales, was crowned the Empress of India.

By 1890 Calcutta was thoroughly British, except those parts of it that were thoroughly Indian. A short distance from Fort William, past Eden Gardens, were Government House and the High Court; around the corner was the Imperial Museum and, a block farther, the United Service Club. Under the Gothic clock tower of the red brick Sir Stuart Hogg Market building sat all the shops one could possibly need. The Calcutta Turf Club, more popularly known as the Race Course, was just south of Fort William. The streets had names like The Strand, Grey Street, Wellesley Street, and Cornwallis Street, and broughams and chaises took the English sahibs and memsahibs on their rounds of shopping and visiting.

On the other hand, the Calcutta waterfront was on the Hooghly River, not the Thames. A ten-minute stroll from Government House would find the wanderer in a warren of twisting, narrow dirt lanes, where cows, goats, chickens, beggars, and rats fought off the flies and mosquitoes. If one continued along Lower Chitpur Road, skirting past wagons and carts of all shapes and sizes, drawn by bullocks, donkeys, and unbelievably skinny men clad in dirty white dhotis, dodging the emaciated cows that ambled anywhere they chose, secure in their sacred status from human molestation, one would pass within blocks of the Leper Asylum and Alms House, and the Hindu Female School, before reaching Bagh Bazar Street. Troops of jackals roamed the city in the night, breaking the silence with their barks, coughs, and howls.

The first assaults to the senses of the European visitor to Calcutta were the heat, the glare, and the smell. The sights came shortly after— the palatial structures housing the British colonial administration and the very rich, mostly within sight and easy running distance of Fort William in case the natives should get restless once again; and all around them the narrow streets fronted by ancient brick buildings, and even more ancient stone buildings, squeezed next to wooden buildings of indeterminate age, with narrow alleys leading to other buildings, possibly of wood, and narrow doorways in walled-off areas with buildings constructed of God-knows-what and older than anyone would care to speculate.

And the whole filled with street stalls selling just about anything you might possibly want, along with a variety of things that the visitor couldn't begin to identify and a few things that he would avert his eyes from. There it was: a chaotic jumble of structures that assaulted the eye, twisting and turning along the constricted, improbable streets and alleys.

That was extraordinary enough; but the odors! Cinnamon and allspice and coriander and turmeric and cow dung and camel dung and oranges and lemons and horse dung and more cow dung and cedarwood and sandalwood and olibanum, which we know better as frankincense, and sweet pastries and human excrement and the olfactory ghosts of curries long gone, and still more cow dung, and a thousand years of this and that and long-forgotten those. The odors assaulted the nose of the visitor, not all at once, but in an ever-changing mosaic of smells that shifted and combined and recombined as the visitor moved about the city.

* * *

Margaret St. Yves, the only daughter of Brigadier General Sir Edward St. Yves, stood in the middle of Agincourt Street holding a large white umbrella over her head, and stared up at the house she'd be living in for the next few months. "I suppose one gets used to it after a while," she said.

General St. Yves looked over at his daughter from where he was supervising the transfer of trunks, boxes, cases, and other large, bulky items from the army goods wagon into the house. "I'm sure one does, m'dear," he said. "Get used to what?"

"The odor," she told him. "The all-enveloping stench of—of—various things, some of them, I believe, unmentionable."

"Oh," her father said. "Oh, yes. One does eventually get used to the odor. On occasion, as it changes in intensity and, ah, composition, one is strongly reminded of it. One never grows very fond of it, I'm afraid."

"One would think the rain would wash the smells away, but instead it seems to intensify them."

Her father looked up speculatively. "One would not call this a rain," he said. "More of a heavy mist. When it rains around here, you know it."

"Well," Margaret said, "it's misting all over my bonnet, and I wish it would stop. And it doesn't seem to have any effect on the heat. When it rains in Britain, the rain cools the air. Here the air heats the water."

"Yes, m'dear," her father said. "Why don't you go inside?"

Margaret stepped sharply forward to allow an oxcart to clatter its way past them. "I prefer standing out here for now," she told her father.

"Of course, m'dear. Silly of me."

Brigadier General Sir Edward Basilberg St. Yves, Bart., I.C., D.S.O., was the commanding officer of the Duke of Moncreith's Own Highland Lancers. The Lancers were not at the moment in the Highlands, but had been stationed for the last four years in India, "upcountry," as it was called by their English compatriots lucky enough to spend their winters in Calcutta. It got too bally hot in Calcutta during the summer, and the viceroy and all of official Anglo-India retired to the summer capital at Simla, high in the foothills of the Himalayas.

For the last two years Margaret St. Yves had been upcountry with the Lancers. She had elected to join her father in India rather than staying with a pair of maiden aunts in Bournemouth, after her widowed Aunt Louise, who had taken care of her for the past ten years since her mother died, had decided to remarry. Louise was marrying a Livonian prince, and moving with him to his ancestral castle in Kurzeme. Neither the maiden aunts nor the mouth of the River Bourne had held much interest for Margaret, but India was unknown and promised at least mild excitement and a modicum of adventure.

Margaret had arrived in Calcutta in March 1888, stayed for three days, and then been whisked off by her father to the Highland Lancers' camp in Assam, farther from Calcutta than Bournemouth was from London. General St. Yves had spent the year suppressing what were described in the dispatches as "minor disturbances" in Assam and Bhutan, and an outright rebellion in Oudh, and Margaret, an extremely bright and curious young lady, had used the time to pick up more than a bit of Bengali, a touch of Urdu, and a smattering of the native customs and history.

Now, on February 12, 1890, a steamy, rainy Wednesday, the Duke's Own had trotted back into Calcutta, and with them came eighteen-year-old Margaret St. Yves. The troops and the junior officers were quartered in Fort William, and the senior officers were finding housing wherever housing could be found. General St. Yves and Margaret were taking over a house that had been loaned to them by an absent civil servant, a public school classmate of St. Yves who was returning to England for a sabbatical.

* * *

Lieutenant Gerald Ffoukes-Just, the young officer whom Margaret was currently allowing to annoy her with his attentions, was overseeing the transfer of the officers' accoutrements to the officers' mess. The regimental battle flags had to be hung around the room; the regimental silver plate to be unpacked and polished; the regimental table linen to be ironed and stored; the regimental china to be carefully uncrated and sideboarded; the regimental mascot, a thirty-four-inch-high bronze statuette of a dancing girl acquired during a previous sojourn in India, that they called "the Lady of Lucknow," to be placed in an appropriate position of honor in the room. Gerald considered the job to be one of trust and responsibility; Margaret thought it was just a ruse of her father's to keep Gerald occupied and away from her.

"We won't even bother unpacking most of this stuff," St. Yves said as the last of the trunks disappeared into the house. "We'll just be p-packing it up again in a short while." He gave a few coins to the wagon driver. "Let's go inside, m'dear," he said.

Margaret linked arms with her father, and they entered the house. The waiting house servant confiscated Margaret's umbrella and helped her out of her rain cape almost before she knew it, and then quietly disappeared. "Efficient," Margaret commented. "Your friend has a good staff."

"His wife wouldn't have it any other way," St. Yves told her. "I don't know how she's going to manage back in England, where the servants are only moderately obsequious."

"I doubt whether they could manage a house quite this large back home," Margaret commented. She peered into the front parlor. "This must be where they stable the gazelles," she said.

"Perhaps we could p-pitch a tent in the library," St. Yves suggested. "We wouldn't want to get used to all this munificence; after all, I'm only a poor soldier boy."

Margaret leaned over and gave her father a kiss on the cheek, to which he reacted as one might expect a British father to react: He affected not to notice.

"I'm looking forward to going home," Margaret said. "I've only been here two years, but it's long enough to realize that, were I to stay here for twenty years, I still wouldn't truly understand the culture."

St. Yves nodded agreement. "And if you did start to really understand, then they'd probably move us to another part of the country where they do everything differently, and you'd have to start all over again."

Margaret smiled. "If I *really did* start to understand," she said, "then all the memsahibs would murmur that I've gone native, and shun me in the streets."

"Well, there is that," St. Yves said.

TWO

HIDE AND GO SEEK

Look round the habitable world! How few
Know their own good; or knowing it, pursue.
JUVENAL (TRANSLATED BY JOHN DRYDEN)

At six minutes before nine in the morning of Friday, the fourteenth of February 1890, a four-wheeler pulled up in front of the town house at 64 Russell Square and four angry and determined men emerged. They marched as one up the front steps and paused at the door. A hand reached out for the bellpull and then drew back, as a brief but animated discussion began, accompanied by much arm-waving. Then the hand reached out again, and the bell was pulled. Moments later the door was opened. A shoving match began, as they attempted to push their way inside en masse, but they were blocked by each other and by the massive, stolid butler facing them. They remonstrated and there was more arm-waving. Finally the butler allowed them inside and closed the door carefully behind them.

When Mr. Maws felt irate—which was seldom, as by nature he was inclined to be placid—the muscles in his back and shoulders bunched up and his earlobes turned red; a prelude to the sort of fighting fury that had made "Gentleman Jimmy" Maws bare-knuckles heavyweight champion of England for three years running back in the early seventies. For over a decade now, since he had given up the ring to serve as butler and occasional bodyguard for Professor James Moriarty, Ph.D., F.R.A.S., his essentially peaceful nature had hardly ever been tested, but now, as he stood in the doorway of Moriarty's dressing room, his earlobes were tipped with red.

"There's four of them downstairs," Mr. Maws told the professor. "The same ones as has been trying to see you for the past two days, and didn't want to hear that you was out of town. They would have searched the place had I let them. I do believe they would have torn the place down, had I let them. They are impatient, uncivil, and intemperate of language. They wish to see you now. They said 'now' several times, along with other words which I shall not repeat. And they call themselves gentlemen; or at least two of them do. The other two, being Scotland Yard detectives, quite possibly do not. I tried putting them in the drawing room, but they wouldn't go. They're waiting in the hall. I think they're afraid you'll sneak past them and out the door."

Moriarty took the pocket watch from his dresser and clicked it open. "A hair's-breath before nine," he said. "They've shown admirable restraint. Or perhaps they had trouble getting a cab." He adjusted his cravat, slipped into his gray jacket, and started down the stairs with a measured tread. The knot of angry men awaiting him in the hallway below glared upward with an intensity that would have done him severe damage if the claims of several prominent psychics were true, and mental power alone could have a physical effect. The professor seemed unmoved by the almost palpable anger of those below. He paused on the landing to survey the group. "Inspector Gregson," he said. "Inspector Lestrade... Dr. Watson... and you must be Sherlock Holmes's brother Mycroft—the resemblance is quite evident, despite the difference in your, ah, girth," he said. "You wish to speak to me?"

"Yes, sir, we do!" Mycroft Holmes affirmed, his voice filling the narrow hallway.

"Wish to speak with you?" Dr. Watson screeched, and then fell silent, in the grip of some powerful emotion, unable to continue.

"Very good, then," Moriarty said, and continued down the staircase.

The men parted grudgingly for him as he reached the ground floor and passed between them. "I believe I know why you're here, gentlemen," he told them, opening the door to the left of the stairs. "Please step into my office."

Dr. Watson was unable to contain his feelings. "Know why we're here?" he moaned, stalking into the room behind Moriarty. "Damned right you know why we're here!"

"Quiet, Watson, control yourself," Mycroft murmured, gliding into the room behind the doctor. The two detectives, bowler hats in hand, tramped into the office after Mycroft and closed the door.

Moriarty rounded his desk and lowered himself into his heavy oak desk chair. "Seat yourselves, gentlemen," he said. "I think you'll find that armchair by the window particularly comfortable, Mr. Holmes." As he spoke, Mr. Maws opened the door and silently entered behind the glowering quartet, taking his place against the wall in case he was needed.

The four men advanced to the front of the desk, rebuffing or possibly merely ignoring Moriarty's suggestion that they sit down. Watson clamped his walking stick between his left arm and his body. Palms flat down on the well-polished desktop, he thrust himself over the desk, his jaw tight, his face rigid with barely restrained rage. Lestrade stood stiffly to the side of the desk, twisting his hat about in his hand, looking uncomfortable but determined. Gregson pushed himself belligerently forward, holding his reinforced bowler as though it were a billy club and he was restraining himself from using it. Mycroft Holmes kept his imposing bulk slightly back from the desk and glowered down at Moriarty, his chin firmly tucked into the great tartan scarf which wound several times around his neck.

Moriarty leaned back in his chair and surveyed his guests one at a time. Whatever emotion he might be feeling was not evident in his face or posture. With his high, domed forehead over a prominent nose and deep-set eyes that seemed to see more than ordinary mortals are permitted to see, the professor resembled a great bird of prey. Once, in the Museum of Antiquities in Cairo, an Egyptian dragoman leading a small tour group had come upon Moriarty by surprise and, convinced that he was seeing the hawk-faced god Horus incarnate, crossed himself twice, spat three times, and handed an elderly clergyman back the wallet that he had just filched from his jacket pocket.

"All right, Moriarty," Mycroft Holmes's booming voice shattered the silence, "where is he?"

A trace of a smile crossed Moriarty's face. "I said I knew why you'd come," he told them. "I didn't say you were right in coming." He closed his eyes for perhaps twenty seconds and then opened them again. "It was predictable that, given Holmes's inane insistence that I have been responsible for every major crime committed on these islands since the murder of Thomas à Becket, his friends would hold me responsible for his disappearance. A lie, if repeated often enough, attains the semblance of truth."

Moriarty took a newspaper clipping from his pocket and put it on his desk facing his guests. "I am just back from my establishment at Crimpton-on-the-Moor," he told them. "This was in this morning's Gazette. Is it essentially accurate?"

They leaned forward to read the clipping.

RENOWNED CONSULTING DETECTIVE DISAPPEARS
Sherlock Holmes's Whereabouts Still Unknown
Foul Play Feared

Mr. Sherlock Holmes, the noted consulting detective of 221B Baker Street, whose exploits over the past decade as a private enquiry agent have been recounted to the British reading public by his friend and companion Dr. John H. Watson, has not been seen since his sudden and unexpected disappearance on Wednesday the 15th of February last. The police have commenced enquiries into his whereabouts.

Clothing identified as that of Mr.

Holmes was found in the possession of Bertram Claymer, a currently unemployed horse groomer who lodges in Keat Street, Whitechapel. Claymer stated to the police that he found the apparel on Saturday the 8th in a dustbin in Newgate Street. The area for several blocks around the dustbin was immediately searched by the authorities, and several articles of apparel that might or might not have belonged to Mr. Holmes were found.

Anyone having any information as to the current whereabouts of Mr. Sherlock Holmes is requested to communicate with Scotland Yard.

A summary of Mr. Holmes's more notable cases will be found on p. 17.

Mycroft was the first to straighten up. "Those are essentially the facts as we know them," he affirmed.

"And on the basis of that you come storming into my house and accuse me of... Exactly what is it that you are accusing me of doing—spiriting Holmes away, denuding him, and throwing his clothes into a dustbin?"

Watson took two steps backward and dropped into a chair. His gaze rose to look Moriarty searchingly in the face, and then fell. "What was I to think?" he asked. "At first, after the accident, I thought Holmes was dead. But then when they found his clothes..."

"What accident?" Moriarty demanded.

"Before we continue," Inspector Lestrade interrupted stolidly, "I must ask you formally, Professor James Moriarty, do you have any knowledge of the present whereabouts of Mr. Sherlock Holmes? I warn you that anything you say will be taken down and used in evidence against you."

Moriarty took his pince-nez glasses from his jacket pocket,

polished the lenses carefully with a large piece of flannel from the top drawer of his desk, and then fitted them on the bridge of his nose and turned to his questioner. "I'm ashamed of you, Giles Lestrade," he said severely, a grammar-school master lecturing an unruly pupil. "After all we've been through together, you and I; and, yes, Sherlock Holmes, too. We have averted several major tragedies, with his help, and solved several perplexing crimes. And was I the 'master criminal' in those cases? No! Even Sherlock Holmes had to admit that it was so, though the words came grudgingly from his lips. You know that he's been accusing me of major crimes for most of the past decade. You also know that he has never been able to prove one word of these accusations. Not one word!"

Lestrade twisted his hat between his large hands. "That's so, Professor," he acknowledged. "None of Mr. Holmes's accusations have ever been proven, not so's you could take them to court. But, between us, it's always seemed to me that there were a few drops of truth in the mix. Now, I don't know how many, and I don't know how much of what Mr. Holmes claimed about you was true, but in some cases it always seemed to me that it was nothing but sheer luck and your own deuced—excuse me, Professor—cleverness that kept you out of the dock."

Moriarty stood up. Gregson, who was the only one still leaning across the desk, bolted backward as though he were afraid the professor was going to stick a pin in him. "Between us, is it?" Moriarty asked. "All right, then. Just between us, just in the confines of this office, I will admit that the mores, morals, and laws of this time in which we find ourselves living are not ones that I adhere to gladly. I will further admit that I find Sherlock Holmes's incessant dogging of my footsteps to be a bit... tiring. The man has set watch on this house disguised as an out-of-work navvy; he has followed me about in the guise of an itinerant bookseller or a bargee on holiday or even, once, a professor of philosophy. Indeed, his ability to adopt different disguises at a moment's notice is quite remarkable."

"I have not seen Holmes in any of the costumes you mention," Watson protested.

"He maintains rooms in several locations about the city for the purpose of donning and discarding one or another of these disguises," Moriarty told him. "I know of two, but there are probably more. He is a thorough and persistent pest."

"Really!" Watson said.

"But if he has any effect on me or on my plans," Moriarty continued, "it is only to make me more aware, more careful, more precise. If I can avoid the attentions of a bloodhound like Sherlock Holmes, then I can assuredly avoid the notice of the simpleminded bulldogs—your pardon, Lestrade—of Scotland Yard."

"What are you saying, Professor?" Mycroft asked.

"I'm saying, Mr. Holmes, that I would find a world without your brother in it to be a most dreary place indeed, and that I would never willingly be a part of any effort to remove him from it." Moriarty dropped back into his chair.

"So you say," Watson said, his voice more under control but the strain still showing in the exaggerated pauses between his words, "but he's gone and you're here."

"Yes," Moriarty agreed. "And I would like to think that, were the situation reversed, I would have a cadre of loyal friends assaulting 221B Baker Street and demanding to know what had become of Professor Moriarty. But he would be forced to answer, as I do, I have no idea. I repeat my question, Dr. Watson: What accident?"

Watson looked over at Mycroft, who shrugged his shoulders perhaps a quarter of an inch.

"Come, come," Moriarty said. "If I am guilty of what you suspect me of, then surely I must already know. If I am not—perhaps I can be of some assistance."

Watson considered for a moment and then spoke. "Holmes was down a manhole into the central drains when it happened," he said. "We spent much of the morning looking for the right manhole, and when he located it, he removed the cover and dropped into the tunnel. I awaited him on the street by the entrance, and he went some distance into the drain. He'd been down, I would judge, some fifteen minutes when a great rush of water flowed through the tunnel. It might have been a release from some reservoir, I don't know. Holmes whistled for help and that—that was the last I heard from him."

The silence stretched on for a second, and was interrupted by the office door opening. Mrs. H., Moriarty's housekeeper, bustled in with a folding table, which she set up in front of the desk. A serving girl came in behind her with a great silver tray of pitchers, cups, saucers, plates, and silverware, and placed it carefully on the table.

"Coffee and tea, gentlemen," Mrs. H. said. "You may serve yourselves." Then she sniffed and bustled out of the room, pausing at the door to turn and add, "As though Professor Moriarty would harm one hair of that ungrateful man's head," and closed the door with exaggerated gentleness behind her.

The gentlemen did help themselves, except for Gregson, who stared suspiciously at the teapot and then turned away.

"What was Holmes doing down a manhole?" Moriarty asked.

"What's that?" Watson looked up from pouring cream into his coffee. "Oh. Investigating a possibility."

"A possibility of what?"

"I don't know, and I can tell you no more than that. I can't discuss the case he was working on."

"Fair enough." Moriarty paused to consider. "So at first you thought he was washed away?"

"Yes. We found the police whistle he had been carrying set on a shelf, but no other sign of him."

"Until Mr. Claymer turned up wearing Holmes's clothing."

"Yes."

"Exactly what items of Holmes's apparel was he wearing?"

"His inverness," Watson began, "and, ah—"

"Jacket, trousers, waistcoat, inverness, hat, and shoes," Mycroft said, dropping down into the comfortable chair by the window. "All of which showed the effects of being submerged in water for some time."

"Fairly complete outfit," Moriarty commented. "Shirt?"

"No."

"Anything in the pockets? Any of Holmes's personal belongings?"

"No."

"Mr. Claymer might have pawned them or sold them," Moriarty suggested.

"We questioned him thoroughly on that. He says he didn't. Offered him five pounds if he could produce any personal items of my brother's or tell us where they could be found. He was quite sorrowful that he was unable to collect."

Moriarty went to the window and stared out. "Several things come to mind," he said.

"I must warn you again," Inspector Lestrade began, "that anything you say—"

"Oh, be quiet, Lestrade!" Mycroft bellowed. "Let the man talk."

"Let us create a chain of inductive reasoning," Moriarty said, "and see where it leads us."

"Go on," said Mycroft Holmes.

"Either Holmes intended to disappear or he did not intend to disappear," Moriarty began. "If he intended to disappear, would he not have left my friend Dr. Watson at home, or at least in a more comfortable place than sitting atop an open manhole? And would he not have said simply, 'Watson, I plan to be away for a few days'?"

"We figured that out for ourselves, Professor," Inspector Gregson said, trying not very hard to suppress the sneer in his voice. As far as he was concerned, Moriarty was a crook, and all the fancy houses and cultured accents and strings of letters after his name couldn't change a thing.

"Ah! Did you?" Moriarty asked mildly. "Then we must proceed with our inferences and see how far they take us. If Holmes did not intend to disappear, then his disappearance was the result of something that happened while he was down in the sewer tunnel. And what we must consider is whether the disappearance was voluntary or involuntary." He looked politely at Gregson. "As I'm sure you'll agree, Inspector."

"Yes," Gregson said. "Of course."

"Let us examine the two scenarios separately," Moriarty said. "If Holmes's disappearance was voluntary, then after a 'rush of water' which may have soaked him, or even carried him away, he recovered, left the sewer at some point other than the one at which he entered it, took his outer clothes off, and vanished. Why did he take his outer clothes off? Well, quite possibly because they were water-soaked. Why, then, did he throw them in the dustbin? Could they not be washed and ironed and returned to serviceability?"

"Perhaps someone else disposed of them," Inspector Lestrade suggested.

"Again, why?" Moriarty said. "We must close our eyes and imagine possible answers to these questions."

"I have been doing so," Mycroft affirmed.

"To what effect?"

"None, yet. The first thought was that the clothes were too soiled to wear, but I examined them and that was not so. If my brother disposed of his clothing himself, the reason eludes me."

"Then let us look at the other possibility. It could be that Holmes's vanishing was involuntary; that someone removed him from the sewer tunnel, took his clothes off, and spirited him away."

"It was that possibility that brought us here this morning," Mycroft observed wryly.

"Yes," Moriarty said, "but consider what that implies. First, that someone, some enemy of Holmes's, knew that he was planning to investigate the sewer system. Second, that this unknown person knew which entrance to the tunnels Holmes would use; a fact that Holmes himself didn't know, according to the faithful Dr. Watson. Then this person would have to know which way Holmes would turn when he entered the tunnel, and know just where to lie in wait for him."

"That's so," Watson agreed.

Lestrade looked from one to the other of his companions. "But that would be impossible, wouldn't it?" he asked.

"Not quite," Mycroft offered. "If he knew what my brother's object was, that is, what he was investigating, then he might be able to surmise where Sherlock would probably appear."

"True," Moriarty said. "Or if he were keeping a watch on the object of Holmes's interest, Holmes might have stumbled into a situation he couldn't control."

"Even so," Mycroft agreed.

"But then," Moriarty continued, "the question remains. Why did Holmes's captors remove his outer clothing? And why did they put it in a dustbin, where it had a good chance of being found? Why not burn it? Why not, for that matter, kill Holmes, if he stood between them and the object of their underground attention? Why bother capturing him at all?"

"That thought had also occurred to me," Mycroft said.

"Have you checked the medical schools and teaching hospitals?" Moriarty asked.

"First thing we did, Professor, of course," Lestrade said. "Mr. Holmes hasn't been admitted to any hospital in London. We are having hospitals farther away checked by the local authorities."

"I assumed that," Moriarty said. "What I meant—"

Watson sat back, looking startled and almost spilling his coffee. "My God!" he exclaimed. "What a distressing idea. Still, I should have thought of that!"

"I did," Mycroft said. "No body resembling Sherlock has been brought to the dissecting mortuary of any medical school in the past week."

"Ah!" Moriarty said. "That's reassuring, but it leaves the mystery intact. We can be reasonably sure that Holmes survived the temporary flooding of the tunnel, but what became of him after that we cannot tell at present. Perhaps the next few days will bring us additional information."

"I fear that every minute that passes makes that more unlikely," Watson said.

"Nonsense," Moriarty said. "I can think of a dozen—a hundred— scenarios that would explain what has happened to Holmes. The difficulty is that we have no reason to favor one of them over another. But I have sources that, let us say, are not available to my friends from Scotland Yard. I shall set inquiries in motion immediately. I am not hopeful that they will discover anything useful, but who can tell?"

Mycroft pushed himself to his feet. "Do you positively assert, sir, that you had nothing to do with my brother's disappearance?"

"I do, sir," Moriarty said solemnly. "On my honor as an Englishman."

"I thought you were Irish," Watson said.

"My father was, Dr. Watson, but my brothers and I regard ourselves as Englishmen, having grown up in Warwickshire."

"Ah!" Watson said.

"We must continue our search," Mycroft Holmes said. "Goodbye, Professor Moriarty, we will not trouble you any further today."

"We'd best get back to the Yard," Lestrade said. "Perhaps some word has come in."

"Very well," Mycroft said. "We shall accompany you back to Scotland Yard, and ponder what to do from there."

"I wish I had some useful suggestions, gentlemen," Moriarty said, rising to his feet, "but at the moment nothing suggests itself."

"Well, then—" Watson said.

"If you think of anything, or hear anything," Mycroft said, "a message to the Diogenes Club will reach me in short order."

The four visitors filed out of the room and to the front door in a calmer state of mind than they had entered. Only Gregson still glowered at Moriarty as they left, but he said nothing.

Mr. Maws let them out, and then returned to the professor's office. "That was very good, that was," he said. "They came in like lions and went out like lambs. And here I thought I was going to have to assist you as you were physically assaulted. At least two of them were prepared to commence pummeling you where you stood; I recognize the signs. But your soft answers somehow turned away their wrath, as the Bible says. I don't know how you do it, Professor. I saw it being done, but I still don't know how you did it."

"I showed them the error of their ways," Moriarty said. "I was clothed in the armor of my innocence."

"You mean you actually had nothing to do with Mr. Holmes's disappearance?" Mr. Maws asked, looking surprised.

"Mr. Maws!" Moriarty said, shaking his head sadly. "Not you, too!"

THREE

THE SCHEMERS

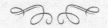

*Wer mit Ungeheuern kämpft, mag zusehn, dass er nicht dabei zum
Ungeheuer wird. Und wenn du lange in einen Abgrund blickst, blickt
der Abgrund auch in dich hinein.
[He who fights with monsters must be careful not thereby to
become a monster. And if you stare too long into an abyss,
the abyss stares back at you.]*
FRIEDRICH NIETZSCHE

It snowed most of the day on Monday, February 17, 1890. As dusk fell over London and the midwinter shadows grew longer, the east wind picked up and what had been a light snow turned to hard-driven sleet. Ice formed in the Thames, and crusted the rigging and mooring lines of the ships in the mélange of docks along the river. The streets of the city were deserted except for the occasional hansom cab or four-wheeler, its horse and driver braced against the icy wind, looking for one last fare before retiring for the night.

In the back room of a rags and old clothes store in Mincing Lane, within sight of the Tower of London if you stuck your head out the window and looked sharply to your left, five men gathered around a massive oak table and schemed a mighty scheme.

First by the door was the Artful Codger, a small, wiry man, his thin, narrow face suggesting the cunning and weaselly soul of the man himself. He sat, legs crossed and tucked under him like a dervish, on a flat wooden chair with no back.

To his left was Cooley the Pup, who had cultivated the look of an innocent fresh-faced boy of fourteen until he was thirty-five. He looked now, at forty-five, ancient and wizened and like a man whose years were filled with unimaginable sins. He had pulled a dilapidated easy chair over to the table and was now sunk into its cushions until all that could be seen of him in the dim light was the tip of his nose.

By his side was Angelic Tim McAdams, a bullheaded, massive ex-navvy, head of a gang of toughs known to be rentable for all occasions, with set prices for broken arms, legs, ribs, or bashed skulls; killing extra. He sat foursquare on a heavy wooden stool, his hands lying motionless and flat on the table.

The Twopenny Yob, whose appearance and mannerisms were enough like those of the younger son of an earl to gain him unquestioned admittance to the best social gatherings, and whose habits and morals were enough like those of a guttersnipe to get him kicked off the swell mob for conduct unbecoming even a pseudo-gentleman, was taking his ease on the far corner of the table, his legs swinging back and forth like a well-clad metronome.

The fifth man, the one who had called this meeting of equals in depravity and lawlessness, was the enigmatic Dr. Pin Dok Low. Possibly Chinese, somewhere between forty and ageless, infinitely knowledgeable in the ways of crime, he towered above the others in intellect and force of will. Now he sat in a high-backed armchair, its back to the rear of the room, smiling a slight inscrutable smile and nodding a tight nod across the table at his companions. "It is good that you have all come," he said.

"Coo-ee, and how could we stay away?" the Artful Codger asked, clapping his hands together twice and then running them through his hair. "A million quid, you said, this job is worth."

"You meant just that, I sincerely hope?" McAdams asked, leaning forward and thrusting his chin in the general direction of Pin Dok Low. "A million pounds? A real, touchable million pounds? I'd hate to be sitting here and find out you've been laying it on. I'd hate even worse to be where you're sitting when it happens that I find that out, if you catch my drift."

Dr. Pin nodded again. "A million pounds, I said, but I confess that the figure quoted was not an exact one. I picked a number that I knew would draw you here," he said, looking impassively at each of them in turn.

McAdams rose and glared at Pin like a great bull preparing to do serious damage to the matador. "I don't like being diddled," he said flatly.

The Artful Codger leaped to his feet. "I'll just be going," he said to the others. "Do with 'im"—he waved a negligent hand toward Pin—"as you like."

"The real figure," Dr. Pin continued, the slight smile reappearing on his face, "might have frightened you away before I had a chance to speak with you. It is certain to be higher than a million pounds, much higher. I wouldn't be surprised if each of us clears a million, even after splitting with our assorted, ah, henchmen."

The Twopenny Yob laughed. "I knew it!" he said. "A Chink with a nose for money. I always thought you'd make me rich someday, Pin, while doing a bit of good for yourself, of course."

McAdams sat back down. "I still don't like being diddled," he said. "Let's hear it, and it better be good."

"In brief, gentlemen," Pin said, "there is a shipment of bullion—several tons of pure, unalloyed gold—arriving in London soon by steamship for storage in the vaults of the Bank of England."

"Gold!" Cooley the Pup spit the word out inadvertently, and looked rather startled that he had said anything.

"The Bank of England," the Codger said, shaking his head mournfully. "Can't nobody break into the vaults of the Bank of England. Can't be done, and that's flat!" He spoke with the sad assurance of someone who had given the subject much thought in the past.

Dr. Pin looked around, the smile on his face even broader. "Ah, yes, maybe so, maybe so, but I know when the gold is coming, and where it's coming, and how it's coming. And, as you will see, I have devised a workable method of relieving the authorities of this dreadful burden before the Old Lady of Threadneedle Street has a chance to put her protective arms around it."

"And you need all of us to be in on it?" the Codger asked.

Dr. Pin nodded. "You and your assorted associates and assistants—you will pick the ones you need. Obtaining the gold is not enough. It must be recast—one cannot trade in gold bars with the Bank of England seal on them—and transported and sold gradually and over a wide area."

The Twopenny Yob lowered himself into a chair and flicked a spot of dust off his collar. "It sounds as if you might have something worth saying, old man," he said cheerfully. "I'll listen attentively, both ears and all that, but you're going to have your work cut out to convince me that it's a doable proposition. And if I don't think it's doable, then I'm not in."

"My dear young man," Dr. Pin said, "if I did not myself think it was, as you say, doable, then I myself would not be in. The wise man does not flee from shadows."

McAdams crossed his arms at shoulder height, his elbows jutting forward like ram's horns, and glared at Pin. "Let's hear it, then," he said.

Pin Dok Low talked slowly and continuously for the next half hour, and his companions listened, and their interest did not wane. When he finished there was much shuffling of feet and rapping of knuckles on the table as they considered what he had told them.

"So the swag's to be divvied up even?" Cooley the Pup demanded.

"As I said," Dr. Pin told him. "After we've disposed of the gold itself, which will take several months at least, the profits will be divided up five ways, one part to each of us. You, in turn, are responsible for all expenses, including paying your own men."

"There's the flaw," the Artful Codger observed. "With this kind of money, someone's going to start buying up the entire East End, and the busies are going to catch wise. And if they get one of us, the others'll soon tumble into the net. A million pounds don't do you no good in Dartmoor."

"That is a problem," Pin admitted. "One possible solution would be to withhold the profits for an extended length of time after the robbery. But which of us is prepared to do without, knowing that a vast sum of money awaits him? And which of us will the others trust to hold the loot?"

"I'll take care of my own share, thank you very much," McAdams growled.

"There, you see? No, each of you will receive your share as soon as it is available, as soon as the gold is turned into coin of the realm or something else immediately negotiable. After that you are each responsible for seeing that you keep away from the long arm of the authorities. And, if you are wise, you will insulate yourself from the failure of others."

"I notice you have not given us the date the bloody boat's coming in, or the location of the wharf at which the thing's tying up," the Twopenny Yob commented.

"Nor even the name of the craft," the Artful Codger added.

"Of course not," Dr. Pin said. "Not until I know you're all in. Even then, not until the last minute. The best way to assure that we trust each other is to give as few opportunities as possible for deceit."

"Yeah, there's something to that," Cooley the Pup agreed, looking around at his companions. "There's something to that. There's a couple of gents in this 'ere very room that I wouldn't trust with the time o' day. Mentioning no names, o' course. And I ain't looking at anyone in particular."

"When you get home, look in the mirror," the Artful Codger suggested, "if it's clean enough to make out your own face."

"None of that, now," McAdams barked. "We're all friends and companions in here, and we're going to stay that way if I have to break a few bones to see to it."

"No fisticuffs, please," the Twopenny Yob said, drawing the sleeves of his immaculately tailored jacket down over his shirt cuffs just the right amount. "It's rude!"

The Codger looked at him and snorted. "So you say," he said. "But that sword cane you're carrying makes a pretty rude slice in a fellow. And that palm pistol you're wearing under your left arm makes a pretty rude hole."

"Indeed," the Twopenny Yob agreed, unabashed. "I don't believe in fighting, you see. I believe in winning, and as quickly as possible."

McAdams looked over at Pin Dok Low. "You want me to take that stuff away from him? I can do it easy, with nobody getting hurt except maybe his tender feelings."

"If the gentleman feels safer with his impedimenta," Pin said, "let him keep them. I assure you he will not use them in this room."

The Twopenny Yob looked around nervously at the implied threat, examining the walls for what, or who, might be hidden behind them watching his every move. "I have no animosity toward anyone here," he said. "The weapons are for self-defense only. And as we're all friends here—"

"Just so," Dr. Pin agreed.

"There's going to be an awful shake-out among the criminal classes if this 'ere scheme of yours comes off," the Artful Codger commented. "The rozzers will be laying their heavy hands on everyone what ever copped a apple from a pushcart, or mistook someone else's house for his own, and that's the truth!"

"They'll call in Sherlock Holmes," Cooley the Pup agreed mournfully. "They're bound to. A job this big. The Old Lady 'erself will put him on the case. And he can see things what others can't."

Dr. Pin looked from one to the other of his colleagues, and the smile on his face grew larger and more inscrutable. "Of one thing I can assure you," he told them, "Mr. Holmes won't be bothering us."

"'Ow can you be so sure of that?" Cooley asked.

"Mr. Holmes has disappeared," Pin explained. "And he isn't going to reappear anytime soon."

"And just how do you know that?" McAdams growled. "Did you disappear him yourself, by any chance?"

"Not I," Pin said. "Indeed, I cannot say just how I know that Mr. Holmes will remain, ah, unavailable. But I feel sure that this is so. Besides, even were he to reappear, his attention and the attention of Scotland Yard will be drawn in an altogether different direction."

"How's that?" the Artful Codger asked.

"A small but necessary part of my modest contribution to this endeavor," Dr. Pin told them. "In addition to obtaining the necessary information, devising the plan, and picking each of you as my, shall we say, staff—"

"Shall we say get on with it?" the Artful Codger snapped. "We all know how clever you are, don't put your arm out of joint patting yourself on the back."

Pin Dok Low glared at the Codger for a second before closing his eyes and doing a baritsu exercise which tensed and relaxed the muscles from his toes up through his body to his eyebrows, and removed all stress, making him once more at one with the universe. "The true master would not allow himself to get annoyed at such trivialities," he said, sighing softly and opening his eyes. "However, there is no true master within three thousand miles of this place."

"Well, as you're the one we're speaking to, master or no master, just what sort of plan do you have for taking the heat off us and getting the busies from Scotland Yard to, as you say, look in another direction?" the Codger demanded.

"I'm going to, as you might say, Codger, throw in a ringer. I'm going to give the police someone else to suspect, along with adequate signs that he is, indeed, the guilty party."

"And just why might they think that this gent done the deed instead of looking our way?" McAdams asked.

"Because they are already primed to believe the worst of this gentleman."

"The worst?"

"Yes. Sherlock Holmes has been blaming him for every major crime that happens anywhere in London—in all of Europe, for that matter—for the past decade. The police will naturally think of him. I will merely reinforce that thought."

"Professor Moriarty!" Cooley the Pup gasped.

"Just so. Professor James Moriarty. The perfect scapegoat."

"I don't know, Pin," the Twopenny Yob said, shaking his head. "It ain't smart to get on the wrong side of the professor."

Pin leaned back in his chair. "That is why I dislike revealing my plans in advance," he said. "Someone such as yourself always responds to the outline before hearing the details. I have thought this out carefully, and we have nothing to fear from Professor Moriarty."

"And just why is that?" McAdams asked.

"Because he won't know he's being attacked. He'll believe that it's merely another case of the police hounding off in the wrong direction because they see evil in everything he does, even if they've never been able to prove it."

"The way I hear it," the Codger said, "it's Holmes that sees the professor behind every bush, and he's never been able to convince the police."

"Yes, but now Holmes has disappeared. They're sure to suspect Moriarty of that. And when a major robbery happens shortly after..."

"You have a point," the Codger conceded.

"Of course. By the time the professor figures out that he's being set up, he'll be in it too deep to get out. And he won't know from what direction the frame is coming."

"I don't know," Cooley the Pup said. "The professor's been a big help to a lot of us over the years."

"A million pounds each," Pin Dok Low reminded them.

"I'm in," Angelic Tim McAdams declared.

"I suppose the professor can take care of himself," the Artful Codger decided.

Pin Dok Low turned his gaze toward the other two, and after a few seconds received a nod from one and a shrug from the other. "Sensible," he said. "Very sensible."

FOUR

THE MAHARAJA'S GOLDEN HOURI

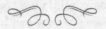

Small is the worth
Of beauty from the light retir'd;
Bid her come forth,
Suffer herself to be desir'd,
And not blush so to be admir'd.
EDMUND WALLER

It was late afternoon on Wednesday, the nineteenth of February, when the stocky man with the sharp blue eyes presented himself at the door to 64 Russell Square. He handed his card to Mr. Maws.

> ## COL. SEBASTIAN MORAN
>
> ## ANGLO-INDIAN CLUB
>
> ### Pennsworth Square

"Tell the professor his old pal is back," he said. Mr. Maws put him in the parlor and left Mummer, Moriarty's midget-of-all-work, to watch the stranger through the spy hole in the butler's pantry while he went downstairs to the basement laboratory, where the professor had been working since late the night before.

Moriarty, with his jacket off, his sleeves rolled up, and a laboratory apron covering his vest and trousers, was leaning over his workbench, a test tube in his hand. The area before him was clustered with bottles, retorts, flasks, metal stands, glass tubing, and a stack of reference books. Old Potts, the professor's laboratory assistant, was napping on a cot in the far corner of the room.

"One moment," Moriarty said, slowly passing the test tube back and forth through the flame of a Bunsen burner. "If this turns red, the Mummer is going to have to make a hasty trip to Bilstone in Leicestershire. Whereas—ah!—look; a fine royal—or at least noble—blue. It is as I hoped." He set the test tube on the rack and turned to his butler. "The trip is unnecessary, a life is secure—at least from one of the more obscure alkaloid poisons. Although how it got into the pudding is still a question. Now... ?"

"A gentleman to see you," Mr. Maws told him.

"What sort of gentleman?" Moriarty asked, hanging up his apron and carefully washing and drying his hands at the work sink.

Mr. Maws considered. "Something over forty years of age, I should say. Says he's your 'old pal,' but his face is a new one to me."

He handed Moriarty the man's card.

Moriarty adjusted his pince-nez and peered down at the card. "Colonel Moran," he said, flicking the pasteboard with his thumb. "I do know the gentleman." He put his jacket on and adjusted the large knot on his red cravat. "Let's go see what he wants."

* * *

Colonel Moran sat patiently in the red leather chair for the ten minutes he was kept waiting, hands folded in his lap, back straight and not quite touching the back of the chair. Occasionally he would twist one side or the other of his full mustache or pat the top of his head, where the carefully groomed hair beyond his receding hairline, parted precisely in the middle with a part as fine as the edge of a razor, was just a bit too black to be natural.

As Professor Moriarty entered the parlor, Moran jumped to his feet and thrust forward a tanned, muscular block of a right hand. "Good to see you again, Professor. It's been a while, but you haven't changed a bit. But then you never do—you never do."

Moriarty took the hand and shook it gingerly. "Four years, or just a bit over, I fancy. I perceive that you're quite recently back from Afghanistan, if I'm not mistaken."

"You're not mistaken, Professor," Moran assured him. "But then you're seldom mistaken, as I remember. Has someone told you of my return?"

"I was unaware of it until this moment. But the deduction was not a difficult one. The fact that you are living at your club proclaims that you haven't been back in England long enough to settle into a flat; your tan suggests a hot climate, and a lot of time in the field. The current campaign in Afghanistan fits those requirements well, I believe."

"Quite so," Colonel Moran agreed. "You make these little tricks of ratiocination of yours seem simple."

"Tricks? Come now, Colonel Moran, you must realize that the more you exercise your brain, the more you can expect from it."

Moran smiled. "Exercise, whether mental or physical, seems to benefit some people more than others, or so I've noticed."

Moriarty reached behind him and pulled the bellpull. "I'm going to have a cup of coffee," he said. "Please join me. Coffee or tea, or something stronger if you like."

Colonel Moran twisted one side of his mustache into an even finer point, and then the other. "Well, it is well past the noon hour," he said. "A fixed habit, sir. No indulging in spirits until the sun has begun the second half of his journey across the sky. It is such fixed habits, sir, that save us from utter ruin."

"That may well be," Moriarty agreed. "But now, as it's approaching four in the afternoon?"

"A glass of quinine water, if you have such a thing, with a substantial splash of brandy, would not go amiss."

"Certainly," Moriarty said, and passed the request on to Mr. Maws when he opened the door. "Now, Colonel, what can I do for you?"

Moran leaned back in his chair. A wolfish grin flickered across his face and disappeared. "You have called upon me for assistance on occasion in the past, Professor, as I have called upon you. I believe our relationship has always been mutually profitable in the past. I have a tale to tell that will excite your imagination. After you have heard my story, then we can discuss how we can help each other on this occasion, you and I." He patted his pockets and pulled out a hand-tooled leather cigar case. "May I offer you a cigar, sir? An Indian Lunkah cheroot in style, but not as vile as the native product. Made especially for the officers of the Penwali Scouts."

"No, thank you," Moriarty said, shaking his head almost imperceptibly. "I don't indulge."

"Do you mind if I—"

"No, go right ahead."

Moran took a silver cigar tool from his pocket and clipped off the ends of his cigar. Thrusting the cheroot firmly between his teeth, he held a tubular cigar lighter with an oversized windscreen to the far end and puffed it alight. The process had the air of an oft-repeated ritual. "Ahh!" he said.

He capped the lighter and held it speculatively in his hand. "Used to be a time," he commented, taking the cheroot from his mouth and blowing a stream of acrid-smelling smoke into the room, "when you could impress the natives almost anywhere by producing fire from your fist. Now they ain't so easy. It takes a repeating rifle to have any impression on most of them." He pocketed the lighter.

The maid came in with Colonel Moran's drink in a tall glass, and a cup of black coffee for Professor Moriarty. She set the tray down on the small table between them.

"That will be all, Teresa," Moriarty said. "Thank you." He noticed that Moran's eyes followed the young girl as she left the room.

"Chin-chin!" Moran said, his eyes flicking back toward Moriarty and focusing on the knot in his cravat. He set his cigar carefully on the ashtray to his right, and lifted the glass to salute Moriarty before bringing it to his lips.

"Now, Professor, with your permission, I'll tell you my story. I think you'll find it worth your time."

"Go on," Moriarty said.

Moran retrieved his cigar from the ashtray. "I shall begin, then, with the maharaja of Lamapoor, which as you may know is the second largest of the independent principalities. Not his present majesty, but his—let's see—great-great-great-grandfather. The events I am about to relate occurred, or at least began, in, as close as I can figure, about the year 1734.

"The maharaja of Lamapoor was a drastically obese young man. In the year in question his weight exceeded thirty stone. This, he and his advisors were convinced, was most pleasing to his subjects, since they believed that their ruler should be a man of substance." Moran paused and coughed.

"Once every seven years, in addition to the annual taxes, levies, assessments, fees, fines, tolls, special charges, and bribes that gladdened the hearts of the citizens of Lamapoor, there was a special ceremony where the subjects of the maharaja matched his weight in gold. There is a much-reproduced drawing of the ceremony showing a giant balance beam with a pan at each end. On one pan sits the rotund maharaja on his special throne, and his subjects are dumping gold coins onto the other."

"I've seen the illustration, or one like it," Moriarty commented.

"Yes, well. It's inaccurate in one respect, I'm given to understand," Moran told him. "They actually used small gold ingots especially minted for the purpose, which they had to buy from the state mint—at a small premium, of course. In effect, they had to pay the maharaja for the privilege of paying the maharaja."

"Many governments seem to work on a similar principle," Moriarty observed.

"Even so. But aside from that, that's pretty much what it must have looked like." Moran paused to take a healthy gulp of this brandy and quinine.

"The maharaja had one problem, though, that worried his advisors and his subjects and almost took all the fun out of being the fattest maharaja in India. He had—how can I say this—an inability to perform his connubial duties. He had difficulty in maintaining the requisite, ah, interest, and he was so large that, even during the comparatively brief periods when he could keep his interest up, he couldn't place it where it needed to be to produce a son and heir. And a son and heir must be produced or the succession to the throne would be in doubt—up for grabs, as it were—at his passing, and the future happiness of large numbers of his subjects might be imperiled; or so it seemed to the maharaja and his advisors at the time.

"So the maharaja's nieces and his nephews and his cousins and his aunts, as well as the various functionaries of the court, were taking what in other circumstances might seem a vulgar interest in the condition of the maharaja's member." He paused.

"Continue," Moriarty said, "with as little obeisance to prurience as you can manage."

"The long and short of it is," Moran said, obviously annoyed that his lovely anecdote was going to have to be truncated, "that the prime minister, who was the maharaja's first cousin, commissioned a Scottish engineer named Westerby Mitchell to construct a device that would enable His Highness to, ah, function. Mitchell looked over the situation and, after spending a few weeks taking measurements and computing angles, set to work on a contraption of leather straps and bands and springs, all set into a hardwood frame, and had it installed in the royal bedroom."

"A simple problem, but not without some interest," Moriarty observed. "Did it work?"

"It solved the, ah, mechanical part of the problem. The other part was solved by the importation from Persia of three exceptionally beautiful houris who were well trained in the amorous arts. With the assistance of the device and the houris, the maharani produced a royal heir within the year. I believe that two of the houris also gave birth around the same time."

"What did the maharani think of this arrangement?"

"That is not recorded."

"Ah!" Moriarty said. "A good story, and I appreciate it. And is the stage sufficiently set now? Can we proceed to the denouement of this farce?"

Moran took a deep breath and let it out. "Don't rush me unreasonably, sir," he said. "I'm trying to tell you enough so that you can, you might say, see how it is; so that you can properly understand what follows."

"I think," said Moriarty, "that whatever follows, sir, I will properly understand."

Moran closed his eyes for a long moment, and then opened them and stared unblinkingly at Moriarty. "I am not sure, sir, why you are being hostile to me and my story, when I haven't even gotten around to the, ah, important part, the part that would concern you, as of yet." He rose from his chair and jammed his cigar firmly between his teeth. "I will concede that you are the cleverest man in London, and the best at devising the sort of stratagems that I might require. I have worked with you before, and I know that this is so. Now, if you will direct me to the residence of the second cleverest man in London, I will bid you adieu."

Moriarty chuckled, and then began laughing, a great, full-throated laugh. Moran, startled, took a step backward and almost fell back into his seat before bouncing up again and glaring belligerently at the professor.

"The second cleverest man in London?" Moriarty asked, and then laughed again. "Why, sir, I cannot direct you to the second cleverest man in London, for he has disappeared."

"Indeed?" Moran asked, looking baffled.

Moriarty nodded, and held his hand up for a minute until he had stopped laughing. "Indeed," he said. "And quite possibly it's not very funny at all. He may have been injured, or even killed, or he may be being held by his enemies for reasons unknown."

"Then why... ?"

"Because, sir, his friends fancy that I am his greatest enemy, and they imagine that I have done away with him. I cannot tell you, sir, how amusing that is."

Moran removed the cigar from his mouth. "I see," he said.

"Do you?" Moriarty asked.

"Actually, Professor, I confess that I do not. I assume that you did not actually do away with, er, the gentleman in question?" Moran sounded bemused, rather than alarmed, at the notion.

"The gentleman in question is the self-styled 'consulting detective' named Sherlock Holmes, and, no, I had nothing whatever to do with his disappearance. I rather regret his passing, if indeed he has passed." Moriarty waved Moran back to his seat. "Finish your story. Perhaps I will be able to help you, perhaps not; but at least you deserve a fair hearing." He leaned forward. "Proceed. Continue."

Colonel Moran looked thoughtful. "Sherlock Holmes has disappeared, has he?"

"Indeed."

"And you had nothing whatever to do with it?"

"Even so."

Moran pursed his lips, considering. After a minute he nodded. "We'll put that aside for now," he said. "I have no reason to disbelieve you. Still, it is peculiar."

"It is," Moriarty agreed.

"Well," Moran said, "back to my tale. For his son and heir's fourteenth birthday, the maharaja ordered the construction of a great temple. These maharajas are always building temples, but this was something special in the way of a temple: four tall marble towers with a definite phallic feel to them at the corners of a vast marble dome. The walls of the dome were covered with erotic sculptures done in what I believe is called 'bas-relief.'"

"There are a number of privately printed books of erotica which contain illustrations of Indian temple carvings," Moriarty said. "I have seen and admired a few such; if not for their artistic quality then for the imagination of the sculptor. Erotic carvings would seem to be fairly common on Hindu temples."

"The native sensibility on the subject of erotic art differs from that of the educated European," Colonel Moran affirmed. "And the native women—But surely here I digress. These carvings are said to honor one of the manifestations of the god Shiva. Beyond that, I know nothing. But that, except in passing, is not what interests us."

"Ah!" Moriarty said.

"Four years after the completion of the temple, the maharaja died and his son, now eighteen, ascended to the throne. The son, to honor his father and celebrate his own existence, commissioned two works of art to be placed in the temple. One was a construct in solid gold—full size—of the, ah, apparatus which had enabled his birth. The joints were set out in rubies and diamonds. The straps and belts were woven from the finest golden threads. A representation of the god Padersiyabi—I may have that wrong—lies prone upon the apparatus but with no visible indication of what he might be able to accomplish in that position. The casual observer is left to wonder what the function of the mechanism might be.

"The second object was a statue, some three feet high, representing his father's favorite houri; the woman whose exotic dancing and, ah, exertions, had enabled, or at least encouraged, the son's conception. Pati was her name. She is depicted standing on her right leg, the left leg bent so that her left foot rests on her right knee. Her arms are in front of her, elbows out, palms facing inward, in a particularly meaningful expression. Just what it expresses, I do not know. If the statue is to be believed, she was quite beautiful. The statue itself is worth a king's ransom, to use a hackneyed, but in this case quite accurate, expression. It was also of solid gold, and encrusted with precious gems: emeralds set into the eyes—Pati had green eyes—and necklaces, bracelets, finger rings, anklets, and a coronet, all set with the most precious gems, fitted onto the statue by the finest jewelers in the kingdom.

"You've seen it, then?"

"I have seen a miniature representation; about six inches high, I'd say. Gilded plaster set with semiprecious stones—valuable in itself, but nothing compared to the intrinsic worth of the original. But exquisite. One feels that it would have been pleasant to know the young woman—Pati. The original is missing—looted from the temple in 1857, during the Sepoy Mutiny. It's guesswork, pure guesswork as to whether it was taken by sepoy troops in revenge for the maharaja being pro-British, or later by the British in revenge for the maharaja being pro-sepoy. And your guess is as good as mine. I have spoken to people who were there, and have heard both stories. Which is why I have come to see you."

"You want to determine who took the statue thirty-five years ago?"

"No, thank God, it won't come to that. Or, rather, I should say, it has passed that. I know who has the golden houri now. I don't know for sure how it came into their hands, but that, thank God, is immaterial."

"You wish my help in recovering the work?"

"The current maharaja, Ramasatjit, has commissioned me to find the golden houri and return it to him. He will pay quite well—more than the intrinsic value of the piece, which, as I've said, is outrageously high."

"How well?"

Moran tapped the ash off the end of his cigar. "What would you say to twenty thousand pounds?" he asked.

"I'd say that, invested conservatively, it could bring you an income of six hundred a year. And you could live quite well on six hundred a year. But then there would be my fee to consider, if I agree to help you."

"You misunderstand me, sir," Moran said. "The twenty thousand would be your fee."

Moriarty polished his pince-nez and replaced them on the bridge of his nose. "You jest, sir," he said.

"I never jest about money," Colonel Moran told him. "And I tell you in all honesty, since, if we are to do this, there should be no secrets between us, at least not concerning the task at hand, that my share will be five times that. I hope you have no problem with that."

"None," Moriarty told him. "But in that case I will make sure that if there is any exceptional risk to be run, you will do the running, Colonel."

"Fair enough," Moran agreed.

Moriarty considered. "Two questions," he said.

"You want to know who has the statue now and where it is?" Moran said.

"That will come later," Moriarty told him. "Why is it worth so much to the current maharaja, and how do we know he will redeem it for the agreed-upon fee?"

"Ah!" Moran said. "As to the first: during the hundred years or so that the statue was in the temple, it became known variously as the Goddess of Lamapoor, the Luck of Lamapoor, the Lady of Lamapoor, and the Queen of Lamapoor. You would pray, if you were so inclined, to one of its various aspects to achieve some worthwhile goal. The Goddess of Lamapoor was adept at providing relief to infertile couples. The Luck of Lamapoor assured success in business ventures. The Lady of Lamapoor answered questions and gave advice, by various forms of divination."

"Lovely!" Moriarty commented. He leaned back and closed his eyes. "And the Queen of Lamapoor?"

"In her aspect as the Queen of Lamapoor the lovely Pati protected the maharaja and his subjects from harm."

"Ah!" Professor Moriarty said. "And has she been successful in this endeavor?"

"Until her disappearance, she performed her job quite well. Lamapoor had a hundred years of prosperity and relative tranquillity while she reposed in her niche in the inner temple wall. The area produces pottery and rugs, both of which are of high quality and highly prized throughout India. After the theft, the country rapidly went to whatever the Hindus think of as perdition. The Sepoy War itself took its toll on the local population, with both sides behaving in a most un-civilized manner—if I do say so myself, as a British officer."

"And since the mutiny?"

"One of the principal dyes used in the rug manufacture suddenly became unobtainable. It was made from some shellfish or other, I believe, and the bloody things died out. And the local clay used to make the pottery was becoming increasingly contaminated with, I believe, sulfur, which was difficult to remove and produced weak and unsuitable tableware. And the migrating waterfowl began avoiding the local lakes. This was of only minor import to the economy, but was considered a bad omen."

"Indeed," Professor Moriarty said. "I myself would consider it a bad omen. I can see why he wants the figure back. How do we know that he'll pay for it?"

"I went to school with the present maharaja. St. Simon's Academy. It was where Westerby Mitchell, the Scottish engineer that contrived the, ah, device, had gone, and the maharajas of Lamapoor have been sending their male children there ever since. The present maharaja was one form behind me. 'Little Pook,' we called him. His older brother 'Big Pook,' was about eight years ahead of us. He was the direct heir, but he died in a tiger hunt. So 'Little Pook' is now the Maharaja of Lamapoor. Who would have guessed?"

"So you're counting on friendship to get paid?"

"Friends? He was one form behind me, and he was a wog," Moran said. "But we respected each other. He was, after all, an extremely rich wog. He had some trouble with, ah, hazing, from some of the more thickheaded students, which he solved by paying me to look after him; and I believe I did a good job. He invited me back to India with him before I took my commission. I spent over a year in Lamapoor, at the royal palace mostly. It was a changeabout, you see. There he was of the ruling class—quite literally—and I was, effectively, the wog. Taught me a lot, that year did."

Moriarty surveyed the colonel wordlessly while Moran stared at his highly polished boot, pondering what he had learned. "The maharaja is a man with an extreme sense of honor," Moran said. "If we return the Queen of Lamapoor, we will be paid."

"Why," Moriarty asked, "did the maharaja pick you to retrieve his statue?"

"Direct, aren't you?" Moran set his cigar carefully in the tray. "Well, if the truth be known, he didn't, not exactly. He let it be known that he would pay a reward for the return of his, ah, luck. I heard of the reward. And, purely by chance, I caught the merest hint of the location of the missing lady. I took leave from my regiment and traced down the rumor through the Anglo-Indian army. I traveled to outposts in Kashmir and Baluchistan, and the scent grew stronger. It was a jeweler in Madras who gave me the final clue. I booked passage back to England on the *Star of Belfast* just as she was leaving port. Once here, I proceeded north to Kilmarnock in Ayr to confirm what I had learned. I was right, although I had guessed wrong in one respect. I sent a telegram to His Majesty to tell him that I might have found the object, and that I might be able to retrieve it, and asking him to confirm the reward. He replied—ah—he replied..." Moran dug through the various pockets in his jacket and pulled out a carefully folded bit of paper. "Here it is, his reply." He passed it over to Professor Moriarty.

MORAN: ANGLO-INDIAN: LONDON
REWARD AS STATED STOP PLUS EXPENSES STOP USE
NO VIOLENCE BREAK NO LAWS IN OBTAINING OBJECT
STOP QUEEN OF LAMAPOOR MUST REMAIN UNBLEMISHED
STOP GOOD HUNTING STOP
LITTLE POOK

Moriarty raised an eyebrow. "I see your dilemma," he said.

"Indeed," Colonel Moran agreed. "A little smash-and-grab, no problem. Cosh a couple of skulls in the process; part of the game. One of 'em dies, well, that's the breaks. I mean, it would have been difficult anyway. Deucedly difficult. But possible. I might have come along to see you and asked for a spot of advice, but I wouldn't have had to bother you to the extent of asking you to become part of the operation. No, sir."

"Break no laws, eh? Interesting problem. I assume you can't just buy it from whoever has it, or you wouldn't be here. Well, where is this little trinket, and how are you planning to get at it?"

"As to the getting at it, well, that's going to be your department, Professor, if you accept this little assignment. As to where she is..." Moran took a long draught on his cigar and slowly blew the smoke out. "She's now in the possession—I might say she's the mascot—of the Duke of Moncreith's Own Highland Lancers. She is placed to the side of the ranking officer at the head of the mess table every evening, and the Lancers drink a toast to her immediately after toasting the queen. So much I learned. While the regiment is at home, she never leaves the officer's mess at their barracks at Castle Fitzroberts in

Kilmarnock. Well, a bit outside of Kilmarnock. But the Duke's Own is back in India at the moment, and so the Lady is closer to home than she has been at any time in these past thirty years. In effect, she's being guarded by sixty officers and twelve hundred men. There is no amount of money, nor any inducement that I can think of, that would cause them to part with their lady."

"Do they know what they have?"

"Apparently not. They call her the 'Lady of Lucknow.' The story is that their regimental sergeant major, McQuist by name, came across her in a cart that had been abandoned by the side of the road while the regiment was engaged in the assault and recapture of Lucknow in March of 1858. Somehow, between her disappearance and her discovery she had been brass-plated. Who put her in the cart is anybody's guess. She immediately, or so the story goes, saved the lives of the sergeant major and two subalterns."

"A busy little statue," Moriarty commented. "And just where is she at the moment? Where are the two brigades of the Duke of Moncreith's Own messing down? Kashmir? Delhi? Afghanistan?"

"In Calcutta by now, I believe," Colonel Moran told him. "The officers and men of the Highland Lancers have come in from showing the flag somewhere upcountry, and are gathering to return to England. They will be in Calcutta for a month or so, and then board a steamer for the trip home."

"A troopship?"

The men and horses will go by troopship, but most of the officers usually choose a higher degree of comfort, especially as many of them have their families with them. So they'll be on one of the civilian steamships—first class, of course."

"Ah!" Moriarty said. "And the statue will, I assume, travel with the officers."

"Of course. Then you'll help?"

"Quite possibly. It is an interesting challenge, and the reward is sufficient to the task. I need more information. I'll make you a list of what I need to know. Are you in communication with someone in Calcutta?"

"I have an agent there," Moran told him. "An old messmate, actually. Cashiered out over some trouble involving a deck of cards. It seems that some, ah, marks had been added to the backs."

"I'm shocked," Moriarty said.

"Yes," Moran replied dryly. "I thought you would be."

Professor Moriarty rose to his feet. "If we do this, we'll have to act immediately."

"And do what?"

"Leave for India. We must get there before the Lady of Lucknow starts on her trip home."

"And then what?"

"If we go the fastest way possible, it will take us three weeks to get to Calcutta. That gives me three weeks to think of something."

Colonel Moran stood up and saluted Moriarty. "Right-oh, Professor," he said, pulling on his overcoat and clapping his hat firmly on his head. "I'll pack. It's good to have you on board."

"I've been meaning to go to India for some time," Moriarty remarked, rising and walking Colonel Moran to the door. "I understand that the records of the Indian astrologers go back many centuries, and there are written observations which comment on the supernova which appeared suddenly in the constellation of Taurus in 1054. I'd like a chance to peruse some of their sky charts from that time which might show the exact location of the star."

Moran stared at Moriarty for a second, afraid that he was being made the butt of some obscure joke. But he decided the professor was serious. "Whatever it takes, Professor," he said, tipping his hat. "Whatever it takes!"

FIVE

THE ENIGMATIC DR. PIN DOK LOW

Fate sits on these dark battlements and frowns,
And as the portal opens to receive me,
A voice in hollow murmurs through the courts
Tells of a nameless deed.
ANN RADCLIFFE

The boy's long nose and protruding teeth were set in a face as white as whey, and his large ears protruded abruptly from the sides of his head. He was called Rodent by everyone who knew him, except his employer and mentor, Dr. Pin Dok Low. Dr. Pin called him "Charles." It was a name that had been given him by Dr. Pin, no more his real name than was "Rodent," but then neither he nor anybody else knew whether he had actually had a birth name, or what it might be. He was also necessarily vague as to his age and his birthday. He thought he might be fourteen, but he looked younger. Most children of the London slums, through malnutrition, lack of exercise, and a paucity of sunlight, looked younger than their age until, suddenly, they looked much older.

He had been called Rodent for as long as he could remember. "Hit's not as hif I minds the name," he told Dr. Pin. "I don't—not weally." And indeed, among his comrades, Gimpy, Spits, Fingers, Warty, and the others, his name was not remarkable.

A short while after Rodent and his friends had entered Pin Dok Low's employment, Dr. Pin had taken him aside and regarded him thoughtfully. "From now on," Pin decided, "you will regard 'Charles' as your given name."

"My given name?"

"Yes, because, you see, I gave it to you."

"Ah, I see," Charles said, although he didn't—not really.

"If you want others to respect you," Pin told him patiently, "you must respect yourself. 'Rodent' is not a name to engender respect. And"—Dr. Pin Dok Low prodded the boy's chest with a long forefinger—"you will be much more useful to me if others trust and respect you."

"Yessir," Charles said doubtfully.

Pin sighed a patient sigh. "We have a long way to go before we reach that particular sunny upland plateau."

Charles was meeting with Dr. Pin in the small warehouse on Bank End Wharf where Pin maintained a—what? Residence? There was no sign that Pin actually lived there. Hideout? But everyone who mattered knew that this was where Pin was to be found. Office? If Pin conducted any business out of the warehouse, it was not evident. It was, Charles supposed, Dr. Pin's place, his spot. Everyone had to have a place, and this was Pin Dok Low's.

The Rodent—Charles—was the leader of a group of street urchins called the Limehouse Coneys, who made a precarious living snatching blows, rozzers, and skins—handkerchiefs, pocket watches, and wallets—from such gentlemen as passed through their neighborhood who were well off enough to possess such fineries. He and his associates had recently accepted another sort of employment from Dr. Pin. "They are my eyes and ears throughout London," as Pin had explained to the Artful Codger.

"They're nothing more than a bunch of dirty young hooligans," Codger had responded.

"Exactly!" Dr. Pin had smiled his crafty smile. "And as such they can go anywhere and see anything. They may be met with kicks or blows, they may be forcibly ejected from here or there, but they will incite no suspicion that they are any more than they seem to be. Sneak thieves, scamps, and hooligans, yes. Spies, no. Give someone something bad to think about you and he will be satisfied, and will seldom try to imagine something worse."

And the Coneys were performing their assignments well. For the cost of six shillings a week, Pin Dok Low had eyes and ears all over London. Such was the price of the souls of a dozen boys.

"Well, Charles?" Pin Dok Low demanded, sitting on his high red chair behind his high ebon desk and staring down unblinkingly at the young street arab. "What have you for me today?"

"There's nuffing stirring at the Baker Street crib," Charles replied, hat respectfully in his hands, feet together, eyes focused on the little ivory idol on the desk. "Mrs. Hudson, the landlady, she goes out and comes in 'bout twice a day. That Dr. Watson, 'e come there yesterday for a bit, kind of stared at fings in the study—you could see him fru the winder from the 'ouse across the street—and went away again. But no sign of Mr. Sherlock Holmes."

"Welcome news," Pin said.

"And?"

"And that professor cove in Russell Square—'e's going away."

Pin Dok Low stood up and slapped his hands down on the desk with a sudden noise that made the Rodent jump. "Going away? What do you mean, going away?"

"I means what I says," the Rodent said, trying not to cringe as Pin Dok Low towered over him. "'E put this 'ere great trunk in a growler first fing this morning and sent it off to Victoria Station, didn't 'e? And then 'e followed 'imself with another trunk in a second growler, didn't 'e?"

"Blast!" said Dr. Pin Dok Low. "Where on earth could the man be going?"

"India," Charles told him. "'E's going to India. Calli-cutta, as 'e said."

"Indeed?" Pin sat slowly back down on his chair. "Calcutta, is it? And just how do you know that?"

"Didn't I follow 'im to Victoria Station? Didn't I wisk life and limb by 'anging on to the back of 'is growler? 'E met another cove at the station, see, and I overhears their gab."

Pin leaned forward and fixed his gaze on Charles. "And who was the other gentleman?"

"I didn't 'appen to 'ear that, did I? They didn't 'appen to mention 'is name. Big, 'eavyset cove, struts about like a soldier."

"And what did they do?"

"They booked a first-class carriage on the Continental Express. They're going to cross the Channel tomorrow morning, and take the boat train to Paris. Then they're going to Calli-cutta."

"And how are they going from Paris?"

"They didn't say, did they? I mean, they ain't going to discuss their entire aytinny-arary standing there in front of the station, just so's I can overhear it, now, are they?"

"And you heard nothing more?"

"No, sir," Charles said. "Well, not much. The professor, he said as how he figures that going as far as they can by train will cut a couple of weeks off the time, 'cause of 'ow a train's faster than what a boat is."

"Ship," Pin corrected automatically.

"Yessir, ship. They wants to get there before the regiment sails."

"The regiment. Ah, of course—the regiment. Just which regiment would that be?"

"They didn't say."

Pin Dok Low leaned back and closed his eyes. For several minutes he said nothing, and the Rodent waited with his hat in his hand, unsure of what to do and afraid to make a sound. Finally Pin opened his eyes again. "Interesting," he said. "But for now..." He leaned forward and lowered his head until his eyes were level with those of the young street arab. "You are doing well. Keep it up and don't fail me, and you and your fellows will be adequately rewarded. Keep an eye on sixty-four Russell Square, in case Professor Moriarty should suddenly return. Keep watch on the house of Mr. Sherlock Holmes, and regularly report who goes in and comes out."

"Yessir," Charles the Rodent said.

"For now"—Pin scribbled a note on a sheet of foolscap, folded it, and passed it to Charles—"you know where to find the Twopenny Yob?"

"'Is digs is off Bensby Street."

"Ah, yes, Barnesbury Street it is. Go and find him and give him this note."

"Yessir," Charles said, stuffing the note into the pocket of his tattered jacket.

"Very good." Low reached into his pocket, pulled out a small cloth purse, and extracted a few coins. "Here's a week's wages for you and your boys. Be off with you now!"

* * *

The Twopenny Yob appeared at the warehouse about two hours later. "I wish you'd send your notes by someone that looks a mite more respectable," he said. "You never know just whom I might be entertaining. I hope this is important, 'cause you pulled me away from what could be a promising evening with the pasteboards. I found me a mark from Newcastle who thinks he's hot stuff, and I was aiming to cool him down five or ten pounds' worth."

"Have you ever been to India?" asked Pin Dok Low.

"Naow," the Yob answered, stretching out the vowel until it sounded like a complaining tomcat. "What on this earth would I ever want to go to India for? I went to Paris once; it was raining. I might go back sometime when I hear the rain has stopped. I went to New York once. I was working the ocean liners. Nothing to do but play cards for upwards of three weeks. Bridge, poker, and euchre—the Americans like euchre. A man can make an honest living on the ocean liners, if he knows how to cold-stack a deck and can do a convincing second deal. On this one crossing on the *Teutonic* the purser was starting to give me the eye, so I got off at New York to wait for the next ship, whichever it might be. Got into a friendly poker game on the Bowery, and narrowly avoided getting shot. Probably won't go back to New York. But India? I never considered India. I never intend to consider India. What has India got that I might want?"

Pin waited patiently for the Yob to stop talking. "Pack," he said.

"Excuse me?"

"Professor Moriarty and a companion just left for Calcutta. The gold is shortly to be shipped out of Calcutta. It could be a coincidence. I don't believe in coincidences, do you?"

"I'm with you there, Pin, but just what do you want me to do about it?"

"Does Professor Moriarty know what you look like?"

"Well, I've never met him formally, but with the professor you never know."

"We'll take the chance," Pin said. "I want you to catch up to him and stay with him. Stalk him like you would a dangerous animal. Observe his every move; read his every thought. At the same time, I want you to remain invisible to him, and keep from him our interest in his whereabouts and his doings." He tapped his finger on the desk. "You won't even come close to this ideal, but approach it as nearly as possible. With an emphasis on not letting him know of our interest."

"I see," said the Twopenny Yob.

"Keep me informed of your progress by telegraph. Once you have established where he is, where he is going, and what he is doing, let me know and I will send someone to meet you."

"Oh? For what purpose?"

"All in all, I think it might be wise to alter our plan in one respect. Rather than use the professor as a foil, I think we should find out what his plans are, and, if they conflict with ours, have him eliminated. Perhaps even if they don't conflict with ours, it might be simpler."

"Do we not need the agreement of the others for such a move?" the Yob suggested.

"I will call a meeting. But if any disagree, I will be very curious as to why. You have no problem with eliminating Professor Moriarty, I assume?"

The Twopenny Yob nodded calmly, as though Pin had just suggested stepping on a bug. "I wouldn't want to attempt it myself," he said. "But as I'm just to catch up to him and follow him, you can do what you think best."

"Thank you," Pin Dok Low said, with a slight bow. "And now you'd best be on your way."

"And just how am I to catch up with him?"

"He and his companion just took the Continental Express to Dover. They're planning to cross the Channel tomorrow morning. We will hire a special, which should get you to Dover sometime late tonight. With luck, you'll be on the same ferry."

"I'll pack," the Yob said. "Give me an hour."

"I'll see about hiring the special. Meet me at Victoria Station. You will need all your wits if you are to accomplish anything."

"I'll be sure to bring them along," said the Twopenny Yob.

SIX

GOVERNMENT HOUSE

When 'Omer smote 'is bloomin' lyre,
'E'd 'eard men sing by land and sea;
An' what 'e thought 'e might require,
'E went an' took—the same as me!

RUDYARD KIPLING

When the red and white carriage carrying Brigadier General Sir Edward Basilberg St. Yves, I.C., and his daughter suddenly pulled to a stop, in the middle of Kalutala Street, right past the Temple of the Seven Winds, St. Yves hitched his dress sword around to a more comfortable position, put his cocked hat carefully beside him on the seat of the coach, lowered the window, and stuck his head out as far as dignity would allow. "Blast and d-damnation," he said after a few moments, withdrawing his head back into the carriage.

Margaret St. Yves attempted to look shocked. "Father!" she said sternly, suppressing an urge to giggle.

"It's cows, Peg," he said. "It's always b-bally cows."

"Cows?"

"In the road," he explained, tapping on the window glass with his knuckle. "Just standing there in the middle of the b-bally road, with no interest in moving in any direction, doing their b-bally bovine-headed b-best to make us late for the viceroy's dinner."

"Really?" Margaret considered. "Do you suppose they're afraid we're going to eat one of their relatives?"

"There isn't enough beef on any of these scrawny creatures to be worth eating," St. Yves said. "Although I suppose if you b-boiled one for long enough you'd get some sort of stew."

"Well, then," Margaret suggested, "perhaps they're trying to save us from having to listen to the viceroy's speech. If we arrive late enough, perhaps his speech will be over."

"No chance of that, I'm afraid," St. Yves said, patting his daughter on the shoulder. This was as close to a show of affection as the general allowed himself.

"Oh, dear," Peg said, letting her eyes go round. It made her look winsome and innocent, and when she was sixteen she had practiced it in front of her looking glass. "Is Sir George going to be aiming his speech at us?"

"Probably at least a small part of it," St. Yves told her. "This burra khana is being held, at least partly, for the officers of the Duke of Moncreith's Own, so it's not likely that he'll start without us."

"Burra khana?" Margaret asked.

"Banquet or b-big feast, or something of the sort."

"Yes, I know what it means. I've learned a little Hindustani, you know."

"Yes," St. Yves said, patting his daughter on the knee. "Quite a lot, apparently. And I do admire you for it. You've learned more about Indian customs and, er, that sort of thing in the past two years than I've picked up in the five years I've been here. But I will say that staying up-country with me since you arrived in India has saved you from learning about some of the more unsavory sides of Anglo-Indian life."

"Like banquets and balls and fetes and the like?" Margaret asked, smiling.

"Exactly," her father agreed. "Damn nuisances. Overdressed people stuffing themselves with indigestible food and making conversation about matters in which they're not interested or know nothing whatever about."

"Yes, Father," Margaret agreed. "Thank you for saving me from that."

He looked at her suspiciously, but she smiled sweetly at him and turned to peer out the window.

The three cows that had been standing in the road with their heads together, as though plotting the overthrow of some bovine autocracy, moved off in single file, in search of greener roadways. The carriage gave a jerk, and another. St. Yves pushed his nose up against the window glass. "Ah! We seem to be moving," he said.

"Well," Peg said, holding firmly onto the leather handstrap, "I suppose up-and-down is a form of motion."

Brigadier General Sir Edward Basilberg St. Yves, I.C., commanding officer of the Duke of Moncreith's Own Highland Lancers, lately returned from suppressing minor rebellions in Assam and Bhutan, sank, or rather bounced, back into the unyielding leather of his seat. Why, he wondered, was it so bally difficult to have a talk—a real man-to-ah-woman talk—with his own daughter? There were things that a parent was supposed to say to his child—that a father was supposed to say to his daughter—and St. Yves had managed to avoid saying most of them. But over the past two years, since Margaret had come out from England to join him in India, the feeling had been growing on him that something must be said. He might, for instance, say, "Peg, m'dear, we'll be going back to England shortly. I think I shall open the house in London. Retire my commission. What would you think of that? What would you like to do, that is, with yourself, I mean?"

Or then again, no beating about the bush. Perhaps the more direct approach: "Peg, m'dear, you're eighteen years old now. Don't you think it's time you considered getting married?"

He might say that, but he couldn't even imagine the words coming from his mouth. Then again he might say to his beautiful, blond, gray-eyed daughter, "Peg, every young unmarried officer in my command is under your spell. I do wish you would do something about it."

But then, could he bring himself to say that, she might well answer, "But, Daddy, what would you have me do?" And he would have no reply, since, as far as he could see, she was not casting any spell beyond bland indifference to the lot of them.

"M'dear," he said.

She turned in her seat to face him. "Yes, Father?"

"What do you think... you know... I mean, as a father..." He could feel himself getting red in the face. Why should talking seriously to his beloved daughter be worse than facing a board of inquiry from the War Department? He didn't know, but there it was. "That is, d-dash it all, how do you think I, as a father, am doing? That is, with you, as a... er... daughter?"

Seeing by his expression that he was in earnest and a humorous response wouldn't suffice, Margaret thought about it seriously for a long moment. That was her way: Humor sprang to her lips unbidden, but when a serious reply was required, a serious reply was forthcoming. Sometimes all too serious.

"I haven't had much experience, you know, with other fathers," she told him, patting his knee gently. "But from what I can tell, you're right up there, bung-ho, a top-drawer dad."

"Is that good?" he asked.

"The best," she assured him, and leaned over and kissed him on the cheek.

"Well," he said, with a feeling that he'd accomplished something, although he couldn't have said what. "Glad to hear it. I do my b-best, you know."

"I know." Margaret adjusted the bodice of the green satin dress she was wearing, and straightened the pink silk flowers that decorated her shoulder. Then she took a small hand mirror from her purse and carefully examined her face. "I just wish we'd arrived in Calcutta a week earlier, so I would have had time to go to the dressmaker's before this evening. I'll probably be the only woman there in last year's dress."

"M'dear," St. Yves said, "there won't be a man in the room who won't think you're the most b-beautiful woman for ten leagues in any direction. And they'll be right."

Margaret laughed. "Thank you, dear Father," she said. "But you must surely know that women don't dress to please men; they dress to impress or annoy other women."

The carriage pulled up in front of Government House, a massive hundred-year-old building in classical Anglo-Roman style, somewhat grander than the average palace; the sort of structure that the British nobility back home had been building as country houses through the seventeenth and eighteenth centuries.

A native footman standing by the oversized front entrance popped over to the carriage, popped the carriage door open, and popped the steps into place. St. Yves adjusted his dress sword and his jacket, tucked his hat carefully under his arm, and descended from the carriage before helping his daughter down onto the wide green carpet that had been laid from the curb to the large double doors.

The majordomo, who awaited them at the entrance, was a splendid personage from his ornate gold-laced tan turban and short, thick, black beard to his long, thin, pointed-toed shiny black shoes. Over his puffy tan pantaloons he wore a green and white dress jacket with oversized gold buttons and a pair of tails trailing almost down to his ankles. "I greet you with much gladness, General sahib," he said, eyeing St. Yves's uniform. "Welcome to Government House. The viceroy would speak with you ever so briefly before the dinner gong is struck."

"The viceroy wants to see us?"

"That is so." The majordomo gestured and a short, dark footman detached himself from a line of waiting footmen and trotted over. The majordomo whispered something in the footman's ear.

"Pliz to follow me," the footman said, making a small but expressive come-along gesture with his right hand.

The footman trotted confidently ahead, and they followed in his wake. "Well!" Margaret said. "Why does Sir George want to see you?"

"Haven't the slightest," St. Yves told her. "We'll know soon enough."

Margaret hitched the skirt of her dress up slightly to negotiate the steps of the wide marble staircase. "It will be quite a conversation-stopper when we're back in England," she said. "I can say, 'Shortly before I left India I was at Government House and the viceroy told me—in confidence, of course'—oops!"

"Oops?"

"I almost tripped. Do you suppose, Father, that you could get Sir

George to tell me something in confidence? Some slight, unimportant thing of little consequence?"

"You must ask him," St. Yves said. "I'm certain he will oblige."

"Pliz to come this way," the footman said at the top of the staircase, pointing down a long corridor to the left with dark wood doors evenly spaced along the green walls. He promptly trotted off in the direction of his pointing finger.

"You were at Boxley with him?" Margaret asked.

St. Yves looked at his daughter. "B-Broxley. Yes, sort of. He was three years ahead of me."

"So you weren't close?"

"No, that's so."

"But you call him 'Messy.'"

"That's so. And he calls me 'Tubs.' But we weren't close."

"Tubs?"

"Yes," St. Yves said, looking slightly embarrassed. "I wasn't always as, ah, slender as I am now."

"I see," his daughter said, having the wisdom not to laugh, or even smile.

The doors along the corridor had small brass plates with names on them: "Mr. Ffaulks," read one; "Mr. Abernatty," the next; "Sir Toby Bentham," after that, and across from them one that said "Customs," and one that said "Writers," and then an unmarked one, in front of which the footman stopped.

He knocked on the door, three precise knocks, and then pushed it open. "Pliz," he said, standing aside for them to enter.

The room was a good-sized library, with walls full of books, a long table down the center, a small desk at the far end, a pair of red damask-covered easy chairs, and a scattering of wooden chairs with tooled-leather seats and backs. Sir George Demassis Montague, Her Britannic Majesty's Viceroy for her Indian Empire, in a fluffy dress shirt, chalk-white trousers, and high black boots, was sunk deep into an easy chair, his feet up on a wooden chair he had pulled over for that purpose, reading a book. The rest of his viceregal regalia, a red jacket with gold braid, a wide plum-colored sash, and a chest full of medals, was hung carefully over the back of another chair. A dress sword with several large gemstones in the pommel rested in its gold scabbard on the desk.

A ruddy-faced man of average stature, with reddish brown hair, a prominent nose, and wide sideburns that almost met at his chin, Sir George had the knack of commanding loyalty from his subordinates and respect from those he dealt with; a fact that came as a continual surprise to him. As St. Yves and his daughter came in, he put the book aside and pushed himself to his feet. "General St. Yves," he said. "Tubs. Good to see you."

"Messy," St. Yves said. "It's been a while."

The viceroy reached for his jacket. "Djuna!" he called. "Where is that boy? Ah, well." Philosophically, he struggled into his jacket by himself.

"No need to dress on our account, Your Excellency," St. Yves said.

"Only polite," Sir George said. "Besides, it's almost time to go in." He beamed at Margaret. "Your daughter, I assume."

"My daughter Margaret," St. Yves affirmed. "Peg, Sir George Montague, my old schoolmate, who has made something of himself since leaving B-Broxley."

"It all comes of having the right parents, don't you know," Sir George said, struggling to fasten the sash over his jacket. "Hard work and a certain flair for the diplomatic"—he let go of the sash, and it promptly bounced up to his chin—"combined with a tendency to tell other people what to do, are all very well, but arranging to have a father who is an earl, even an Irish earl, can make all the difference."

"Here, allow me," Margaret said, stepping forward and pulling the lower end of the sash into place.

"Thank you, young lady," the viceroy said. "I don't want to give the impression that I can't dress myself, but this fancy dress costume I'm called upon to wear requires assembly and construction. One can't simply get into it, one has to build it around oneself. There's the sword that goes with it, but I absolutely refuse to wear the sword this evening. It will bang and clatter about my legs, and serve no useful purpose, and probably trip me up at some inopportune moment. If there's to be any swordplay, I'll let your father defend me. He's much better at it than I am, no doubt, anyway."

St. Yves clutched the handle of his dress sword. "I doubt if this thing's sharp enough to do much damage," he said. "B-but you show me which of Her Majesty's civil servants you wish skewered, and I shall make the attempt."

"Really!" Margaret said, stepping back to examine her handiwork. "You are a pair of bloodthirsty gentlemen."

The viceroy took a pair of white cotton gloves from the pocket of his jacket and slipped them on. "But well dressed," he said, "and with excellent manners." He examined himself in the slender mirror in the wall behind his desk. "Thank you, my dear," he said.

"We should precede you into the hall," St. Yves said.

The viceroy lowered himself into the chair behind his desk and waved them into nearby chairs. "I must speak with you before we go in," he said. "Please sit down."

"Certainly, Your Excellency," St. Yves replied.

Sir George nodded. "Two things," he said. "The first is official." He turned to Margaret. "It's also confidential. I won't ask you to leave the room, that would be rude, and we English gentlemen may be blood-thirsty, but we are never rude. So I will merely ask you not to mention it to anyone until, ah, until you reach England."

"Asking me to keep a secret is never 'mere,'" she told him. "But"— she made the mark of a large X across her chest with her forefinger— "I solemnly promise that whatever secrets you may share with us will never be divulged by me. Never."

"Excellent," Sir George said, smiling. He turned his gaze back to General St. Yves. "You are returning to England momentarily, I believe."

"Yes, Your Excellency. The Highland Lancers have been relieved, as you know. The men will be embarking on the troopship *Egypt*, probably at the end of this coming week. Most of the officers, particularly those with family here, will be taking whatever passenger ship leaves soonest after the *Egypt*." St. Yves smiled a wry smile. "The passenger ship will be more comfortable and faster, but Her Majesty's government will not pay for mere comfort for enlisted men. Or for officers, either, if it comes to that, but we can afford the passage. So we'll p-probably be waiting on the dock for the men when the *Egypt* arrives."

Sir George leaned back in his chair and stared steadily at St. Yves. "In this case," he told him, "you and your officers and some of your men will be traveling on *The Empress of India*. Rather fitting, all things considered. Her Majesty's government will reimburse you, since you will be on the queen's business."

"I see." St. Yves thought this over, but no possible reason for this unexpected governmental munificence came to mind. "I sense that you are about to tell me something that I will not like," he told the viceroy, "although what it might be exceeds my grasp."

There was a knock at the door, and a small young man in an oversized turban and baggy shirt and trousers came into the room.

"Ah, Djuna," the viceroy said, "there you are. Where were you when I was trying to fix this sash? Never mind, it's done now; this charming young lady did it for me."

"So sorry this babu was called away, sahib," Djuna said, bowing several times briefly, giving the general appearance of one bobbing for invisible apples. "So happy that the memsahib was able to help. The job of personal secretary to the sahib viceroy involves affixing cravat and sash, making tea, tending to visitors, beating shoe-wallah for not properly shining shoes, chasing away native job seekers and mendicants who would invade viceroy's office pleading for baksheesh. All is time-consuming, and sometimes functions overlap. I sincerely abase myself."

"First of all, you're my valet, not my personal secretary," Sir George said crossly. "You can't go around making up any title that pleases you. Last week it was—what was it?—social assistant. What on earth is a social assistant? Second of all, if I ever catch you beating the shoe-wallah—do I have a shoe-wallah?—I will personally beat you severely."

"Yes, sahib, you will," Djuna agreed. "There is native person to see you. A merchant of some sort, perhaps; although there is something of the hill tribesman about him. He says he has news. I have put him in the waiting room to your office."

"At this hour?" the viceroy grumbled. "Tell him to come back during the day."

"He says it is important even now. He says, 'To be or not to be.' Is quote from famous English playwright-wallah Shakespeare."

"Ah!" the viceroy said. "Bring him some tea and have some food sent to him. Tell him I'll be with him in a bit."

"To be or not to be?" Margaret asked.

"It is a, ah, sort of password," Sir George explained. "The native must be a member of what we call the 'Scouts.' They travel all over India and gather information in which the government might be interested. I'll see him after the burra khana."

Djuna bowed. "You wish me to assist you with your sword before I depart?" he asked.

"I am not wearing my sword."

"That is self-obviously so. You desire assistance putting it on?"

"I am not wearing my sword, and I do not intend to wear my sword. You may put my sword away in the cabinet."

"Big painting on wall of dining room shows viceroy wearing fancy dress, gold stripes, sash with medals of many shapes and colors, and great gold sword."

"That was painted a hundred years ago. Lord Wellesley wore a sword. I choose not to."

"The hoi and the polloi at the burra khana will expect to see viceroy-wallah altogether decked out in full splendiferous costume," Djuna insisted.

"But without the sword, my young friend. Now get out of here before I either wallop you or dock your pay."

Djuna shrugged. "Okey-doke. But please for the wallop. My wages already insignificant enough." He circled the desk, picked up the sword, and trotted out of the room.

"So," St. Yves said, "the hoi and the polloi are going to be among us at the dinner. Just how hoi, and which polloi, if you don't mind my asking?"

Sir George dropped heavily back into his chair. "It's my wife's idea," he said. "The common people must get a chance to mingle with their governor at least twice a year. Just not too common, and mostly European. The natives we invite are mostly of higher status than many of the Anglos."

"Very democratic," Margaret remarked.

The viceroy looked at her contemplatively for a moment, and then turned back to St. Yves. "Here's the situation regarding *The Empress of India*," he said. "I want you to pick, say, five of your officers and thirty of your most dependable men to sail back with you on her."

"To do what?" St. Yves asked.

"As it happens, you'll be guarding a treasure. Unofficially, or let me say semiofficially, but that's what I want you there for."

"A treasure?" St. Yves asked. "What sort of treasure?"

"The *Empress* has been refitted with a large strong-room," the viceroy told him. "When she arrives here in the middle of next week, it will be emptied of the first shipment of a new paper currency that we are about to introduce. Then it will be filled with a great amount of gold bullion, to a value of some four million pounds, that is even now being assembled, under heavy guard, at Fort William. The gold is to be taken back to the Bank of England, where it will be used, among other things, to back the currency."

Margaret raised her hand to interrupt the flow of conversation. "If you don't mind my asking what I'm sure is a silly question," she said, "what is the advantage of taking gold away and issuing paper money, if the gold is going to be used to back the paper money? Why not just turn the gold into coins?"

The viceroy shrugged. "It's not a silly question," he said. "It's one I've asked myself. And the only answer I can give you is that the banking-wallahs say it's a good idea. Something about convertibility. For every rupee's worth of gold that we're keeping in the vaults, we can issue ten or twelve rupees of paper. Don't ask me why, but I'm told we can do that. Not only that, but the gold can be loaned out and earn interest at the same time as it's backing the currency; and even when it's loaned out it never physically leaves the bank."

"Oh," Margaret said.

St. Yves leaned back in his chair and stared fixedly at the viceroy. "My question is: Why are we to guard the gold, and from what exactly are we guarding it?"

"Another good question, and the answer is: I don't exactly know.

But come now, we must go join the, ah, crowd. It would never do for the viceroy to be late for his own burra khana." Sir George patted his old school chum on the shoulder. "Return here after dinner and we'll work out the details. All will be made clear to you. And perhaps even to me."

SEVEN

WEST OF SUEZ

Go on my friend, and fear nothing;
you carry Caesar and his fortunes in your boat.
JULIUS CAESAR (AS QUOTED BY PLUTARCH)

The boat train from Calais pulled into the Gare du Nord at three-fifteen in the afternoon, and a cloud of visiting *Anglais* and returning *Francais* flowed out to the platform and quickly dissipated onto the streets of Paris. Professor Moriarty and Colonel Sebastian Moran were among the last to leave the first-class carriage, acting on the years of experience that had taught them that caution is most valuable when there is no apparent need.

After a few moments, they were joined by Mummer Tolliver, Moriarty's servant and "midget of all work," accompanied by a blue-jacketed porter pushing a hand truck. "This gent assures me that if I give him the baggage ticket, he'll bring us our luggage," Mummer said. "Either that or I have two sick dogs in the handbag of my aunt. He seems to be speaking some foreign language, which I am trying to follow along as best I can out of thissere book."

"French, perhaps?" Moriarty suggested.

"That's what he'd like us to think," the mummer said darkly, "but can we be sure?"

Moriarty sighed and shook his head. "Give the porter the baggage tickets," he told Mummer. "We'll take the risk."

"As you say," the mummer agreed, and he handed the flimsy documents over to the porter, who shrugged a fatalistic Gallic shrug and headed off in the direction of the baggage car.

"Now, my friends, comes the moment of decision," Moriarty said. "Mummer, when the porter returns with the baggage you'll have to have him take them to the *salle des bagages* so the French authorities can signify their approval of our possessions. Then check them in the cloakroom—the sign says *consigne*—and join us."

"Course I will," the mummer said with a tip of his hat. "Who says I won't? Join you where?"

Moriarty thought for a second. "The Café du Chien Soured, I suppose, on the Rue de Maubeuge, about a block away to the right."

A light snowfall welcomed them to the street, and the air smelled of coal, wood, and charcoal fires; and wet horse from the row of carriages pulled up outside the station. Moriarty and Colonel Moran belted their greatcoats, pulled up their collars, settled their hats firmly on their heads, and braved the block and a half to the café. They settled at a table by the window where they could watch the snow falling against a background of grimy train station. Moriarty ordered a cappuccino and a plate of bread and cheese. Moran, a whiskey and soda, "and that will do me nicely, thank you."

Moriarty spread open an *Indicateur Chaix*, the French version of a railroad timetable, and stared down at it with amused intensity. "One can devote one's life to studying the innermost mysteries of the universe," he said, "or the intricacies of a French railroad timetable, but not both. Not in the same lifetime."

"The British are not much better," Moran observed. "And the Anglo-Indians have a certain quality of operatic intensity and futility about them. They make dramatic promises that one knows they're not going to keep."

"Well," Moriarty said, "this one seems to claim that if we are at the Gare d'Est at eight-seventeen tomorrow morning, we can board the Express d'Orient. Although, it assures us, it would be of the preference of the railroad and the simplicity of the traveler if we purchased our *billets simple* from La Compagnie Internationale des Wagons-Lits at their offices in the Rue Savoyard, or at the Gare, or through the concierge of any major hotel in advance of our attempting the voyage."

"It says that, does it?"

"Even so. This will put us in Munich the morning of the second day, and Vienna early the morning after. And then on to Budapest, Bucharest, and Giurgiu."

"Giurgiu?"

"It's on the Danube. We detrain at Giurgiu."

"Why?"

"Evidently because there's no bridge. We take a ferry across the Danube to a city-town-village or whatever called Ruse, which is in Bulgaria."

"*Serveuse!*" Moran called, waving his empty whiskey glass in the air. "I can see," he told Moriarty, "why I've always taken a ship. It may take an extra two weeks, but it's less athletic."

"In Ruse," Moriarty continued, flipping a page in the *Indicateur Chaix*, "we hop back on a train, which is a continuation of the first train, so the *chef de train* will see to our *bagage*, and after seven hours we find ourselves in Varna, which is on the Black Sea."

"The Black Sea? So after this we take a ship?"

"Yes, for fourteen hours. And then we find ourselves in Constantinople."

Colonel Moran stared at Professor Moriarty. "There is an overland route from Constantinople to India," he said. "But it is only negotiable by camel, goes through, among other places, Afghanistan, which is not a good idea at the moment, and it takes many months."

"Fond as I am of riding on the backs of camels, we will forgo the pleasure," Moriarty said. "From Constantinople we can either take a train to southern Greece and a ship across the Mediterranean, or we can try for a ship to Port Said directly from Constantinople. This timetable is of no use for either of those possibilities. At Port Said we can embark on the next British passenger ship headed through the canal to India. If we can make reasonably quick connections, we will save over two weeks on the passage to India. If that's what we want to do."

"And why shouldn't we do that?" Moran asked.

"We probably should," Moriarty told him. "But it's a bit risky. If we miss connections, we could be stranded for a week in Varna, or even Constantinople."

"And the option?" Moran asked, smiling broadly at the proprietress, who was bringing him his second whiskey and soda. With a great effort of will, she did not retreat hastily from the table. Colonel Sebastian Moran's broad smile had been known to stop a band of marauding hill tribesmen in their tracks and cause them to seriously consider taking up sheep farming.

"One option would be to proceed directly south from here and see if we can intercept an outgoing ship at Naples or Palermo—which would also involve a ferry ride. That way we will save a week at most, but we're more sure of getting a ship."

Colonel Moran pondered for a second. "I say go for broke," he said.

"Broke it is, then," Professor Moriarty agreed. "We can put up for the night at the Hôtel Gerard on Rue des Brigadiers—they know me there—and send the concierge out for our billets."

Moran's white teeth flashed in a brief grin. "Here I am in Paris, and on my own, so to speak," he said. "I do have to send a telegram to my agent in Constantinople, make sure nothing's gone astray in the past week. I'll have him reply to Munich. And after that, I fancy I can find a useful way to spend a night in Paris on my own, Professor, if you've no objection."

Moriarty raised an eyebrow. "None, my good man, as long as you make it to the train in the morning."

"Never fear," Colonel Moran said. "I never allow pleasure to interfere with my obligations."

EIGHT

THE JADOOGAR

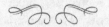

And who, in time, knows whither we may vent
The treasure of our tongue, to what strange shores
This gain of our best glory shall be sent,
T'enrich unknowing nations with our stores?
What worlds in th'yet unformed Occident
May come refin'd with th'accents that are ours?
SAMUEL DANIEL

The burra khana was held in the Presentation Dining Room. The largest of several, it was spacious enough to hold a small circus with its menagerie, elephants and all, and a good bit of its audience. The walls were covered with elaborate brocade hangings, and three rows of crystal chandeliers, like great opalescent squid, filled the room with the bright light of hundreds of recently installed gas mantles.

Small tables were spattered about the room with a random hand, to create a casual, informal feeling to the banquet. The guests likewise had been spattered among the tables with reckless intermingling, the better, as the viceroy's wife, Lady Montague, put it with an expansive wave of her gloved and bejeweled hand, to make new friends and experience new ideas. Although anyone who expressed truly new ideas would certainly not have been invited to the viceroy's February burra khana.

Margaret's father was sitting up with the viceroy at one of three tables at the front of the room, an area which had the floor raised just enough so that one could tell that people at the tables there were above the common herd, metaphorically as well as physically. Margaret was at a six-person table somewhere near the middle of the room, with two other women, two men, and an empty chair. The man to her left had a full mane of graying hair, a trim beard, and a thin, wide mustache, turned up at the ends and twisted to fine points, along with piercing blue eyes and a wide nose that was, unfortunately, a bit too red to suggest a life of total sobriety. His dinner jacket fitted him precisely, but the lapels were a bit too wide, and the tips a bit too pointed for a proper English cut. And did not his shirt have just a few more pleats on it than an English gentleman would have thought proper?

To that man's left sat a heavy, angular elderly lady whose dark green satin gown, bespeckled with diamonds, was too heavy by far for the climate—but the proprieties must be observed. A large diamond ring ornamented each of her forefingers, and from the rope of pearls encircling her neck descended an even larger diamond. For variety's sake, a pair of large sapphires were pinned to her ears, but the diamond theme was recaptured by the tiara nestled in her tightly curled hair.

To her left, directly opposite Margaret, sat a short, slightly tubby, distinguished-looking Indian gentleman with dark eyes and pitch-black hair that came to an exaggerated widow's peak and lay so perfectly flat on his head that it seemed to have been painted on, or perhaps glued in place. He wore an elaborately embroidered white and tan kurta—the knee-length garment that looks like a cross between a frock and a jacket—and his gold-rimmed glasses had oversized, round lenses which gave him a look of perpetual astonishment.

And then an empty chair. And then, to Margaret's right, completing the circle of the table, was a young woman in an unassuming light blue gown. Her hair was blond and not quite under as much control as might be wished, her eyes were a mild, impassive blue in a face of such perfection that men might think of angels, or, perhaps, of other things. A plain gold bracelet was her only adornment aside from what nature had provided.

As the waiters ladled the thick yellow mulligatawny soup from a great silver tureen into the waiting bowls, the French-looking gentleman cleared his throat. "Permit me to make the assumption that it would be proper, considering the occasion, if we were to introduce ourselves back and forth to one and another," he said, looking around the table. "I believe we have been seated all hobbilty-cobbilty to permit of such informality. And I do not have the objection if it falls upon me to begin. Myself, I am named Professor Gerard August Demartineu. I have done the traveling about India for a time now, and I have discovered much of interest. I find that I have a great admiration for the Indian people, and a great respect for what I see that you English are attempting to do to them. Or is it for them? These English conjunctions are of the utmost difficulty to acquire."

The older lady turned a stern gaze at Demartineu. She gave the clear impression that stern gazing was nothing new to her. "You speak with an accent," she accused him. "Are you some sort of foreigner?"

"Ah, but, madam," Demartineu said to her, "are we not all foreigners here?"

"Humph!" the lady replied.

"Except, of course, for my friend Mamarum Sutrow," he continued, indicating the short man in native garb on the lady's other side.

"Alas," the little man said, "I myself would be counted as a foreigner in this place. I am most originally from Kalat, even beyond Sind, and one would have to pass through many kingdoms of various sorts and sizes before reaching my homeland."

"There, you see," Demartineu told the lady. "We are indeed all foreigners here."

Margaret smiled. "Everyone is a foreigner in this world," she said. And she quoted:

"'Into this Universe, and Why not knowing
Nor Whence, like Water willy-nilly flowing;
And out of it, as Wind along the Waste,
I know not Whither, willy-nilly blowing.'"

The young woman to her right clapped her hands together. "*The Rubáiyát!*" she cried, her voice full of sighs and youth. "How wonderful, and yet how sad."

"Even so," Mamarum Sutrow said, breaking into a broad smile. "Omar Khayyám. Another foreigner. Translated from the Persian by an Englishman named Fitzgerald."

"And it's true," the young woman said, her eyes shining. "As true as only poetry can be true. We are—all of us—foreigners, visitors for a time to this world, and then we pass beyond. As Omar said, 'The Wine of life keeps oozing drop by drop, / The Leaves of Life keep falling one by one.'"

The older woman looked at the younger and her faced cracked into what might have been a smile. "I remember having a passion for *The Rubáiyát*, it must be a quarter century ago. 'The moving finger writes, and having writ, moves on....' It is, indeed, so beautiful and so sad. But I found its constant allusions to drinking rather off-putting; as though drunken carousing could solve anything or provide solace for the ills of the world."

"It serves as well as most other things, madam," Demartineu said. "One or two glasses of wine make the world seem brighter, and a few more glasses make it go away entirely, if only for a while." He dropped his spoon into the soup bowl as it was being taken away. "The soup was good, yes? I have high hopes for the fish."

"Was Omar really referring to wine?" Margaret asked. "I always thought that Fitzgerald translated it as wine for his English audience, but that, as Muhammadans are strictly forbidden to drink alcohol, Omar probably was actually referring to the smoking of kef or bhang."

"Ah, yes," Demartineu said. "The leaf and bud of the *Cannabis sativa*. It could well be." He looked over at Sutrow. "What do you think, Mr. Sutrow?"

The little man shook his head. "I have never read the original," he said, "and I would not venture an opinion. Although I admit that the lady's notion might be a good one."

"Well," Demartineu said. "We are pleased to share the table with a lady with a good notion, who has so far remained nameless."

He rose to his feet and bowed to Margaret.

"Pleased to meet you, Professor," she said, extending her hand across the table. "My name is Margaret St. Yves. My father is an officer in the Lancers."

"Oh, yes." Demartineu bowed over her hand and then released it. "Brigadier General Sir Edward St. Yves, I.C., commanding officer of the Duke of Moncreith's Own Highland Lancers. The boss man, your father. I myself would not like to have a general for a father, I think. He is too accustomed to giving orders, and too used to having them obeyed. It would, I think, fray on one, that."

"I believe that Father has stopped trying to give me orders," Margaret said. "Or, perhaps, I've just stopped noticing."

"Oh, I'm sure not," Demartineu said, his eyes wide. "I cannot but imagine that you, so lovely and well mannered, are the dutiful daughter."

"Perhaps so, Professor," Margaret said, nodding her head to acknowledge the compliment, "but sometimes one has a positive duty to ignore one's parents, don't you think? It's for their own good. If one is too obedient, then the slightest disagreement is cause for endless worry and discussion. Whereas if one disagrees with one's parents on a regular schedule, then they come to expect it and think no more about it."

Demartineu stared thoughtfully at her for a long moment, and then chuckled. "Ah, Miss St. Yves, I fear that you are having me along, is this not so? You are making of the sport with this old professor."

"Not at all, Professor," Margaret said, smiling at him.

"And you, mademoiselle," Demartineu said to the young *Rubáiyát* fan, "will you do us the favor of an introduction?"

"Oh, sorry," she said. "I am Lady Priscilla Montague. Pleased to make your acquaintance." She extended a hand.

With another bow, Demartineu took her hand, pressed it slightly, and released it. "Ah!" he said, raising a forefinger of enlightenment. "The viceroy, is he not also a Montague?"

"My father," she explained.

"Do you hear that, Mr. Sutrow?" Demartineu asked, reaching behind the bejeweled lady to poke his friend in the arm. "We are surrounded by the younger generation of the British Raj; and a charming younger generation it is." The bejeweled lady frowned at him, and he smiled broadly back at her. "And you, madam, would you do us the supreme honor of identifying yourself. Please?"

Madam looked at him. "I will tell you my name," she said. "But under no circumstances are you to consider this an introduction."

Demartineu looked at her sadly. "Ah, yes," he said. "You, perhaps, put more of the burden on the term 'introduction' than I had intended. Rest yourself assured that I have not the intention to invite myself to weekend at your house, or borrow the money."

There was a pause while Madam tried to decide whether she had just been insulted. "I am the Dowager Duchess of Tynesdale," she announced finally. "You may call me 'your ladyship,' or 'my lady.'"

Demartineu beamed at her. "I shall, my lady," he said. "I shall do so constantly. My word."

"Hmmph!" she said.

After the fish came platters of curried lamb, deep dishes of stewed chicken, sliced pork roast with mangoes, and a baked egg and cheese dish with a reddish brown sauce that tasted much better than it looked. The side dishes that appeared at one's elbow every twenty seconds or so included a variety of vegetables in the mildest possible curry, a smaller selection of vegetables in a significantly stronger curry, an assortment of vegetables lightly fried, and a potpourri of cabbages briefly boiled, along with three different sorts of bread, one of them stuffed with onions. The conversation faltered and slowed as the diners allowed themselves to be overwhelmed with food.

Margaret had drunk the soup, nibbled the fish, and now found herself almost unable to eat. She pushed some food around on her plate so as not to appear conspicuous. "Tell me, Professor Demartineu," she said after a while, "just what is it that you profess?"

"What is it that I—" Demartineu paused and stared across at her for a moment. "Oh, I see it now. English, it is such a remarkable tool. You can say just about anything in English, and it means what it means. In French, if you assemble words in any but the correct manner, they lose their meaning and you are speaking the nonsense.

I myself am adept at speaking the nonsense."

"You are, perhaps, a professor of French?" Margaret asked.

"Not at all," Demartineu said. "Well, perhaps in a way. I am—I have been, let me say—a professor of the drama, of the theater. I do not, you understand, teach how to do it; how to write the plays or how to act. That would be useful, perhaps, and no university student desires to be taught anything useful. I used to profess, as you say, at the Université de Languedoc."

"How interesting," Lady Priscilla said.

"You think so?" Demartineu asked. "Why, then, perhaps it is. I instructed the youth of France on the works of such artists as Molière, Racine, Corneille, and Beaumarchais, as well as your Shakespeare and Marlowe. I gave a seminar on the works of the too-little esteemed Jean-François Regnard, including deep dissections of *Attendez-moi sous l'orme*, *Le Légataire universel*, and what is perhaps his masterwork, *Le Joueur*. I have an abiding knowledge of the lives and works of many French and English playwrights who have been dead these past two centuries and more. With the modern world, I am not so familiar."

The dowager duchess produced a lorgnette from her reticule and peered through it at Demartineu. "Tell me," she said, tapping him on the back of the hand with her spoon. "It is a matter of some interest to me. Do you think Shakespeare wrote his own plays?"

"On that I have no opinion, my lady," he said, snatching his hand away. "I have heard of this dispute that goes about in some literary circles in your country, that perhaps Shakespeare did not write the plays to which he is attributed. That, perhaps, Sir Francis Bacon wrote them instead." He shrugged. "It does not matter. We have the plays, and whether Shakespeare was Shakespeare, or Bacon was Shakespeare, or perhaps someone else entirely was Shakespeare, this Shakespeare was indeed a master playwright, second only, perhaps, to Molière."

"Well!" the dowager duchess sat up straight and glared down at the French professor. "It certainly does matter. To perpetrate a fraud upon the English people, indeed upon the people of the world, for the past two hundred and fifty years, would be disgraceful, and should be set to rights as soon as possible."

Margaret leaned back, folded her hands carefully in her lap, and looked down at her plate. She would resist all temptation to goad the duchess on. Besides, the duchess did not look as though she required goading. It was a good thing, Margaret thought, that the duchess had not noticed Demartineu's reference to Shakespeare as being second to Molière, or there'd be blood on the table.

Demartineu shook his head sadly. "I do not agree, but I sympathize," he said. "I, too, was once involved in a dispute over the provenance of the works of a long-defunct playwright. It seems that whenever genius is displayed, someone must leap to his feet and claim that there is no genius, merely humbug."

"Humbug?" Margaret looked across the table. "And was it humbug in this case?"

"I do not think so," Demartineu told her. "The playwright in question was the great Molière himself. A Professor Hanoutaux of the École des Arts in Paris published a monograph in which he asserted that he had determined, without a doubt, that the comedies of Molière were actually written by the tragedian Pierre Corneille. Without a doubt, mind you. The fact that they were attributed to Molière and only Molière during his lifetime, the fact that Molière himself acted in several of them; these were of no consequence. Molière was only an actor and, according to Professor Hanoutaux, could not possibly have the richness of vocabulary necessary to write his own plays. I ask you, what does an actor possess if not richness of vocabulary?

"He cited Plautus, a Roman playwright, as having a great influence on both Molière and Corneille; which is undoubtedly true. What that might prove, I know not. Hanoutaux examined scenes from *L'Amour Médecin* and *Sganarelle*, where he claimed to find proof of his thesis. Particularly convincing, he felt, was the paltry output of Corneille. Why did Corneille write so few plays of his own? Because he was busy writing plays for Molière. His reasoning was flawed, and his examples proved nothing.

"I replied in a monograph of my own. I pointed out that the reason Corneille wrote so few plays was because he was a slow writer. He wrote tragedies—*El Cid*, you will recall, was one of his. It is slow work, writing tragedies. One must cry a lot. I pointed out several other errors of logic and gross misunderstandings in Hanoutaux's monograph. He was crushed."

"What did he do?" Margaret asked.

"What could he do? He challenged me to a duel, of course."

"No!" Lady Priscilla's hand went to her mouth. "Really?"

The dowager duchess sniffed. "Dueling," she said firmly, "is against the law."

"This is so," Demartineu acknowledged. "Even in France, for these past thirty years it has been forbidden. Nonetheless, there is no other way for men to settle questions of honor. And, in France, every dispute concerns a question of honor. You say the Earth goes around the Sun; I say the Sun goes around the Earth—a duel will discover the truth. You say Napoleon was the savior of France; I say he was a scoundrel and his reign was a disaster. We will meet on the field of honor to decide which of us is right."

"So, did you accept?" Margaret demanded.

"But yes, of course. Not to do so would have been unthinkable."

"What happened?"

Demartineu leaned forward. "You must understand," he said, "that in France today a duel is more of a, how you say, ritual than a blood sport. There are rules and formalities. What is going to happen is preordained, and understood by all."

He held up one finger. "First, the challenge."

Another finger. "Then the acceptance."

Another finger. "Then the meeting of the seconds, and the choosing of the weapons, the time and the place."

Yet another finger. "Then the seconds ask the duelists whether an apology is acceptable. 'Cannot we avoid this senseless bloodshed?' is the usual formula."

All five fingers. "The refusal. 'Honor must be satisfied!'"

Demartineu raised both hands for a second, and then dropped them back down onto the table, and continued his description fingerless. "Then the morning of the duel dawns. By tradition it should be cold and drizzly, but if that is not achieved, the affair will continue nonetheless. The duelists go separately to the field of honor with their seconds. A doctor arrives in a third carriage, which awaits somewhat to the side of the festivities. It is all very tense and dramatic."

"Yes?" Lady Priscilla asked breathlessly. "And?"

"One last time one of the seconds asks each of them: 'Will you not apologize? Will you not accept his apology?' 'No,' each replies firmly. Honor must be satisfied.

"They stand facing each other. The referee drops a handkerchief between them. If the weapons are épées, the duel begins at that moment. If pistols, the formalities continue. They wheel about and walk off ten paces each. Then they wheel back and stand, rock still, facing each other. 'You may begin,' the referee calls."

"And?" asked Lady Priscilla.

"Each fires into the air, over the head of the other. Honor is satisfied. Everyone breathes a great sigh of relief, and they all go home."

"So," Margaret asked, "that was your duel?"

"No," Demartineu said. "That was every other duel in France for the past twenty years, with very few exceptions. But the gods of risibility were circling about me in this occasion." He raised a finger again, but dropped his hand back to the table after a second. "My second, an old friend and one of France's better known actors, communicated with Professor Hanoutaux and his second, the Viscount de Someplace-or-other. The viscount told my second, in strict confidence of course, that Professor Hanoutaux had determined to kill me. He was not going to fire over my head, but into it. *Alors*, what could I do? I did not wish to kill the professor, but I certainly did not wish for him to kill me."

"What did you do?"

"A brilliant plan occurred to me. In my youth I was the backstage assistant to a magician called Laces the Magnificent. He did, as part of his repertoire, a trick of the name 'The Bullet Catch.' He had retired and was now living in a villa in Provence. I went to him for assistance."

"You were going to catch the bullet?" Margaret asked.

"The essence of the trick," Demartineu told her, "is that the gun goes off, with a cloud of smoke and even a recoil, but a bullet is not really fired."

"Ah!" Margaret said.

"Laces had a pair of matched percussion-cap pistols especially made for performing this trick. Very beautiful weapons they are, too, with ivory handles and silver chasing on the barrels. And the trick mechanism is so carefully hidden that a committee of experts can come on-stage to load the guns, and to examine them carefully, and they will pronounce them genuine."

"Ah!" Margaret said.

"I borrowed the pistols. On the appointed day we met on the Champs de Mars. The guns were loaded in front of my adversary. He suspected nothing. He picked one, and I took the other. We paced off the distance and turned. On the referee's word, we both fired."

"Honor was satisfied," Lady Priscilla said.

"Acting on some caprice, I know not why," Demartineu continued, "perhaps to somehow get even with Professor Hanoutaux perhaps due to some deeply submerged urge to perform, I grabbed at my chest, staggered, and fell to the ground."

"You didn't!" the dowager duchess exclaimed.

"For a few long moments I lay there, silent and still. I don't know what I expected to hear," Demartineu said. "Perhaps exclamations of shock, perhaps some words of remorse. What I heard instead from Professor Hanoutaux was a gloating laugh. This was too much! I rose to my feet. 'You,' ah, 'dirty person,' I yelled at him, approaching him and shaking my fist. This had an unexpected result."

"I'm not surprised," Margaret murmured.

"The professor, you understand, thought that I was dead. When he saw me rise and stalk toward him, it was a tremendous shock to his system, as I soon discovered. Clutching his heart, Hanoutaux gasped and fell over. His seconds attempted to force cognac down his throat to revive him, but it was no use. Within a few moments, he was dead."

"Oh, my," said the dowager duchess.

"My sentiments precisely," Demartineu told her. "The gods, they were laughing at that one."

"What happened?" Margaret asked.

Demartineu paused while the dinner plates were removed, the table was scraped, and finger bowls were put at each place. "Word of the duel spread quickly," he said, "but it changed in the telling. By the time the story got back to me, I was a villain dyed in the black. I had, it seemed, performed some devious and underhanded trick designed to efficate—is that the word?"

"Effectuate?" Margaret suggested.

"Yes? But is not 'efficacious' a word?"

"It is," Margaret agreed. "But efficate is not."

"English!" Demartineu shrugged. "It is almost as bad as French."

"The duel," Lady Priscilla reminded him.

"Oh yes. Well, it was said that I had somehow, ah, caused the death of Professor Fernand Hanoutaux. This was not rational, and the French claim to be the most rational of peoples. On this point they lie."

"Pardon me," Lady Priscilla said, "but how was this not rational? I mean, it was mistaken, but might it not have been true? We have only your word that you did, ah, what you did, by accident."

"Ah, you see," Demartineu said, wiggling a finger in her direction. "Even you, and knowing only my side of the story, have your doubts. It is that I have not the honest face, yes? Well, you see, it is this: Recollect that we were having a duel. We were using trick pistols, to which only I knew the trick. If I had wished simply to kill him, would I not have simply shot him dead? I would have needed neither the hocus nor the pocus."

"Oh," Lady Priscilla said. "I guess...."

"Such things do happen in duels occasionally, even in France. People do, by some chance, get killed. It is a regrettable accident. Sometimes, in the actuality, it is murder, but to the face, it is a regrettable accident. You see?"

"I see," Margaret said.

"So, had I wanted a regrettable accident, I would have done what, as it happens, Professor Hanoutaux was planning to do to me. Only I would have done it first."

The finger bowls were taken up and replaced with little dessert dishes, each supported by a little fork and a little spoon. A silver bell was rung for silence, immediately aided by a dozen or so spoons clinking against the sides of a dozen or so wine glasses. The room quieted, and the viceroy rose and spoke. It was traditional for the viceroy to speak during the dessert. It was expected, if not looked forward to. The viceroy himself did not look forward to it, but what must be done must be done, as he had said back in his office. Tonight the speech was unusually perfunctory. The viceroy introduced General St. Yves, and the other staff officers of the Lancers, who were suitably scattered about the room, spoke briefly of the British burden in administering and educating a subcontinent full of natives, some of whom welcomed the administering and many of whom seemed to resent it, and then sat down. Gradually the chatter in the room began again.

"Finish your story, Professor," Margaret said, turning back to the table.

"I thought it was fairly well finished," Demartineu protested.

"Oh, no, Professor," Lady Priscilla told him. "Why, you were just getting to the good part."

"Really?" Demartineu asked, looking at her innocently. "And what part is that?"

"The part where everyone in Paris thought you'd deliberately murdered that Professor What's-his-name."

"Hanoutaux," Demartineu said. "It wasn't everyone in Paris. It was, perhaps, ten or twenty people. But the story followed me back to Languedoc, and the *université* was not so happy with me as once they were. So I left and commenced to wander about the world, here and there, which is something I had always wanted to do in any case. And so"—he shrugged a great gallic shrug—"here I am."

"And where will you be going next, Professor?" Margaret asked.

"Ah! As to that, I am done with professing, I have decided. I am instead reverting to my old profession. With the aid of my new friend, Mamarum Sutrow here"—he smiled over at the little man from Kalat—"we are going to astound audiences all over Europe with performances of the astounding legerdemain and prestidigitation. In a word, a magic act."

"You are going to become a magician?" Margaret asked.

"No, no, I am going to regain my old position of backstage person extraordinaire, but my friend Mr. Sutrow here..." He waved a hand grandiloquently at Sutrow. "He will emerge on the British stage—we are going to work first in England, as the audiences there are less critical—as the world-famous Indian fakir Mamarum the Great! Note you that he has the presence, he has the temperament, and, although short in stature, he has the bearing to be a great personage on the stage."

Sutrow contrived to look embarrassed.

"But is he world-famous, then?" asked Lady Priscilla. "Are you, Mr. Sutrow? Should I have heard of you?"

"Alas, no," Sutrow acknowledged.

"Why would anyone choose to become famous as a faker, Professor Demartineu?" demanded the dowager duchess.

"Not 'faker,' your ladyship, but 'fakir,'" explained the professor, drawing out the final syllable to emphasize the difference in pronunciation. "A fakir is a beggar, a street performer, like the omnipresent snake charmers, or one of the religious mendicants who scarify themselves for the pleasure of their god and the amusement of the crowd. But through some sort of linguistic transformation, it has come in Europe to signify Indian magicians or other sorts of exotic Asian entertainers. These magicians perform the swords-through-basket trick, which would not fool a small child, and talk about the Indian rope trick, which would be a true miracle if anyone could do it. Actual Indian magicians, able to perform many miracles and held in high repute by their countrymen, are known as jadoogars. My friend Mr. Sutrow here comes from a respected family of jadoogars. Is this not so, my friend?"

"I have that honor," Mamarum Sutrow agreed. "I will be the first jadoogar in my family to bring his skills to the fabled West," he said, with a serious expression in his dark eyes. "I shall have much to live up to. I will do my humble best."

"You'll have them standing on their seats begging for more," Demartineu told him.

"Oh, I sincerely hope not," said Sutrow anxiously. "The theater owners would surely object!"

NINE

THE PHANSIGAR

What's past, and what's to come is strew'd with husks
And formless ruin of oblivion.
WILLIAM SHAKESPEARE

It was past ten in the evening when Margaret and her father returned with the viceroy to the library. "Now, about this gold we're to be guarding," St. Yves said. "Why does it need to be guarded, and why us?"

Sir George settled into his easy chair and waved General St. Yves and his daughter to seats. "It is in the nature of gold to be guarded," he said.

"True," St. Yves admitted. "And there must be some more usual means for guarding it."

"This is an extraordinary case," the viceroy explained. "I received a telegram from the governor of the Bank of England, a chap named Bergarot, claiming that an attempt might be made to steal the gold. When or where, he doesn't know, except that it will be sometime before the gold is put into the bank's vault."

St. Yves pursed his lips. "Insufficient information," he said. "I'm not altogether sure that I want to be responsible for four million pounds' worth of gold, not with five officers and thirty men. Not, for that matter, with ten times five officers and thirty men. Four million pounds is enough to... well, it's enough to b-buy a small country and make yourself a king."

"A good point," the viceroy said. "And let me reassure you. Technically you won't be responsible for the gold. Although we both know that it won't do your career any good if someone should make off with it during your watch. The bally gold is my responsibility until it's loaded aboard the ship. And then the ship's captain signs for it. He is, by maritime law and usage, responsible for anything and anyone on his ship, from the smallest belaying pin, whatever that may be, to the most valuable cargo. His responsibility doesn't end until the cargo is off-loaded at Queens Dock in London."

"So we'll merely be helping the captain guard the gold," St. Yves mused.

"Just so," the viceroy said. "And let me say that I don't really expect any trouble. Bergarot is being overly cautious. Not that I blame him; his job, after all, is to see the gold safely into his vaults. No, I believe you'll have an uneventful voyage home. My daughter Priscilla will be on the ship with you. Her mother wants her in London for the season, and I certainly wouldn't let her go if I thought there was even the slightest danger. Although I will admit that the knowledge that there'll be thirty of your Highland Lancers on board will make me sleep even easier during her voyage."

Sir George swiveled around as the door burst open suddenly and Djuna flung himself into the room. "In the name of Krishna, sahib, you come, come quickly, come!"

"Krishna?" the viceroy asked.

"Any god you like, sahib, but please come, come now!" And Djuna flung himself back out of the room.

"I suppose we'd better follow the little beggar," Sir George muttered, coming to his feet. "Probably nothing; these people are so excitable." But the speed with which he hurried to the door belied his words.

Djuna trotted down the corridor head up, arms at his sides; the gait of someone who is in a great hurry but doesn't want to be seen running. The others managed to stay close behind without quite breaking into a run. The group turned the corner and there, ahead of them at the end of the corridor, were the great bronze doors of the viceroy's office. As they approached they could see that the polished dark-wood door to the right of the bronze doors stood open, and one of the ubiquitous footmen stood next to the door in a stiff approximation of attention, but his exaggerated posture and the hint of panic in his eyes strongly suggested that he would rather be somewhere else.

Djuna stopped his quick walk at the open door, and the others narrowly avoided piling into him. "In there, sahib," he said, pointing.

The viceroy took two steps into the room and stopped. "God—bless me," he said.

Margaret peered around the doorway. This was the anteroom to the viceroy's office. It was about ten or twelve feet wide, and half again as long, and lit by two gas fixtures in the wall which were turned low, leaving the corners in palpable darkness. The walls were covered with a wallpaper the color of desert sand. There were two small desks to the right, and a row of file cabinets behind them. Several glass-front display cases to the left were fairly crammed with artifacts from the various peoples and places on the Indian subcontinent that the British had roamed over in the two-hundred-plus years they had been there.

There was a man in the room, presumably the native who had been waiting to speak to the viceroy. In his yellow cotton kurta jacket, baggy trousers, and brown turban and sandals he looked to be some sort of merchant. Not a street vender, but perhaps someone with a stall in the bazaar. He lay on the floor inside the doorway, with his head at an unnatural angle and a long white scarf twisted around his neck and knotted. His eyes bulged from his head, giving him a look of great astonishment. Even from where Margaret stood she could see that the whites of the eyes were filled with jagged red marks, like frozen lightning bolts, circling the sightless pupils.

Margaret took several deep breaths, closed her eyes, and attempted to swallow. It didn't work. She could hear the beating of her heart. She took several more deep breaths and stepped back until her shoulders were against the wall on the far side of the corridor.

St. Yves knelt by the body. He cut the scarf off with a small silver pocketknife and put two fingers on the man's neck to feel for a pulse. "He's dead," he said. "Not that there was much doubt, but I thought, you know, just in case..."

"Yes," the viceroy said, "quite." He looked down at the body for a long moment and cleared his throat. "Djuna, go to the card room and get Chief Constable Parker. He should be there by now. Bring him here. Tell him what happened—but only him. Don't mention it to anyone else. Keep your mouth closed—hear me?"

"Yes, Viceroy sahib," Djuna said. "I go now." And he raced off down the hall.

"Strangled," St. Yves said, coming to his feet. "Right here in your office, while the building is full of military officers and civil service officials. I've never heard of anything like it. Looks like a Pathan tribesman, but the clothes—"

"Perhaps he dressed up for his visit to the city—or perhaps he didn't want to be recognized," the viceroy suggested.

"Could well be, something of the sort," St. Yves agreed. "Some sort of local dispute, I would imagine, or a robbery. Perhaps the chap was carrying something of value and the other chap knew it. But the b-bally nerve of the killer, coming right into Government House to do his deed."

"Not robbery, surely," said the viceroy. "There are several articles of considerable value about the room"—he indicated the display cases with a wave of his hand—"and none of it's been touched. Besides, the chap still has his purse tied to his belt."

"Not robbery, then," St. Yves agreed.

"I don't think it's any sort of local dispute, Father," Margaret said, slowly crossing the corridor toward the doorway.

"Eh? What's that? Margaret, I'm not sure you should be looking at this, m'dear."

"Well," she said practically, "it's too late to worry about that now, isn't it? I think I'll be all right."

"What did you mean, you don't think it was a dispute?" Sir George asked.

"That scarf with the knot in it," she said, pointing. "I've seen pictures of it."

"What's that? Pictures of this scarf?"

"Well, I mean ones like it. It's the sort used by the Phansigar. I read a book about them."

"The Phansigar?" St. Yves asked. "Peg, m'dear, what sort of books have you been reading?"

The viceroy stepped back. "The Phansigar—of course. The Thuggees!" he said. "By Jove, I think she's right, about that scarf at any rate." He picked up the scarf and examined it. "She is right," he said. "There's a small knot at each end of this thing—here where the ends are tied together and each of the knots has a coin tied into it." He pulled one of the small knots loose. "A silver coin. It's the ritual killing-scarf of the Phansigar."

"*Rumal*, I think it's called," Margaret said. "That's the scarf they wore around their waist and used to dispatch their victims."

"That sounds right," the viceroy agreed. "We have a small museum of Thuggee artifacts downstairs, and there are a few scarves like this in it."

"I've heard of the Thuggees," St. Yves said. "But I thought they were all killed off forty or fifty years ago."

"Perhaps not," said a voice from the doorway.

Margaret looked up and saw a British army officer standing in the doorway, peering into the room. He was a tall young man with a face rather too rabbity to be truly good-looking, immaculately turned out in the dress uniform of a lieutenant in some regiment with which she was unfamiliar: blue regimentals with two thin red stripes running down the trousers, and a double-breasted jacket with wide, red-trimmed lapels and oversized gold buttons. He appeared to be taking a considerable interest in the proceedings. His words, "Perhaps not," had been uttered in a flat tone intended to impart information rather than shock or alarm, but Margaret found them all the more alarming for their matter-of-fact delivery.

"Perhaps not?" Margaret asked.

"There may be one or two Phansigar still roaming about, don't you know," he explained. "There are signs—"

Margaret's father, who had been staring at the young officer for a long moment, interrupted. "Just who are you, Lieutenant, and what are you doing there?" he barked.

"Oh, sorry, sir." The man in the doorway brought his heels together, stiffened to attention, and saluted. "Lieutenant Peter Pettigrew, carrier pigeon officer of the Seventh Foot, reporting, sir!"

St. Yves returned the salute briskly. "Carrier pigeon officer?"

"Well," the young man said thoughtfully, looking from St. Yves to Margaret to the viceroy, "not exactly."

"How's that?"

The man considered carefully, and then replied, "I'm not really a lieutenant, and my name isn't really Pettigrew. I don't know whether or not there really is a Seventh Foot, or just what it might be if it did exist, and I don't know the least about carrier pigeons. Aside from that, everything I told you is the absolute truth."

Margaret's eyes widened and she bit her lip to fight off an impulse to giggle. This was neither the time nor the place for even the slightest giggle.

The viceroy turned to face the young nonlieutenant. "Of all the effrontery," he said, some powerful emotion evident in the timbre of his voice. His face had turned just the slightest shade of red. "Please identify yourself, sir, and explain what you're doing here and why you are wearing a uniform to which you have just admitted you are not entitled."

"Sorry, your lordship." The young man shifted from his rigid position of attention to a close approximation of parade rest. "This is my Lieutenant Pettigrew, ah, persona, as it were. Actually my name is Collins. Peter Collins. The 'Peter,' at least, was honest, you see. I happened to be with Chief Constable Parker when your boy ran him down. He immediately sent your boy off for Dr. McWarren, and then went off to see to it that all the exterior doors to Governor's House were locked and guarded, except the front door, of course, and he sent me along to see if I could be of any help. I'm with the Special Department of the Constabulary, you see. The doctor should be along presently, I imagine."

"I don't think McWarren can do much good," the viceroy commented. "The chap is dead, you know."

"What 'special department'?" St. Yves demanded. "I never heard of a special department."

"Parker seems to feel that nobody is dead until Dr. McWarren says he is dead," Collins told the viceroy. And then he shifted his attention to General St. Yves. "Our official name is the Department of Special Intelligence. We are not widely known, which is a good thing, for the most part."

"The DSI, eh?" the viceroy said. "You chaps keep popping up in the oddest places." He indicated the corpse with a nod. "Then was this chap one of yours?"

"You think he might have been a Scout?" Collins asked. "That hadn't occurred to me. I'd better have a look." He went over and knelt by the corpse.

"According to my boy Djuna, the chap had a message for me," the viceroy told Collins as the young man examined the body. "The chap told Djuna to say, 'To be or not to be.'"

"Ah!" said Peter Collins. "He did, did he?" Collins peered closely at the body and said, "Hmmm." And then he said, "Damn!" And then he said, "Excuse me, miss. Didn't mean to curse in front of a lady."

"Don't mind me," said Margaret, who was trying to remain as unobtrusive as possible so that her father wouldn't notice her and send her away.

Collins took a small ivory-cased pocketknife from his trouser pocket and carefully slit open the seam in the ornate collar of the corpse's garment. "This man was, indeed, one of ours," he said, removing a tightly rolled tube of white silk, no longer than a cigarette and no thicker than a toothpick, from where it had been concealed inside the collar. He unrolled it and showed it to the viceroy.

"A rose," the viceroy said.

Margaret leaned over to look. A stylized image of a red rose, its petals tightly closed as though concealing some roseate secret, was stamped on the fabric.

"It's our, ah, sigil, so to speak," Collins said. He flipped over the left lapel of his uniform jacket, revealing a small silver pin of an identical rose, with petals of red enamel.

"So he worked for you people, did he?" the viceroy asked.

General St. Yves pulled his ear thoughtfully. "As he was coming here to pass some information on to you, using the password and all," he told the viceroy, "I would think that makes the idea of it being a robbery less likely. It is probable that he was killed to prevent him from speaking with you." St. Yves turned to Collins. "What do you say, young man?"

"It's extremely probable," Collins agreed. "And it must have been something both important and extremely urgent for him not to go through the usual channels." He peered closely at the ornate collar and allowed a puzzled frown to cross his face, and then pushed himself to his feet.

"Can you find out who he is?" asked the viceroy. "I suppose we must notify his relations, so they can take his body. I think we should pay for the funeral pyre, assuming the chap was a Hindu—the least we can do. Are there any arrangements made for the relatives to collect back pay, or any kind of death payment?"

"I'm afraid that a funeral pyre won't do," Collins said, moving over to a nearby wooden chair and sitting down. "This gentleman will require a proper English burial."

"Excuse me?" said St. Yves.

"The collar of his, ah, garment," Collins explained. "If you look closely at the collar, you will notice a slight—very slight—discoloration along the inside."

St. Yves knelt down by the body to look. "Right enough," he agreed. "So he didn't wash his neck as well as he ought."

"This discoloration, you will note, is the same nut-brown color as the man's skin," Collins explained. "Skin color does not come off, unless it was artificially applied. Looked at in that light, I must assume that he is an Englishman disguised as a native."

"An Englishman?" asked the viceroy, sounding startled. "How can you be sure?"

Collins shrugged. "English, Scots, Irish, Welsh—what you will. He could even be French, German, or Russian, I suppose; but then the question of why he came to Government House to speak to your lordship, and just what he had to say, becomes unnecessarily complicated. I think Mr. Occam would vote for one of Her Majesty's British subjects of some flavor. I think we will find," he continued, "that he had some explicit warning to pass on to your lordship, that it was urgent, and that he was killed to prevent him from delivering it."

"So that's your opinion, is it, young man?" the viceroy asked.

Collins flushed and stood up. "I don't mean to seem to be giving suggestions to you gentlemen," he said. "It must sound awfully presumptuous. It's just that this is my, ah, field, you know."

"Nonsense," said the viceroy. "Any suggestions, comments, or special knowledge that you have, now is the time to share it. If you can throw any light on this"—he indicated the dead man lying at his feet—"we certainly want to hear it."

"Yes," Margaret agreed. "For example, what did you mean, 'perhaps not'?"

General St. Yves looked over at her with a frown, as though just realizing that she was still there, but he said nothing.

Collins pondered for a moment. "What do you know of the Phansigar?" he asked.

"They were known as Thuggees in the north," St. Yves said. "Bands of thieves. Used to waylay and rob travelers. Wiped out by the British authorities some fifty years ago. But we still hear stories, of course. The amahs frighten small children with them, like the bogeymen."

"And bogeymen indeed they were," Collins began. "I've had cause to do some research on them in the past few weeks. Their customs, habits, and beliefs were enough to frighten any small child, and most adults. The cult of the Phansigar—the Thuggees—was many hundreds of years old. Quite possibly well over a thousand years."

"Incredible!" the viceroy said. "A thousand years?"

"There are carvings dating back to the eighth century in the cave complex at Elura in Maharashtra state, known as the Rock Temples. A series of panels show the Thuggees in operation: one depicts garrotting the victim, another dismembering the body, and so on."

"A thousand years—at least," the viceroy said. "A thousand years of robbery and murder. Amazing."

"When they were suppressed there were, perhaps, ten thousand of them scattered about the Indian subcontinent," Collins said. "They lived in small villages; which is to say that the entire village, men, women, and children, would be Phansigar. They practiced murder and robbery as a religious duty, consecrated to the goddess Kali. They had absolutely no pity for their victims, but would slaughter them as you would kill a chicken."

Margaret shuddered. "How can people just murder other people like that," she asked, "without feeling anything?"

Collins shrugged. "Ask Tomás de Torquemada," he said, "or the gentle folks of our own race who burned witches and heretics at the stake for most of a thousand years. The Phansigar believed they had a religious obligation to do what they did. It doesn't excuse it, or really even explain it, but there it is."

"Obligation?" asked the viceroy.

"Just so. According to the Hindu creation myth, a great demon ate up all humans as fast as they were created, and Kali came along and killed the demon with her sword. But from every drop of demon blood, a little demon was created with the same appetites. According to traditional Hindu belief, Kali solved the problem by licking up the demon blood before it could drop. But the Phansigar believe that Kali grew tired of this, and created two men and told them to kill the demons without spilling any blood. To accomplish this, she gave them long scarves. The men killed the demons and returned to Kali to give her back her scarves. But she told them to keep the scarves, and to make their living from them, strangling other men as they had strangled the demons. It was their duty to obey."

"That's awful!" Margaret said.

"So it is," Collins agreed. "In Europe in the Middle Ages bishops used to ride into battle against the infidel. But they were forbidden by their church from shedding blood. So they carried great maces—clubs—in order to smash in the heads of their enemies without shedding their blood."

"Enough of that, young man," St. Yves said severely.

"Sorry, sir," said Collins. "But, at any rate, the Phansigar considered what they did both a job and a religious duty."

"Wouldn't people learn to shun their villages?" Margaret asked.

"You would not notice anything unusual about their villages if you chanced to visit one," Collins said, "except perhaps how closedmouthed the women were with their gossip when you were present. Indeed, they were considered models of morality. The men did not ply their craft—or practice their religion, if you prefer—within a hundred miles of their own village. They would sometimes follow their intended victims for many miles—remember, this was before the railroads, and all travel was extremely slow—and await just the right location to commit their crimes. They would strangle everyone in the party with the rumal, their ritual scarves, leaving no witnesses, excepting only small children, whom they would bring back to their village and bring up as their own. The bodies of their victims would be ritually dismembered and buried."

"Ugh!" said Margaret.

"How could they have gotten away with these predations year after year?" the viceroy asked.

"I suppose because of the length of time any journey took," Collins replied. "Even if everything went well, a long business trip might take three or four months. So a traveler wouldn't be expected home for at least six months. By the time he was missed, there'd be no way to tell where or when anything had happened to him, or whether it was the result of Phansigar, or bandits, or accident, or whether he'd just decided to stay away. Of course, there were awful rumors whispered about the Kali-worshippers who murdered travelers, but nobody knew anything about them."

"But we wiped them all out, didn't we?" the viceroy asked. "Back in the thirties. Fellow named, ah..."

"Steeman," Collins said. "Sir William Steeman. He studied everything there was to know about the Phansigar, and spent his career eliminating them. By the late 1840s it appeared his job had been done."

"But you don't think so?" asked the viceroy.

"He may have missed a village," Collins said cautiously. "And the Thuggees may have stayed dormant these four decades, awaiting the chance to begin again. They would have to take their time to develop new techniques to keep up with the changing times: railroads, the telegraph, and the like."

"Is this just your theory, Collins," the viceroy asked, "or is their something to support this idea?"

"There have been some reports recently of travelers—merchants, mostly—who disappeared, and have not been heard of since."

"Bosh!" said General St. Yves. "Regular, old-fashioned bandits or dacoits. I've had some dealings with them myself upcountry."

"Yes," Collins agreed, "there is a certain amount of banditry going on. Always will be, I imagine. But they don't go out of their way to hide the bodies. Most of them would just as soon rob without killing at all, if they have no trouble subduing their victims."

"That's true enough," St. Yves acknowledged. "But people do disappear, you know. Just disappear."

"With all due respect," Collins said, "no, sir, they do not. There's always a cause. We might not find it out, but it's there somewhere. And when we can't find a hint of a cause, and when neither the people nor their bodies turn up, and when the number of people who have developed this distressing habit seems to be increasing, and they're all from the same general area of the country, one might wish to search a bit deeper for the cause."

"You think," the viceroy asked, "that the Thuggees have returned?"

"I'm not sure they ever left," Collins told him.

The viceroy shook his head. "I could have been back in Roscommon, riding to hounds like a gentleman, or collecting incunabula, whatever they are, but here I am, Viceroy of Her Majesty's Realm of India, with a resurgence of Thuggee murders to occupy my time."

"Here, now," cried a deep voice from the doorway. "What have we here?" A heavyset man with muttonchop whiskers peered in at them.

"Dr. McWarren, sorry to impose on you," the viceroy said. "We have here a, ah, injured man."

"Dead, you mean," McWarren said, glaring at the body with a critical eye. "Well, let's have a look."

TEN

PUNCTUATED EQUILIBRIUM

For the first few days the trip east was rapid, but it proved unexpectedly eventful. A bullet shattered the window of Moriarty's compartment in the Express d'Orient at seven A.M. the first morning, as the train sped through the Moselle Valley. "It's those accursed hunters," muttered *le conducteur* who came to investigate, writing in his little notebook. Moriarty accepted the profound apologies *le conducteur* offered on behalf of La Compagnie International des Wagons-Lits, and was moved to another compartment. When the train stopped briefly at Strasbourg, Moriarty stepped outside to inspect the damage, and discovered that a discreet white X had been chalked beneath the shattered window.

In Munich, Moriarty and Colonel Moran narrowly missed being run down by a runaway Jaegerlager Bier wagon, and had to step nimbly to avoid being struck by one of the great kegs of beer that came bouncing off the wagon as it jounced down Kaiserstrasse. A day later in Vienna, a crazed man with a knife attacked Professor Moriarty in the Café Figaro on Neustiftgasse, and succeeded in slashing the back of Moriarty's arm before Colonel Moran was able to bash him on the head with a chair.

Thus reinforcing Colonel Moran's stated belief that coffeehouses were dangerous places, and that one should spend one's time in *bierstuben* or other establishments for the consumption of alcoholic beverages. The Viennese police came and took the man away, and even apologized to their foreign guests for this regrettable incident. Moriarty waved away their offer of a trip to the hospital and bandaged up his arm with the aid of Colonel Moran and a strip of clean tablecloth. Stitching up the sleeve of his jacket would have to wait.

"Why didn't you use that pigsticker you've got hidden away inside your walking stick?" Moran asked, indicating with a twitch of his chin the black stick with the golden owl handle that Moriarty carried everywhere. "That gent could have done you serious damage."

Moriarty smiled grimly. "I had the utmost faith that you would come to my aid in time," he told Moran. "And I didn't want to give the police any excuse to hold us here and cause us to miss our connection."

"Right," Moran agreed. "Curious set of coincidences we're getting here," he added.

"It seems certain that the gunshot in France and the beer wagon incident in Munich were no accidents," Moriarty said. "In which case they must have been planned and prepared before we arrived. You will remember that the gunshot came at exactly seven in the morning. Someone computed just where the train would be at that time. And the shooter knew which window to aim at—someone on the train had marked it with a small X. Likewise, the beer wagon must have been awaiting our passage at the top of that street. And the gentleman here in Vienna who just tried to practice his carving on my chest must have been notified of our pending arrival, and somebody must have pointed us out to him. Which means that our unknown adversary has someone following us. Or, more accurately, traveling along with us."

Moran shifted in his chair and quickly looked around the coffeehouse. "Who?" he asked.

"I think I have the man spotted," Moriarty said. "Although he may not be the only one. He's been on the train with us since Paris, at least, but I suspect that by now he has reinforcements. He's a very

British-looking gentleman with the air of either one of the minor nobility or a cardsharper."

"One of the swell mob, eh?" Moran said.

"Quite possibly. I have the mummer watching him, to see if we can determine anything from his movements, or his friends."

Moran sat silent for a few minutes, musing into his oversized cup of *kaffee mit schlag*, and then slapped his hand on the table. "I'll be damned if I can figure out how anyone knows of our going after the statuette, except the maharaja, and I can't believe he'd try to stop us. What would be the point?"

"I agree," Moriarty told him. "I think there's something deeper afoot here."

"What?"

"That remains to be seen. Notice, they—whoever they are—seem to be concentrating on eliminating me, rather than you, which would not be the case if they were trying to prevent us from attaining the statuette. But just what they hope to accomplish, or who is behind them, I have no idea at the moment."

"I'd say they were trying to accomplish your death," Moran commented.

Moriarty nodded. "Yes, but what are they trying to accomplish by my death? What goal is it toward which my continued existence is an impediment?"

Moran shook his head. "It's a puzzle to me," he said. "But I think we'd best do our own eliminating right quick. I suggest we dispose of those who are following us before they get really annoying. And besides, they might get lucky." He made a twisting motion with his hand. "A dark alley, a knife in the ribs, and who's to be the wiser? Eh?"

Moriarty raised an eyebrow. "Let's hope it doesn't come to that," he said.

"No better way of discouraging the opposition," Moran said. He slapped Moriarty on the back. "Don't get yourself killed, Professor. At least not until after I get my hands on the maharaja's golden houri."

"It gives me a warm feeling to know that you care," Moriarty said dryly.

"I was jesting, Professor. Certainly I was," Moran said, leaning back and smiling his best smile. "Why, I wouldn't see anything happen to you for all the cigars in Egypt. My word I wouldn't."

"I am reassured," Moriarty said. "I can continue on now with a new spring in my step." He drank up the last of his coffee. "And I think it would be wise to spring in a new direction," he said, rising from his chair and throwing some coins on the table. "Come, my friend, let us do something at least halfway clever to eliminate this nuisance."

"Good!" Moran said, jumping to his feet. "'Any action is preferable to standing still' has long been my motto. Where to, Professor?"

"Trieste," Moriarty told him.

Moran stopped in mid-stride. "Trieste?"

"Trieste is the smuggling center of the northern Mediterranean. We are going to hire a fast boat to smuggle us to Port Said. It will have the added advantage of cutting two or three days off our journey."

"But our bags are checked through to, where? Varna."

Moriarty switched his walking stick from his left hand to his right, and struck it sharply against a lamp stand. "We have our overnight bags. The rest we must abandon."

Moran sighed. "My favorite weapon is in my large trunk," he said. "A Mannlicher-Schoenauer eight-millimeter that I had especially customized by Von Goertl of Innsbruck."

"When this is over, we'll have the Wagon-Lit people return our luggage," Moriarty told him. "You'll see your rifle again." He stopped at the corner and stepped quickly over to the building. Taking a small piece of French chalk from his pocket, he made a series of simple geometric figures on the granite wall, none larger than two inches square, some connected to the others, some standing alone. When he was done, he stepped back and examined his handiwork, which resembled nothing so much as the meaningless scribblings of a ten-year-old.

"What have you done there?" Moran asked.

"Left a message for the mummer," Moriarty explained, "telling him where to find us."

"In Trieste?"

"No, at the train station at ten o'clock tonight."

"Ah!"

"In the meantime, we must make some effort to evade anyone who might be watching our movements." He pocketed the chalk and set off down the street again.

Matching the professor's stride, Colonel Moran took a large clasp knife from a sheath hidden inside the waistband of his trousers and concealed it up his sleeve with a swift, practiced motion. "Sounds right to me, Professor," he said. "You just point 'em out to me, and I'll do the evading right enough."

Moriarty looked at his companion as though seeing him for the first time. "All very good," he said, "but keep that folding scimitar up your sleeve unless you need it for self-defense. I had a less drastic idea in mind for our, ah, foes. Excessive violence might be counterproductive."

"I am of the belief that there is nothing excessive about killing someone who is trying to kill you," said Colonel Moran. "And it's a damn good idea to do it first. The stakes are a little too high and the game is a little too final to be overly sporting about it."

"The term 'sportsman' is not one I would think of applying to you," Moriarty told him. "You, as I remember, are of the belief that there's nothing wrong with killing someone on the slightest provocation, or, for that matter, for a reasonable fee."

"True," Moran said, unabashed. "I'm not squeamish about killing. Shouldn't be a soldier if you're going to be squeamish about killing— or about dying, for that matter. Her Majesty seems to be quite willing to sacrifice us when it's in her interest. Following her royal lead, I am quite willing to sacrifice others when it's in my interest. It's the way of the world. Always has been, always will be. Those who don't understand that are probably not going to remain in this world for their full three score and ten. As for sportsmanship—running about on a field of mud kicking at a pig's bladder, and yelling 'Well played!' or 'Good sport!' when a teammate breaks his rib or someone else's leg, has always seemed to me to be pointless, useless, tiring, and painful."

"There are other sports," Moriarty said.

"There are other objections," Moran replied.

"At any rate, sportsmanship was not my objective," Moriarty said dryly. "Let's try to do what's necessary without drawing any unnecessary attention to ourselves, and let's not accidently extinguish any innocent passersby. The idea is to elude our foes, not to eliminate them. Our adversary has a limitless number of henchmen, as thugs and toughs are for hire in any major metropolis and most of the lesser ones. On the other hand, they are not highly motivated, as evidenced by their success rate so far."

"I can see that, Professor, but they only have to succeed once to, as it were, take the prize."

"Quite," Moriarty said. "And thus—Trieste." He paused in mid-stride, causing Colonel Moran to do a quick two-step to avoid running into him. "That," he said, pointing across the street with his cane, "is an interesting shop, over there."

Moran looked where Moriarty was pointing. "The luggage store or the apothecary?" he asked.

"I'm not sure yet," Moriarty told him. "Let's cross the street and see."

The two of them crossed the road, nimbly avoiding a cluster of four-wheelers and an omnibus drawn by two horses of enormous size. A policeman standing in the middle of the road at the corner and attempting to direct traffic glared at them, but made no effort to leave his post.

"I know," said Colonel Sebastian Moran as they reached the sidewalk. "We'll go first to the apothecaries and have them concoct a potion—perhaps a mixture of the juices from the pod of the *Papaver somniferum* and the nut of the *Nux vomica* in the ratio of three to two—then we can dash over to the luggage store to buy a nice black leather case to keep it in."

"It's a seed," Moriarty said.

"Pardon?"

"*Nux vomica* is not a nut, it's a seed," Moriarty told him.

"Nut—seed; tell me why you just endangered our lives in dashing across the street." He stopped walking and took the professor's arm. "If you're trying to establish a reputation for erratic behavior, I'm willing to swear to it without you're actually performing the same."

Moriarty swung around to face him. "Keep talking," he said, taking his pince-nez glasses off and thrusting them into his vest pocket. "And wave your arms about a bit, so that it will appear to an observer that we're having an argument."

"I'm perfectly willing to have an argument with you anytime you find it convenient," Moran exclaimed, shaking his fist in Moriarty's face. "What do you mean, an observer?"

"There is someone following us," Moriarty told him, brandishing his walking stick. "Not the man from the train, but, we must assume, one of his agents. Don't look around just yet."

"This is getting tiresome," Moran observed, blocking Moriarty's swing with his own stick. "What does he look like, when I do look?"

"Short, stocky, bearded, dressed in black, wearing a sort of floppy cap, carrying a rolled-up newspaper," Moriarty said. "The shape of his mustache, the size of his heavy boots, designed for stomping one's opponent, and the fact that his rolled-up newspaper appears to be concealing a heavy object, presumably a length of lead pipe, mark him as one of Vienna's criminal classes."

"What shall we do?" Moran asked, jabbing Moriarty in the chest with his forefinger, a ferocious scowl on his face. "We can't stand here poking at each other for the rest of the day. I could knock you down, I suppose, and then be so overcome with remorse that I help you to your feet and we go off arm-in-arm for a consoling beverage."

"I suggest that you take a step or two backward, shake your fist at me once more, and then angrily exit into—I think the apothecary would be best. I shall wave my walking stick furiously at you and then march off down the street, well rid of you. If I'm right, our follower will follow me. Give him a one-block lead, and then come after. I'll march on for ten or fifteen blocks, and then turn into some convenient alleyway; he will come in after me, and you will close the exit."

Moran crouched in a street fighter's crouch and glared at the professor. "Why don't I just cosh him?"

"Because I want him able to talk. I want to find out who sent him."

"He probably doesn't even know," Moran said, jabbing at Moriarty's face with his left a couple of times.

Moriarty easily evaded the jabs. "Perhaps so," he admitted, "but it's worth a try."

"Very well," Moran agreed. He took two steps backward, lowered his arms, and breathed heavily for a second. Then he shook his right fist in Moriarty's face. "Look around nervously when you approach the alleyway," he told Moriarty in an undertone. "You'll draw him in faster. 'The bleating of the lamb excites the tiger,' as we say."

Moriarty dropped his stick to his side and glared convincingly at Moran. "Hunting tigers for sport," he said. "Seems like a waste."

"Of tigers or men?" Moran asked. "We only went after the man-eaters. The maharaja wouldn't let us touch any others. Funny thing is, the man-eaters were usually the ones that were too old or too injured to catch their regular game. Men are easy prey, for a tiger." With that, Moran wheeled and stalked off to the apothecary, turned to glare at Moriarty for a second, and then flung the door open and entered.

Moriarty shook his walking stick at the retreating Moran, then paused to gather himself, straighten his clothing, and affix his pince-nez glasses firmly on the bridge of his nose. He then started off down the street with the rapid, heedless stride of a thoroughly irritated man.

On the right-hand side of Moriarty's pince-nez, at the very edge, Moriarty's artificer Old Potts had affixed a small mirrored rectangle so that Moriarty could have a glimpse of what was happening behind him without turning his head. As Moriarty strode forward he peered into the little mirror with a practiced eye, and observed his follower trotting across the street and taking up a position about half a block behind.

Moriarty kept up the rapid pace for a dozen blocks, peering into his minuscule mirror occasionally to make sure that his follower was still following. The first few blocks were mainly large residential buildings with storefronts lining the ground floor. But then the storefronts petered out, and the buildings looked more as though they were used for light manufacturing. A sign on the second floor of one building read: "*Felix Hermann–Schokolade Erschaffungen.*" On the next block was "*Schmendl Schuhfabrik.*"

Moriarty paused and consulted a blank piece of paper which he produced from an inner pocket, looking around as though he were trying to locate a specific building or address. The man behind him paused also, and leaned against a lamppost, breathing deeply. *No stamina*, Moriarty thought. *There should be mandatory exercise for the criminal classes.* He looked cautiously around for Colonel Moran, and finally spotted him walking unconcernedly along about a block down on the other side of the street. This seemed as good a place as any to end this clandestine parade; the streets were practically deserted and the ground-floor windows were mostly shuttered—a sign of what sort of neighborhood this became after dark.

Moriarty forged ahead more slowly now, peering at signs and numbers as though looking for a specific address, until he found a narrow walkway between two buildings. He peered in timidly, checked his blank piece of paper, and looked about suspiciously as though fearful that this was some sort of trap. His pursuer darted between two horse carts at the curb, causing the rear horse to shy nervously and back up a couple of steps with a clatter of hooves. Moriarty affected not to notice. There was an iron-bound door at the end of the passageway, and no windows at the ground level on either side. Perfect. After a few more moments of feigned hesitation, he started bravely down the walkway.

Tiger hunters in India don't try to chase the tiger; it is far faster and more agile than the hunter. Instead they stake out a young lamb or kid and conceal themselves nearby. The bleating of the lamb, as Colonel Moran had said, excites the tiger, and lures him into the trap.

The tiger in question crossed the sidewalk and, flattening himself against the side of the building, peered down the alleyway. He saw Moriarty walking slowly toward the iron-bound door at the far end. Moriarty seemed intent on what was in front of him, and unaware of what might be behind him. The tiger allowed the rolled-up newspaper he was carrying to fall away from the lead pipe it concealed, and started silently down the alleyway after the lamb.

When the tiger was about ten yards into the alleyway, the lamb suddenly stopped and turned. Moriarty smiled and advanced toward his pursuer. "You had best put down that piece of pipe and sit on the ground with your hands over your head," he said in German. "You can't escape."

"Escape?" the man looked surprised, but then he laughed. "It is not I who have to be concerned about escape, *mein herr*." But he stopped and held the pipe in front of him as though he were preparing to lead a marching band. "I have a job to do," he said. "It will hurt less if you do not resist."

Moriarty sighed. "For your own good, give up all thought of hurting me, or of getting away. Your exit is blocked."

"My exit?" The man shook his head as though he could not believe what he was hearing.

"You ain't going nowhere, buddy," drawled Colonel Moran in German from somewhere behind. The man spun around and saw Moran standing at the entrance to the alleyway, leaning against the building, looking dapper and dangerous.

"Your German is very colloquial," the professor called out to Moran.

"I learned it at a very colloquial spot," the colonel replied.

The man between suddenly leaped toward Moriarty, who was no more than five feet away by now, and, with a savage yell, kicked swiftly and heavily at Moriarty's groin. Moriarty easily sidestepped the blow. The man followed through in one continuous move, transferring his momentum from legs to arms, swinging the lead pipe viciously at Moriarty's head. Had the blow connected, it would assuredly have killed him. Moriarty moved aside just enough so that the blow whistled harmlessly past his ear, then he caught the man's arm and twisted it as it came down by turning his own body, causing his attacker to drop the pipe, and poked the man in the stomach with the head of his stick.

The man doubled over, the breath knocked out of him, but a second later he had grabbed the lead pipe on the ground and straightened up, closing with Moriarty and grappling, trying to get in a solid blow with the pipe. Moriarty dropped his stick and the two swayed back and forth, each trying to get mastery of the pipe. Moran raced forward but, just before he reached them, the man was thrust to the ground, facedown, and in a second Moriarty had his knee in the man's back and was twisting his left hand behind him.

"That was a neat move," Moran commended. "Just what was it you did there? I thought I saw it, but I didn't exactly grasp what happened."

The man on the ground squirmed and yelped. "You pig of a dog! Get off me! I think you've broken my arm!"

"It's a move in baritsu," Moriarty told Moran. "One of the more obscure Oriental martial arts. Very useful. It takes years of practice, but the effort is well repaid." Then he leaned down to the man on the ground. "It isn't broken yet," he told him, "but it will be if you keep squirming. And calling me names isn't going to help your case in the hereafter."

"I shall yell for an officer of the police if you do not release me."

"Yell away," Moran said grimly.

"What is it that you gentlemen want?" the man cried. "Why have you assaulted me? What do you mean, 'the hereafter'?"

"Assaulted you?" Moriarty smiled an unfriendly smile. "Now, that's an interesting way to look at it."

"I was just walking down the street when you gentlemen jumped me," the man insisted.

"Yes?" Moriarty asked. "And just what business had you down this alleyway? And why were you carrying a lead pipe? And why did you attack me with it?"

"A man's got to defend himself," the man insisted.

"Enough of this," Moran growled. "I'll just kill him, and we'll be out of here." A large knife suddenly appeared in his hand.

The man looked up at the knife and his eyes got very large. "No, no," he yelped. "I am not ready for the hereafter. I meant you no harm—argh!" The last as Moriarty twisted ever so slightly more on the arm he was holding. "I mean, it was just a job. No need to take it personal. I failed—I'll admit that. I underestimated you, and I lost. Let's call it quits, fair and square, and I'll just be off."

"What's your name?" asked Moriarty.

"Why—ah!—they call me Plum. Ask anyone. That's my name, Plum."

"Well, Plum, why were you trying to kill me?" Moriarty asked. "Who sent you?"

"Trying to kill you?" Plum laughed weakly. His face, pressed against the pavement, was turning white from the pain inflicted by Moriarty's scientifically applied baritsu hold. "I think you are dislocating my shoulder. Perhaps you could let up a little, just a bit, no more. No, *mein herr*, I was not trying to kill you. I see the confusion now, and an honest mistake it was indeed. You thought—But no, I had no intention of trying to kill you. Indeed not!"

"What then?" Moriarty demanded.

"I was just to break a few bones, that's all. A few small, unimportant bones. Just to keep you here for some time."

"Keep me here?"

"That's what I was told. That's all I know."

"Who hired you?"

"Hired me?"

Moriarty applied more pressure to the arm.

"Argh! *Gott*, but that hurts. When this is over, and we are friends again, perhaps you will teach me that move."

"Perhaps," said Moriarty. "Who hired you?"

"I got the job from the Crow. He gives out all the work assignments."

"Work assignments, is it?" Colonel Moran said savagely. "And a fine sort of work it is."

"He's the head of your gang?" Moriarty asked.

"It's not so much of a gang, as an informal association," Plum said. "The Crow is more like the secretary, if you see what I mean. He works out the assignments and tries to keep everything fair between us. If you'll let go of my *gottverdammt* arm and let me up, I'll be pleased to discuss the system with you."

"And just why did the Crow want two passing Englishmen beaten up?" demanded Moran.

"Not two Englishmen," said Plum. "Just him." He pointed his chin at Moriarty. "The Crow described him and told me where to find him. He said there was someone with him, but you were incidental. I could beat you if I had to, but I wouldn't get paid anything extra for it."

"I've been slighted," said Moran. "I should find this Crow and ask him what's wrong with me that I'm not to be beaten up along with you, Professor."

"And who is paying the Crow for this job?" asked Moriarty.

Up until now Plum had looked phlegmatic and resigned, for all that he was facedown on the sidewalk with his arm being twisted. Being beaten up was, after all, part of the game. Suddenly he looked frightened and tried to pull away, and he screamed at the sudden unbearable pain as his arm was twisted well beyond where nature had intended it to go.

"You brought that on yourself," Moriarty told him. "You're not permanently injured yet, but don't do that again. Now, who is paying to have my bones broken?"

"I don't know," Plum whined. "He didn't tell me. Honest."

"You're lying," Moriarty said dispassionately.

Moran bent down and brought his knife to within inches of the man's face. "Left eye or right eye?" he asked pleasantly.

"*Mein Gott!*" cried Plum. "You wouldn't." He shuddered and looked up at the leer on Moran's face. "You would, yes, you would. I can tell you. The Crow was bragging about it, his first assignment from the world-famous English master criminal."

"What English master criminal?"

"Professor Moriarty is his name. An English gentleman employed the Crow on behalf of his chief, the famous English Herr Professor Moriarty to break your bones so that you could not leave Vienna for some weeks. You will not tell on me, will you?"

Colonel Moran leaned back on his heels, folded his clasp knife, and broke out laughing.

"Tell me about this English gentleman who spoke for the master criminal Moriarty," Moriarty said.

"I know nothing about him," Plum insisted. "He dealt only with the Crow. I swear!"

Moriarty released his hold on Plum and pulled him to his feet. "I believe you," he said. "A touch; a distinct touch. You may go now."

Plum moved his right arm gingerly, and seemed surprised to see that it still worked properly. "Yes," he agreed. "Yes, I will go now." He trotted down the alleyway to the street, never pausing to look back, and disappeared around the corner.

"Well, Professor," Moran said, shaking his head. "You've set a new record for the master criminal's devious behavior. You've sent someone out to break your own bones." He burst out laughing again. "Isn't that too much?"

"I'm flattered that my name has acquired such currency throughout Europe that someone would use it to establish his bona fides as a master criminal," Moriarty said sourly. "I must find out whom to thank for the honor."

ELEVEN

THE GAME'S AFOOT

There is a time for some things, and a time for all things; a time for
great things and a time for small things.
MIGUEL DE CERVANTES

An old, long-disused wharf squatted over the muddy water where Covington Street met the Thames, its rotting planks and slimy pilings concealed from view by the sagging wooden fence that kept drunks and children from falling through the unsafe relic into the river below. The barge tied up to the wharf had not been new during the Napoleonic Wars, and was slowly sinking in place, its small deckhouse tilting at a crazy angle on the afterdeck, the whole rotting away from age and neglect.

Or so it was meant to look to a casual observer.

It was early evening on this Saturday, the first day of March, 1890. The sun had disappeared behind the shops and warehouses and a light snow was falling, which further obscured the arrival at the wharf of four of what the commissioner of the metropolitan police described as "London's most undesirable residents." They were all known by name to the chief inspector of the detective division, who would happily have given a week's pay to put any one of them away for a stretch in Dartmoor Prison. Angelic Tim McAdams and Cooley the Pup arrived moments apart, and disappeared into the depths of the barge. The Artful Codger came perhaps five minutes later, looked carefully around to be sure he was unobserved, and then, settling his leather cap more firmly on his head, proceeded cautiously down into the blackness of the hold.

After another minute the bottom half of the door in the small deck-house opened, and Dr. Pin Dok Low scurried forth like a fox emerging cautiously from its burrow. He paused to savor the smells coming off the river, drinking them in like the steam off a cup of the blackest souchong tea, then hurried to join his compatriots below the deck.

Behind the door to the hold was a double curtain of black muslin, keeping in the light from the two oil lamps that swung from the ceiling.

Cooley the Pup looked up as the curtain was pushed aside, his hand to the back of his neck, where a slender leaf-bladed throwing knife was concealed. As Pin Dok Low emerged through the doorway, he dropped his hand back into his lap. "Well, Pin, about time you got here," he whined. "We thought you'd be here waiting for us, seeing as how it was you asked us to this here meeting."

"Oh, I was, I was," Pin said smoothly, going around to sit at the head of the table, the spot instinctively reserved for him by the others. "I awaited you at a vantage point from which I could assure myself—and you—that you were not being followed."

"I can look after meself, without no help from you nor anybody else," growled Angelic Tim McAdams.

"Self-reliance is a wonderful thing," Pin agreed. "Very useful, I believe, in prison."

"Here, now; what has prison got to do with it?" demanded the Pup.

"Nothing, I sincerely hope," Pin said smoothly. "But it pays to remain alert. 'Eternal vigilance is the price of freedom,' would be a good adage to engrave above the portal of every criminal enterprise."

"Is that so?" said the Artful Codger, leaning back in his chair until it was teetering on its back legs. "Then who's watching the store at present?"

Pin took a pair of black-framed glasses from the pocket of his tunic, polished them on the hem of the garment, and settled them onto his nose. "One of my associates is in the deckhouse, keeping the area under surveillance," he told the Codger. "If he sees anything that should concern us, a bell will direct our attention to the fact." He pointed to a spot on the ceiling, where a small bell had been fastened. "We will have sufficient time to consider the possibilities and act as seems best."

"Well, then," said McAdams, "just what are we doing here? I got better things to do than to hang about in a stinking barge."

"Stinking is right," the Codger agreed. "There's a smell of bilge water about this place that all the perfumes of Araby couldn't cover up."

"Ah, such ingratitude," Dr. Pin said. "And I thought it would make you gentlemen feel right at home."

"How come you got so many little hidey-holes, Pin?" the Codger asked. "Every time you call a meeting, it ain't for the last place we met at, it's for some new place altogether. Why is that?"

"Yeah, that's a good question," McAdams agreed.

"You would think so, McAdams," Pin said, smiling a gentle smile. "It must be very frustrating to have your minions keep watch on that old clothes shop in Mincing Lane, or the Friends of the Benighted Heathen Missionary Society warehouse for days on end, through rain, sleet, or snow, as the expression goes, and catch not a glimpse of myself or my companions."

"So you got companions, do you?" the Codger asked. "My friends and I, we were kind of wondering."

"Perhaps I speak metaphorically," said Pin. He held his hands in front of him, palms up. "My ten fingers and my brain are all the companions I need, and all you need to know about."

"And what information do you and your ten fingers wish to impart?" asked the Codger. "You going to open up a bit more on the gold shipment? When is it coming in? Just how are we going to take it away from them as are undoubtedly sitting on top of it with loaded blunderbusses?"

"The gold has not left Calcutta yet," Pin told them, "but it is due to be loaded aboard the steamship *Empress of India* shortly for its voyage to the vaults of the Bank of England."

"That's good, that's good," McAdams said, rubbing his massive hands together. "My boys have been growing a bit impatient, what with me trying to keep them out of trouble until the big moment."

"Wait just a blooming minute," Cooley the Pup interrupted. "If the ship is just getting ready to leave India, why, then, it won't be here for at least—what?—five weeks. Is that right?"

Pin nodded. "I could not fail to disagree with you less," he said.

McAdams thought that over for a long moment. "Say," he said finally, "is that a yes or a no?"

"It will be about a week before the *Empress* arrives in Calcutta, then a week or so there, and then five weeks, or perhaps a bit more, before the gold arrives in Southampton," Dr. Pin said, "if it arrives at all."

"If it arrives?" asked the Pup.

"Say, what do you mean by that?" asked McAdams. "You been stringing us?"

"I don't like the sound of that *if*," commented the Artful Codger. "Perhaps you'd better go on."

"Yeah," said the Pup. "Go on. Do go on."

Dr. Pin Dok Low leaned back in his chair and surveyed his companions. "Professor Moriarty has left London," he told them.

"We know that," said McAdams. "The Yob is following him, ain't he?"

"The Twopenny Yob is indeed on his, ah, tail," Pin agreed. "Four attempts have been made on the professor's life. None have been successful. Not that I expected that any of them would succeed. If Professor Moriarty could be stopped that easily, he would have been stopped long since."

"I don't hold with killing unnecessarily," said Angelic Tim McAdams unexpectedly. The others around the table turned to look at him.

"Well," he insisted, "I don't."

The Artful Codger turned back to Pin Dok Low. "So?" he asked. "The professor is out of the way. You can't use him as a—what?—as a decoy for the rozzers anymore, but by the same chance, he ain't around to get in our way or foul up our plans."

Pin Dok Low scowled. "Moriarty is making his way across Europe," he told them. "The Twopenny Yob was close behind him but, at the moment, this is no longer so. As far as we can tell, he's on his way to India."

McAdams slapped his hand on the table. "Good," he said. "The farther away the better for that cove. He's a mite too wise for playing him the way you wanted to, and that's what I think."

"I'm glad it relieves your anxiety," Pin said smoothly, "and I hate to be the one to raise it in another quarter, but, as I'm sure you will realize after a moment's thought, there is one most interesting possibility that we must not overlook."

"And what's that?" asked the Pup.

The Artful Codger half rose from his chair, and then fell back down. "Calcutta!" he exclaimed. "Calcutta!"

"Exactly," Pin Dok Low agreed. "Why would Professor Moriarty, the most brilliant criminal mind in England, possibly in all Europe—present company excepted, of course—be headed to India at just this moment? Could it be a coincidence that a large shipment of gold is being prepared to leave Calcutta in about two weeks? I think not."

"So," McAdams said, a fierce scowl growing across his face, "the professor's going to beat us to the gold."

Pin Dok Low smiled at him, a beatific smile. "I think not," he repeated.

"So," the Codger said, leaning his elbows on the table and staring across at the wily Oriental. "What's your plan, Pin?"

"Simple," Pin said. "We are going to prevent the gold being stolen until we are ready to steal it ourselves."

"How's that?" asked McAdams.

"You"—Pin pointed a long finger at McAdams—"are going to stay here in London, and you and your boys are going to be ready to remove the gold according to the original plan."

"All very good," McAdams agreed, "only you ain't never told me the original plan."

"A man must have his little secrets," Pin said, chuckling. "But I will explain it now, at the end of this meeting." He turned to Cooley the Pup. "You are going to go to Amsterdam and make the preparations for disposing of two tons of gold."

"Sounds good," the Pup agreed.

"And returning with the money," Pin added.

"Of course," said the Pup, sounding hurt. "What do you take me for?"

"I'll be taking your head," McAdams remarked, "if you attempt to ab-bloody-scond with what's mine."

"I'm not afraid of your threats," said Cooley the Pup, "but I have my sense of honor."

That remark shocked the others into silence, and they stared at the Pup until he started shifting nervously in his chair. "Well," he insisted, "I do."

Pin sighed a long-suffering sigh, and continued. "Codger, you're going to come with me."

"Right-oh. Where to?"

"India," Pin told him.

"India? What's the play?"

"If we're going to steal the gold for ourselves," Pin told him, "we're going to have to make sure that nobody else gets it first."

The Artful Codger rubbed his left ear thoughtfully. "It makes sense," he allowed finally. "It's right-on weird, but it makes sense when you think about it. We're to guard the gold so's we can steal the gold."

"How're you going to get there in two weeks?" McAdams demanded.

"We can't get to Calcutta in two weeks," Pin admitted. "But we can get to Bombay in a bit over that. And the *Empress* should arrive a day or so after we do. We will book passage on *The Empress of India*, and accompany our gold back to England, to make sure that nothing happens to it."

The Codger thought it over for a second. "I fancy a sea voyage wouldn't be amiss," he said. "How are we to get to Bombay?"

"By special train to Naples, and then by a fast steamer through the canal."

"Special train, is it?" asked McAdams. "And how do we pay for it? I hope we ain't expected to lay out the expenses for this venture."

"Pay for it?" Pin Dok Low smiled his inscrutable smile. "What a thought. We'll bill it to the government of Bavaria."

"Bavaria?"

"Yes, and why not Bavaria? I have a printer at work right now making up the necessary official documents and permissions and such. I shall go in disguise as Graf von Falkenberg, cousin to Crown Prince Sigismund. There will be no problems."

"But," said Cooley the Pup, pointing a quavering finger at Dr. Pin Dok Low, "you're Chinese!"

"Am I?" asked Pin. "Why, so I am. But I have always fancied myself a master of disguise. How's your German, Codger?"

"'Bout the same as my French," the Codger said. "As a matter of fact, my German could easily be mistaken for my French."

"Ah!" said Pin. "Well, we'll think of something. Go put on your gentleman's disguise and pack a bag. Meet me at Victoria Station in, say, two hours. We will leave tonight."

"Right," said the Codger. He pushed himself to his feet. "See you gents; I'm off to guard the gold."

TWELVE

THE EMPRESS OF INDIA

I'll have them fly to India for gold,
Ransack the ocean for orient pearl.
CHRISTOPHER MARLOWE

It was late in the afternoon of Friday, March 14, when the steamship *Empress of India* made her way up the Hooghly River and approached Calcutta Harbor. At 652 feet long and 70 wide, the *Empress* was the queen of the Anglo-Asian Star steamship line. Built by John Brown & Company, Clydebank, Glasgow, in 1888, she had a pair of Garrett & Harris quadruple expansion engines to drive her twin screws and, when everything was working perfectly and the sea gods were smiling, was capable of hitting a speed of nineteen knots. She was not quite the longest, nor the heaviest, nor the fastest, nor the most luxurious ship afloat, but she was not far off any of the four.

Two oceangoing steam tugs, *Egbert* and *Ethelred*, had come out to prod the *Empress*, bow and stern, into its berth alongside the Commissariat Jetty, just down from Fort William. Ordinarily one tug would have sufficed, but The *Empress of India* was bringing the new issue of paper currency, and precautions must be taken. The two tugs were crammed with armed men, ready to fend off any possible attempt to filch the lucre. The *Clive*, the viceroy's own steam launch, fitted with a pair of twenty-year-old Schoenfeld-Waters breech-loading two-inch guns, was chasing up and down the river, warning off all other boats. As the *Empress* docked, special armored drays pulled up on the wharf to receive the sealed boxes of currency. The jetty was guarded with a full company of Bengali heavy infantry, which formed a *cordon sanitaire* between the usual army of peddlers, hawkers, mendicants, street performers, hustlers, and pickpockets and the disembarking passengers.

"In a week now we'll be loading the gold for the return trip," said the viceroy, who was watching the proceedings from a window in the Bengali Military Administration offices on the third floor of Fort William. "This is a sort of dress rehearsal for that."

General St. Yves stood beside the viceroy and surveyed the scene. "It looks to me as if you're quite prepared for any sort of t-trouble you might expect," he commented.

"It's the unexpected trouble that I'm concerned about," the viceroy said. "Somebody clever enough to think of something I haven't thought of, or that I've discarded as being too fanciful."

St. Yves smiled. "And here you've been reassuring me that I have nothing to worry about."

"Ah," the viceroy said, "but your situation will be quite different. You'll be on a ship at sea. The *Empress*'s master, Captain Iskansen, is one of the best qualified, most capable ship's officers I've ever known. Anglo-Asian Star is lucky to have him. The *Empress* will be escorted out to sea by the *Clive* and the torpedo gunboat *Sea Lion*. They won't leave until she's about twenty miles out, by which time she's untouchable. Another ship might try to come alongside and board you, but *The Empress of India* is the fastest thing afloat, just about, in this part of the world. There are a couple of naval vessels that can match her for speed, but I can't picture Her Majesty's Navy stealing Bank of England gold. And as for passengers or crew: no one on board the ship will attempt to steal the gold, not after they've thought it out. If they do, where are they going to put it?"

St. Yves stared out at the docking ship and thought it over. "What you said before," he said, "about the unexpected. You know, I think that's what's going to keep me up nights; worrying about how to prepare for the unexpected."

* * *

From his vantage point by the ordnance building, a scant few hundred yards from the Commissariat Jetty, Professor James Moriarty leaned on his owl-headed walking stick and watched the two tugs pushing and pulling at *The Empress of India*. "Look at that sight," he said to Colonel Moran, who stood to his right. "It makes one marvel at the accomplishments of modern engineering. Fifty years ago the wooden sailing ship still ruled the seas, and the few great side-wheel steam ships were dirty, noisy, uncomfortable, and inefficient. Their engines were remarkable more for the fact that they worked at all, rather than anything they were able to accomplish in the manner of speed or reliability. Not a few of them ended up burning up their own furniture and fittings for fuel when delayed by a storm or other natural mishap."

"We've come a long ways," Moran agreed easily.

"I find it remarkable and not a little frightening that science is progressing so rapidly," Moriarty told him. "But what good will come of this remains to be seen, as most men remain for the most part the stupid brutish louts they've always been."

Moran raised an eyebrow. "That's a bleak view of the world you've got there, ain't it?" he said. "It sounds to me like you're a devoted—what's the word?—misanthrope."

Moriarty raised an eyebrow. "I don't think that mankind is irredeemable," he said. "I just think that he's not doing overmuch to be worth redeeming."

"Just as I said," Moran insisted. "You're a whatchamacallit."

"And you're not?" asked Moriarty.

Moran paused to think about it seriously. "I don't think most men are worth the powder to blow them to hell," he said finally. "But there are some—yes, there are some. And as for women, well, I confess I'd go out of my way to save many of them. But I'm not sure it would be for an entirely worthy motive."

Moriarty grunted and returned his gaze to the scene in front of him.

"We're going to need togs, you know," Moran said. "For the ship. A couple of suits, evening clothes, shirts, that sort of thing."

"It was inconvenient, losing our luggage," Moriarty said. "I suppose you're right; there are certain ways in which one does not wish to be unconventional, and dress is one of them. Best to blend in."

"My dear man," Moran said, "I'd rather be caught cheating at cards than not dress for dinner when in society."

"I daresay," Moriarty said.

"I know of a tailor on Bubbling Well Road, by the big bazaar," Moran said. "We let him take our measurements today, and we can have our clothes tomorrow. And they'll fit right, too. Remarkable chap."

"Then by all means let us visit his establishment," said Moriarty. "I'll fetch the mummer, too. I have an important role for him in our coming enterprise. We'd best enlarge his wardrobe so that he can dress the part."

"What part?" Moran asked.

"I think a peripatetic merchant," Moriarty said. "One who travels in statues."

"Statues," Moran said, visibly cheering up. "Then you've thought of a plan?"

"I have."

"Well!" Moran slapped the professor on the back. "I knew I could count on you, Professor. What do we do?"

"Since we can't steal the statue, or hurt anyone in acquiring it," Moriarty said, "our best option is to have it lose its perceived value."

"How's that?"

"We must make the officers of the Duke of Moncreith's Own cease to desire the statue. We must make them think that the statue is not worthy of being kept in a place of honor. We must make them give it to us."

Moran cocked his head sideways and stared at the professor. "They're going to give it to us?"

"Just so. Or, less probably, sell it to us for an extremely reasonable price."

"Very funny, Professor."

"I sincerely hope not, Colonel."

Moran looked suspiciously at Moriarty. The professor had an unpredictable sense of humor; could this be an example? "All right, then. And just how are we going to do that, if I might ask?" A certain tightness in his voice showed that he was repressing some strong emotion.

"Come," said Moriarty. "There's something we have to do as quickly as possible if my plan is to work. I think it best not to ask your friend for help; it might give him ideas. We should be able to locate the assistance we need at or around the bazaar." He turned and headed toward the carriage stand a block away. "Did you know," he asked Moran when the colonel caught up with him, "that I am something of an expert in the ancient and mysterious art of mesmerism?"

Moran looked at him for a long moment, and then said, "Bah!"

Moriarty chuckled.

THIRTEEN

THE SCORPION KILLERS

As I was going up the stair
I met a man who wasn't there,
He wasn't there again to-day
I wish, I wish he'd stay away.
HUGHES MEARNS

At five-thirty the next morning, five men climbed a well-worn staircase in that quadrant of Fort William being used by the Duke of Moncreith's Own Highland Lancers, went down a long corridor decorated with Indian regalia, cricket bats, cases full of sports trophies, ancient Scottish battle flags, faded color prints of great moments in fox hunting, and other impedimenta of the British officer, and knocked on the door to the officers' mess. The five wore white smocks and carried pails and boxes and bottles and rolls of fabric and a pump sprayer. Two of them were English, or at least British; the tall sahib and the broad sahib, as their Indian companions thought of them. If looked at closely, they bore a striking resemblance to Professor James Moriarty and Colonel Sebastian Moran. The remaining three were native Indian, experts at what they did, and were not at all sure why they had allowed themselves to be talked into joining in this farcical and dangerous masquerade. They were, after all, tradesmen and artisans, not brigands and thieves.

"The money," Damodar, who was the eldest, and a well-kept sixty if he was a day, reminded the others.

"Ah, yes, the money." Half already paid, and in the hands of their families. The other half due immediately upon their timely and safe removal from this most dangerous project. "It is quite a sum," agreed Harshil, a short, rotund man who tended to be glum at the best of times. "But is it worth the five years in prison we shall assuredly acquire if we should happen to get caught?"

"Come, surely that will not happen," Farokh said firmly. He had always believed that the gods, being essentially perverse, would be most likely to help those who appeared not to need help. "Look at our leader. Does he look like the sort of man who would lead us into prison?"

"He looks like a man who would be quite capable of leading us anywhere he felt like going," said Damodar, "and out again."

"Just so," Farokh agreed.

Damodar folded his arms. "We are here. We will do what must be done; what we agreed to do. And the rest is in the hands of Vishnu."

Harshil stared at the others bleakly. "It is written," he said, "that if you would make Vishnu laugh, tell him your plans."

"It is also written," said Farokh, "that he who worries constantly about the future has no joy in the present. And we live in the present."

"Yes," Harshil agreed morosely, "until the future arrives with a loud noise and blows out the candles."

"What?"

"Never mind. Look like you know what you're doing; here comes the guard."

The man approaching the door in answer to their knock was not actually a guard. He was the second under-cook; a corporal name of Pippins. "What can I do for you gents?" he asked, pushing the door open.

"Actually," Moriarty said, unfolding an official-looking bit of paper and handing it to the cook, "it's more likely to come down to what we can do for you, mate."

Corporal Pippins perused the document as best he could. Why these military orders and such couldn't be written in plain English was beyond him. Sorting through all the "whereas's" and "hereby requested and directed to's" to figure out just what it was those gentlemen of limited intelligence that God and the British government had put in command over him wanted him to do, was a constant pain; half the time they never actually stated what they wanted him to do, but if he guessed wrong he'd probably lose his stripe.

This one seemed to want the professional gentlemen in front of him to spray the dining room for scorpions and other pests. Scorpions?

"I ain't never seen no scorpions in or around thissere room," said the corporal.

The tall gentleman who seemed to be in charge had pushed through the door and was surveying the dining room with a critical eye. "Well," he said, "someone seems to have done. Maybe it was just a great jumping spider or something of the sort. You want us to spray or to go away? It's all the same to me."

"Jumping spider?" Corporal Pippins looked concerned. "We ain't got no jumping spiders around here, do we? I mean, the snakes is bad enough."

"It's like Mr. Darwin said; it's a question of survival of the fittest," Moriarty explained. "Usually your snakes eat your scorpions. But your jumping spiders, now, there isn't much will eat one of them."

"Oh," said the corporal, looking around the room with a renewed interested in cracks, corners, and crevices.

"Don't worry about it," Moriarty assured him. "The spray we use will eliminate spiders, jumping or nonjumping, scorpions, ants, roaches, centipedes, millipedes, mice, rats, snakes, cats, dogs, pigs; and it will do a pretty good job on people if you don't take the proper precautions."

"Damn!" said the under-cook feelingly. "What about all the silverware and glasses and plate and such?"

"I hear as how you're shipping out any day now, isn't it?" Moriarty asked.

"Well, the officers is, anyway," Pippins admitted.

"Well, then, you'll have to wash all that stuff anyway before you packs it up," Moriarty said. "And what skin is it off your nose?—it ain't you as does the washing."

"And besides," added Moran, "you don't want to be taking no

scorpions back to England with you, now, do you?"

"Scotland," corrected Pippins.

"Ah, now," said Moran. "Scotland. That's different."

"Wait a minute," said Corporal Pippin.

Moran held up a placating hand. "Just a joke, mate. Your poisonous invertebrates should not be permitted to make their way back to Scotland, either. My word."

"Shouldn't send no scorpions back to Scotland," Pippins insisted.

"Even so," said Moran. "Even so."

Corporal Pippins thought it over. "I'll have to check with Cookie—Sergeant Ostogood—about thissere. You just wait right here—I'll be back in a bit."

As Pippins left the dining room, Moran leaned over to Moriarty and intoned, "Your parents must have moved around a lot."

"How's that?"

"I'm no expert," Moran said, "but it seemed to me that you had about three different London accents going for you in the space of as many minutes. Not that yon corporal noticed."

"You're right," Moriarty agreed. "I get carried away summat." He smiled. "I'll endeavor to be more consistent."

The corporal returned a minute later. "Cookie says that you are to go ahead, but that I'm to keep watch on the silver plate and such."

"Fair enough," Moriarty agreed. He gestured to the waiting native artisans, and they pulled out white head scarves and face masks and wrapped their heads in the white cloth as they had been shown by the professor earlier. Theirs was not to reason why; theirs was but to follow instructions and get paid.

"We don't have any extra headgear for you," Moriarty told the corporal. "But if you hold your breath, you should be all right. And take a good shower after we're done."

"Hold my breath?" Pippins held his breath experimentally for a few seconds and then let it out with an explosive sound. "For how long?" he asked.

"No more than, say, half an hour," Moriarty assured him, through the two layers of white cloth that he had tied around his mouth and nose. "We'll be done by then."

"Say, I can't hold my breath for anything like half an hour!" Pippins complained.

"Really?" Moriarty asked, sounding surprised. "No, I don't guess you can. Silly of me." He thought for a second. "Tell you what," he said. "You stand outside the door to make sure we can't sneak out or anything. And then when we're done, we'll wait here while you check the spoons and such to ascertain that they're all there. Right?"

Pippins nodded slowly. "Right enough," he agreed.

Moriarty shooed the corporal back into the kitchen and closed the connecting door. He and his crew then made sure all the doors were tightly shut and closed the cracks beneath and above the doors, using some rags they had brought along and, when they ran out, the brigade's tablecloths.

"Pardon, sahib," said Damodar, who was stuffing a tablecloth under the double doors to the corridor. "But this does not seem, somehow, just."

Moriarty paused. "I respect your opinion, Damodar. What is it that does not seem just?"

"This—" Damodar gestured. "This using of the tablecloths of the brigade officers. It will surely increase their laundering costs."

Moriarty nodded thoughtfully. "There is something in what you say," he said. "I'll make an anonymous donation to the officers' mess fund."

Moran nodded agreement. "Seems only proper," he said.

Damodar smiled and spoke to the others, and they nodded and were satisfied. These were God-fearing, just, and understanding men, whatever the strangeness of their desires.

Corporal Pippins peered through the little window in the door to the kitchen, and watched the depesting proceed. First the men sealed off the room. Then they unrolled the rolls of fabric and spread them about. Then they took the pump sprayer and sprayed here and there, misting up the room until it was hard to see anything whatsoever. They were over there by the shelf on which resided the Lady of Lucknow. Pippins tried to see what was happening, but couldn't quite make it out. He could have sworn that they took the statue and lowered it into a bucket. Whatever for? If anything happened to the Lady, well, wouldn't the officers just about have a fit. And they'd blame him, right enough.

But then the tall man had pulled something out of a case on the other side of the room. Was that a scorpion? By gad, that was a scorpion. So there were scorpions in the dining room. And he'd been going in there and putting his hands in the various cupboards for the past six weeks. And maybe they'd brought the creatures back from upcountry, and he'd been sharing a dining room with them for the last two years. Wasn't that something to think about?

And the tall man had shoved the scorpion into a sack, and now came the mist again. What was that he had to look at? Oh, yes—the statuette. Couldn't see anything now, but he'd keep an eye out.

But then the men went about spraying once again, and when the mist had cleared he could see that the Lady of Lucknow was right up there on her shelf where she'd been.

It was a total of about forty minutes before the scorpion killers pulled the stuffing away from the doors, opened the windows, and declared the room free of dangerous pests. Corporal Pippins entered cautiously. The room smelled of something acidic and something burnt, but he wasn't sure what. The men waited patiently while the corporal checked the silverware and the plate, and declared all of the brigade's valuables present and accounted for. Then they nodded pleasantly to him and toddled off, carrying with them their assorted pails, bottles, boxes, and fabric rolls, and a perfect gutta-percha mold of the Lady of Lucknow.

* * *

Once outside the fort, Damodar, Harshil, and Farokh accepted the envelope containing the other half of the agreed-upon stipend, shook hands solemnly with the tall sahib and the broad sahib, and headed back to their foundry, where they were to immediately begin the production of fifty copies of the little statuette over the next three days. An arduous task which would require the assistance of most of their family members, but the sahibs needed them in time to ship them aboard *The Empress of India* when she left on Wednesday morning, and the sahibs paid generously.

After they had left, the tall sahib turned to the broad sahib. "I leave you to sort out the details for the next few days," he said. "I'll be taking a short trip. Mummer Tolliver will give you any assistance you need. You've seen by now how capable the little man is. Get our tickets for the voyage, and make sure the statuettes are crated properly and put aboard."

Moran stared at the professor. "You are full of surprises," he said after a moment. "A short trip to where, may I ask?"

"You may," Moriarty said. "Do you realize that there are no English translations of any of the more important Indian works of astronomy or mathematics?"

"No," Moran said. "I didn't realize that."

"Disgraceful!" Moriarty said. "Consider that there are Vedic texts on astronomy that are over three thousand years old. Surely they must be worth perusing."

"You would think so," Moran agreed. If there was a degree of insincerity in his voice, Moriarty affected not to notice.

"I am going to see Dr. Pitamaha, head of the Department of Astronomy at the University of Calcutta," Moriarty told him. "I have sent him a telegram telling him to expect me. He is attempting English translations of the *Grahanayayadipaka* by Paramesvara and the *Yuktibhasa* by Jyesthadeva. I am going to offer to help finance his work."

"The *Grahanayayadipaka*?" said Moran. "Really? Who would have guessed?"

"Bah!" said Moriarty. "See you in two or three days."

FOURTEEN

SHIPMATES

A loftier Argo cleaves the main,
Fraught with a later prize;
Another Orpheus sings again,
And loves, and weeps, and dies.
A new Ulysses leaves once more
Calypso for his native shore.
PERCY BYSSHE SHELLEY

With her boarding pass and stateroom reservation in her right hand, and a large bouquet of Oriental lilies cradled in her left arm, Margaret St. Yves strode up the gangway and boarded the S.S. *Empress of India.* A blue-jacketed purser checked her boarding pass at the head of the gangway, and a white-coated, blue turbaned steward took her stateroom reservation and led her down, up, around, through, over, up again, along, and over again, to her stateroom. She had "A" deck stateroom number 72, two doors over from her father's number 76. The door between turned out to be reserved for what was in effect a dayroom for the officers of the Duke's Own, for whom the pleasures of the ocean voyage were being tempered by their need to be ever vigilant against whatever threats might arise against the two tons of gold stored in the special vault below.

"Here you are, memsahib," the steward said, pausing at the

stateroom door. He pushed it open and stood aside, holding out the door key. "I present you to your key, gracious memsahib. Please to go in now. If there's anything you require, I am placed at the end of the hallway in a small closet wherein are the towels and linens. My name is Taleem, and I am the cabin steward for this very hallway."

"My luggage..." Margaret began.

"If you will be pleased to enter your stateroom momentarily, you will find that the steamer trunks and such as you wished to partake of in your stateroom are present now, as are the trunks of your companion. The baggage you wished maintained in the hold is yet already in the hold being held. A stewardess should be along shortly to assist you in the unpacking and show you how to operate the new electrical lights which have been recently installed." He touched the bill of his cap with his forefinger. "I shall continue in my endeavors to aid some of the other passengers now, memsahib. I shall be back directly if you should require of me."

"Yes, of course." Margaret tried not to look surprised. The question was, she thought as she watched Steward Taleem scurry off down the corridor, just who was this "companion" whose trunks were already in her stateroom. It might be some mistake. But the last thing her father had said to her when she saw him last about two hours before was, "Dear, there's something I've been meaning to tell you—" before he got pulled away by his adjutant to deal with the latest in the never-ending crises that always occur in any sort of troop movement. So perhaps... She took a couple of steps through the open door and peered cautiously into the stateroom.

On the far side of the room, next to the oversized porthole, a young blond girl was staring into an open steamer trunk with an expression of distaste. She looked up as Margaret opened the door. "Miss St. Yves," she said. "How good to see you again so soon."

"Lady Priscilla!" Margaret said.

Lady Priscilla Montague's expression of distaste did not change as she eyed the new arrival.

"I'm so glad our fathers arranged for us to share this stateroom for the voyage," said Lady Priscilla Montague, plopping down suddenly on her unopened steamer trunks with something of a bounce.

"So," Margaret said tentatively. "We're to share a stateroom."

"I'm sure that we shall be the best of friends," Lady Priscilla declared. Margaret could only see her from the nose up over the open steamer trunk, but both nose and cheeks were flushed with red, which showed even through her Indian tan.

Margaret took two more steps into the room and closed the door behind her. "When anyone says 'we shall be the best of friends' to me in that tone of voice," she said, "I know that she means the exact opposite."

"Then you have had some experience in this matter?" asked Lady Priscilla sweetly.

"Tell me, Lady Priscilla," Margaret continued calmly, "how have I managed to offend you so thoroughly in such a brief acquaintanceship? I will be able to make use of the knowledge directly, as there are several people whom I have been trying to offend for quite some time, and they never seem to notice."

Lady Priscilla folded her arms and stared fixedly at the statuette she had just placed on the bureau: a porcelain representation of a small mouse sitting at a small-mouse-sized school desk, reading a small book. "Offend me?" she said. "Offend me? Ridiculous! How could you possibly offend me? Just because my own father doesn't trust me to take a simple voyage from Calcutta to London without thrusting someone in my very own cabin to watch over me as though I were a schoolgirl...."

"Actually, you are a schoolgirl," Margaret pointed out.

"That doesn't matter."

"And I am neither your governess nor your duenna. I have no desire to watch over you. I have quite enough trouble watching over myself, thank you."

Lady Priscilla moved from the steamer trunk to the bed with another bounce. "I would like to believe you," she said. "Perhaps, with some years of practice, I shall achieve that happy state."

"Deep breathing might help," Margaret suggested. "I didn't even know we were to be cabin mates until I opened the door and found you within. Perhaps there has been some mistake."

"No mistake." Lady Priscilla shook her golden locks. "My father said that we'd be sharing a stateroom. That you would act as my chaperone until we reached England."

"Then it was your father's doing and none of my own," Margaret told her. "I did not volunteer for such an assignment and, as a matter of fact, I was not asked."

"Do you swear it?" Lady Priscilla asked, looking solemnly over at her cabin mate.

Margaret thought of telling her that ladies do not swear, but decided to forgo the opportunity. "I do," she said solemnly, raising her right hand.

"Cross your heart?"

Margaret crossed her heart.

"My father did not arrange for you to be in this cabin with me so that you could watch over me?"

"He may well have," Margaret said, "but he said nothing to me about watching over you, and I have no intention of doing so. Perhaps he suggested it to my father, who intended to mention it to me. But Father did not do so, therefore I have neither the inclination nor the authority to be your duenna."

Lady Priscilla nodded. "Then I'm sorry I assumed otherwise," she said.

Margaret stretched her hand out to Lady Priscilla. "We will keep each other's secrets," she said, wondering just what sort of secrets Lady Priscilla had that she was so desperate to keep.

* * *

One deck below, Professor Moriarty stood in the middle of his small cabin and looked around with distaste.

"It's the best I could do," Colonel Moran told him. "All the first class cabins were gone. I was assured that this was—how did the booking agent put it?—the very first class of the second class. Our tickets are actually first class, and entitle us to the use of all the first-class facilities. So we can mingle with the gentry, if we've a mind to. I was being facetious," he added quickly, as Moriarty gave him a less-than-pleased look. "I thought it best if we each took a whole cabin, rather than doubling up. The booking agent wanted us to double up, but I was quite firm."

"Double up?" Moriarty asked in disbelief, stretching his arms apart and touching both walls.

"They stack the beds," Moran told him. "All the larger staterooms, even second class, were gone before I booked. It's this bloody gold. The ship is crowded with the Duke's Own officers and men, who fancy that they're guarding it."

Moriarty raised an eyebrow. "You're sure that our crates got on board?" he asked.

"I am," Moran assured him. "And I spread around a little baksheesh to make sure they were put where we could get at them easily."

"Very good." Moriarty shook his head sadly. "It seems such a waste."

"And what would that be?" Moran asked.

"To come all this way merely to turn around and go back after four days. Do you know that the Department of Astronomy at Calcutta University has the archives of the observatory at Burrah? And I barely had time to admire them, much less examine them."

"A pity," said Colonel Moran.

Moriarty poked at his bunk tentatively with his walking stick and sat stiffly on the edge of it. "The Burrah Observatory is over three thousand years old," he told Moran. "They were taking naked-eye observations of celestial events for over two and a half millennia before the telescope was invented. They have records of transits of Venus from the fifth century before Christ."

"Fancy that," said Colonel Moran.

Moriarty rested his chin on the gold handle of his walking stick and gazed up at Moran. "When you and I are long gone," he said, "the stars will still be in their places, and the planets will still be orbiting majestically around the sun."

"And a fat lot we'll care," Moran commented.

A faint smile flickered across Moriarty's face. "Sometimes it does one good to contemplate the infinite," he said. "It serves to put things in their proper perspective."

"When I want to feel small," Moran said, "I contemplate my bank account."

"And when I wants to feel small," said a voice in the doorway, "I looks in the looking glass."

Moriarty turned around. His midget-of-all-work was standing in the doorway looking unusually elegant in a new suit of broad green and yellow checks with wide lapels and cuffs on the trousers and jacket sleeves. "Mummer! I wondered where you'd gotten to."

"They's got me two decks down, gov," the mummer said, swaggering into the room. "Down with the cows and the sheep and the pigs and the like."

Moran laughed. "He lies," he said. "The booking agent assured me that his is a nice little cabin."

"True," the mummer admitted. "With 'little' being the word of choice. They got no respect for the mercantile classes, which is what I'm traveling as, you might say. Course, I ain't got it as bad as the servants. They got 'em four decks down where there ain't hardly any windows and they puts 'em six to a room." He pulled himself up onto the wooden chair that went with the small built-in desk in a corner of the cabin. "Course, even them ain't got it as bad as the soldiers, and they ain't got it as bad as the native crew, who really do sleep with the cows and the sheep and the pigs; or at least on the same level, which is way below the waterline."

"I'm surprised they believed you were anything as sober as a merchant," Moriarty said. "You look like a busker in that suit. You ought to be outside the Gaiety Theatre in London entertaining the crowd with a twirling cane and a fast buck and wing."

"This is my traveling merchant's disguise," said the mummer, looking offended.

"Ah!" said Moriarty.

"And I'm practicing that pitch, what you told me, about them statues," the mummer said. "Thinking over what they might ask, and how I might answer. I'm ready to go anytime."

"We'd best wait a few days," Moriarty told him. "Give Colonel Moran a chance to get chummy with the officers of the Duke's Own."

"Course, I really did have an 'andsome suit o'lights once, with little mirrors sewed into it all over and everything. My mother made it for me when I were six years of age. I was not much smaller than I am now, but, of course, I looked considerably younger. I used to do an act with two other six-year-olds and Morty—he was seven, but he looked six. We would dance and sing." The mummer stood up and did a shuffle, and sang in a high-pitched voice, "I want—to be—alone—with you—for just—an hour or two." He stopped and sat down. "And other suitable material," he concluded.

"You must have been beautiful," Moran said.

"'Andsome," said the mummer, looking annoyed. "'Andsome, I was."

"Sorry," Moran said. "Handsome, then."

"Morty, now—*he* was beautiful," said the mummer.

FIFTEEN

ALL THAT GLISTERS

To gild refined gold, to paint the lily
To throw a perfume on the violet,
To smooth the ice, or add another hue
Unto the rainbow, or with taper light
To seek the beauteous eye of heaven to garnish,
Is wasteful and ridiculous excess.
WILLIAM SHAKESPEARE

Viceroy Sir George Montague, in consultation with General St. Yves and Captain Iskansen, of *The Empress of India*, had decided to wait until the passengers and crew were all aboard the *Empress*, and steam was up, before transferring the maharaja's gold to the specially constructed vault deep inside the ship. Normally this would be done well before sailing, so as not to draw attention to the cargo, but as it seemed that attention had already been drawn, the triumvirate determined that strength and speed would have to make up for the lack of stealth.

When the last passenger was safely aboard, the gangplank was removed, and the ship's officers conducted a walk-through of the ship looking for anything untoward or unusual, aided by such of the crew as were believed to be absolutely reliable—although how reliable any man will prove when faced with the possibility of making off with some part of two tons of gold was a question that had already kept St. Yves up for several nights. At the same time two companies of the Pandiwar Foot, a highly dependable local regiment, conducted a sweep of both banks of the Hooghly River for a couple of miles in either direction.

When all was declared normal by the sweepers on and off the ship, a phalanx of guards descended on Commissariat Jetty, a cargo door in the side of the *Empress* was opened, and six reinforced goods wagons emerged from Fort William and proceeded to the pier.

It took the best part of four hours to effect the transfer of the boxes of gold from the wagons to the specially prepared vault, what with the checks and rechecks and precautions-in-depth against every eventuality that the viceroy or his most misanthropic aide could imagine. Divers were sent down to examine the exterior hull of the ship. Had there been a military observation company within two days' travel, the viceroy would have sent up a hot-air balloon.

The gold had been cast into uniform bars, each of which weighed twenty-one pounds four ounces. They were packed six to a box, the boxes being wooden frames that constricted, without concealing, the six bars. When the gold was stowed and had been checked, counted, recounted, and several bars had been selected at random, freed from their boxes, and shaved of minuscule slivers of soft gold for assay (and those bars put aside for reweighing), the consignment was signed over by Sir George, signed for by Captain Iskansen, put on the manifest by the ship's purser, and the vault's inner door of specially hardened steel bars was locked, and the key put into an envelope and sealed with some scarlet tape and a blob of wax, upon which was impressed the viceroy's seal, and the envelope put into an inner pocket of the captain's dress jacket for stowing in the small safe in his quarters, then hands were shaken all around, the cargo door was closed and sealed, and the captain headed up to the bridge to give the command to get under way.

* * *

"There's an outer door and an inner door to the vault," Colonel Moran told Professor Moriarty, who was lying on his bunk reading as the ship weighed anchor. "The outer door is solid reinforced steel, and the inner is tempered steel bars, like a prison cell. The walls, floor, and ceiling of the vault are half-inch steel plate, riveted every six inches along the seams."

Professor Moriarty looked up from his book, *Advances in Organic Chemistry* by Janifer, and frowned. "Why are you telling me this?" he asked.

"In case anything should come to mind," Moran said. "The outer door's going to be left open all day," he continued doggedly, "and only shut at night. Anybody can wander along the corridor on C deck and peer in at the gold through the steel bars of the inner door whenever they've a mind to. In the evening, right before the first seating for dinner, the captain and a covey of his officers go down and peer at the gold for one last time and then close the outer vault door for the night. Three of those new electrical lights, and very bright ones they are, have been rigged up in the corridor to keep the corridor and the vault doors illuminated at all times, day and night. And there are two inside the vault itself, lighting up the whole inside so bright that it hurts your eyes to look."

Moriarty stared at the far wall for a second, lost in thought, then he closed his book and sat up. "You don't say?" he said. "How odd."

"The Lancers are posting their guards at both ends of the corridor all day," Moran continued, "and at the top of the stairway, which I understand is called a 'ladder' on a ship. And right smart they look, too."

"You don't say," Moriarty repeated. "How interesting."

"You're mocking me," Moran complained.

"Not at all," Moriarty said soothingly. "I'll wager this conversation is being repeated in half the cabins on the ship, and most of them occupied by people of a much more, ah, honest turn of mind than you or I. There is something about large sums of gold that brings out the speculative nature in people."

"That's so," Moran agreed. "The problem as I see it is not so much how to get the gold out of the vault as what to do with it once you have accomplished that. After all, when you're on a ship in the middle of the Indian Ocean, there aren't very many places to which you can abscond."

"I trust you are considering this merely as an intellectual exercise," Moriarty said.

"Even so, even so," Moran replied. "I may wander by the vault occasionally and stare wistfully through the bars, but I won't do anything foolish. Not with this other matter so well in hand. It is well in hand, is it not?"

Moriarty chuckled. "Have faith," he said. "Your job is to get to know General St. Yves. Befriend him, and fascinate him with your tales of military derring-do, or whatever. Exchange stories of killing large animals. Play cards with him and don't cheat."

"Don't cheat?" Moran asked plaintively.

"And do your best not to win. You are a retired colonel of independent means. You play only for the relaxation and enjoyment."

"That's so," Moran agreed. "But I do enjoy winning."

Moriarty peered at him over the top of his pince-nez. "Restrain yourself," he said. "Think of the larger picture."

Moran grinned. "Oh, I know, I know," he said. "I just like to see the annoyed expression you get when you contemplate my inability to refrain from cheating at cards."

* * *

It was past four in the afternoon when *The Empress of India*'s horn sounded a series of low, mournful bellows, and the ship backed away from the dock and started down the river, flanked by the oceangoing tugs *Egbert* and *Ethelred*, and accompanied by the steam launch *Clive*. Behind her, following her closely into the Bay of Bengal, was the torpedo gunboat *Sea Lion*. Ahead of her, flags and pennants flying, was the Maharaja of Najipur's paddle-wheel steam packet *Maharaja of Najipur*, given this position of honor in recognition of the fact that Najipur was one of the few Indian states to have its own navy, as well as the fact that almost a quarter of a ton of the gold in the *Empress*'s vault belonged to the maharaja.

Margaret and Lady Priscilla stood forward on the port side of "A" deck with a smattering of the other first-class passengers who weren't too preoccupied or too blasé to watch the ship's embarkation. It was a grand sight. The *Maharaja of Najipur* was about five ship lengths in the lead, with all the sails on its two masts furled, and its paddle wheel churning away amidships. Sailors in spanking-new white uniforms with red hats and sashes stood perched on the *Maharaja*'s masts, rigging, and yards as though they were frozen in motion, eternally caught at the moment they were about to hoist the sails.

And, standing at attention at the prow of *The Empress of India*, facing forward, clad in the gloriously colorful full regimental uniform of the Duke of Moncreith's Own Highland Lancers, was the Lancers' piper, Master Sergeant Warren Bruce of that ilk, and the eerie wail of the "Lament for Douglas" sounded even over the throb of the ship's engines and the slapping of the waves.

Margaret spread her arms and lifted her head high to allow the wind to blow against every part of her. The skirts of the red silk frock she wore pressed against her knees and billowed behind her. "I can feel the infinite possibilities of the future approaching!" she exclaimed. "I must be ready to grab at life as it passes, and cling to it firmly and with resolve."

Lady Priscilla turned toward her companion and wrinkled her nose. "I have no idea," she said, "what you're talking about, you know. But I admit that it has a jolly sound to it."

"Whenever something comes to an end," Margaret told her, "something else begins. And one has a very short opportunity to influence the direction this new beginning is to take."

Lady Priscilla nodded and stared thoughtfully at the men on the rigging of the *Maharaja of Najipur*. They were engaging in an elaborate aerial dance, where they all shifted position rapidly and recklessly and according to some design that was not readily apparent, showing off for the watchers on the *Empress* and along the shore. "Tell me," she said to Margaret, "if one wished to ascertain the cabin number of a particular person, how would one go about it?"

"Ask the purser or the cabin steward," Margaret told her.

"Yes, but if one did not wish anyone to know of one's interest in the, ah, location of this person?"

Margaret dropped her arms to her sides and turned to look at her companion. "Oh, I see," she said.

Lady Priscilla turned faintly red about the face. "No, you don't," she insisted. "For there is nothing to see. I asked out of idle curiosity, that is all."

"Of course," Margaret said. "Well, if you will entrust me with the name of this person whom you're idly curious about, I'll find out his cabin number for you."

"What makes you think it's a man?" Lady Priscilla demanded.

"Really!" said Margaret. "And why would such caution and secrecy be necessary were it a woman?"

"Oh," said Lady Priscilla. "His name is Welles. Lieutenant Welles."

* * *

General St. Yves and his two adjutants, a stout, red-faced colonel named Morcy and Major Sandiman, a tall thin man with a thick mustache under a prominent nose, met Captain Iskansen in the corridor leading to the gold vault. The newly posted guard at the end of the corridor snapped to attention and wished fervently that he'd been more attentive in memorizing the special orders of the day as all the well-pressed uniforms pockmarked with brass insignia and entwined in gold braid passed him.

"You wanted to see us?" St. Yves asked the captain.

"Yes," Iskansen said. He was a large man whose face was weathered, his blond hair mostly gray, who wore the stripes of command with an easy familiarity. One felt just by looking at him that he would bring the *Empress*, its crew, and its passengers through any storm, past any reef, safely to port. "Come."

He led them to the door of the gold vault. "This is my responsibility," he said ponderously, pointing through the bars of the inner door at the crates of gold that gleamed in the cold light of the powerful electric bulbs in the ceiling fixtures. "The vault is my first line of defense, and you and your men are my second."

"That is so," St. Yves agreed.

"Go over with me one more time how you're positioning your men and just what their orders are," the captain said.

"Colonel Morcy has made the dispositions," St. Yves said, indicating his adjutant.

Morcy nodded. "The watch is divided into four six-hour shifts per day," he said, ticking off the points on his fingers as he made them. "Each shift contains a corporal of the guard and ten or eleven men. The two posted guards, one at each end of the corridor, are relieved every two hours, the rest of the men staying on call in the guardroom at all times. All the men are armed with the Martini-Henry carbine and bayonet, and carrying a whistle. They also each are equipped with a bull's-eye lantern to light in case the electrical power should fail. Their standing orders are to allow passage through the corridor but to keep alert for anything untoward or out of the ordinary. If they see anything in the least unusual, they are to blow the whistle and all the men in the guardroom will immediately turn out. One man is immediately sent to the officers' dayroom, where one of us or another senior officer will always be on duty in case of need."

"And the guns," Captain Iskansen asked, "they are loaded?"

"Yes, sir. The men are under instructions to shoot if threatened."

"But the bayonets? I don't see the bayonets."

"Because of the close quarters," Morcy explained, "the bayonets are kept in their scabbards, only to be drawn if needed."

"Ah," said the captain. "I see. Is there anything else I should know?"

"What sort of thing?" asked St. Yves.

Iskansen lifted his hands expressively. "Any contingency plan, any clever little secret plot to better guard the gold?"

"No," said St. Yves, looking faintly puzzled. "That's all of it."

"Good," Captain Iskansen said firmly. "I want to know everything that's happening on my ship. I hate surprises."

"So do we," St. Yves assured him. "Let us hope that we don't encounter any during this voyage."

"Then we understand each other," said Iskansen.

"Have you any other questions or suggestions?" St. Yves asked.

The captain thought for a moment. "No, no," he said. "It sounds quite well done. Thank you." He nodded at them and walked off.

"Well," Major Sandiman said when Iskansen had rounded the bend. "What do you suppose that was about? He surely knew all of that already."

"Chain of command," suggested Colonel Morcy. "He wants us to clearly understand that he's at the top of the chain."

"As long as we're here," St. Yves said, "let's drop in on the guardroom. Make sure everything's shipshape. Then I'll stand you both to a drink."

"Good plan," approved the colonel.

"Very good, sir," said the major.

SIXTEEN

BOMBAY

Genius is the ability to see things invisible, to manipulate things
intangible, to paint things that have no features.
JOSEPH JOUBERT

The steam sloop *Endymion*, a thin stream of oily black smoke wafting out of its tall, pencil-thin smokestack, oozed its way into Bombay Harbor at a bit past eight in the morning. Passing Oyster Rock Battery, it glided along the line of piers, basins, yacht clubs, dockyards and a row of large stone elephants, their trunks upraised in eternal challenge, and pulled up alongside a grimy pier at a dilapidated boatyard, whereupon it promptly shut down its engines and coasted to a stop.

Pin Dok Low, slender and immaculate in a loose white muslin jacket and baggy white pants, stood atop the steering house closely studying the flock of docked and moored ships as the *Endymion* passed them in the harbor. "It isn't here yet," he called down to his two companions waiting on the deck below.

"How do you know it ain't been here and left already?" Cooley the Pup yelled back at him.

The Artful Codger stomped his feet noisily. "Now, wouldn't that just be something to write home about, wouldn't it just?"

"Highly unlikely," Pin Dok Low said. "But we will, of course, check that eventuality out immediately." He lowered himself into to the steering house and spoke briefly to the captain, and then leaped like a great bird of prey onto the deck below. "Now, gentlemen," he said to his two companions, "the adventure begins."

"It seems to me, Pin, that thissere adventure begun the first time I run'd acrost your name," said Cooley the Pup. "It's been nothin' but ups and downs ever since."

"Don't mind him, Pin," the Artful Codger said. "He's suffering from *mal* of the *mer*, which makes everything shine in a baleful light."

Dr. Pin Dok Low smiled at the Codger, showing an uneven row of yellow teeth. "Why, Codger," he said. "That's almost poetry. 'Shine in a baleful light.' However did that occur to you?"

"I think I read it somewhere," said the Codger, determinedly not looking embarrassed.

"I didn't know you could read," said Pin.

"It don't come up offen," the Codger said. He squinted at Pin in the morning light. "You know, Pin, when you ain't dressed like a Chinee, you don't look hardly Oriental at all. You could almost pass for a white man."

Pin smiled broadly, the gold caps on two of his teeth flashing in the sun. "What a compliment," he said. "I am honored to almost resemble a member of your uncultured and barbaric race."

"This ain't getting us nowhere," said Cooley the Pup. "Here we are in Bom-bloody-bay, and it seems we got here before *The Empress of India* pulled in. What I wants to know is, what does we do from here? After we make sure that the *Empress* ain't been and gone already, o'course."

"Yes," Pin agreed. "Always making sure of that, of course. We find the booking office and book passage on *The Empress of India*. Whereupon we set about watching the gold in the ship's vault as though it were our own—which it shortly shall be."

"Oh, great," groaned Cooley. "More pitching and tossing about."

"The *Empress* is quite a bit larger than the *Endymion*," said Pin. "You shouldn't get sick."

"I'll get sick," said Cooley.

"Why didn't you think of that before you come with us?" asked the Codger.

"Well, I didn't know I was going to get sick, did I? I mean, it ain't like I ever been on a bloody boat before."

The captain of the *Endymion*, a corpulent giant of a man who said his name was Georgidios and claimed to be a Greek, thumped down from the steering house to the deck. "We are tied off now," he boomed. "You can go ashore." He slapped Pin on the back. "Did I not tell you that I could get you to Bombay in ten days, if the blessed boilers did not burst?"

"Indeed," Pin admitted.

"And the blessed boilers did not burst, and so here we indeed are." Georgidios beamed and patted the ship on its cargo hatch. "The *Endymion*, he is a good, speedy little craft, he is."

"I thought all ships were called 'she,'" said the Codger.

"The *Endymion* is a boy," Georgidios said. "Named for a Greek shepherd, a lad who was so beautiful that the goddess Artemis, whom you call Diana, fell in love with him and bestowed many kisses upon him." Georgidios blew several kisses into his plump hands and bestowed them onto the air in front of him.

"We're going to leave you now, Captain," Pin told Georgidios "Many thanks for your prompt and efficient traverse of several seas and a rather long canal."

"Yes, yes," Georgidios said. "And thank you for your more-than-adequate payment."

"I told you we should have argued him down a bit more," said the Codger in an undertone. Captain Georgidios heard and glowered at him, and he glowered back.

"Have one of your deck hands bring our luggage from the cabin," Pin told Georgidios. "We'll send a runner for it as soon as we locate a hotel."

"Aye, aye," said Captain Georgidios. "Good luck on your venture, whatever it may be."

SEVENTEEN

ALL AT SEA

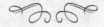

Man never knows what he wants; he aspires to penetrate mysteries
and as soon as he has, he wants to reestablish them. Ignorance
irritates him and knowledge cloys.
HENRI FREDERIC AMIEL

On the third day at sea Colonel Sebastian Moran was invited to join General St. Yves and the officers of the Duke's Own at their table at the last seating for dinner. His stories of hunting man-eaters in the Himalayas and fighting the Mahdi and his dervishes in Egypt—basically true and told with even more than the usual British understatement—made him a desirable dinner companion for these professional soldiers. After all, they had been together for many years, and had listened to their own stories many times.

"Remember in Bela when the parrots used to flock around every afternoon to get fed?" Major Sandiman reminisced.

"Parakeets," Colonel Morcy corrected. "*Psittacula alexandri*, as a matter of fact. The red-breasted parakeet. They were enamored of bread crumbs, which the wallah used to throw down at three every afternoon but Tuesday, for some reason."

The others nodded. Tuesday. They remembered.

"At the foot of the Himalayas," Moran began, staring into his cigar smoke, "by that swash of jungle called the Terai, there's a bit of grassland abutting the forest where my chaps and I used to go on maneuvers every spring."

The officers of the Duke's Own turned to listen. They'd never been to the Terai. Moran's story, if nothing else, would be new.

"One day a Hindu in my service, a bright chap named Jivana who went on to become something big in the Kashmir-Afghanistan Railway, told me there was a great *tamasha*—a sort of spectacle—to be seen at a temple nearby. He assured me that it would not violate any taboos if we went to watch, so the next evening five of us went to see what it was all about. We skirted the woods for about half a mile, and came to a great stand of bamboo, perhaps two hundred yards on a side. Jivana led us through a winding path to a clearing in the center of the bamboo thicket. At the far end of the clearing was a small Hindu temple, a whitewashed clay structure of indeterminate age. The roof of thatched elephant grass sat on ancient teak beams, the ends of which were carved like gargoyles, but in shapes to which the Western eye is unaccustomed. A large bronze bell inlayed with words in an alphabet I did not understand stood to the side of the temple doorway."

Moran paused to puff on his cigar. "Go on," one of the listeners urged, and several others nodded; as good a tribute as a standing ovation from a different audience.

"Across the long side of the clearing there was a row of small, unadorned huts, in front of which sat a row of dhoti-clad priests, each of which was cooking *chappattis* over a wood fire in front of him. A thin line of blue smoke rose up from each of the fires, and they spread out and joined perhaps a hundred feet up, forming a layer of blue haze that obscured the mountains. The priests ignored us entirely, as though we were meaningless, or perhaps invisible watchers at some ancient and inevitable ceremony."

Moran paused again, and a lieutenant named Jimlis interjected, "That can't have been the show—a dozen half-naked Hindu priests sitting around frying bread."

"That's how it began," Moran told him. "Jivana motioned for us to be quiet and stand there, and so we did. I noted that the *chappattis* were singularly large and course, more cakes than bread.

"Just as the last rays of the sun were coming over the bamboo, the chief priest, an ancient man clad in white robes, emerged from the temple and began striking the great bronze bell with a great bronze hammer. A deep thrumming sound filled the clearing, and the bamboo shivered to the vibrations emitted."

Moran took another puff on his cigar, stared moodily into it, and went on: "Something brushed by my leg, and I looked down to see a jackal, a great brute of a beast with red eyes and a foul breath, enter the clearing and pause, sitting on its haunches and staring at the chief priest as he continued to stroke the bell. The animal was totally fearless and unconcerned about our presence there."

Moran's audience of hardened professional British officers sat entranced; here was a story they hadn't heard before. "Go on," said General St. Yves.

Moran nodded. "More of the beasts gathered, coming through subtle pathways in the cane, until there were perhaps a score of them. As each one emerged from the thicket, it sat as the leader had, silently observing the stroking of the gong. Finally, when all had assembled, the priests gathered their rough *chappattis* and went around the compound, breaking off a bit by this stone, a chunk by that bit of earth, a morsel on top of that flat rock, and so on, until all the cakes were crumbled and distributed and the priests had resumed their cross-legged positions in front of their small huts.

"Then, all at once the head priest stopped stroking the great gong and, as the reverberations died away, the pack of jackals came forward to eat, each to his or her assigned spot, with no fighting or squabbling or any great fuss. After perhaps five minutes they all, as though at a signal, turned and faded away into the cane. The one I think of as the leader went last, again paying me no more attention than if I were a stone or a clot of earth."

Captain Helsing, who thought he was wise in the ways of all animals, especially jackals, smiled a superior smile. "Jackals don't behave like that," he said.

"These did," replied Colonel Sebastian Moran.

"Did you discover why or how this ceremony began?" asked Colonel Morcy.

"I asked the head priest, each of us managing to communicate in bad Hindi, the only language we had in common. His native language was Oriya, I believe. At any rate, I asked him how this observance came about, and he said he had no idea. The priests of this temple had been feeding the jackals in his great-grandfather's time, and would continue it as far into the future as Brahma would allow."

The officers of the Duke's Own nodded. That was the sort of answer they understood. They could look forward to many more stories from the experiences of Colonel Sebastian Moran. A pukka sahib, Colonel Moran.

And then there was the trading of names:

"Yes, Binky came out to the Soudan in, I think it was '84. He was a captain then..."

"I knew him when he was a subaltern at Kings; hadn't got his title then, you know..."

"Danforth and old Muzzy were great pals. You remember Muzzy? Son of the Earl of Roberts. Christian name David, I believe. Muzzy."

"Aide-de-camp of General FitzPacker, back in '77, I remember."

"Oh, yes. Old 'Hannibal' FitzPacker."

"Hannibal?"

"That's what they called him. Older than the moon, and incredibly skin-and-bony. Had a fixation on using elephants in the army. Wanted the War Department to buy a couple of dozen Indian elephants and start an elephant cavalry brigade. He was overly fond of brandy, I believe."

The officers' postprandial cigars were taken strolling about the deck and discussing portents and the state of the world.

"Hot."

"Deuced hot."

"Been hot for a while."

"It'll get hotter."

"Not in England."

"No, not in England."

"Glad to be going home."

"Deuced responsibility, all that gold."

"Nothing to worry about. Our boys'll guard it well enough."

"Deuced responsibility. The chaps aren't trained for this. Should have used marines. The marines are trained to guard things on a ship."

"Didn't have any marines."

"That's so. All the same..."

Colonel Moran interjected, "You think there's some danger, then?"

"Wouldn't think so, no," said General St. Yves. He took a long puff on his cigar and stared contemplatively at the ocean below. "I watched Captain Iskansen closing the outer vault door yesterday evening. He makes quite a ceremony out of it."

"How do you mean?" asked Colonel Morcy.

"Well, he has this little c-coterie of officers—ship's officers, I mean—who come along with him. Won't let anybody else near while he twiddles the locks and such. We even have to move our guards farther away during the procedure. He keeps his little secrets, does the captain."

"Same thing when he opens it in the morning," volunteered a plump major named Bosch. "Banging and twisting and standing this way and that." He illustrated with emphatic arm gestures. "As seen from afar, of course. Even his own officers clustered about him during the process look away while he's messing about with the outer door locks. It makes you wonder why he bothers keeping the thing open during the day."

"So we can all see for ourselves that it's still there, I suppose," General St. Yves said. "But all the same..."

"There's something about gold," Moran offered. "Why, I remember once in the hills above Mawpatta..."

* * *

After breakfast the next morning Colonel Sebastian Moran carefully selected a cheroot from the twelve tightly rolled Lunkah cheroots in his tooled black leather cigar case and rolled it speculatively between his fingers. "General St. Yves and his officers, they're good soldiers, all. British to the core," he told Moriarty, who was sitting in the leather chair across from him in the small, overly furnished upper deck smoking lounge. "I understand them and they understand me."

"I don't think they understand quite everything there is to know about you," Moriarty said dryly.

Moran spent some time poking the end of his cheroot with a toothpick and lighting it before replying. "There are some things, Professor," he said finally, "that even *I* don't know about me."

Moriarty looked at the colonel with some surprise. "Come, now," he said, "that's a statement redolent of moral philosophy. Don't tell me there beats the heart of a Benthamite under that thick skin of yours."

Moran puffed cautiously at his cigar for a minute before replying. "I couldn't say one way or the other," he said, "not knowing just what it is you're talking about."

Moriarty grinned. "No matter," he said.

Moran lowered his voice. "I don't suppose you've had any further thoughts on the gold, have you?"

"No thoughts at all," Moriarty admitted. "I find it futile to speculate when I'm possessed of so little information."

"Well, I can add to your store a bit," Moran told him. "I doubt if it will help, but just for the sake of completeness..." and he told Moriarty what he had heard of the captain's ceremonial opening and closing of the outer vault door, complete with arm gestures copied from Major Bosch.

Moriarty nodded as Moran finished. "That's actually interesting," he said.

"Fascinating," Moran agreed. "Does it give you any ideas?"

"Actually, it does," Moriarty told him. "But they're of no immediate use. For now let us concentrate on retrieving the statuette. Have you had an adequate opportunity to examine the Lady in question?"

"I have poked at her and prodded her admiringly at two dinners now. They bring her out with the soup and place her on a sideboard against the wall behind General St. Yves's chair. Do the rooms on ships have walls? Bulkheads, perhaps, or scrimshaws, or some such."

"'Wall' will do," Moriarty said. "I assume you've verified that it's the right statue."

"Under the brass skin of the Lady of Lucknow beats the bejeweled heart of the Queen of Lamapoor, all right," Moran said between puffs. "There's no doubt about that. None at all. The brass plating can't be very thick because it appears to be wearing off in a couple of places. I fear that if the mess stewards keep up their industrious polishing of our little Lady, they're going to start seeing gemstones peeping out from under the brass."

He tapped his cigar against the edge of an oversized ceramic ashtray. "The question is, how are we going to induce the officers of the Duke of Moncreith's Own Highland Lancers to part with their little brass goddess before that happens. That's the question. And that's your part, Professor. I think I have my part well in hand. When does your part begin?"

"My part?" The professor polished his pince-nez with a small square of blue flannel and adjusted them on the bridge of his nose.

"Yes. You and that midget friend of yours in the suit of many colors. What is it that you're planning to do, and when does it commence?"

"It has commenced as we sit here," Moriarty said. "The mummer is hawking our little statues in the first- and second-class lounges. He's also passing out a few to the purser and others of the ship's company who may be expected to display them here and there about the ship. And, of course, he's telling the tale."

"That's it, then?" Moran held his cigar about a foot from his face and stared expressionlessly into the twisting column of smoke rising from its tip.

"One other thing," Moriarty said. "We have procured a supply of plaster of Paris from the ship's pharmacy, and the mummer is turning one of our brass statues to stone."

Moran thought about that for a moment, and then turned his cigar outward and thrust it in the general direction of the professor's nose. "Are you sure you're as smart as you think you are?" he asked belligerently. "'Cause I have no idea what this mumbo-jumbo's in aid of, and whenever you try to tell me, I seem to get that much further from figuring it out."

"Just worry about your part of the job," Moriarty told him firmly, pushing the cigar aside. "You brought me in on this to solve a difficult and intriguing problem, and I am doing so. Whether you can grasp every strand in the pattern is unimportant as long as you understand your part and do your job. And you're doing it admirably so far. I have no complaints and, whether you know it or not, neither do you."

"Well," Moran said, somewhat mollified by Moriarty's positive attitude. "I'll leave you to it, then. But you might tell me a little ahead of time when I've to do something, and warn me of what you're doing, so we don't cross each other by accident."

"I'll be careful," Moriarty assured him.

"Then what's next?"

"At dinner tonight," Moriarty said, "you will take the next step."

"I will, will I?" Moran put the cigar in the ashtray and pressed his thumbs together. "And what will you be doing?"

"I will be arranging with Captain Iskansen to have a steam launch meet us when we drop anchor in Bombay Harbor."

Moran picked up his cigar with the thumb and forefinger of his left hand and, holding it in front of his nose, stared at it as though close study would reveal some imponderable secret. When it failed to produce anything but smoke, he looked back up at Moriarty. "And how," he asked, "will Captain Iskansen accomplish this?"

"Signal flags, Colonel," Moriarty told him. "Signal flags. He will run the appropriate one up the mainmast as we approach, and a steam launch will await us."

"They have one for that?" Moran asked.

"Perhaps more than one," Moriarty allowed. "But the signals officer should certainly be able to do it in one string."

Moran nodded thoughtfully. "And what's my part in this charade to be?"

"You are going to inform General St. Yves and any other officers who might be interested that your good friend Professor James Moriarty is arranging for a steam launch to take a selected group of interested and serious-minded friends to Elephanta for the day. We probably won't be leaving Bombay until the next morning, so we'll have a long day to explore."

"Well, you'd best make certain of that before we go haring off to—where?—Elephanta? I thought that was some sort of African disease."

Moriarty raised an eyebrow. "Elephanta is a small island off the coast of Bombay. It is redolent with caves that have, for centuries, been dedicated as temples to this god or that. The carvings are quite miraculous, or so I'm told."

"And what will induce a pride of British officers to visit these carved-up caves?"

"They are quite educational and uplifting. They will, of course, take their wives, who will enjoy it immensely."

"The ladies are fond of being educated and uplifted, I'll grant you that," said Moran. "But as to the gentlemen..."

"There is one cave that ladies are not permitted to enter," Moriarty told him. "The officers will find that one quite, ah, uplifting."

"Ah!" Moran said. "Now you're talking. Fun for the whole family, eh? I'll see what I can do."

* * *

Margaret and Lady Priscilla had lunch together in the Ladies' Dining Room, and then Lady Priscilla went off to pursue her interests—a subaltern named Welles whom she was permitting to pay a certain amount of polite, proper, and discreet interest in her. Margaret settled into a deck chair under the canvas canopy on the first-class promenade deck, where she could enjoy the almost cool ocean breeze, and worked at transliterating the Devanagari alphabet in the badly printed English-Hindi military phrasebook she had found discarded at the post library. She was determined to increase her Hindi vocabulary by at least two words a day, picked at random from the pages of the phrasebook and devised into the silliest sentences she could imagine. Margaret had found that silliness was a great aid to learning, and a military phrasebook was a great aid to silliness.

She stopped reading as a man in a light tan linen suit paused by her chair to light a cigarette. The match flared, the man puffed, and a stray bit of wind blew the first puff of smoke in Margaret's face, sending her into a fit of coughing.

The man turned to her, an expression of dismay on his face. "I apologize most terribly, madam," he said. "Allow me to—Why, it's Miss St. Yves. How do you do? Well, I see how you do, and it is the fault of myself. I am most horribly sorry."

After a minute the coughing became sporadic, and then ceased, and Margaret peered up at her inadvertent tormentor. "Well!" she said. "Professor Gerard August Demartineu. I didn't know you were aboard the ship."

"Why, you have remembered the whole of my name," said the French professor, plumping down on the chair next to Margaret's and extending his arm out to the side to keep the smoke from his cigarette far from Margaret's face. "I am honored. Yes, it is that I am aboard *The Empress of India*, as you can plainly see. My, ah, partner and protégé, Mamarum Sutrow, and I are headed to England to begin our career as prestidigitators of the first water."

Margaret looked around, but did not see the little round-faced jadoogar.

"Mr. Sutrow is in our cabin with a sickness of the stomach," Demartineu told her, correctly interpreting her visual search of the deck. "He believes that it is the result of something he ingested, and feels sure that some beef was inserted in his lamb curry. I feel sure that he has the sickness of the sea, since it began shortly after we left port and ceases not. But he insists that he is a good sailor and never suffers from the sickness of the sea. But, as he has never been to sea before, I do not understand how he can be so positive of this."

"You've been painting, I see," Margaret said.

"Painting?" Demartineu looked startled. "Why do you say that?"

Margaret pointed to the professor's shirtsleeve, which peeped out from beneath his jacket on the outstretched arm. "Slight traces of brown paint on the cuff of your white shirt," she said. "I could think of more complicated explanations, but the simplest is that you've been painting."

Demartineu looked down at his sleeve with an expression approximating horror. Then his face cleared. "Ah, now I see," he said. "Yes, I have been horribly remiss. Painting some props—props? Yes, that is the word—that we will need for the act. Captain Iskansen has requested that we perform for the passengers some evening. It will be a change from large women singing about birds in gilded cages, I think. I should have rolled up the sleeves for the painting, *hein*? But it so un-British, the rolling up of the sleeves, that I could not bring myself to do it whilst on a British ship. I will change the shirt after the lunch. If I return to the cabin before the lunch, the groanings of Mr. Sutrow will put me off eating entirely."

Margaret shook her head. "Poor man," she said. Whether she was speaking of Mr. Sutrow or Professor Demartineu wasn't clear, but the professor didn't ask.

After a moment Demartineu stood up. "So nice," he said vaguely, and then moved off farther down the deck, to where he could enjoy his cigarette without offending.

Margaret returned to her reading until, some minutes later, a voice interrupted her.

"I say," the voice said. "If it isn't Miss St. Yves."

It was a voice she recognized, but had never expected to hear again. She looked up. Did her heart beat faster? Perhaps. "Well!" she said. "You do get around. Pray tell me, who are you today? Or shouldn't I ask?"

The young man who was not Lieutenant Peter Pettigrew, carrier pigeon officer of the Seventh Foot, was standing at the foot of her chair looking sadly down at her. What he was sad about, she couldn't tell. "Today, surprisingly, I'm Peter Collins," he told her. "The name my mother knows me by. But I don't know how long it will last. I may feel another name coming on anytime now."

"Try taking asafetida," she suggested. "I believe it is indicated in cases of this sort."

"Thank you," he said, sitting down on the chair next to her.

"Perhaps I shall." Then he suddenly leaped to his feet again. "I say," he said. "I mean, I didn't mean, that is—do you mind if I take this chair?"

She thought of replying, "Not at all, where do you intend to take it?" but decided against it. "Please, sit down," she said instead. "We can't have you hopping about."

"Good," he said, lowering himself back into the chair. "I've given up hopping about in favor of reeling, writhing, and fainting in coils." Peter signaled to a passing deck steward, and ordered a pot of tea and two cups.

"How nice of you not to ask me if I desired any tea," Margaret said sweetly. "I do so hate having to make decisions."

"Would you like some tea?" Peter asked. "Or must I drink the whole pot myself, using both cups, just to prove I wasn't being unbearably rude?"

"That would be rude," Margaret told him.

Peter sighed a deep sigh. "There I've done it," he said. "Whenever I find myself feeling, ah, fond of a girl, I behave in an unbearably rude manner toward her, thus relieving myself of the necessity of trying to ascertain whether she might possibly develop a fondness of me, given sufficient passage of time."

Yes, her heart was beating just a bit faster. "How clever of you," she said. "Tell me, if it isn't rude of me to ask, what are you doing here? On the *Empress*, I mean. When last I saw you, you were hunting the wily Phansigar. Don't tell me there are Thuggee brigands lurking about the ship?"

Peter laughed. "Not s'far as I know," he said. "No, I've been called back to London by the Foreign Office."

Margaret looked at him quizzically. "I didn't know you worked for the Foreign Office," she said.

"Neither did I," Peter admitted. "But when your boss says to you, 'Here's your steamship ticket and one pound two shillings thruppence for expenses. You're to report to Whitehall,' you pocket the kale and board the bloom—er, boat."

"How exciting!" said Margaret. "Perhaps they're going to appoint you prime minister."

"I'm afraid I'd have to turn it down," Peter told her. "I haven't the requisite wardrobe."

Margaret laughed. "Is that the only reason?"

"Why, of course," Peter said. "Aside from that I'm eminently qualified. I know nothing about anything, and am prepared to give you my opinion on any number of subjects at the drop of a topper, with complete conviction and an air of ineffable authority."

"I've often thought that those were the qualifications for many high government offices," Margaret agreed.

A short, pudgy Indian steward in ballooning white pantaloons and a white steward's jacket that hung loosely over his narrow shoulders appeared, set up a small portable table in the space between the two deck chairs, and went away. A minute later he reappeared and covered the table with a teapot, two cups, a pitcher of cream, a sugar bowl, and a plate of scones; and then went back for crocks of butter, two kinds of jam, two small plates for the scones, silverware, and linen napkins. Then he took three steps backward, as though retreating from royalty, bowed three times, and attempted to scurry off down the deck. He had barely taken four steps when he doubled over as though in sudden acute pain, stumbled to the rail, and heaved up whatever had been in his stomach.

Peter grabbed one of the napkins and crossed to where the steward was clutching the rail. "Here," he said, handing it to the man. Margaret, who had come up behind him, stayed tactfully silent.

The steward wiped his face, coughed, gagged, coughed again, and stood up weakly. "Dank you, sor," he said.

"Are you going to be all right?" Peter asked, looking the man over critically. "I think you'd better go lie down for a bit."

"No, dat's fine, sor. I feel better now."

"Seasick?" Margaret asked sympathetically.

"No, mo'om. Is something going about with the crew. Maybe onetwo dozen boys are sick even now. Maybe something bad was eaten."

"I see," Peter said. "Sorry."

"I be all right now, sor," the steward said, and staggered off down the deck.

A PROFESSOR MORIARTY NOVEL

Peter looked thoughtful as they returned to their seats.

"What is it?" Margaret asked.

"I don't know," he told her. "Nothing, I hope. Nothing beyond a mild case of food poisoning. Bad curry, perhaps."

"Don't be mysterious," she said. "It makes me nervous."

"If there's anything to tell you," he said seriously, "I promise I will."

"Thank you," she said, sitting back down and taking up her book.

"Tea?" Peter asked, hefting the teapot.

Margaret nodded and Peter poured. "What are you reading?" he asked.

She showed the book to him. "It's a generally annoying English-Hindi phrasebook," she said. "It assumes that one knows things that one, or at least I, don't. I am trying to increase my knowledge of the language, but this book imparts its information grudgingly and with an air of cringing superiority."

Peter smiled. "A Uriah Heep sort of book?"

"That's it. Always wringing its hands and apologizing, but you know that in the dark heart of its innermost pages it's sneering at you."

"Say," Peter said, "does that 'increase your knowledge' mean that you do speak Hindi?"

"That would be an exaggeration," she said. "I can speak and understand simple phrases—on the level of 'Please, I would like to acquire a healthy camel for the transportation of household goods'—if simply and clearly spoken."

"I can see how useful that would be," Peter commented.

"Tell me," she asked, "did you find out who that man was?"

"Man?"

"On the floor. In the viceroy's office."

"Oh. Yes, we found out who he was."

"Was he English?"

"British, actually. He was a Scot."

"Poor man."

"I don't know—he might have liked being a Scot."

Margaret's face flushed. "I didn't mean—"

Peter raised a placating hand. "I know. I'm sorry. That wasn't very funny. Yes, poor man. His name was MacCay. Ian MacCay. He was one of us—a DSI officer."

"Why was he dressed up like a native?"

Peter shrugged. "Some of our chaps do that on occasion. It's not exactly encouraged, but it's da—deucedly useful. Gathering information firsthand, don't you know. MacCay was Anglo-Indian. Grew up somewhere in Rajputana, I think. His father was something-or-other with the railroad. In his youth MacCay probably dressed like a native until he went back to Britain for school. Spoke Hindi better than he spoke English."

"Why had he come to see the viceroy? And why in native dress?"

"That we still don't know. Perhaps he had no access to his normal garb. Perhaps he had no way to get the stain off his hands and face. Perhaps he had no time. He must have run across something of interest, and it must have been both important and urgent enough for him to have not taken it up through the regular channels. But as of when we left, there had been no signs of anything out of the ordinary happening in the native population. Of course, we aren't exactly sure where in the vastness that is India he had been practicing his little deception."

"It's frightening to think that a man could be murdered right there in the viceroy's office," Margaret said. "It makes one feel, not unsafe exactly, but as though the entire world were not as stable and orderly as one has been led to believe."

"It is," Peter agreed, looking suddenly serious. "It's more frightening to consider the possible messages that MacCay might have been trying to convey."

EIGHTEEN

STIRRING AND TWITCHING

What in me is dark
Illumine, what is low raise and support,
That to the height of this great argument
I may assert eternal Providence,
And justify the ways of God to men.

JOHN MILTON

*T*he *Empress of India*, white smoke billowing from its red-and-gold-barred smokestacks, steamed into Bombay Harbor early in the morning of the fifth day after leaving Calcutta. Here it would fill up its coal bunkers, debark a few passengers, unload one bit of cargo and pick up another, embark a few passengers, restock on fresh fruit, vegetables, and meat, and refill the fresh water tanks. Here it would allow the passengers who were going on to England to go ashore until four o'clock the next afternoon—with a very stern warning, writ large on a sign by the gangplank put up by the chief purser's chief assistant:

THOSE PASSENGERS INTENDING TO RECOMMENCE THEIR JOURNEY WHO DO NOT ENCOMPASS THE RETURN OF THEMSELVES TO THE SHIP BY THE FOUR O'CLOCK IN THE P. M. HOUR OF THE MORROW MAY BE DISCOMFITED BY THE PASSAGE ONWARD OF THE STEAM VESSEL EMPRESS OF INDIA WITHOUT THE PRESENCE OF THEMSELVES

Here it would get replacements for about thirty of the native stewards and deckhands who had to be put ashore, still in the throes of acute distress from the curious incident of the epidemic among the crew. Here the ship and its precious cargo was guarded by a ring of British gunboats, a gaggle of local constables, a brigade of the Bombay Heavy Infantry, and a company of the Khairpur Light Horse, an all-native regiment with both British and Indian officers. Here the enigmatic Dr. Pin Dok Low and his associates boarded the ship.

After seeing that their trunks were properly stowed in their second-class cabins—there was nothing available in first class, not even when the request was accompanied by the suggestive clinking of a couple of gold sovereigns—they went off to discover the route to the dining room, the location of the storeroom holding the gold, and the whereabouts of Professor James Moriarty. Locating the gold was no problem; everyone aboard knew where it was, and everyone knew all of the secrets concerning how it was kept and guarded—some of them even true.

"It's down belowdecks in a special vault," explained the Artful Codger, as he and his two companions huddled around a table in the Second-Class Gentlemen's Smoking Lounge. "Anybody can go see it anytime when the ship's at sea, see; but not now because the ship ain't yet at sea, if you see what I mean."

"You're making me see-sick," Cooley the Pup groaned.

"What do you mean, 'Anybody can go see it'?" Pin inquired, frowning.

"Just that. There's a corridor which goes by the vault door, and it's lit by these here electrical lights which is on all the time. And the outer vault door is open all day and closed by the captain—name of Iskansen—his very self every night."

"Open?" the Pup said incredulously. "You mean you could walk right in amongst the gold?"

"Not walk in," the Codger explained. "There's an inner door what is kept locked, but it's made of bars what you can see between and see what's inside, which is the gold. So you can sort of like peep in. And there's even a couple of those electrical lights in the vault itself, so you can see it real good, if you see what I mean."

"You're making me see-sick again," the Pup complained.

"So one can peer between the bars and stare at the gold," Pin mused. "Most peculiar."

"Did I mention the guards?" the Codger asked. "There's a couple of British soldiers on guard outside the door all the time—day and night. And they carry loaded rifles, so I understand."

"Have you seen this yourself?" asked Pin.

"I walked by the vault. But, like I said, the outer door's closed while we're in port. And it's the sort of door what would look comfortable on any bank vault you've ever seen. And them two soldier-boy guards is standing there nonetheless, spick and span, rifles gleaming. The rest of it I got from a couple of gents at the bar, who told me all about it."

"Well, now," said Cooley the Pup. "What do you suppose the professor is planning to do about it? How's he going to squeeze that gold out of that there vault when it's being watched all the time?"

"That's right," the Codger agreed. "Not only by the soldier boys, but by any random passenger who happens to wander by."

"Several possibilities occur to me," said Pin. "Which one exactly Moriarty and his henchmen will adopt remains to be seen."

The Artful Codger looked quizzically at him. "Moriarty has henchmen? I've never heard that he works with a crew. Don't he usually just mastermind a job for a piece of the action, and let someone who has a mind to boss the operation? That's the way I've heard he works the business."

"I heard the professor says he don't like to give orders, 'cause he knows so few people capable of following orders," said Cooley the Pup. "That's what I heard."

Pin Dok Low looked at his companions with distaste. "It really doesn't matter, gentlemen, what the relationship between Professor Moriarty and his—let us call them helpers, aides, assistants, slaveys, lackeys, attendants, auxiliaries, lieutenants, followers, troops, or associates—is, our problem is to discover how he and his, ah, men intend to purloin the gold, and prevent them from doing it."

"Well, it should be a cinch to keep an eye on the gold the way they've got it set up," the Codger remarked.

Pin looked from one to the other of them. "Doesn't it strike you as odd," he asked, "that they keep the outer door to the vault open all day? They're going out of their way to keep the gold on display."

"Perhaps they want everyone to know it's really there," the Artful Codger suggested.

"Perhaps so," Pin agreed. "And perhaps that is because it isn't really there at all."

The Pup looked startled. "What do you mean?" he asked, his voice squeaking out from between clenched teeth. "Where do you think it is?"

"I'm not sure," Pin said. "Perhaps it's going on a different ship, and this is just a bluff. Perhaps it's in a different, sealed compartment. Or perhaps it's there after all, and I merely suspect everyone else of having as devious a mind as I."

"Perhaps we'd best make sure," the Pup said. "We don't want to be guarding the wrong hole and let the rat slip through somewheres else, do we?"

"We don't," the Codger agreed. "Indeed we don't." He turned to Pin. "You think of the damnedest things."

"Thank you," said Dr. Pin Dok Low.

* * *

Peter Collins knocked on Margaret's stateroom door shortly after breakfast. She opened it to find him leaning against the opposite wall of the corridor, his white linen suit spotless, his face scrubbed, and his hair kempt with care. "Morning," he said, pushing himself off the wall and giving a slight bow. "Your father tells me you're coming along on this expedition to see the elephant, so I thought I might, ah, as it were, accompany you. With your permission."

Margaret was silent for a long moment, unsure how to reply. A tiny voice deep inside her wanted to shout out, "Yes, yes, of course. Wherever you go, I shall follow!" But she dare not. Her self-respect, her upbringing, her sense of dignity would not allow it. *Why this man*, she thought, *out of all the others?* He was good-looking, but she had known better. He seemed to like her, but others had seemed more deeply smitten. He seemed to be quite bright, but time would tell. She knew—*knew*—that he had all the attributes she required of a man: kindness, a cheerful disposition, a loving nature, a willingness to share, a willingness to value her opinions, the desire and ability to put her above all other women or men, as she would put him....

What *was* she thinking?

How could she know all that, or any part of it, about this man she scarcely knew?

She must keep her head firmly in control of her heart. If this was love at first sight, she wanted none of it. She would have to step back and take a long, hard second look before she allowed herself to be swept away.

And yet...

The moment was stretching on, and Peter was looking increasingly nervous. "Have I said something?" he asked. "Was I too forward? Shall I abase myself?"

"No, no, not at all," she told him, gathering her thoughts and putting them aside. "I was considering what to wear. I tend to stare off into space a lot, as you'll see. Usually I'm considering what to wear."

"Say no more," he told her. "My great-aunt Dorothea spends copious amounts of time considering what to wear, although she always ends up clad in black taffeta and a hat that resembles a blancmange. A black blancmange. Actually a noirmange, I suppose."

"I think it would be great fun to join the expedition to Elephanta," she told him, "although I know nothing of it save that it's an island. Is there actually an elephant?"

"So I understand. Professor Moriarty, the chap that's arranging this outing, says there's a giant statue of an elephant. It would seem to be why the Portuguese named the island thus, although there are no actual living elephants. The local name for the island is Gharapuri."

"Gharapuri? That means fortress town, I think."

"If you say so," Peter agreed. "Unexpectedly useful, learning a language with a military phrasebook. Although I don't think there are either a fortress or a town on the island. Just a giant elephant statue. But since an elephant is pretty big to begin with, a giant elephant should be impressive. And then there are the caves, full of religious sculptures which were apparently carved out of the solid granite in the sixth century. Dedicated, I think, to the god Shiva."

"I tremble with anticipation," Margaret said. "Give me a minute and I'll be with you. I'm just about ready." She withdrew inside the cabin and, true to her word, reappeared in just over a minute, adjusting an oversized straw sunbonnet to just the right angle on her head.

"What of Lady Priscilla?" Peter asked. "Is she joining us?"

"Lady Priscilla and her beau, a Lieutenant Welles, have decided to wander about in the bazaars of Bombay," she told him. "A Mrs. Bumbery, a respectable lady who must be in her fifties, is to accompany them as chaperone."

"Ah, well," said Peter. "If the respectable Mrs. Bumbery is in her fifties, then she will certainly countenance no sort of immoral behavior. But can you be sure that she isn't merely forty-nine?"

"What a shocking idea," Margaret said.

NINETEEN

ELEPHANTA

Oh busy weaver! Unseen weaver! Pause! One word!
Wither flows the fabric? What palace may it deck?
Wherefore all these ceaseless toilings? Speak,
weaver! Stay thy hand!
HERMAN MELVILLE

Gharapuri Island is a slab of basalt roughly two miles square squatting in the Sea of Oman six miles north east of Bombay Harbor. Sometime in the fifth century, possibly during the reign of Chandragupta II, the greatest of the Gupta rulers, skilled artisans hewed a series of interconnected caves, both great and small, into the native rock of the island 250 feet above the sea. Pillars to support the caves' high ceilings were carved in place. Images of the god Shiva in many of his aspects, warrior and farmer, creator and destroyer, corporeal and inanimate, male and female, were sculpted in high relief on all surfaces. Visually powerful and undoubtedly beautiful, the Gharapuri caves had for over a millennium evoked awe and reflection among all who visited.

The Portuguese acquired the island from the Sultan of Gujarat in 1534, and found a giant stone statue of an elephant by the landing site. And so they renamed the island Elephanta, as though a thousand years of history could be blotted out with the change of a name. The elephant fell and broke into pieces when the British tried to ship it to England in the 1860s and by the end of the nineteenth century it lay by the shore in several great chunks.

The steam launch *Efrit* was a side-wheeler with a mango-orange funnel, a cabin that took up most of the deck, and a great hoop of a wheel amidships on the port side, the like of which hadn't been seen in European waters for a quarter century. She maneuvered among the dhows, ghanjahs, baghlahs, caïques, sloops, and assorted other vessels moored around the island and pulled alongside the dock. The deafening whine and clatter of her ancient walking beam engine died down, only to be replaced by a not-quite-as-loud hissing sound as the captain vented a great dollop of steam, a reflection of his joy at having made one more trip without mishap.

Twenty-two people of assorted sizes, ages, sexes, and costumes came ashore and gathered about their de facto group leader and expedition organizer, Professor James Moriarty, at the foot of the steps going up the side of the hill leading to the caves. Shortly thereafter a squad of dhoti-clad native porters emerged from the innards of the boat, six of them carrying large wicker picnic hampers and two lugging a sheet metal camp stove suspended on poles between them. The squad started up the steps, accompanied by a small man in a brown-and-white-checkered suit. Right after them came three men from the *Empress*'s dining room staff, clad in oversized immaculate white jackets, carrying carving knives, whisks, ladles, serving forks, and other impedimenta of office.

"Our lunch goes ahead of us," Moriarty said, gesturing to the passing hampers and crew. "We shall follow shortly." He took a breath and struck a lecturing pose. "Although this is known as the 'City of Caves,' there are but eight main caves on the island," he told the group. "They form an intricate complex of courtyards, grottoes, shrines, inner cells. I have read intensively about them, and I'll try to give you a brief explanation of what we see as we go along." He adjusted his pince-nez and peered around the group. "I see there is a gentleman here who, by his native garb, is possibly better able to expound on the religious meanings of these images than I. Perhaps he would like to comment?"

The small, dark-skinned man in the white kurta and dusky red turban performed a graceful half bow as the others turned to look at him. "I have the honor to be Mamarum Sutrow, a humble fellow passenger on this voyage of discovery," he said in a high, clear voice. "By religion I am Zoroastrian, and know little of the icons of the Hindi gods, except that they express and represent deep religious and philosophical concepts encompassing history, art, and morality."

"Where is your colleague, Professor, ah, Demartineu?" Peter Collins asked.

"He is upset of the stomach," Sutrow explained. "He wished greatly to come, but felt not upworthy of the effort of such an expedition."

I see," Peter said.

"Poor man," said Margaret. "This is certainly upworthy of anyone's effort."

Moriarty clapped his hands together three times, in the time-honored way of dispelling demons and attracting attention. "Let us head up the path now and commence our visit to the caves," he said. "I will not entreat you to stay together; you are not children, wander where you like. I will, however, remind you that the picnic lunch will remain with the main party. And when you hear the boat whistle in four and a half hours it would be a good idea to return to the dock with reasonable speed."

Margaret and Peter made their way slowly up the steps not talking, allowing other people to pass them on the way up. They found that they had a lot not to talk about. Margaret held Peter's hand as they climbed the stairs and wondered about the rightness of things. She had held the hands of many a young man—well, fairly many, although she wasn't sure what the standards were—and they had felt cold and clammy, those that didn't feel hot and sweaty. But Peter's hand felt strong and secure and friendly (friendly?), and it felt somehow right that she should be holding it. She had walked beside an assortment of young men and had felt, at best, a vague sort of interest in those aspects of life, and physique, and attitudes, and thought processes that made them different from young women. But she felt an almost desperate desire to know all there was to know about this rather rabbit-faced young man who climbed the stairs beside her whistling "With Cat-Like Tread," from *The Pirates of Penzance*.

* * *

"They're coming up!" Mummer Tolliver whispered, peering around the entrance to the cave and watching the tour group ascend the stairs. "We'd best hurry!" He turned around to see that the three porters with him had stopped what they were doing and were staring at him questioningly. "You blighters don't speak English, do you?" Tolliver trotted back to where they were standing. "Silly me. Here, lets get this statue back into the corner there." He made lifting-up and pushing-back motions with his hands. The native porters followed his mimed instructions and lifted the plaster-coated brass copy of the Queen of Lamapoor, currently known as the Lady of Lucknow, and thrust it deep into an otherwise empty niche along the wall of the cave. For one with a discerning eye for Indian art and artifacts, it was stylistically as different from the artwork surrounding it as a Rembrandt is from a da Vinci, but the closest one with such a discerning eye was in the Department of Antiquarian Studies at the University of Bombay, some fifteen miles away, and his opinion was not asked.

"That's perfect," the mummer said, making the universal sign for "that's perfect" with his hands. While the porters watched indifferently—they had long since stopped trying to understand why the crazy European tourists did any of the things they did—he scrambled up onto the ledge and took a small packet of quick-drying cement powder from one pocket and a vial of water from another, poured the water into the powder, and stirred it to produce a thick white goo. He tilted the statue and applied the goo under it and all around the bottom. Then he jumped off the ledge, produced a small brush, and brushed the floor, gathering up the dust into a small pan. He then blew the dust onto the statue. Although its pallid whiteness could not be totally disguised, this gave it a semblance of age and permanence. It looked different from the other images in the small cavern, but not quite an only-been-here-for-the-past-ten-minutes difference.

"Now quick!" the mummer said, making a brushing motion with his hands. "Back to the main cave and let's get busy helping the others unpack the lunch hampers and set up."

* * *

The visitors from the *Empress* straggled out along the steps going up to the caves, some 250 feet above the landing. A troupe of red-faced monkeys scampered over the rocks to chatter at them and demand back-sheesh as they arrived at the top. When no food or shiny playthings were offered, the monkeys scolded the arrivals and departed as they had come, except for two who settled, one on a flat rock above the cave entrance and the other on a stone post in the clearing, leaned back on their haunches, and stared at the visitors, immobile as graven images of their primal monkey god.

Most of the *Empress* group went with Professor Moriarty into the central cave with the stone pillars and he gathered them in front of the twenty-foot-high three-headed statue known as the Trimurti. Moriarty lit the brass bull's-eye oil lamp he was carrying and shone its beam on the heads, so far above their own heads. They represented, he explained, three major aspects of the godhead that was Shiva: Lord Brahma the creator, Lord Vishnu the preserver, and Lord Shiva the destroyer. This provoked a spirited discussion on how a god could be all three, and with three separate names at that.

"Nothing will provoke such hilarity and disbelief in a man as another man's religion," Moriarty said dryly. "And that goes whichever man is considering the beliefs of whichever other man—or woman."

Margaret and Peter sat outside one of the larger caves, in the shadow of its high, vaulted ceiling, holding hands, ignoring the others, and talked softly about something they could never recall later. In a while, when the sounds of conversation from inside grew fainter, they stood.

"Shall we walk?" asked Peter.

"Let's." Margaret adjusted her bonnet and smoothed her skirt.

They wandered through the hall, pausing to admire one or

another of the carvings which filled the walls almost continuously, talking about this and that.

"So you're going to be in London for a while?" Margaret asked casually.

"As far as I know," he told her. And then, after an elaborate pause: "And you?"

"My father will be going to Castle Fitzroberts, the Highland Lancers' headquarters outside Kilmarnock. But he plans to spend a couple of weeks in London first, attending to family business. I've been thinking of asking him if I could stay on. My aunt Constance would be glad to have me, I'm sure. She has a house in Belgravia."

"I was thinking of taking some leave time after I report," Peter said. "I have a month or so coming."

"Really?" asked Margaret.

They stopped in front of a figure delicately carved in relief on the left wall. It depicted a smug-looking man dancing. He had a secretive smile on his face and an extra arm, which was stretched above his head holding what seemed to be a small person. Even with the third arm he looked realistic and energetic, as though he could dance off the wall and join them, if he chose. If, perhaps, he found them as interesting as they found him.

"Striking," Peter said.

"Beautiful," Margaret agreed. "But incomprehensible. You have the feeling with so much of this art that it is meant to convey some deep feeling, or relate a truly meaningful story, but it's someone else's story, and you aren't meant to understand it."

"I do, indeed, have that feeling," Peter agreed. "But I felt the same way for the whole week I was in Florence staring at a peck of Renaissance masterworks. I am resigned to accept the fact that I must merely enjoy fine art without hoping to understand it. And then there was the opera I went to. *Tosca*. I didn't understand a word of it. It was as though it were in a foreign language."

Margaret suppressed a giggle. "Philistine!" she murmured.

* * *

After a bit over two hours of exploring, examining, and contemplating the caverns of infinite delight and perpetual torment, abode of the masculine force and the eternal feminine, the living incarnation of Shiva, the perpetual inanimate and eternal avatar of the godhead, Moriarty and his followers returned to the main grotto to find the picnic hampers unpacked, six light tables set up and surrounded with canvas camp chairs, the serving tables pushed together and piled with provender of an Anglo-Indian sort: whole roast chickens and tandoori chicken, roast leg of lamb and roast lamb cubes on skewers, three different kinds of chutney, basmati rice with yogurt, pureed eggplant, nan bread, and more. Two servers with dazzling smiles stood behind the tables in their white aprons. A third was removing more platters of hot food from the camp stove even as the group formed into a line and reached for plates. A cool breeze blew in from the sea, and all agreed that tramping about in caves staring at stone figures can make pausing for food seem like an awfully good idea.

General St. Yves and his two adjutants, Colonel Morcy, whose waist was larger and whose face was redder than when the trip commenced, and Major Sandiman, whose mustache was thicker and whose visage was more dour, sat at a table with Colonel Moran and Professor Moriarty, discussing Hindu art and other matters of mutual interest as they ate.

Colonel Moran waited until what he judged was the proper moment in the meal to dangle the bait. When the pace of eating had slowed and the others were beginning to look restless, he began. "I understand that one of these caves has some carvings of a more, ah, if I can borrow a term, sensual nature," he said, leaning forward and speaking in a confidential tone.

"That's so," said Professor Moriarty, setting the hook. "The book in the ship's library mentioned them. Without going into any great detail, of course."

"I wouldn't mind taking a dekko at them, if it can be managed without offending the others," Moran said.

"It would be very interesting," Moriarty agreed. "The carvings have a deep religious significance, I understand, even if to our eyes they seem a little, well, risqué."

"Religious significance, you say?" St. Yves asked.

"So I've been told.

"Seems to me," St. Yves commented, "that everything on this bloody subcontinent has a religious significance, even the b-bloody insects."

"I have had a similar feeling myself," Moriarty admitted. "But it would certainly help with our understanding of the various peoples of India if we had a deeper knowledge of their traditional beliefs and religious practices."

"True," St. Yves agreed.

"After all," Moriarty added, "despite the 'poor benighted heathen' image that the overseers of the British Raj try to project, India had a highly developed civilization back when the people of Britain were still painting themselves blue and worshipping trees. Our overlordship of India is the result of better guns, not a superior culture."

Moran gave the professor a quick warning glance. This was not the time for one of Moriarty's little rants on the evils of modern society, or just who was calling whom uncivilized. "Perhaps we should go look at these carvings now, if we're going to go," he said, determined to get the conversation back on the rails again. "Then we can be back by the time everyone else has finished eating."

"It might be amusing," St. Yves agreed, pushing his chair back. "Do you know where this particular chamber is, Professor?"

"I believe so," Moriarty said. "We'll take a stab at it." He relit his oil lamp and, with as little fuss as possible, the small group left their companions and headed back into the caves.

The mummer joined the group as it left the large cave, and Moriarty introduced him to the others as "my friend Mr. Tolliver, a dealer in Indian curiosities."

"'At's right," the mummer agreed. "And the curiouser the better, says I."

Moriarty led the group through a not-quite-maze of little chambers, grottoes, and connecting corridors to a cave with a high, narrow opening to the outside, letting in a wide blade of light that progressed about the room as the day advanced.

"I believe this is it, my friends," Moriarty said, casting the beam from his lantern about the room. More of the wall space seemed to be unfinished in here than in most of the other chambers. But the carvings that were there were well and carefully done by a true artist with a feeling for the human form. The far wall displayed a series of images of strong men and supple women, or perhaps the same strong man and supple woman, engaged in erotic dalliance of an imaginative and athletic nature, assuming positions of which the average European had never conceived, and several that he or she would have deemed impossible.

"Well, there you are, gentlemen," Moriarty said. "The people who built this had an enlightened attitude toward the sensual aspects of human relations fifteen hundred years ago. They have pictured here acts that we would be embarrassed to admit we know the names for."

"I'd just as soon not know the name for that one," Colonel Morcy said, pointing to a carving of a couple particularly intricately entwined. "It looks intricate and not particularly pleasurable."

"I'd just as soon not know the names of any of them," said Major Sandiman, who was standing at a position of parade rest and determinedly looking straight in front of him. Where, as it happened, was a carving in high relief of a woman's leg wrapped around a man's torso, her toes pointing joyously toward the ceiling. "A gentleman does not do that sort of thing!"

"No kidding, cove?" asked Mummer Tolliver, sounding intrigued. "What sort of thing does a gentleman do, then?"

Colonel Moran peered into a niche in the wall a little farther along. "Well, I'll be damned!" he exclaimed. "Bring that lamp over here, will you?"

"Certainly." Moriarty strode over to Moran with the lamp. "What have you found?"

"Shine it in there—in that recess." He pursed his lips and stared at the illuminated statue in the niche. "I'm damned if that doesn't look like a stone version of that statue you gentlemen of the Lancers go to dinner with," he said, turning to General St. Yves.

"Here, now, what's that?" Colonel Morcy demanded, wheeling

around and stalking over to where Moriarty and Moran were standing. "A statue resembling the Lady of Lucknow? Wouldn't that be something? Perhaps we can discover something of her provenance if it's so."

"It has been something of a mystery where she came from," Brigadier General St. Yves said, coming over to examine the statue. "Hmmm. Curious. It does look like her, at least superficially, I'll admit."

The mummer elbowed his way between the men and squinted at the statue that he had put in that very niche barely two hours before. "Well, I'll be packed in putrid pickled peppers," he exclaimed, "if that ain't Fatima the Dancing Dolly."

"You know this statue?" St. Yves asked.

"Not this very one, o'course," the mummer explained. "But I got a couple of hundred just like her in the hold of the ship. Only made out of the purist brass. I calls her 'Fatima the Dancing Dolly,' and plans to sell them to the tourist trade in London and Brighton, and such-like."

"A couple of hundred?" asked Major Sandiman, looking annoyed.

"I would have gotten more if I could," the mummer said. "The last batch went in nothing flat."

"The last batch?" asked Major Sandiman, looking even more annoyed.

"You say you call her 'Fatima'?" asked St. Yves. "Does that mean you don't know the actual provenance of the statue?"

"Oh, sure I does," the mummer said breezily, "but I couldn't very well call her by her right name, now, could I?"

"Why is that?" asked Colonel Morcy.

"Why, middle-class morality, that's why. Middle-class morality would have none of it."

"Really?" asked Professor Moriarty. "Is it an immoral statue we're looking at, then?"

"The way I sees it, the immorality is in the eyes of them as looks at the statue, not in the Harlot of Hajipur herself," Tolliver said, drawing himself up and looking self-righteously around the group surrounding him.

Major Sandiman grimaced. "The, ah, 'Harlot of Hajipur,' you say?"

"Not me," the mummer explained. "I don't say that. But I've been given to understand by them as supplies me with such stuff that thissere lady"—he pointed a thumb at the statue—"is the goddess of what you might call 'ladies of the evening.' If you get what I mean."

"Their goddess?" General St. Yves queried. "This statue?"

"Yes, sir, that's it. Brings 'em luck, and, eh, clients, and keeps 'em safe. Or so I'm told. There's a brass copy of thissere lady in the back room of every brothel from Yezd to Rangoon. Or so I'm told."

"It is a suggestive pose," added Moriarty, looking at the statue closely through his pince-nez. "Resembling the passive-receptive postures outlined in the *Kama-Sutra*."

Major Sandiman frowned. "The *Kama*—"

"An ancient Indian manual of, ah, lovemaking. Very instructive, or so they say," Moriarty told him.

"And you have brass copies of this very statue?" a thoughtful Colonel Morcy asked the mummer.

"When we gets back to the ship," the mummer told him, "you can come take a dekko at one, and see for yourself."

"Yes," said Colonel Morcy. "That will be nice."

* * *

When Peter and Margaret made their way back toward the steam launch there was a man standing at the bottom of the stairs busy brushing lint off the lapel of his white linen jacket. He looked up as they passed and removed his hat. "Excuse me," he said, "but are you Inspector Collins?"

Peter turned to him. "I am positively he," he admitted. "What can I do for you?"

The man looked from Peter to Margaret and back. "Ah..." he said.

"It's all right," Peter assured him. "This lady's with me."

"Right, then," the man said. He took an envelope from his pocket and handed it to Peter. "From H," he said. "Urgent."

"Ah!" said Peter.

"A pleasure meeting you," the man said, bobbing his hat in each of their directions. "My name's Phitts, by the way." Jamming the hat back on his head, he turned and loped off down the dock to where a small sailboat was tied up. He jumped in, cast off, raised the sail, and waved at them in one continuous motion, and then the boat had caught the breeze and pulled handily away from the dock.

Margaret caught Peter's arm. "So you're an inspector," she said.

"So I am," he admitted. "We're all inspectors, except those of us who are Scouts, or district inspectors, or commissioners. But there's only three of them."

"H," she said.

"My boss," he told her. "His title is high exalted poo-bah."

"Short name."

"Yes."

"Hadn't you better open that letter?" Margaret asked. "Or are you tactfully waiting for me to go away?"

"Please don't go away," Peter said. "Don't ever go away." He ripped the envelope open and took out a folded sheet of paper. For a second he paused, looking at Margaret, who was peering over his shoulder expectantly.

"I won't look," she said, and turned her head away.

"I don't think it will matter," he told her. He unfolded the paper. "Look," he said.

She turned back and looked. She saw a jumble of letters. Neatly arranged, but a jumble nonetheless:

GSJCA	QTMAW	RHKGH	ONBFR	RWRGN
KWHRE	OQFAB	GXCTF	BFSTN	DXGRH
OHUMM	LEOTB	RBTHM	JRHAF	MLOEW
EPRIC	TQLYE	OFCDL	TMLOE	WEOBK
QVQCB	KTRRH	LRQDW	GPLTC	PMRWR
TCHVM	FORHR	XQPNB	PRYZ	

"Well," she said. "Very informative. Some sort of code, no doubt."

"It's done in what's called the Playfair Cipher," he told her. "Safe and simple to use. I'll have to wait until we get back to the ship to translate it."

"I thought you said it was simple."

"Simple but time-consuming," he explained. "And it uses a key word which changes from time to time. I'll have to look up this one back on the ship."

"Oh," she said, looking disappointed.

"It's probably quite dull," he told her. "These things usually are. Of course," he reflected, "when they're not dull, they tend to be very exciting indeed."

TWENTY

A NUMBER OF THINGS

Happy Thought
The world is so full of a number of things,
I'm sure we should all be as happy as kings.
ROBERT LOUIS STEVENSON

The Artful Codger came into the second-class lounge at something between a fast walk and a canter and stopped at Pin's table. His breathing was rapid and his face was flushed. "I seen him," he gasped.

"Breathe deeply," said Pin. "Relax. You should never run on board a ship; all the books say so. Sit down. Let me pour you a cup of tea."

Dropping into a seat, the Codger put his hand to his chest and took several slow deep breaths. "He's back on the ship," he said.

Pin finished pouring the tea and put the teapot carefully down. "Who is?"

"Who else? Professor Moriarty."

"Of course he is. Where else would he be? The *Empress* is about to leave port."

"Yes, but he really is here. I've seen him. He was getting off this old side-wheeler. I don't think he saw me."

"Are you sure it was him?"

"Tall bloke, stands straight as a lamppost; big head, with them nose-pinching glasses; deep-set eyes, cold as blue ice, looking like they could read what you're thinking and not liking it much; topper; gold-handled cane."

"That's an apt description of Professor Moriarty. Does he know you?"

"I don't think so, but they do say that the professor knows everything."

Pin's eyes widened and he seemed about to say something, but he refrained.

A waiter came by the table and paused, salaamed, bowed, looked obsequious, and wished to know whether the masters would like anything else be brought to them that they might partake of, if it pleases your worship.

They said no. The waiter backed away and left.

"And this is why you were running?" Pin asked.

"Actually..." the Codger said, looking embarrassed, "actually I got lost."

"Lost?"

"Well, it's a big ship," he said defensively.

Pin nodded and ran a hand over his sleek, black, well-groomed hair. "So the professor has returned," he said. "Where has he been?"

"He's been out with a bunch of folks looking at the elephants, is what they told me."

"Elephants?" Pin asked, looking suddenly alert. "For transporting gold, perhaps?"

"I thought of that, I did." He took a breath and added, "Which is why I was running."

"Ah!" said Pin, and then lapsed into a thoughtful silence.

Cooley the Pup strolled over to the table and joined them, hands jammed deep in the pockets of his light gray flannel pants. "How's yourself?" he asked. "I thought you might like to know the professor has rejoined the ship."

Pin came out of his reverie and looked sharply at his companions. "So I just heard," he told the Pup. "Off looking at elephants, was he?"

"I hadn't heard that," said Cooley. "I heard as he was on some island looking at statues."

"Maybe," suggested the Artful Codger, "they was statues of elephants."

The long, mournful blast of the ship's horn reverberated through the room.

"We're about to leave Bombay," said Pin. "Go down and casually pass in front of the gold vault door every so often. If the captain is as faithful as they say about opening the outer door once we leave port, you should be able to see something."

"Right enough," said the Codger. "What am I looking for?"

Pin grinned a tight-lipped grin. "Gold," he said.

* * *

It was early evening when the *Efrit* returned the Elephanta visitors to their ship, and *The Empress of India* was already preparing to depart. The cargo hatches were closed and battened down, the purser was fretting about the few as-yet unreturned passengers, the last of the fresh water had been brought aboard, and the replacements to the crew had been fitted out in fresh uniforms and given their instructions.

Margaret and Peter shook hands decorously, although perhaps their hands remained together rather longer than either of them expected and separated in the main corridor to return to their cabins. Margaret pulled open the door to her stateroom, saw that Lady Priscilla had not yet returned, and flung herself on her bed to consider life. In his cabin Peter sat at the small writing desk and, banishing the image of Margaret as best he could from floating in the air before his eyes, took the Tauschnitz pocket edition of British poetry from a side pocket of his portmanteau and flipped through it.

By an abstruse process devised by some clerk in the coding office who never had to decode a message as though anything more important than his lunch were at stake, Peter determined that the fourth word in a poem by Dryden was to be the key word for the cipher. On looking it up, he found that the word was "Cleopatra." Peter made a five-by-five grid of the alphabet on a sheet of lined paper, starting with the letters in "Cleopatra," and took the letter from his pocket and smoothed it out on the desk:

GSJCA	QTMAW	RHKGH	ONBFR	RWRGN
KWHRE	OQFAB	GXCTF	BFSTN	DXGRH
OHUMM	LEOTB	RBTHM	JRHAF	MLOEW
EPRIC	TQLYE	OFCDL	TMLOE	WEOBK
QVQCB	KTRRH	LRQDW	GPLTC	PMRWR
TCHVM	FORHR	XQPNB	PRYZ	

Slowly and carefully he wrote out the clear text of the message above the cipher text:

INFOR	MANTV	ERIFI	ESTHA	TXTHU
GXGEX	ESACT	IVEAG	AINBU	TWHER
EISUN	CLEAR	TRANS	FERCA	NCELX
LEDFO	RNOWL	EAVEC	ANCEL	XLEDI
MXMED	IATER	ETURN	TOCAL	CUTXT
AOFXF	ICERE	QUEST	EDXY	

Or, removing the nulls and putting the proper spacing and punctuation in, he read:

Informant verifies that thuggees active again, but where is unclear. Transfer cancelled for now, leave cancelled. Immediate return to Calcutta office requested.

As he was transcribing the clear version, Peter heard the ship's horn sounding its doleful message of farewell to the city of Bombay. He could, he supposed, swim ashore, but that seemed a bit drastic. The next place he could leave the ship would be Suez, in about five days. The Thuggee hunters would just have to do without him for a bit longer. He thought of the telegram he'd like to send from Suez: DO YOU STILL NEED ME STOP THERE'S THIS YOUNG LADY...

No, he didn't suppose that's what he'd actually send.

*　*　*

The Empress of India pulled out of Bombay Harbor accompanied by two Royal Navy steam frigates and a motley flotilla of sailing craft. Lady Priscilla returned to her stateroom looking flushed and happy and insisted on telling Margaret all about her day's adventures with Lieutenant Welles and the wonderfully near-sighted Mrs. Bumbery, who was much more interested in shopping in the bazaar than chaperoning her two charges.

Curious, Margaret thought, she had no impulse at all to tell Lady Priscilla about Peter Collins, even though his image crowded most other thoughts from her brain. It wasn't that she and Priscilla weren't such close friends, although they actually weren't, but that she didn't want to share Peter with anyone, not even verbally, not yet.

*　*　*

Professor Moriarty took his pince-nez from his waistcoat pocket, polished the lenses with a bit of flannel, and adjusted them on the bridge of his nose. "I think it went well," he said.

"You do?" Moran asked, looking around the first-class lounge and signaling for a waiter.

Moriarty nodded. "We have planted the seed," he said. "It will sprout and grow into a bitter weed."

Colonel Moran looked at his companion in feigned admiration. "My, how you do talk," he said. "A 'bitter weed' indeed. And just how will this profit us?"

Moriarty leaned back in his chair and regarded Moran over the top of his pince-nez. "You and I," he said, "have different approaches to the world around us. Let us take, for example, the matter of dealing with other men. We both would try to persuade them to do our bidding, but you would use a blunt object atop the head, or the threat of one, where I would use superior knowledge and what the American philosopher William James would call 'psychology.'"

Moran frowned. "Is that some sort of insult?" he demanded.

"Not at all," Moriarty assured him. "I think what I'm commenting on is a difference in outlook. I don't doubt your native intelligence. You made quite a good living playing cards for several years, I recall, and that demands a fine intuitive mathematical skill and a quick wit."

"It does," Moran agreed. "But when possible I much prefer the direct approach. I confess it. It makes no sense to me to do otherwise."

A waiter with a well-scrubbed face, dressed in new and spotless whites, came to the table, bowed, scraped, groveled a bit, and took their order: gin and tonic for Moran and a cognac for Moriarty.

"The staff has gotten a bit obsequious, have you noticed?" Moran asked. "It's all 'Would the sahib like this?' or 'Can I bring the sahib that?' or 'Let me brush the sahib's jacket off, pliz' or 'It would be an honor for me to shine the sahib's splended black boots.' It's those new people that came aboard in Bombay. And they all have this smile that isn't a smile pasted across their faces."

"They were probably hired just for this passage," Moriarty surmised, "and they hope to keep their jobs past the one trip. Even the meager pay offered by the Anglo-Asian Star line to its waiters and stewards is probably triple what they could make at home. If, that is, they could find jobs at all."

"Well, all that bowing and scraping—they make me nervous," Moran said.

Moriarty chuckled as the waiter brought the drinks, groveled a bit, and left. "Turnabout," he said. "I'm sure you make them nervous."

Mummer Tolliver appeared at the table in a brand-new suit of many colors—mostly grays and greens—and straddled a chair. "Evening," he said. "I has a favor to ask of you, Professor."

"If it is in my power to grant it to you," Moriarty told him, "it is yours."

"What?" asked Moran in mock astonishment. "Without even knowing what it is?"

"Mr. Tolliver would not abuse my trust," Moriarty said. "Any more than I would abuse his. There is, after all, honor among, ah, close friends." He turned back to the mummer. "What do you need?"

"Well, it's like this, Professor," Tolliver said, looking a little embarrassed. "Have you heard as how they're opening up the ballroom in a day or so?"

"No," the professor told him. "I hadn't heard."

"Well, they are. They was fixin' the floor, laying down new parquet flooring and such, and now they're done with the fixin'."

"Disgraceful!" said Colonel Moran. "I shall write to the *Times* about it. The idea of traveling aboard a ship without a functioning ballroom. Why didn't they put the new flooring in whilst we were at dock, I ask you?"

"It's taken a gang of seven men two weeks to do it," Moriarty commented. "That's two weeks of paying wages and keeping steam up without going anywhere, if they were to do it at dock. It's more profitable for the company to keep the ship working while they do minor repairs."

"I thought you didn't know about this here ballroom work," Colonel Moran said querulously.

"I like to know everything I can about everything there is," said Moriarty. "I merely meant I hadn't heard that they'd finished the job."

"They've finished it off near enough so's they're going to have a little show on the stage and some dancing after," the mummer said. "And so I want your help, Professor."

"You'd better ask Moran," Moriarty said with a chuckle and a gesture. "He's assuredly a much better dancer than I. Have him join you."

Moran recoiled a few inches. "Not on your life," he said. "I'm not a dancing master sort of gent, if you don't mind."

"I'm capable of dancing quite nicely all on my lonesome, thank you very much," said the mummer, twisting his face into the grotesque frown of a greatly insulted man. "That ain't nohow it."

"Then how may I aid you?" Moriarty asked.

"I'm going to perform a few songs at thissere show they're putting on, and I'd be properly pleased if you'd accompany me."

"The professor—sing?" Moran asked. This time the astonishment was not mock.

"On the piano," the mummer added quickly. "I would like you to play the piano for me, and perhaps join me in a little patter; a bit of back-and-forth banter, don't you know. Which banter we will carefully work out aforehand, o'course."

"Well, Mummer, what a nice thought," said Moriarty. "It's been a while since I trod the boards."

"The stage lost a great talent when you decided to become a mathematics professor, if you don't mind my saying so, Professor," said the mummer.

"What do you know—who would have guessed?" asked Moran. "The piano, no less."

Moriarty turned to him with an unreadable expression. "I'm also a virtuoso on the bassoon," he said.

Moran stared at him, his mouth open. "I don't know whether you're putting me on, Professor," he said. "But I reckon it don't much matter if you want to have your little joke."

"No, I don't suppose it does," Moriarty said. "How are you doing in the distribution of our lovely Lady, Mummer?"

"I've put out a smatter of the statues where they're sure to be noticed, as you suggested, Professor."

Colonel Moran swirled his gin and tonic around in the glass and stared at the professor. "How's that?" he asked. "Perhaps, as we're this far along, you should explain just what it is you expect to accomplish with this sleight-of-statue business. We can't switch them out for the real one, 'cause that would be stealing and contrary to the agreement."

"True," Moriarty agreed.

"We could buy the thing from them, if they'd sell it. That would be legal and proper. But I don't see how having a hundred of our own is going to get us any closer to that desirable consummation. Maybe we could get them to buy a couple of copies from the mummer here, but where would that take us?"

Moriarty looked thoughtfully at the portrait of Queen Victoria on the far wall. "What we are endeavoring to do," he told them, "is to convince the officers of the Duke of Moncreith's Own Highland Lancers that the statuette they call the Lady of Lucknow would be a disgraceful and improper object for them to bring back to Castle Fitzroberts. After all, their wives and children—including daughters— dine at the officers' mess at least three times a year."

"But it's been there for years," Moran objected.

"Ah, yes. But for those years they were in ignorance. Now their eyes have been opened. With the proper assistance they shall purge themselves of this, ah, half-century lapse in judgment."

Moran thought it over. "If you say this trickery will accomplish the desired result," he said, "then let's get on with it. I will happily watch and learn."

Moriarty nodded. "It stands an excellent chance of doing the job."

"And ain't nohow illegal," said the mummer. "Not as I can see."

Moran nodded. "And that's what counts, isn't it? I've never been overly enamored with morality, that I've noticed."

"Nor legality, either, as I recall," Moriarty added.

Colonel Sebastian Moran looked insulted. "I've never done anything just because it was illegal," he insisted. "There has to be some monetary incentive."

TWENTY-ONE

THE LONELY SEA

These are much deeper waters than I thought.
SIR ARTHUR CONAN DOYLE

An evening's entertainment in the newly reopened ballroom was scheduled for the second day out from Bombay. Most of the entertainers had been recruited from among the passengers themselves except for a trio of sailors who were rehearsing traditional sailors' chanties (the bowdlerized versions) and Third Officer Beagle, who was going to play the mandolin and sing doleful songs about lost love. Doleful songs about lost love were very popular.

The highlight of the evening, according to the daily bulletin posted in various places about the ship, was to be Mamarum Sutrow in his very-first-ever public performance as "Mamarum the Great, Prestidigitator and Magician Extraordinaire."

Chairs were set up in the ballroom, which had a stage at one end and was used for such entertainments. Electrical footlights and spotlights had been installed to illuminate the stage, and the chandeliers over the audience also held electrical bulbs capable of being dimmed slowly until they were out. This modern electrical lighting was, for much of the audience, as much of a novelty as anything they might see onstage. After the performance the chairs would be struck and the ship's orchestra would play for the passengers to dance far into the night.

Most of the first- and second-class passengers and those among the ship's officers and crew who didn't have other duties had filled the room by seven, when the foolishness was scheduled to begin.

The first performer was a large woman in a copious pearl-gray dress singing about her "Willie," accompanied at the piano by a small, thin woman in black, wearing a hat with a large feather. The bobbing of the small woman's head as she played caused the feather to come loose from its moorings and droop in front of her left eye. She blew it out of the way with a well-placed puff of air until, two bars later, it fell again. Again the puff of air, and again...

The audience was soon holding its collective breath in anticipation of each fall of the feather and, when the song came to an end, rewarded the performers with rapturous applause and even some cheering from a pair of eight-year-olds at the front. The ladies were startled at this, and very pleased. The singer's husband, who was in the audience, never dared tell her the reason for their great success.

The sailors came next, three hearty young men singing "Hearts of Oak" and "Blood Red Roses," with great volume and enthusiasm, and bashfully accepting their applause.

Peter and Margaret sat in the back row next to Lady Priscilla and her subaltern suitor and watched the show with divided interest. To Margaret's eyes, Lady Priscilla was almost bubbling with suppressed excitement, while Lieutenant Welles seemed a mite subdued and worried. Sometime while the handsome white-tied young violinist was playing Pablo de Sarasate's "Fantasy on Martha," with his buxom and overly made-up mother at the piano, Lady Priscilla murmured something about taking a stroll on the promenade deck, and she and Lieutenant Welles slipped out of their seats and left the room.

"I worry about her," Margaret whispered to Peter.

"I would say you should worry about him," Peter replied softly. "I think that young lady can take care of herself."

The next on stage was Alfred "Mummer" Tolliver in his neatly pressed red-and-white-checked suit, accompanied on the piano by Professor James Moriarty, in black tie and tails.

Sitting on the far right, about halfway along the files of chairs, were Dr. Pin Dok Low, in his disguise as a minor European nobleman, and his two companions. When Moriarty came out and sat at the piano, Pin leaned forward in his seat and intoned, "Professor Moriarty!" as though the name itself were a curse. "The Napoleon of crime, and he sits there like a respectable citizen. The man's gall has no end."

"You ain't no slouch in the crime department yourself, Pin," murmured the Artful Codger.

Pin turned to glare at him as the mummer began addressing the audience.

"Evening, all," said the little man. "I'm going to sing for you a couple o' songs what me father taught me. 'E used to sing 'em in the music halls 'imself, 'e did—till the ushers threw 'im out." He struck a pose. "Maestro, please!"

Moriarty played a few odd-sounding chords, peered closely at the sheet music on the piano in front of him, and played a few more. The mummer opened his mouth to sing—and then closed it again. "No, no," he yelled at the pianist, "that ain't it."

Moriarty pointed at the sheet music. "This is what you gave me to play, little man, and this is what I'm playing."

"'Little man,' is it?" The mummer staggered, visibly hit by the slings and arrows of outrageous fortune. Straightening up, he bellowed, "I'll have you know I'm taller than I look!" He faced the audience and assumed his singing pose again. "Let's take it from the top."

Moriarty began again: the same distressing chords.

The mummer strode over to the piano, hoisted himself up on it, and walked across the closed top until he was standing over the keyboard. He looked down at the sheet music. Then, with an exaggerated sigh, he reached down and turned the music over end-for-end. Jumping off the piano, he returned to center stage. "It was upside down," he confided to the audience. "Let's try it one more time."

Moriarty studied the newly righted sheets for a second, and then commenced playing again and the mummer listened carefully and nodded. "That's more like it," he said. He struck his pose, waited for a few beats, and began:

"As we drive to the Derby in a four-in-hand, a four-in-hand, a four-in-hand As we drive to the Derby in a four-in-hand..."

After the first two verses, he interrupted the lyric for a soft-shoe shuffle, which got wider and higher and more energetic every moment, until it seemed that the stage could hardly contain the little man. The man wielding the follow spotlight had trouble keeping him in its beam.

And then the music stopped and, instantly, so did the mummer: frozen in motion, one foot in the air, one arm outstretched. After holding the pose for a few seconds, he folded himself into a bow and swept his arm out to the audience before scampering off the stage.

"The little chap's done that before," Peter murmured to Margaret through the applause.

She nodded. "He is certainly energetic."

Lady Priscilla and her beau returned to their seats just then. Was her face a little more flushed than when she left? It was hard to tell in the subdued light. And besides, Margaret reminded herself, strictly speaking it was none of her business. As she had assured Lady Priscilla on the first day of this voyage, she was not her stateroom mate's keeper.

The lights came up briefly, and then dimmed again. And then— magic!

A curtain toward the rear of the stage was raised to reveal the painted backdrop of an open square in an Indian bazaar, the painting so lifelike that you felt you could walk up to it and feel the hard-packed earth under your feet, touch the wooden stalls, fondle the fresh fruit on one stand, smell the dried fish on another. So lifelike that it took a moment to realize that the table against one of the stalls, covered with a variety of not-quite-recognizable objects of brass and lacquered wood and ivory, was half painting and half actual table, jutting out from the backdrop.

Mamarum the Great came out from stage left. He didn't look quite as short (platform shoes?) or as tubby (perhaps a girdle?) as Margaret remembered. Indeed, in his gold and white kurta with the wide red sash and pointy red shoes, he looked handsome and dignified. He bowed at the audience and several scattered people applauded for a few seconds. He smiled and stood motionless until the applause and the nervous coughs had died out. Then he reached to the table behind him and picked up—from the half that was real table, and not part of the painted backdrop—a large, ornate brass pot and held it chest-high in front of him. He put his hand in the opening and ran it about inside, to show that the pot was empty. He turned the opening to the audience so they could see for themselves that there was nothing in it. He then held the pot upside down and shook it, and indeed nothing fell out.

Mamarum peered into the air in front of him, as though looking for something suspended there that he could see but the audience could not. Holding the pot with his left hand, he reached for this invisible object with his right and snatched it out of the air. Then he tossed it, still invisible, into the pot, where it landed with a loud *clink*.

He snatched another object out of the air, and then another and another, tossing each into the pot with a great clinking sound. He came to the edge of the stage and reached out over the audience, and grabbed. A gold coin appeared in his hand. He twisted it around and through his fingers, and bent down to show it to the mother of the two eight-year-old children sitting in the front row. He handed it to her and indicated that she should examine it, which she did, that she should try to bend it and flex it to make sure it was solid, which she did. That she should bite it, which she declined to do. She handed it back to him and he tossed it in the pot. *Chunk*.

And another. *Clink*. And another. *Clink*. You could see the gold coins appearing in his hand, appearing out of empty air, and hear them as they were thrown into the pot. *Chunk*. And then rapidly, one after the other, as fast as he could grab: *clink, clink, clink, chunk, clink*. And then he put the pot on the stage in front of him and reached up with both hands and a cascade of shiny gold coins rained into the pot.

Then he smiled and shrugged, as if to say it was nothing, any master of the mantic arts could have done the same. He picked up the pot and held it over the front row and poured—and nothing came out. The pot was once more as empty as it had been. The gold coins vanishing into air, into thin air.

He bowed for his applause. It came.

Mamarum then clapped his hands thrice, and an assistant—a young Indian lad clad in an oversized dhoti—came out carrying a rolled-up rug perhaps six feet wide and ten feet long, which he proceeded to unroll in the middle of the stage. He then raced offstage to return with a wicker basket about large enough to hold a small goat if it lay down and curled up, which he carefully centered on the rug.

Mamarum pulled the top off the basket with a flourish and pointed the opening toward the audience so they could see inside. It was an empty wicker basket. Putting it back down with yet another flourish, he reached into it and pulled out a long red scarf. There was a slight gasp of surprise, but not a large one. After all, it was only a scarf—easy to conceal—we didn't look that closely in the basket, did we?

Waving the scarf gently, so that it rippled in front of him as he walked, Mamarum left the stage. He came down the central aisle, looking to the left and right, peering into the audience, considering, until about halfway down he stopped by the side of an attractive though stern-faced young lady. He offered her the end of the scarf. She took it tentatively. He pulled on it, urging her to stand up and come along. She let go of the scarf and shook her head.

Mamarum shook his head questioningly and shrugged. Smiling that it was all right, he continued down the aisle to the last row and offered the end of the scarf to Lady Priscilla. She shrank from it. He nodded encouragingly. She took the end delicately, unsurely. He nodded his encouragement again and pulled gently. She stood up as one hypnotized and, clutching the scarf, followed him back up the aisle until they reached the stage.

Lieutenant Welles was not happy. He glowered at Mamarum. "Why the bloody hell she agreed to this is more than I know," he muttered.

The lieutenant, Margaret decided, was jealous. Not a good trait in a suitor.

Mamarum the Great took Lady Priscilla's scarf hand and kissed it in a proper, respectful, and genteel manner and led her by the hand onto the stage. In the back row, unnoticed, Lieutenant Welles growled.

With gestures and silent encouragement, Mamarum had Lady Priscilla step into the wicker basket and lie down, smoothing her outer garments and curling up until she was out of sight within the basket. Mamarum picked up the lid and, with a swift, practiced motion, set it on the basket. A few in the audience saw that he had allowed an apparently unnoticed few inches of the fold of Lady Priscilla's dress to stick out at the join of lid and basket.

The assistant now returned to the stage, wheeling out a rack holding about a dozen long, sharp swords with bejeweled handles. Mamarum and the assistant pushed the rack to the front of the stage and allowed several people in the front row to examine the swords and feel their points and edges. Mamarum then pointed to various people farther from the stage and silently invited them to come forward and examine the weapons. Several did at first and then, impelled by curiosity and a desire to be one of the knowledgeable few, a sizable number left their seats and came to the edge of the stage to see and feel for themselves that the swords were, indeed, swords. Several were actually invited onstage where, for the edification of the rest of the audience, they pulled, pushed, and prodded the various swords to demonstrate that they were real, solid, and sharp.

When the audience members, satisfied that there was no trickery at least in the edged weapon part of the illusion, returned to their seats, Mamarum picked up one of the swords, slapped the flat edge against his open palm to reemphasize the hard-steel reality of the blade, and then thrust it quickly and roughly through the wicker basket until its point protruded through the other side.

Rapidly, and with a smooth economy of motion, Mamarum circled the basket, thrusting swords through the wicker high and low, until the basket was crisscrossed with swords, and it was clear that nobody inside could have escaped being pierced by at least one of the blades, and probably a good half dozen.

The audience knew they were being fooled, but they were caught up in the spectacle, and in the story of what was supposed to be happening, and they waited breathlessly to see how it came out. Then, as Mamarum placed the last sword, there was a murmur from some of those watching, an excited whisper, a gasp here, a sharp intake of breath there. For what Mamarum seemed not to have noticed as he danced around the basket was the trickle of blood coming through the side of the basket, staining the wicker, dripping onto the carefully placed rug.

That was too much for Lieutenant Welles, who suddenly jumped to his feet. "Damn you," he bellowed, "you bloody wog, can't you see what you're doing? Get her out of that thing!"

Startled, Mamarum stopped circling the basket to peer out into the audience. "Beg pardon?" he said calmly. Only the fact that he had spoken at all showed the intense emotion the taunt must have provoked in him.

The spell was broken. The magician had spoken.

"The girl—you've cut her," someone yelled.

"There's blood all over the place," contributed someone else.

An angry woman's voice trebled, "My God, my God! What a tragedy!"

A surge of anger and panic swept the audience and some jumped to their feet, some pushed themselves up heavily from their chairs. Most remained frozen in their seats, but there was no telling how long their hesitation would last.

Mamarum threw up his hands in despair. "Patience, my friends," he said in a surprisingly loud and powerful voice. "The illusion was to end otherwise, with a drawing out of the swords and much ceremony. But you would have it thus." And with that he tilted the basket toward the audience and pulled off the lid.

The nested swords gleamed and sparkled in the spotlight's beam, and Lady Priscilla...

...was not there.

The swords pierced empty air, the rag that had seemed part of Lady Priscilla's dress was just a small silk rag, and the blood on the basket's side had come from nowhere, as far as anyone could see.

"You see?" Mamarum's voice carried through the room. "No unnecessary spilling of blood. No one injured. Only a disappearing lady, the very essence of magic, the heart of the mystery. Where is she? I leave that to you to solve!" And with that Mamarum turned and walked slowly and deliberately off the stage.

"Well, I'll be damned!" said the Artful Codger. "I seen her climb into that there basket, and I had my eye on it the whole time since, and she sure ain't in it now."

"It's all done with mirrors," said Cooley the Pup with the air of a man who's in the know.

Pin turned to Cooley. "Really?" he asked. "And just where were these mirrors placed?"

"Maybe there was a trick bottom in the basket," offered the Codger. "And she dropped through a trap in the stage."

"That's what I said," the Pup agreed, nodding. "Mirrors."

"Notice the lovely Kasham rug that the magician thoughtfully placed under the basket," Pin said with just a trace of irony in his voice. "Perhaps there's a trapdoor in it, also."

"Perhaps," agreed the Codger, who was invincible to irony.

The audience was still balanced in their seats, unsure whether to go forward or back, when someone in the back of the room started to applaud. And then someone else took up the clapping, and another, and another, and the applause became general and anger and apprehension were forgotten and everyone sat back down in their seats and relished the way they had been fooled.

"You're so clever," Margaret said, touching Peter's arm.

Peter turned to her. "What?"

"Starting to clap like that. You may have prevented a riot."

"Sheer genius," Peter admitted modestly.

Lieutenant Welles was still standing, and looking around the room like a marksman seeking a target. "Where is she?" he asked the room. "If the wog's so bloody smart, what has he done with her?"

It seemed like a good question, and was about to be answered. The wog in question had returned to the stage and was peering out into the audience. "Lady Priscilla!" he called. "Come forth now, please!" When he got no response, he jumped down from the stage, looking puzzled. "She should be at the back of the room," he said.

"How'd she get there, then?" called someone.

"Perhaps we should wonder about that later," Mamarum replied. "For now, let's see where she, indeed, is at this moment."

The lights came up in the room, and everyone looked around. Lady Priscilla was nowhere to be seen.

"She should have come back in through that door," Mamarum said, pointing to a door on the right side rear of the large room.

"How'd she get back there?" the man demanded again.

Mamarum struggled for an answer. A magician never reveals his secrets. "Later," he said finally.

"Well, she's not here. So where is she?" Lieutenant Welles demanded.

Mamarum shrugged. "I don't know," he confessed. "Perhaps you frightened her away."

Welles took two steps toward Mamarum, and then reconsidered and stopped. "I'll settle with you later," he said. "We have to find Priscilla!" He trotted toward the indicated door, an invincible force in his blue and white Lancers' uniform.

From somewhere on the ship, outside the room, came the distant sound of a sharp explosion. A shot? A firecracker? People in the audience stood up and murmured to each other, but none seemed to have any clear idea of what to do.

Welles reached the door and pushed. Nothing happened. He jiggled the handle and pushed again. Nothing happened.

"Who locked the door?" Welles demanded sharply. "What the bloody hell is going on here?"

"Please, sir," an elderly man in a frock coat admonished him. "Watch your language! There are ladies present."

Welles stopped and turned. "Sorry, sir," he said. "I do apologize for my profanity, but as we seem to be locked in here, for no discernible reason, and with one of our group missing, I thought it proper for me to express my concern." His voice had started low and intense, but it grew louder as he went on, ending in a bull roar. "If this is some sort of joke, it's no longer funny. I'd suggest that whoever locked this door get over here right now and unlock it!"

More sharp cracking sounds from outside, these seeming to come from a different direction.

Audience members headed for all the exits. There were eight of them. They were all blocked. The ballroom was right next to the promenade deck on "B" level, and six large windows fronted the deck. The metal weather shutters had been drawn over the windows to keep light out during the show. One of the ship's officers broke the central window to get at the shutter. It had somehow been locked from the outside and would not budge. The hysteria mounted, and passengers broke out the other windows with the same result.

"There's something wrong," Margaret said with heroic understatement, rising to her feet. "I think I'd better go find my father."

"There's a lot wrong, if I'm any judge," Peter told her. "I think your father's going to be quite busy for the next little while. I'd suggest, if you don't consider it too much of an imposition, that you stay with me." He took her arm and pulled her back to the rear wall. "We'll be out of the way here," he said. "Which might be a good thing. Until we can figure a way out of this room."

Margaret turned to face him and saw that he had produced from somewhere a short, two-barreled pistol, which he held casually in his left hand, pointed at the floor. Her eyes widened, but she decided not to say anything about it now. Not now. "What do you think is happening?" she asked.

"I'd say someone's making a try for the gold," he told her.

* * *

"Blast!" said Pin. "I should have seen this coming."

Cooley the Pup pulled at a string fastened around his neck under his shirt, and a long, wicked-looking knife slid from its mooring up his sleeve and fell into his hand. He pulled off the thin leather sheath and discarded it. "You think this is it?" he asked.

"They've got most of the passengers and crew in here," Pin said, flexing his shoulders angrily. "What better moment to go after the gold?"

"But look," the Artful Codger objected. "There's your pal the professor up there. If his men were taking the gold, wouldn't he be with them?"

Pin looked up at the stage, and saw Moriarty and Mummer Tolliver standing together at the left side, looking out at the auditorium, as though they were just as puzzled at what was happening as everybody else.

"Clever!" Pin said. "I'll give him that."

The Artful Codger had taken off his tie and slipped a pair of brass knuckle dusters on each hand. "We'd better get a move on," he said. "The question is, where to and how?"

* * *

Colonel Sebastian Moran made his way through the restive audience over to where Moriarty and the mummer were standing. "Well, Professor, you said someone would make a try for the gold before the trip was done, and it looks like you were right. I can't think of anything else that could be happening, unless it's the natives on the crew mutinying because their curry isn't hot enough. But, if it is the gold, the question is who's doing it, and how are they planning to manage it?"

"I think we'd better do our best to put a stop to the attempt," Moriarty told him.

"Ah!" said Moran. "Then I'd best go see which of our companions in involuntary incarceration has devised the best chance of getting us out of here. I'll be back in a trice." He sprinted off toward the front, where several men were already pounding at the locked door.

Moriarty looked thoughtful. "Perhaps we can turn the hueing and crying to our advantage, that is if we succeed in beating off these attackers."

"How so?" asked his small companion.

"Mummer, I have a job for you."

"You mean I has to miss the fighting?" the mummer stamped his foot in irritation. "We short people never have any fun."

"You might find this exciting enough to satisfy you for a while," Moriarty told him. "Here's what I want you to do...." And for the next two minutes he explained what had to be done.

224

Moran returned a few minutes later. "It's going to take them a while," he said. "Perhaps we can find a quicker way out of here."

Another gunshot sounded in the distance.

"Perhaps we'd better," said Moriarty.

TWENTY-TWO

HUGGER-MUGGER

If you can keep your head when all about you
Are losing theirs and blaming it on you,
If you can trust yourself when all men doubt you
But make allowance for their doubting too...
RUDYARD KIPLING

At first it was not clear just who was trying to do what, and with what, and to whom. Captain Iskansen entered the Lancers officers' dayroom at five after seven. "Not going to the big show, I see," he said. General St. Yves and the two junior officers with him looked up from the oversized table strewn with documents.

"Paperwork," St. Yves said. "The bane of the military. Everything written down, signed, and filed, never to be looked at again. Not that the idea of watching dowagers sing or juveniles play the piano is that compelling. What can I do for you, Captain?"

"I thought the question was what I can do for you," Iskansen said. "I was informed that you wished to see me. What do you need?"

St. Yves pushed his chair away from the desk. "I wanted to see you? Who said so?"

"Why, one of the stewards told the first officer, who told me." Captain Iskansen frowned. "Is this some sort of joke?"

"Not on my part," St. Yves assured him, rising to his feet. "We'd better get to the bottom of this." He turned to the two subalterns. "Lieutenant McPride, take over in here. See to the changing of the guard if I'm not back in time. Lieutenant Pinton, come with me."

A pair of white-coated stewards appeared in the doorway holding pewter trays under their arms and Webley service revolvers, which were pointed toward the officers, in their hands. "Pliz, I beg of you, remain quiet and stay contentedly where you are," one of the stewards said firmly. "We would not like to have the shooting of you."

St. Yves sat slowly back down. No point in charging a man with a Webley. Good revolver, the Webley. Great stopping power. "What do you blighters want?" he demanded, trying to put a veneer of nonchalance over what was actually more anger than fear.

"Only just for you to remain where it is you are," the steward told him. "All of you. Pliz."

Lieutenant McPride, a beefy, red-faced young man with that lack of fear and common sense so useful in junior officers, started forward. "Damn you! You can't just—"

The steward pointed his Webley at the ceiling and fired once. The sound in the small room was deafening and hurt the ears.

"I must insist," the steward asserted, his voice sounding thin and distant in the wake of the booming of the pistol.

Captain Iskansen stood still where he was, white-faced and trembling. "By God, I've got a ship to run!" he said. "You can't do this!"

The talking steward smiled a gap-toothed smile. "Have," he said.

The silent steward came into the room, carefully not getting between his partner and the Englishmen, and relieved the three army men of their sidearms. Then the two stewards backed out of the room.

"If you bang on door, I shoot through it," the talkative one said. And they left the stateroom, pulling the door shut behind them.

"They're after the gold!" Captain Iskansen slammed his hand down on the desk. "I should have foreseen this. It must be those new porters and stewards that came aboard in Bombay. But how are they planning to get away with it?"

St. Yves waited for a minute, and then went to the door. "Up against the wall, everyone," he whispered. "Just in case." He tried the door. Nothing happened. He twisted and jiggled the knob. No shots came through the door, but neither did it open.

"What the blasted hell," he mouthed, yanking and jerking at the door, "have they done to this thing?"

"There is a way of fastening the door from the outside," Captain Iskansen told him, dropping into a nearby chair. "If the room is to be used for storage, for instance."

"D-damn," said St. Yves. "I suppose they don't want to kill us unless they have to."

"Kill us?" Lieutenant Pinton leaped out of his chair and stared grimly at the closed door, looking even taller, slimmer, and more intense than usual. "Excuse me, sir, but they wouldn't dare. Would they? I mean after all, we're British officers."

"D-damn!" St. Yves repeated. "You're right, Captain. We should have seen it. This thing's been well planned. Damn convenient, all those people getting sick all at once. They're after the g-gold, of course."

"I have a ship to run," Iskansen reiterated, slapping his open palm once more on the edge of the desk. "I've got to get out of here. It's bad enough that they're after the gold, but the Good Lord knows how much damage they'll do to the ship in attempting to get it."

"You see what they've done?" asked St. Yves rhetorically. "They've removed the top of the chain of command from the ship's crew and the military by locking us in here. Our subordinates will be needing orders, and we won't be there to give them."

Captain Iskansen jumped to his feet. "The porthole!" he exclaimed.

General St. Yves looked at it critically from across the room. "Too small," he said. "None of us will fit through it."

"If we remove eight bolts," Iskansen said, "we can push out the brass framing and gain an extra six inches or so. One of us should be able to get through it then."

A rifle shot sounded from somewhere below. And then, about twenty seconds later, another.

"Those are our rifles," said Lieutenant Pinton.

"One of the guards at the gold vault," said McPride. "Or both."

"Tools!" said St. Yves. "Do we have any tools?"

* * *

"The loft!" said the mummer. "I'll wager they ain't got that closed off."

Moran looked around. "Loft?"

"Behind the stage and up a ladder," explained the mummer. "There's a loft for the stage canvas and such-like what has a door to the upper deck."

"So there is," said Moriarty. "Let's go!"

The three of them clambered back onto the stage and headed for the rear wall behind the backdrop painting of a street bazaar in Hyderabad. "Here's the ladder," said Moriarty.

"I'll go up first," Mummer said. "I'm the shortest."

* * *

"Take a glim over there on the stage," said the Artful Codger. "It looks like the professor and his friends are making a break for it."

"I knew it!" exclaimed Pin, seeing Moriarty disappear behind the backdrop. "Quick! After them."

Pin raced down the aisle and leaped onto the stage, followed with a bit less agility by Cooley and the Codger. Behind them in the ballroom some of the men had taken a long table from the side wall and were using it as a battering ram against the main exit doors. Some others were at one of the side doors taking turns kicking at it with little effect.

After a bit of searching, Cooley the Pup located the ladder. "This must be where they've gone," he whispered hoarsely.

"We'd better follow them," the Artful Codger said, coming over. "You first."

"Yeah, right," said the Pup, "why am I not surprised?" He stuck his knife between his teeth like a storybook pirate, and scrambled up the ladder. The Codger was right behind him, and Pin, anxious not to lose his prey, crowded along behind.

A single shot sounded somewhere in the distance. They paused on the ladder to listen, but it wasn't repeated.

"That was the fourth shot so far," said the Codger, "unless I've missed one."

"Where do you think it's coming from?" the Pup asked in a loud whisper.

"No way to tell," said the Codger.

"What do you think it means?" asked the Pup.

"No point in speculating, we'll find out soon enough," snarled Pin. "Let's get on with it."

The room at the top was filled with rolls of canvas, racks of wood slats, coils of rope, containers of dried fish glue, jars of paint pigment, and boxes of metal pegs, hooks, screws, hinges, and whatnots. Moriarty and his merry band had passed through without stopping, leaving the exit door open.

"Where are we?" the Codger whispered.

"We must be on 'A' deck," Cooley the Pup ventured, peering out the door. "But this ain't a passenger cabin corridor, and I don't know what it is."

"Come," said Pin, leading the way into the corridor. "We must locate Moriarty and that colonel and their midget friend and stop them as quickly as possible."

"They seem to have helpers," said the Artful Codger.

"Cut off the head of a snake," Dr. Pin Dok Low said grimly, "and the body will die."

* * *

"Do you hear that?" Peter put his ear close to the ballroom wall.

"What?" Margaret leaned over and listened. "I can't hear anything over the banging and thumping of our fellow prisoners."

"The ship's engines are slowing down," Peter told her.

She listened and it was so: The steady *thumpita thumpita* of the engines was more pronounced and slower than it had been, and it slowed down even more as she listened. "What does that mean?"

"It means the ship is stopping."

"I know that," Margaret said testily. "I meant, what does that mean?"

"It means we'd really better get out of here."

"That's what I've thought all along," she said. "Engines slow or engines fast, it's not a good idea to be locked up in the ballroom while strangers with uncertain motives are rummaging through the rest of the ship."

"Their motives are fairly certain, I think," Peter commented.

She nodded. "They're after the gold. Well, all right, let them take the gold and go away. Then we can get on with the trip."

"It's more than that," Peter told her, trying to speak as calmly as he could given the surrounding chaos. "I think we've found your Phansigar."

Margaret was still for a minute, letting her mind absorb the implications of that suggestion. "Phansigar."

"I think so."

"Thuggees."

"I'm sorry, but—yes."

"Why do you think so?"

"The message I received. It said that the Phansigar were rumored to be active again, but my superiors didn't know where they were planning to strike. Well, I think we've just found out."

"But," Margaret objected, "according to the old stories, they kill all their victims so as to leave no witnesses. Why haven't they tried to kill us, then?"

Peter shrugged. "Why bother?" he said. "They have to transfer the gold to another ship. They must have a ship somewhere close. And reinforcements. There can't be more than thirty of them on the ship now—the replacement porters and stewards who came aboard in Bombay, if I'm right. And they can't bring the *Empress* into port anywhere, they'll have to sink her after they get the gold. So there's no point in killing us one by one when we're all going to die anyway."

"Oh, dear," said Margaret, bringing her clenched hand to her lips. "There are so many things I wanted to do before I reached thirty, but dying was not one of them."

Peter reached down and took her other hand. "I'm sorry," he said, "I didn't mean to upset you. I spoke without thinking."

She lifted her chin and her eyes were clear. "No, no," she said.

"Don't ever tell me less than the truth. If there is an 'ever.'"

Peter fought back an emotion that threatened to spill from him. There might possibly be a time when showing emotion was an appropriate response to something-or-other, but this wasn't it. "There will be lots of 'evers,'" he assured her. "The truth is that I plan to get us out of here, and stop these Thuggees from stealing the gold or sinking the ship." He made a good solid fist out of his right hand and shook it in front of him. "Not necessarily in that order."

"Good," she said. "I am relieved to hear it. Tell me about your plan?"

"I plan to get us out of here," he said.

"How?"

"I haven't worked that part of the plan out yet."

"Oh," she said.

"It's what we're taught," he told her. "First, establish clear goals."

"And second?"

"I didn't take that class," he told her. "We'll have to improvise."

Margaret considered. "I should think the first thing would be to release all of these people," she said. "With this many passengers running around, it should discommode our antagonists and make it easier to put your plan in effect. When you develop a plan, that is."

"Some of them may get injured, maybe killed," he said.

"And if they stay here?"

Peter nodded. "Release it is, then."

"How?"

He considered. "I think the first question is, where? They're expecting us to come through the main doors, or one of the two side doors, if we come at all. I think we'd better come at them from an unexpected quarter. Perhaps the promenade deck."

"The windows are sealed," Margaret reminded him.

"But the walls are thin." He snapped his fingers. "Damn!" he said. "Excuse the language, but there's something of which I should have thought earlier."

"In this situation a little foul language is acceptable, perhaps even appropriate," she assured him. "What?"

"The stage," he said. "It's a real, that is to say professional, stage."

"Yes?"

"Come on!" he said, thrusting his pistol into his belt and heading toward the stage. "All professional stages in London are required to have a fire axe by the side of the stage. It's to sever the rope holding up the curtain in case of fire."

She hurried along behind him. "We're not in London."

"Let's hope the requirement has become a habit." He hoisted himself onto the stage and hesitated, looking to the left and right. He went left.

The fire axe was there, fastened to the wall to the left of the proscenium. Peter pulled it loose and leaped off the stage. "Right here should do," he yelled, swinging the axe against the wall.

In three swings he had made a serious dent in the wall. In five he had a hole. Other men gathered around, shouting encouragement. After about a dozen swings, the hole was about the size and shape of an upside-down long-stemmed flower vase. He paused for breath and a seaman took the axe from his hand and attacked the wall with an air of professionalism that quickly enlarged the space until a small child could have squeezed through. And then an older child, and then an adult. And then he stopped and pushed through the hole, axe in hand, and looked around for someone to hit. Peter and Margaret came through next, and cleared out of the way for the stream of people following.

Peter tapped the axe man on the shoulder, and then dodged back as the man swung around, hefting the axe. "Friend," he said. "If you have nothing particular in mind," he said, "perhaps you'd like to come along with me."

"You got some idea what to do about all this?" the man asked.

Peter nodded.

"All right, then—I'm with you."

"Where to?" Margaret asked.

Peter considered. "I think the most important thing is to get the ship under way again. If I'm right and there's another ship out there looking for us, we should make it harder for them to find us. Then we've only got the thirty or so attackers already on board to deal with." He took her arm, and hesitated. "I'm not sure where to tell you to wait where you'll be safe."

"I'm not waiting anywhere," she said firmly. "I'm coming with you. Besides, there's no place that's any safer than any other place, as far as I know."

"But there are some places that are certainly more dangerous."

"I'm coming with you."

* * *

Colonel Moran was in the lead as they moved cautiously down the corridor and through a door to the upper promenade deck. It was almost nine o'clock, and night had fallen with its usual thump. The darkness on deck was interrupted only by light spilling from a few portholes and an occasional dim oil lamp on a bracket marking a door or ladder. The electrical lights, it seemed, were limited to a few areas of the ship, and the generator was not run continuously.

Moran paused and turned as they reached a ladder going down. "So far, so good," he said. "Not a soul in sight. What's the plan?"

"Downstairs," Moriarty said. "Our attackers must be spread thinly about the ship. General St. Yves's Lancers were probably surprised in their sleeping quarters and somehow confined. If we could get to them, we might be able to do something."

"Their weapons are all under lock and key in the guardroom," Moran said. "That must be the first place our adversaries, whoever they are, secured. They may have taken the guns for themselves, which would present us with a pretty problem."

"I think I'd best leave you here and go on for'ard," the mummer said, "and contribute my mite to the success of our little venture."

"What are you going to be doing?" Colonel Moran asked.

"Throwing statues overboard," the mummer told him.

"What? Whatever for?"

"Ask 'im," said the mummer, pointing a thumb at Moriarty.

Moran turned to look at him, but the professor shook his head. "Later," he said. "No time now." And, as if to emphasize his words, another single gunshot sounded from somewhere below them.

TWENTY-THREE

THE GATHERING STORM

How pleasant it is, at the end of the day,
No follies to have to repent;
But reflect on the past, and be able to say,
That my time has been properly spent.

JANE TAYLOR

Pin and his henchmen rounded the corner of the passageway and came on deck just in time to see Moriarty and Moran pass under the dim oil lamp hanging over the ladder to the lower promenade deck.

"No one else around," whispered Cooley. "What do you suppose they're up to?"

"Meeting up with their pals, no doubt," said the Codger, "and seeing about removing the gold."

"We will creep after them," Pin whispered, "and see what they do."

"Creep it is," the Artful Codger whispered back hoarsely.

* * *

Moriarty pressed a stud on the head of his cane when they reached the bottom of the ladder, twisted the gold ring connecting it to the body, and pulled out the eighteen-inch-long slender steel blade thus concealed. The body of the cane, freed from its stiffening sword, was a flexible yew staff with a lead weight at the bottom, a dangerous if not mortal weapon in its own right. "Take your choice," he told Colonel Moran, "saber or cosh."

"As you reminded me recently," Moran told him. "I have a certain fondness for bashing people about the head. Cosh it is."

Moriarty handed him the length of yew. "A gentle tap will render your foe unconscious," he told Moran. "A heavy swing to the head will kill."

"Clever," commented Moran, swishing the end of the stick around speculatively.

Two men and a woman came around a corner of the deck and stopped when they saw Moriarty and Moran. "You're Professor Moriarty," said the tall, slender man. The other man, Moriarty noted, was one of the ship's crew, and he was hefting a fire axe.

"I am," Moriarty acknowledged. He peered into the dark. "And I believe you and this young lady accompanied us on our visit to Elephanta, correct?"

"That's right. Peter Collins at your service. And this is Margaret St. Yves." The two of them stepped forward.

"The general's daughter?" asked Moran.

"That's right," she acknowledged.

"I admire your father," Moran told her. "Fine officer. Pukka sahib."

"Thank you," said Margaret. "I've always found him rather admirable myself."

A distant shot echoed faintly past them, and then another.

"No time for reminiscence now," Colonel Moran said, holding the length of cane under his arm like a swagger stick and glaring at some unseen object in the distance. "Battle, murder, and sudden death—that's what's on the menu. The next hour should separate the dogs from the puppies!"

Peter and Margaret turned to look at him in wonder, but he didn't notice.

"Unfortunately, the colonel's right," Moriarty said. "Although he doesn't phrase it in the way I—or anyone else in the known world—would. And we'd best get to it. How did you people get out of the ballroom?"

Peter explained about the hole they had chopped through the wall on the port side of the deck and the stream of people who were even now escaping from it.

Moriarty nodded. "That will add to the confusion, which is all to the good."

A green flare streamed up into the sky from somewhere on the upper deck and burst high in the air.

"That's not a good thing," Peter said, watching the green ball of fire slowly descend into the sea.

"There must be a ship following us," Moriarty said. "It's probably trying to find us even now."

"That's what I thought," Peter said. "My idea is to make our way to the bridge and try to get the ship going again."

Moriarty shook his head. "Won't work," he said. "Come with us."

"Why won't it work?" Peter asked, "They've got to be spread pretty thin. They can't have many men up there." He exhibited his small pistol. "And I should be able to take out a couple of them, for starters."

"They almost certainly control the engine room also," Moriarty said. "Your signaling to resume speed from the bridge will only alert them to their new problem."

"Well, sir," Margaret said, "do you have a better idea?"

"I believe so," Moriarty told them. "The guardroom for the Lancers is on a lower level by the gold vault, and it holds the rifles and bayonets for the whole force. I believe that the occasional gunfire we hear is a sign that it is being assaulted but has not yet fallen. If the villains had the guns, I believe we'd either hear a lot more gunfire or a lot less, depending. We should attempt to rescue it before our opponents, whoever they are, get the weapons."

"Phansigar," said Margaret.

Moriarty turned to her. "Excuse me?"

"Our unseen enemy," Margaret said. "We believe they're Phansigar."

"Damn!" said Colonel Moran. "Excuse my language, miss. Thuggees—I should have guessed!"

"Thuggees," Moriarty mused. "Phansigar. I've read about them, of course, but I thought they disappeared forty years ago."

"Nothing that evil—and that successful—ever disappears," said Moran.

"I'm afraid he's right," Peter said. "We heard they were possibly active again, and here they are."

"We?" asked Moran.

"I'm with the DSI," Peter told him.

"The Department, eh? Good chaps. I knew some of your people in Afghanistan. Eric Leakirk. Young chap. Dark hair. Blank stare. Smarter than he looked. Had a good seat on a camel."

Peter shook his head. "Don't think I know him," he said.

"Save that for later," Moriarty interrupted. "Are you with us or not?"

"We should try to get something to fight with," said Peter. "I have a two-shot derringer pistol, but nothing else."

"I have this," said the seaman, hefting his axe. He pointed toward the lifeboat tied down at the edge of the deck. "And each of them lifeboats has a flare gun with eight or ten shells in a watertight compartment abaft."

"Good thought," said Moriarty. "What's your name, seaman?"

"A.B. Hickscroft, sir."

"Well, able-bodied Seaman Hickscroft, I'm Professor Moriarty, this is Colonel Moran, and we're pleased to have you with us. You, too, Collins, and Miss St. Yves."

Those spoken to murmured "Thank you," and "Right on." None of them seemed to object or think it odd that Moriarty had assumed de facto command of their little party.

"It's time to get on with it," Colonel Moran growled. "Are you ready?"

"Just let me near them, sir," Seaman Hickscroft rumbled.

"That's the spirit!" Moriarty said. "Mr. Collins, do you want to retrieve the flare gun from that lifeboat?"

"I do indeed," Peter said, and suited action to word, opening a corner of the canvas covering the lifeboat and slipping into the boat like a well-greased ferret. A few seconds later he emerged. "I wondered why the rope was undone in this corner," he said. "Look what—or should I say who—I found." He ducked into the boat again, and reappeared with the head of Lady Priscilla. He pulled and heaved, and the rest of her appeared. She had been manhandled, tied up, and gagged, and was now bruised, angry, and very irritable, which they discovered as soon as Peter pulled the gag off.

"Thank God you found me," she said, spitting the remains of the gag from her mouth while Peter was busy releasing her from the rope that was wound around her like spider webbing around a fly. "I've never been treated like that before in my life. In my life! Trussed up like a sack of God-knows-what and tossed into a lifeboat. And by native stewards! I have no idea what they think they were doing, but when my father hears about this—prison is too good for them—they should be flogged!"

Peter helped her out of the lifeboat, and then dove back inside to emerge less than a minute later with a flare gun in one hand and a tin box of extra flares in the other. "It's not lethal, I think," he said, dropping back down to the deck, "but it should slow them down."

"Lady Priscilla, how did this happen to you?" Margaret asked, going over and putting her own scarf around her cabin mate's quivering shoulders.

"I was doing that trick, you know, with Mr. Mamarum, and when I arrived outside the ballroom door—"

"How did you do that?" Margaret asked.

"Does it matter?" she asked. "I'm not supposed to tell."

"Actually, it might matter," Moriarty said.

"Well..." Lady Priscilla said. "I suppose.... Do you remember when Mamarum and his boy brought that rack full of swords out? Well, he put it between the basket and the audience and I scrambled out the top of the basket while you couldn't see me."

"Come on!" Margaret said. "That rack wasn't solid. I could see right between the swords."

"You *thought* you could," Lady Priscilla told her. "But when they set it down, they released a rolled-up strip of canvas fastened to the rear that was painted to look like the back of the set. And I crawled behind it and put on a black robe and cinched it so it would look like a dress, if you didn't look too closely. When that crowd of people came up to examine the swords, I joined the crowd. When they left the stage, I left the stage with them, and I kept going until I was outside the doors."

"Gor!" said Seaman Hickscroft. "Who would'a thought?"

"And," Lady Priscilla continued, getting down to the part that was the source of her aggrievement, "no sooner did I step outside the door than these two stewards grabbed me, stuffed a wad of cotton in my mouth, and tied me up. Then they returned to what they had been doing, which was securing the doors to the ballroom with strips of wood and screws and wedges and whatnots, leaving me tied up in a corner. When they finished with the doors, they jabbered at each other for a minute, then one of them tossed me over his shoulder like a sack of flour and took me over to the lifeboat and threw me in."

"How fortunate!" said Professor Moriarty.

"Excuse me?" Lady Priscilla backed away from him, bobbing her head like an irate pigeon.

"My lady, had it not been for the fortunate circumstance of your early departure from the room," Moriarty said, smiling at her as though she'd purposely done something clever, "and your friend the officer's distress at your disappearance, then we should all still be in the ballroom watching amateur clog dancing, and by the time we emerged—or found out we couldn't emerge—it would have been too late."

"Too late for what?" Lady Priscilla asked.

Margaret explained to her as quickly as possible what had been happening.

"Well, I'll be—" Lady Priscilla said.

Another green flare went up from the bridge of the ship.

"That other ship must be having trouble finding us," Moriarty commented. "We'd better get on with this before it does. We have at most thirty of them to deal with now, and if we manage to release the Lancers and their weapons we'll have a good shot at it. But there's no way to tell how many are aboard the ship." He turned to Margaret. "I don't know where to tell you and Lady Priscilla to stay until this is all over," he said. "Perhaps you should return to your stateroom."

"I think I'll go around to the other side—the port side?—of the deck and see if I can find Lieutenant Welles," Lady Priscilla said. "He's very good in situations, if he has someone to tell him what to do."

"Very well, my lady," Moriarty agreed.

"As for me," Margaret said, "were I to return to my stateroom I should go crazy wondering what was happening. And have palpitations at every sound. I'm not sure what palpitations are, but I'm sure I would have them."

"You can't talk her out of coming with us," Peter told Moriarty, "and we'd best not waste time trying." He held out his little two-shot pistol to Margaret. "Do you know how to use this?" he asked.

"Am I my father's daughter?" asked Margaret. "I've been firing sidearms since I was six years old. I'm also a dead shot with a forty-pound bow, and I can handle an épée reasonably well."

"A sure recipe for domestic bliss," Peter said, handing her the pistol. "Watch out for this one. It's a single-action with a light hammer pull and a hair trigger."

"This way," Moriarty said, leading them along the deck to the next stairs down.

* * *

The Artful Codger, who had been stretched out along one side of the ladder between the decks, his head lower than his feet, to hear what Moriarty and his minions were planning, pulled himself up and twisted his head from side to side to relieve a neck cramp that had overtaken him while he was unable to move. "They're going down to the guardroom to try to free the guards and get their weapons," he reported to Pin. "It sounds like they're getting ready to fight the Thuggees, so maybe they're not on their side after all."

"The what?" Pin asked. "They're going to fight the what?"

"Thuggees," the Codger repeated. "That's what the other bloke called them. He said it several times. Thuggees."

"I thought they were all killed off many years ago," said Pin.

"That's what the professor said. But apparently they ain't. Who are they, then, when they're at home?"

"A vicious gang of murderers. They made a religion out of theft and murder."

"I got some acquaintances like that," commented Cooley the Pup.

Pin considered. "No profit in staying here," he said. "We'd best follow along behind them and see which way the wind blows. Perhaps Moriarty and I are both trying to prevent the gold from being removed by some third party."

"Now, wouldn't that be something?" commented the Artful Codger.

"Teaming up with the professor," said Cooley. "Now, that would be—"

Dr. Pin Dok Low glared at him.

"—wrong," he finished hastily. "That would be wrong. Interesting, but wrong."

* * *

Lieutenant McPride gave one last pull and the inner rim of the porthole frame came free of the wall, sprang from McPride's hand, and bounced around the room, narrowly missing General St. Yves. "Sorry, sir," he said. He dropped the twisted and bent spoon he had been using and pushed at the porthole itself. It resisted his efforts at first, but then budged slowly and grudgingly outward.

Lieutenant McPride fell back, exhausted, and Lieutenant Pinton took over for the final push. It took another few minutes before the brass porthole, mount and all, was pushed out and fell with a clatter to the deck below.

Pinton stepped back and examined what he and McPride had wrought. "It still seems a mite small," he said.

"I think you're the, ah, slenderest of us, Lieutenant," St. Yves said. "If you can't make it through, then none of us can."

"I'll give it a try, sir," Pinton said. "If we could move the desk over to the hole so I don't have to balance in midair while I'm trying to pull myself through, it might help."

They pushed the desk over and moved all the papers, a box of cigars, and a small ornate jar of snuff off the desktop. Lieutenant Pinton took his jacket off, climbed up on the desk, and stuck his head through the porthole. Then he backed out again. "It's my shoulders, sir," he said apologetically. "I always thought of them as being too narrow, but now it seems they're not narrow enough."

"Are we b-bereft of options, then?" asked General St. Yves. "There must be some way we can escape this confounded room."

"Perhaps if I put one arm through first..." said Pinton, considering the hole. He stretched out his right arm and thrust it through the hole, followed by his head. "By God, sir," he called from the outside. "I think this might do it!"

Pinton continued wiggling and squirming and pushing and pulling, until he succeeded in getting his body through the hole and fell, shoulder first, on the promenade deck below. He stood up and peered back inside. "I've done it, sir!" he announced.

"So we see," said St. Yves. "Can you—"

"Yes, sir; I'll go right around and see about freeing the door."

"You're cut," St. Yves said, seeing blood running down the lieutenant's arm.

"Nothing, sir. Just a scrape. Be right there, sir." And he ran around to the corridor.

A few moments later those inside the room heard some thumping, scraping, and cursing from outside the door, and then it was opened. "It was a bolt, sir," said Lieutenant Pinton, hefting a three-inch-long bolt.

Captain Iskansen was the first out the door. With a "Got to get to the bridge. Thank you, Lieutenant," he was off down the deck and up the nearest ladder.

"Well, gentlemen," said General St. Yves. "We'd better go and see how much damage these chaps have been able to do, and set it to rights."

"Yes, sir," his lieutenants said.

"And perhaps do a bit of damage of our own," added Lieutenant McPride.

TWENTY-FOUR

THE MARQUIS OF QUEENSBERRY DOESN'T RULE HERE

I 'listed at home for a lancer,
Oh who would not sleep with the brave?
AE.HOUSMAN

A battle was being waged between six Lancers and an indefinite number of Thuggees on the deck holding the gold vault. A slow battle, a battle in miniature, with no bugles sounding the charge, no roar of cannon, no advance at full gallop with lances down, no shouted orders to dismount and form a skirmish line; but deadly nonetheless.

Six of the Lancers were in the guardroom, crouching behind an overturned table in the doorway two at a time, peeking out at the corridor, and firing their Martini-Henry carbines at whatever moved. One of their number—the guard who had been on duty at the far end of the corridor—now lay dead at his post, a Thuggee scarf tight around his neck.

About a dozen Phansigar were blocking both ends of the corridor, hiding behind an overturned couch at one end and a barricade of fifty-pound bags of rice at the other. The six of the Duke's Own were not interested in fighting their way out of the guardroom. It was more important to remain and keep the guns and ammunition stored there out of the hands of their opponents.

All was quiet when Moriarty and his passel arrived at the disputed deck. They rounded a corner in the corridor and saw several men in stewards' white crouching behind an overturned couch about twenty feet in front of them, exchanging shots and insulting remarks with some of the Duke of Moncreith's Own in the guardroom. The electrical lights were still shining brightly in front of the gold vault, and the outer door to the vault was still open. As yet there was no sign that the Thuggees had made any attempt to remove the gold, or even open the inner door. Moriarty waved his group back out of sight around the corner before the Thuggees noticed them.

"Things seem to be at an impasse," Moran commented. "The enemy's advance has stalled."

"It'll pick up again if that ship gets here," said Peter. "If there is a ship."

"It's the only thing that makes sense," Moriarty said. "Which means we'd better do something with reasonable speed."

"Any ideas?" Colonel Moran asked, tight-lipped. "I don't fancy advancing into superior firepower. A flanking attack would be preferable. Sneak up on them."

"How do you sneak up on them in a corridor?" Peter asked.

"The professor's the tactician," Moran told him. "Ask him. I just do as I'm ordered."

"I'd like to thank you for that profound statement of confidence," Moriarty said. "But you're the military man. What did they teach you at Sandhurst besides looting and commissary?"

"Artillery," Moran told him. "I can plot a trajectory with the best of 'em."

"Very useful," Moriarty agreed.

"Speed?" Margaret reminded them.

The door to the deck behind them swung open, and they whirled and pointed various weapons at the three men who came through until they saw that the newcomers were not Phansigar.

"Perhaps we might be of some use," said the tallest of the three. "I am Dr. Pin Dok Low. These two gentlemen are my assistants."

Moriarty silently examined the three men, pausing for a long moment to look hard at Pin Dok Low. For a second he seemed about to say something, and then he didn't. Colonel Moran thought that

Moriarty looked vaguely puzzled, except that was clearly impossible. Professor Moriarty was never puzzled by anything, no way.

"Welcome to our little farrago," said Peter Collins. "You don't happen to have a small cannon anywhere about your person, do you?"

"My walking stick," said Pin, displaying the gold-headed object in question, "has a powerful air gun concealed in its shaft. Unfortunately, it takes entirely too long to reload and pump up the air pressure to make it more than a one-shot weapon. However"—he reached down and took the gold-banded tip off the bottom of the stick—"we may as well have the benefit of that one shot."

"Well." Peter turned back to Moriarty and asked the inevitable question. "What's our plan?"

"I suggest," said Moriarty, "that we rush them in the dark."

"What dark?" Moran asked. "Those damn electrical lights are as bright as the midday sun. Brighter."

"Notice the conduit that runs along the ceiling by the right-hand wall," Moriarty said, pointing to the long tube, which had been painted to blend in with the light green of the ceiling. "Unless I am mistaken, it holds the two wires necessary to supply electricity to the lamps. If we cut the wires, it will suddenly be very dark."

"Say," said Cooley the Pup. "Won't the electricity fall out?"

Moriarty looked at him for a long moment, and then said, "No."

"Make it dark," Peter said. "And I'll fire a flare at them. And then we'll go."

"Good thinking," Colonel Moran agreed.

One of the Phansigar in the corridor yelled an urgent call in liquid and strident syllables. Another replied, longer and louder.

Moran peered around the corner and then pulled back as a bullet whizzed by. "The beggars are up to something. I wonder what they're saying."

"Something about a bomb," Margaret told him. "Rolling a bomb, I think."

"Rolling?"

"I think so. It sounded like he yelled, 'Get back, something... something... roll the bomb.'"

"Glad you speak the language," Moriarty said. "We'd better get out there."

"Let's do it," said Moran.

"You," Moriarty said, pointing to Margaret, "will stay here. If anyone rounds the corner and it isn't one of us, shoot him. Can you do that?"

"I think so," she said.

"It isn't as easy to shoot someone as is popularly imagined," Moriarty told her. "Physically it is not difficult—you point the gun and pull the trigger. But the mind rebels against taking a life. But if one of them does get away from us he will try to bring reinforcements, and he will either go through you or around you. He must not succeed."

"I'll do what I must," Margaret said, clutching the little derringer tightly in her hand.

"So you will," said Moriarty. "Well, come my friends. This should be over very quickly, one way or another."

Another shot came from inside the guardroom.

Moriarty reached up with the tip of his sword-cane and pried the conduit away from the wall. "Are you ready, Mr. Collins?"

Peter opened the flare gun and dropped a cartridge into the breach, slammed it closed, and then flattened himself against the wall and peered around the corner. "All set," he said.

"Colonel Moran?"

"Reminds me of the Pawamatti campaign," the colonel said, swishing his loaded cane through the air and then crouching by the corner. "On a smaller scale, of course. I would suggest a bit of loud yelling and screaming as we advance. It disheartens your adversaries, or so it is believed."

"Screaming it is," Peter agreed.

"Dr., ah, Pin?" Moriarty asked.

Pin looked at his two sidemen. The Artful Codger adjusted his knuckle dusters and nodded. Cooley the Pup held his knife at belly level and jabbed experimentally. "I think, in the dark…" he said.

"We're set to go," Pin said.

"One… two… three… !" Moriarty whispered. On "three" he twisted his sword in the conduit and severed the wire. A bright spark arced out from the tip of his blade, and then all was black.

Peter threw himself out past the bend in the corridor and fired the flare gun, sending a streak of red flame bouncing along from one wall to the other, off the ceiling and floor, until it lodged in a sack of rice on the far side of the corridor, past the guardroom door, and burst into a bright red ball of fire. While Peter paused to reload the flare gun, he felt rather than saw his companions race by him down the corridor. One of them—Peter thought it was Colonel Moran—let out a great cry of, "God for Harry, England, and St. George!" Someone else was yelling something that sounded like, "Bullocks and mare's blood!" but might have been something else.

The closest group of Thuggees were able to let off two shots and two weirdly high-pitched screams before they went down under the sudden onslaught. The group of white-clad marauders farther down the corridor fired a few rounds into the mass of fighting men, not seeming to care who they hit, and then rushed forward to join in the melee, screaming their own screams and brandishing long, curved knives that gleamed wickedly in the light of the single oil lamp that was produced by one of the guards, who was peering out from the guardroom doorway.

Margaret, hardly knowing what she did or why, followed along slightly behind her companions, inching along the wall to keep out of their way, the little derringer held before her like a talisman.

Several more shots rang out, and Moriarty found himself grappling with a man who seemed intent on cutting his nose off. The professor went rapidly through the four baritsu codas of Standing Frog, Reaping Rice Farmer, Leaping Lizard, and Death Comes Calmly, suffering a cut on the shoulder before he was able to twist around and insert the point of his sword neatly between the man's third and fourth rib under the heart. His antagonist sighed loudly, threw his knife heedlessly into the air, and sank to the floor.

One of the Thuggees leaped onto the couch, arm upraised, to throw a round black object into the guardroom. Margaret raised her little pistol, squinted over the barrel, and squeezed the trigger. The man fell forward, and the round black object dropped from his hand

and rolled toward Margaret, sparks hissing from a short wick sticking out from the side. Without pausing to think, Margaret thrust the gun into her belt and swooped up the black object, which felt hard and cold and unaccountably heavy in her hand. She pinched the wick between her fingers, but it burned and stung and refused to go out. Time slowed down and it seemed as if she were moving through molasses as she took six steps back to the turn in the corridor, pitched the object as hard as she could toward the far door, and ducked back. There was a *thump* as it landed and then... nothing.

Margaret slid to the floor as though her muscles were made of rubber, her heart beating faster than it ever had before. Time continued to move slowly for her until what seemed like many minutes later—in reality it was but a few seconds—there came a great, sharp explosion from around the corner, a bright flash of light, and then a palpable acrid smoke billowed up and filled the corridor.

At that moment the six lancers who had been trapped in the guardroom erupted from the door and joined the melee. The affair was over in five more minutes and nine thuggees were either dead, wounded, unconscious, or captured.

In addition to Moriarty's wound, the Artful Codger had been shot through the hand, Peter had a badly scraped shin, although it was unclear how he had achieved this distinction, and Dr. Pin Dok Low, having been grazed by a bullet from somebody's gun, was lying, unconscious, on the corridor floor.

Moriarty knelt by Pin and examined him carefully for wounds. "He seems to have been knocked out," he said. "The scalp wound is superficial, and I can't find any further signs of injury." He leaned close to Pin's head and said clearly: "Holmes! Holmes, can you hear me?"

"What's that?" demanded the Artful Codger. "Holmes? What Holmes is that? Whom the blazes do you suppose he is?"

TWENTY-FIVE

WHO IS THIS MAN?

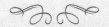

Rise! For the day is passing,
And you lie dreaming on;
The others have buckled their armour,
And forth to the fight are gone.
A place in the ranks awaits you,
Each man has some part to play;
the Past and the Future are nothing,
In the face of the stern To-day.
ADELAIDE ANN PROCTER

There was a loud clatter from the stairway at the far end of the corridor and thirty of the Duke of Moncreith's Own Highland Lancers emerged up the stairs at a gallop. At their head, brandishing a sword in one hand, a pistol in the other, and with the cry of battle on his lips, was Brigadier General Sir Edward Basilberg St. Yves, Bart., I.C., D.S.O. It took him a moment to realize the altered situation in front of him, with those Thuggees left alive being tied up with their own scarves. He tried to stop the charge, but the rush of troops behind him carried him along past the door of the guardroom before those behind had passed the order to halt far enough back for it to succeed.

"Congratulations, sir," said Colonel Moran, coming to attention and giving the general a respectful salute. "I see you've managed to free your men."

"Yes, ah, that's s-so," St. Yves stammered with proper British reserve and humility. "N-nothing much to it, actually. We managed to s-sneak up on the blighters." He looked around at the hodgepodge of couch cushions, sacks of rice, and men scattered about the corridor floor. "What's b-been happening here?"

"We have carried the day, sir," Colonel Moran told him. "Carried the day."

"Not yet," Professor Moriarty reminded them, rising from beside the still-unconscious form of the man who had called himself Dr. Pin Dok Low. "We must prepare for the inevitable invasion, and we must do so at once."

St. Yves gave a will-this-never-be-done-with? sigh and asked, "What b-bloody invasion?"

Margaret, who had been sitting with her head down in a dark section of corridor, stood up just then and said, "Daddy," in a little voice. The small pistol was still in her hand.

St. Yves's eyes widened. "Margaret, my dear," he said, thrusting his sword back into its scabbard and striding over to her. "My dear child. How are you? How did you get here? You haven't been harmed?"

"Oh, Daddy," she cried, clutching the front of his uniform jacket and holding on to him as though he were a life preserver in a stormy sea. "Daddy, I think I've killed a man!"

St. Yves paused, frozen for a second, not sure what to say. Best to be casual, unconcerned, he decided. "Come, now; with that little contraption?" he said with a slight laugh, taking the pistol from her grasp and shoving it into his pocket.

"It was one of the Phansigar," she told him. "He was throwing a bomb and I shot him. I had resolved to do so, but I didn't know that I'd feel—this way—afterward."

"Where did this happen?" he asked.

She pointed. "Over there," she said.

"Well." He considered. "Let's go see what damage you did."

"I'd rather not," she said.

"All right, you stay here," he told her. "I'll go look."

Peter Collins, who had been standing mutely next to them, joined St. Yves as he examined the man. A minute later they both returned. "You didn't kill the blighter," her father told her. "And what you did was extremely brave—throwing the bomb and all."

"You only wounded him in the thigh," Peter said. "I've tied it off to stop the bleeding."

"He'll live to hang," St. Yves said grimly.

"Oh, thank goodness!" said Margaret.

St. Yves turned to Moriarty. "What's this invasion you speak of?"

Moriarty explained to him their theory about the Thuggee ship that must be right now trying to locate *The Empress of India* to retrieve the gold.

"Yes," St. Yves agreed. "That must be their plan. There weren't enough of them here to transport the gold, and they don't seem prepared to open the vault. They must be expecting further assistance." He hopped up on the overturned couch. "Men!" he called.

"Tenn-hup!" came the bellow of a sergeant from somewhere amid the milling troop, and the men snapped to various forms of rigid attention.

"Each of you pick up your weapon from the guardroom along with ten—no, twenty—rounds of ammunition and form up on the port side of 'A' deck," St. Yves told them.

"Excuse me, sir," a ruddy-faced corporal said, making a quarter turn to face his general, "but which side is that?"

"The side you'll find me on," St. Yves told them. "Now hop to!"

"Troop!" the sergeant called. "Get your weapons on the double and report! Dismissed!"

A rapid but orderly exodus began as the men grabbed their Martini-Henry carbines and ammunition packets from the guardroom and followed St. Yves up the outside ladder.

Pin Dok Low groaned and pushed himself up to a sitting position. "Where the devil am I?" he demanded, looking around. "What am I doing here?"

Moriarty squatted down next to him. "You're on *The Empress of India*," he told him. "A passenger vessel of the Anglo-Asian Star steamship line, bound from Calcutta to London by way of Bombay and Port Said. Do you know your name?"

"What do you mean?" Pin asked. He paused for a minute, looking puzzled, and then his face cleared. "My name is Holmes—Sherlock Holmes." He shook his head and peered at his interlocutor. "Moriarty! It's you! I should have known you'd be up to some devilry or other. What have you done to me?"

Cooley the Pup leaned over the sitting man. "Ooo the deuce did you say you were, mate?" he demanded.

"I'm Sherlock..." Holmes groaned, held his head, and looked up. "Cooley the Pup," he exclaimed. "What are you doing here?"

"I might ask you the same thing," the Pup growled. "Sherlock Holmes, are you? A fine story you've been handing us these weeks!"

"And what is it you've done with the real Pin Dok Low?" the Artful Codger added from where Margaret St. Yves was doing a professional job of bandaging his hand. "I knew you didn't look like no Chinaman."

Holmes looked away from his two recent confederates and glared at Moriarty. "What have you been up to?" he demanded. "Why are these people here? Why am I here?"

"As near as I can tell," Moriarty said, "you've followed me across two continents and half of another. Why this should be, I have no idea. Pin Dok Low, is it? How's your head?"

Holmes raised his hand to the wound, winced, and lowered it again. "I saw a flash of light," he remembered, "and then—"

"You were shot," Moriarty told him. "A near miss. Or perhaps I should say a near hit. The bullet just grazed you above the ear. The left ear."

Holmes was silent for a moment. And then he put a finger to his nose and said, "Thuggees."

"That's right," the Artful Codger agreed.

"I remember now," said Holmes. "Thuggees—the ship—gold—the Bank of England—Watson! I must send a telegram to poor old Watson—and my brother, Mycroft."

"Hard to do," Moriarty reminded him. "We're in the middle of the Arabian Sea. What do you remember?"

Holmes thought hard for a minute, staring down at the deck and rubbing his head, wincing once when he inadvertently ran his hand over the fresh wound over his ear. He looked up at Moriarty and grinned ruefully. "You were right," he said. "I was pursuing you. And you were—are—after the gold shipment. Are you not?"

"And you and your, ah, companions, raced from London all the way to Bombay in order to board this ship and prevent me from, ah, acquiring the gold?"

"Well," Holmes said, doing his best not to look embarrassed, "you see, I was after it myself."

"Really!"

"That is, Pin Dok Low was determined to acquire it. And I was Pin Dok Low."

"I'm shocked," Moriarty declared. "And I note that even as Pin Dok Low you did not let up in your continued efforts to harass, even to harm me."

"I did?" Holmes asked.

"Your agents," Moriarty reminded him. "In various locations throughout Europe. I was shot at, bashed at, and pushed in front of moving vehicles."

"That doesn't sound like me," Holmes said, frowning. "But it does sound awfully like Dr. Pin Dok Low." He smiled. "The doctor did have some good in him after all!"

"Very amusing," said Professor Moriarty.

Margaret came over and knelt by Holmes. "Let me see your head," she said. "I found a bottle of MacGregor's Eight-Year-Old in the guardroom which I'll use to cleanse the wound. If you'd like to take a couple of quick gulps before I begin, it might serve to deaden the pain."

"No, thank you, miss," Holmes said. "My head is spinning around quite enough without the aid of MacGregor's Eight-Year-Old."

Holmes gritted his teeth and stared intently at the far wall while Margaret poured a couple of jiggers of Scotch over the wound and patted it dry with some clean cotton bandaging, which she then tied around his head. "That should do it," she said, standing up to admire her handiwork.

Holmes thanked her and attempted to push himself to his feet. After two tries he slumped back down. "Perhaps I should remain here a bit longer," he said. A volley of gunfire sounded from on deck, and then another and another. Then the gunfire became sporadic, as each man reserved his fire for a visible enemy.

"The missing ship has arrived," commented Moriarty.

"We should go up there," Peter said, shoving a clip into the magazine of the carbine he had just snatched from the guardroom.

"We'll join you shortly," Moriarty said. He and Margaret helped Holmes into the guardroom and onto one of the wooden chairs.

"You're really Mr. Sherlock Holmes, the detective?" Margaret asked.

"I believe so," he said. "Although I haven't been for the past few months. The mind is more of a frail and fallible thing than I would have thought previous to this experience."

"Let's hear it," Moriarty said grimly. "Why have you been following me about disguised as a Chinaman dressed as a middle-European businessman?"

"That's who I believed I was," Holmes explained. "Tell me, have you some nefarious scheme to make off with the gold? And if not, what are you doing here?"

"I'll ask the questions for the next little bit," Moriarty told him. "However; no, I have no plans to acquire the gold. As to what I'm doing here, that will have to wait."

"Why should you think that Professor Moriarty is after the gold?" Margaret asked.

"Because he is Professor Moriarty," Holmes explained.

"Let us not wander off into bright byways of speculation," Moriarty said. "What do you mean, you thought you were Pin Dok Low? Is it not just one of your less puerile disguises?"

Holmes blew a thin whistle of air between his pursed lips. "Let me try to clarify my thoughts," he said. "I was asked by the director of the Board of Governors of the Bank of England to help safeguard a shipment of gold." He paused and looked around. "Presumably this shipment of gold."

Moriarty arched an eyebrow. "Yes?" he said. "And then you went down a manhole into the London sewers."

"How did you know that?" asked Holmes.

"Your amanuensis Watson told me," said Moriarty.

"Really?" Holmes shook his head. "I must hear your end of these events after I narrate my own," he said.

"You shall," Moriarty promised.

"I descended into the depths of the London drains to ascertain whether it was possible to violate the vaults of the Bank of England from below," Holmes said.

"So," said Moriarty. "And is it?"

"I never had the chance to find out," Holmes said. "And," he added thoughtfully, "had I, I would keep it to myself."

"What happened?" Margaret asked.

"There was a great onrush of water which I was unable to avoid," Holmes said. "It swept me up and carried me along. For some time I fought it, trying to get my footing or cling on to some projection, but I was unable to do so. Then the back of my head collided with some hard object, and the next thing I remember is lying on a concrete shelf about two feet above the water, which must have deposited me there and then receded."

"Why, you might have been killed!" Margaret said. "That's miraculous!"

"I would have forgone the miracle if I could have avoided the wetting," Holmes told her.

He paused in the telling of his tale and they all strained to listen to the sounds from above. Once again there was the deep explosive crack of a coordinated volley of rifle shots, and then another, and then silence.

"I would judge those are parting shots," said Moran from the doorway. "I believe the Thuggee ship has been beaten off."

The ragged sound of cheering came through the porthole.

"It does sound as if you're right, Colonel," said Moriarty.

"I'll stack the carbines," Moran said, and headed off down the corridor.

"So," Moriarty continued, turning his attention back to Holmes, "how did you get from a London sewer to *The Empress of India*?"

"I awoke with no idea of who I was," Holmes told him. "Indeed, I had no idea of who I really was until just a few minutes ago when I found myself on the floor out there with you bending over me. Truly a shock—until I began to remember."

"Remember?"

"What had happened in between the sewer in London and the corridor floor outside this door," Holmes said.

"After I had recovered sufficiently to rise from the shelf I looked for the nearest exit from the sewer. I crawled through a large overflow pipe that let out above the Thames and found myself at the foot of Watting Road. I recognized the location, and some bits of memory came back to me. Unfortunately, the small memory I recovered set me on the wrong path. I had a room above a grog shop on Watting Road which I used on occasion to don the appearance and assume the personality of Dr. Pin Dok Low, a nefarious Chinese criminal. Of my own invention, let me add. I am the only Pin Dok Low that ever there was. In this guise I had been able to penetrate the London underworld in search of information. What I remembered, on finding myself on Watting Road, was that I was a criminal called Dr. Pin Dok Low. Far from realizing that I was actually Sherlock Holmes, I believed him to be my deadliest enemy."

"You poor man," said Margaret.

"I went up to my room and shed my clothes, which were soaking wet and smelled of—various unpleasant odors. I bathed myself as best I could in the large basin I kept for that purpose and transformed myself into Pin. I then went for a long walk to clear my head, disposing of the clothes I had been wearing in a dustbin somewhere along the way."

"Didn't the act of becoming this Chinaman—the necessity of performing a transformation to assume the identity—tell you that you weren't really him?" asked Moriarty.

"I suppose it did," Holmes agreed. "I knew I was someone playing the part of Pin Dok Low, as it were, but you see, I had no idea of who that other someone might be. So I stayed with the identity I was sure of."

"An Oriental villain."

"And one with the knowledge that someone was trying to steal a fortune in gold—it was the one thing I remembered. And I assumed—being a villain—that the potential thief was I. All else followed from that one mistaken assumption."

"So you came on board to steal the gold?" Moriarty asked.

"No. That was to happen later. I came on board to prevent you from stealing it first."

"Mr. Holmes!" said Margaret. "How can you say such things about the professor?"

"Sometimes I wonder," said Holmes.

Margaret rose. "What time is it?" she asked.

Moriarty pulled his pocket watch out and opened it. "A little past two in the morning, Bombay time," he said. "Which I assume is still the right time, unless we've already passed the seventieth meridian east, in which case it is an hour earlier."

"I'd better go find my father," she said. "I insist upon hearing the rest of this fascinating story later. It was nice meeting you, Mr. Holmes."

"Thank you. I feel the same way myself," Holmes told her.

TWENTY-SIX

MISSING

*The eye of man hath not heard, the ear of man hath not seen, man's
hand is not able to taste, his tongue to conceive, nor his heart to
report, what my dream was.*
WILLIAM SHAKESPEARE

A large black dhow, which had been motorized with some sort
of ancient and infernally noisy engine, was nosed along the
starboard side of the *Empress*, held in place by a brace of lines that
had been thrown over the side by the faux stewards in preparation for
the assault. Thirty or so Thuggees in puffy white pantaloons and long
jackets, with red sashes around their waists and red scarves around
their heads, looking for all the world like particularly villainous extras
in a road production of *Pirates of Penzance*, came boiling up the ropes
and onto the deck. They waved scimitars and blunderbusses and one
or two Martini-Henry rifles and a brace of percussion-cap pistols, and
screamed of the greatness of Kali.

The troops of the Duke's Own assembled on the port side of the
deck and tramped in good order over to the starboard to meet the
threat. They formed a skirmish line and advanced with the stolid
fatalism that is drilled into every British soldier for four hours every
day. The deck was not wide enough to admit much of a skirmish
line, and the men would have been happier on horseback. But it is a

certainty that the horses wouldn't have enjoyed themselves at all, and besides, the few horses that were stabled belowdecks were not very adept at climbing stairs.

The British formed two ranks, kneeling and standing, and fired a volley at the Thuggees, who were no more than twenty feet away. The Thuggees advanced quickly, barely giving the soldiers time for one more volley before they closed with the British line. But those two massed volleys had ripped into them, and there were less of them now.

It was now mainly scimitar against bayonet, and there were a few minutes when the fighting could have gone either way. The forces of good and evil swayed back and forth, exchanging gunfire and grappling in hand-to-hand expressions of ill will. The troops had appeared too quickly and the Phansigar were not prepared to face them. The band of killers, although brave enough, were unused to standing up to an armed and trained opposition. Slowly they were beaten back.

When the battle had clearly turned against them, the Phansigar made for the rail and jumped, dived, or merely threw themselves overboard to a man. Some landed directly on the dhow below, but the dhow cut its lines and put on the steam and, with a great thumping and clattering, pulled out of the range of the Martini-Henry carbines popping away at whoever appeared on deck. The attackers still aboard the *Empress* dove over the side and swam, those who could swim, rapidly after the dhow. Some of them made it, but most perished in the water, refusing to grab hold of the lines lowered by the crew of the *Empress*. Two electrical carbon-arc searchlights mounted toward the bow of the *Empress* were quickly manned, but by the time the carbon rods were trimmed and adjusted and fired up, the dhow was just about out of range. And, black against the black sky and the blacker sea, it quickly disappeared into the darkness.

The wounded and dead men of the attacking party left behind numbered fourteen when they had all been assembled: eight dead and six left to be hanged when they reached port. Of the ship's crew, three were dead; of the lancers, two; and of the passengers, two: an elderly clergyman who probably died of a heart attack, and a young British bank clerk who was found with an unfired revolver in his hand and a Thuggee scarf tightened around his neck.

Captain Iskansen had all the passengers remain in their cabins while the ship's officers searched the entire ship for hiding Phansigar: They thought they had found one squeezed in behind an air shaft, but he proved to be one of the original stewards who had been too frightened to emerge.

The damage to the ship was minimal and easily repaired, and the only things that were discovered to be missing were some statuettes of dancing girls, most owned by one Albert "Mummer" Tolliver, except for one which had been the property of the Officers' Mess of the Duke of Moncreith's Own Highland Lancers. All of which, presumably, had been thrown overboard by the Thuggees in an excess of religious zeal.

"I still got a couple o' crates of them little ladies down in the hold," the mummer told the senior officers after the loss was discovered. "If you'd like, I'll be glad to replace the one what went missing with one of me own."

"We've been toasting her every evening since Sergeant Major McQuist found her back in '58. My father before me, and his father before him," said Major Sandiman, who took pride in the fact that his was the third generation of Sandimans to serve in the Duke's Own. "It will seem odd, no longer doing so. Still, with what we know now about her provenance..."

"I concur," General St. Yves said. "Remember Hiffington and the barmaid. If it ever became known that the regimental officers had been toasting the statue of a tart for thirty-odd years, we should never hear the last of it."

"None of us would be able to show his face in the Army-Navy or White's without a snicker going around the room," Colonel Morcy agreed. "On consideration," he continued, "knowing what we know now about the, ah, little Lady, perhaps it would be best were we to forgo the pleasure of her company."

"It's settled, then," St. Yves said. He turned to the mummer.

"Thank you for your offer, sir. We will not replace our missing Lady with another representation of the same, ah, goddess, no matter how close the resemblance. Perhaps if you are ever purveying brass tigers, or elephants, or kettles, we might acquire one to remind us of days gone by."

"I'll keep that in mind, General," the mummer told him. "See if I don't."

TWENTY-SEVEN

ALTERED PATTERNS

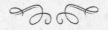

*I may tell them the mysteries that are hidden and concealed, the
wonders of the weaving of the web on which depends the perfection
and glory of the world... the wonders of the path of the celestial
ladder, one end of which rests on earth and the other by the right foot
of the Throne of Glory.*
HEIKHALOT RABBATI

It took a few days for normality to descend once again upon the
ship. Once the bodies were absented, the wounded tended for in
the ship's infirmary, the decks swabbed, the holes, gashes, dents, and
abrasions repaired or painted over, and all other outward signs of the
ordeal removed, the experience took on the quality of a bad dream for
some of the passengers, and of an exciting adventure in which they had
an opportunity to display extraordinary coolness, courage, and martial
ability to some others. At least, that's the way they planned to tell it.

"I will admit, Professor," said Colonel Moran, relaxing in the
upper deck smoking room with his feet up on the chair opposite his
own, "that for ways that are dark and for tricks that are vain, nobody
I've ever known can hold a candle to you. You got that little Lady
away from the Duke's Own with the slickness of Mamarum the Great
pulling those gold coins out of the air."

"I merely took advantage of the opportunity that presented itself," avowed Moriarty from the depths of the next chair to the left, but he looked pleased at the praise.

"Ah, but seeing opportunity where the rest of us saw only danger and confusion is what makes it a stroke of genius in my book." Moran puffed contentedly on his cigar. "While the rest of us are battling the blasted Thuggees, there is Tolliver going about throwing those statuettes overboard. All but one." He swiveled in his chair to look at the mummer, who was almost invisible—all but his nose and the tip of his cigar—sunk into the cushions of the chair in his other side. "Say!" he said. "You are sure you saved the right one, aren't you? I mean, I wouldn't want to show up at the maharaja's with a castoff of the real statue."

"What do you take me for?" protested the mummer. "The little Lady is cocooned quite nicely in layers of cotton batting, sitting in a crate holding eleven more copies of the same. But I don't think you'll have any trouble telling them apart. The real one has a certain fineness of detail which the others lack."

"You might want to leave the ship at Port Suez and take your prize right back to India," Moriarty suggested.

Moran shook his head. "Little Pook has his agents in London. I'll turn the Lady over to them, thus completing the deal. I shall accompany them back to India, of course, but if anything happens to the Lady on the return trip it'll be on their head, not mine."

"Ah!" said Moriarty. "You are not without a certain subtleness of character yourself."

"When it comes to collecting what's mine," Moran said, "I manage."

Sherlock Holmes entered the smoking room and came over to their corner when he saw them. Somehow he no longer looked anything like the sinister Dr. Pin Dok Low. The cast of his face was subtly different: the turn of his mouth, the leanness of his cheeks. His gaze, while still intense, was more direct and forthright than previously. "Do you mind?" he asked, gesturing toward an empty chair.

"Join us, by all means, Mr. Holmes," Moriarty told him. "How are you feeling?"

"Rueful," said Holmes, dropping into the chair and taking a

cigarette from a silver case in his inner pocket. "And both relieved and confused. We seem to have been on the same side in the recent contretemps, and those blackguards were clearly not agents of yours."

"On the other hand," Moriarty commented dryly, "there seem to be a number of blackguards among your current acquaintances."

"Yes," Holmes admitted. "I'm not sure what to do about that. The two of them have realized that my scheme for getting the gold will not be realized, and as I never told them enough about it for them to carry it out on their own, they are a bit miffed at me at the moment. I think the Artful Codger suspects that my turning out to be Sherlock Holmes is some clever ruse on my part to make off with all the gold for myself. At any rate, both of them are currently avoiding me, which is probably all to the good."

"Are you quite recovered from your, ah, experience as your alter ego?"

"I shall probably never be completely recovered," said Holmes, striking a large safety match against the side of the box and lighting his cigarette. "My memory of the events, and of the thinking of Pin Dok Low, has left a bad taste in my mouth and it will take some time to cleanse my palate. I always thought I'd make a good criminal, but I never realized how close to the surface the impulse was." He blew out the match. "Perhaps, in future, I shouldn't be quite so harsh on you, Professor."

"Oh, I'm sure that when you've quite recovered you will manage to be just the dogged bulldog you were before," Moriarty said, a smile tugging at the corner of his mouth.

A wreath of smoke circled Holmes's face and drifted slowly toward the ceiling. "I still can't believe that your presence on this ship, in close proximity to a large store of gold, is purely serendipitous, Professor Moriarty. What are you doing here, if you're not after the gold? Tell me that."

"I don't suppose you'd believe that I have been visiting old Indian astronomical observatories?" Moriarty asked.

"You don't suppose correctly," Holmes told him. "Even while I was immersed in the personality of Dr. Pin Dok Low, I did not lose sight of who you are, or what you might be up to."

"And you attempted to have me killed several times, as I recall," Moriarty reminded him wryly.

"Incapacitated, merely," Holmes asserted. "Perhaps some of my agents—Pin Dok Low's agents—were overly assertive in their interpretation of my orders. If so, I'm sorry."

"I stand corrected," Moriarty said. "Not dead, merely with a number of important bones broken."

"Well..." Holmes smiled ruefully. "At the time we were both after the gold. Now only one of us is."

Moriarty raised his hands in an appeal to absent gods. "I assure you, Holmes, that whatever business I had is complete, that nobody was hurt by it, that it has nothing to do with the gold in the vaults below us, and that I intend to spend the rest of the journey in pleasant contemplation of the vast ocean as we cross it."

Holmes rose from his chair. "I've noticed that you seem to take a perverse pleasure in not lying to me," he told Moriarty, "but trust to subtle indirection to keep me ignorant of your true goals. So I will parse your words at my leisure and see if I can discover what secrets lay within. In the meantime, I might as well make myself useful for the rest of the trip by keeping a close eye on you—and the gold." And with that as his Parthian shot, he stubbed his cigarette out and stalked off.

"Be my guest, Holmes," Moriarty called to Holmes's retreating back. "But do try to get some rest and recapture you old, ah, joie de vivre."

"So that's Sherlock Holmes," Colonel Moran said, watching through a cloud of cigar smoke as Holmes, stiff-backed, pushed through the smoking room door and departed. "The phrase 'unpleasant chap' leaps unbidden to my mind."

"He doesn't go out of his way to make friends," Moriarty observed. "Never has."

"Really?" Moran tapped his cigar against the side of the ashtray. "I hadn't noticed. What is it, exactly, that he suspects you of, Professor?"

"Everything," Moriarty explained. "Everything."

* * *

The Empress of India reached Port Suez three days later and had a one-day stay in port before she could commence the fifty-two-hour passage through the canal early the morning after. Guards were posted at every gangway, entrance port, and periodically along the deck, with orders to look fierce, growl at anyone trying to board, and stomp on fingers or toes if necessary to keep intruders off the deck. "It won't work," Captain Iskansen said, "but we might as well try."

"Who are these relentless boarders that we must repel?" General St. Yves asked, after seeing to the disposition of his men.

"Native shopkeepers," Iskansen told him.

"Shop..."

"Even so. And they will set up shop in any nook or cranny of the deck they can reach: under cover or out in the open, beside the lifeboats, under the lifeboats, in the ladderways; as long as they're underfoot and in the way."

"Ah!" said St. Yves. "I remember them from the trip out. Insistent little beggars. But I thought they were invited on board to sell trinkets to the passengers."

"Inviting them would be quite redundant and unnecessary," the captain told him. "We arrive in port, they arrive on board. It's quite miraculous and damned annoying."

"There is that about miracles of all sorts," St. Yves murmured. "They do tend to be quite annoying."

The gold vault was of course closed, both inner and outer doors, and closely guarded while the *Empress* was in port, as it would be for the entire transverse of the canal. As it happened, some of the ubiquitous "shopkeepers" did manage to come aboard and spread their wares on various parts of the deck, giving the passengers a last chance to buy scarves, hats, dresses, shoes, and various gewgaws of an Oriental flavor until they reached London, where much the same articles could be bought in the East End for much the same price. Captain Iskansen did manage to keep them all from going below, or even inside, and the last of them scurried off into the waiting skiffs as the *Empress* prepared to enter the canal.

* * *

The Artful Codger and Cooley the Pup confronted Sherlock Holmes in his cabin the morning the ship entered the Suez Canal. "Well, I haven't seen you two around for the last few days," Holmes said, sitting on the edge of his bed, wrapped in his Pin Dok Low red silk dressing gown with the embroidered dragons snapping at each other across the front. "Cigarette?" he extended his silver cigarette case toward them.

"That's a start," said the Artful Codger, selecting one and bringing it up to his nose to sniff it. "Cheap tobacco," he opined.

"Strong tobacco," Holmes told him. "Egyptian. Not particularly cheap."

"If you say so," said the Codger, "but it ain't the sort of tobacco I'd be buying if I had my share of that gold down below. I suppose there's no chance of that now."

Cooley the Pup straddled the hard-back wooden chair in front of the tiny desk and waved away the offered cigarette case. "What I want is words," he said. "I want you to explain to me what I don't understand."

"That would take years," Holmes told him, a muscle in the corner of Holmes's mouth twitching as he spoke. "What particular bit of explanation would you like right now?"

"So you're really Sherlock Holmes?" the Pup demanded. "What happened to Pin?"

"Is there a Pin Dok Low?" asked the Codger. "Was there ever a Pin Dok Low?"

"As far as I know there was only the one I created," Holmes told them. "I created Pin Dok Low, I became Pin Dok Low, and now I am no longer Pin Dok Low. Sorry about that."

"Some people we both know are going to do their best to make you very sorry," the Codger said mildly. "Now, me, I take the cruel reverses of life with a smattering of equa-bloody-nimity, but there are those who don't share my inconsequential attitude toward life. And a couple of them are awaiting our arrival in London even now."

"You're not threatening me, are you, Codger?" asked Holmes, an anticipatory smile on his face.

"Not me," the Codger said, raising his hands in mock horror at the suggestion. "Just reminding you of what's what."

Holmes stood up and glowered at his two former henchmen. "If you behave yourselves," he told them, "and cease thinking in terms of impossible crimes, I had it in mind that perhaps I could do something for you."

"What sort of something?" the Codger asked suspiciously.

"On the other hand, if you're determined to threaten me and otherwise show signs of malcontent, why, then you're on your own and the devil take you."

"Easy for you to say, Pin—Mr. Holmes," said the Pup, "but you're the one as got us on this here boat, don't say you're not. Were it not for you and your assurances—"

"Pin Dok Low's assurances," Holmes interrupted him.

"Now, there's a distinction without a ha'penny's worth of difference," sneered the Artful Codger. "It was you and your blandishments what got us here," he said, "and it's up to you to make honest villains of us, as I see it."

"As I see it," Holmes told them, stepping closer until he loomed over them like a gaunt oracle, "the pair of you have hopped over to the other side of the fence, and you might consider staying there for a bit."

"How's that?" asked the Artful Codger.

"What fence?" the Pup asked, moving his head slightly back as though afraid that Holmes intended to bite him on the nose.

"Why, you're both heroes," Holmes told them. "You've helped save the gold. You've even been wounded in the cause, Codger," he added, indicating the Codger's bandaged hand.

"And what of it?" asked the Pup.

"Why, I would think there would be a reward," Holmes told them. "Yes, I'm sure of it. The Bank of England itself will certainly pay a reward to those who helped fight off the Thuggees."

"Well, I'll be..." the Pup said, as the enormity of the idea sank in.

"Now, wouldn't that be amusing," said the Artful Codger.

TWENTY-EIGHT

INTO THIN AIR

We cannot kindle when we will
The fire that in the heart resides,
The spirit bloweth and is still,
In mystery our soul abides.
MATTHEW ARNOLD

Captain Iskansen stood and raised his glass to his guests at the captain's table. It took a few seconds for the hubbub at the table to cease, and the quiet rippled slowly across the room as people turned to hear what the captain had to say. "An ocean voyage is a time for companionship, and for shared adventure," he told the assembled diners, holding his glass high above the pea soup. "Well, we have had our share of both. Indeed, this voyage of *The Empress of India* will be long remembered by all who are aboard her. I am well pleased to have had this—this—throng of heroes aboard, for both crew and passengers have behaved like heroes on this trip, and I thank you one and all."

"Hip-hip," called someone in the room, and the dining room reverberated with a series of cheers. And the toast was drunk and, at some tables, drunk again.

"Eat, drink, and be merry," Captain Iskansen bellowed. "For tomorrow we dock!"

A smattering of applause grew into a fusillade of earnest clapping.

The trip down the length of the Mediterranean had been blissfully uneventful. The *Empress* had rounded Gibraltar and was plowing her way north through rain just heavy enough and a sea just choppy enough for the passengers to feel as though it were a part of their continuing adventure without being truly uncomfortable. They had their sea legs, most of them. They could dine without discomfort despite the rolling motion under their seats.

Cool breezes wisped around the ship. This evening had been cool enough for woolen trousers and tweed skirts to replace the light cotton or linen garments for promenades around the deck. The dreadful attack was in the past, and all signs of it had been removed. The passengers were now feeling exceptionally jolly, and good companionship abounded.

Margaret St. Yves turned to her father after the captain resumed his seat and spoke to him earnestly and in an intense undertone, causing General St. Yves to fidget and look ill at ease. "But dear," he said, interrupting her flow of words, "you want me to agree to let this Peter fellow marry you? Just like that? I'm to give you away to this fellow who thinks wearing an army uniform is some sort of joke? Really?"

"If he should ask you for my hand, Father," Margaret said patiently, "I just want you to know that it would be all right with me if you were to seriously consider it. And then if, after a suitable period of consideration—say, ten or twenty minutes—you were to say yes, I would think that was perfectly fine."

"And when is he going to ask me?" St. Yves inquired.

"I don't know," Margaret confessed. "He hasn't asked me yet."

St. Yves thought this over carefully for a minute. "And what makes you so sure he's going to?" he asked, venturing into territory in which no man is safe.

"A woman knows these things," his daughter told him.

"I see," St. Yves said. "Has he any money? Any expectations? Will he be able to support you?"

"I have no idea," Margaret said, blithely throwing aside the notion that money was of any importance. "Besides, won't I have a sufficient income on my own when I marry? I always supposed I would."

"True," her father admitted. "You come into a sizable sum from your maternal grandfather when you marry or reach the age of thirty-five, whichever comes first. But do you really want a husband who lives off of your money?"

"If we're married," Margaret said reasonably, "then I don't suppose it will really matter whose money it is."

"It might," St. Yves said. "It could come to pass that it would matter a great deal. A man should be able to support his wife."

"If a couple is living on inherited wealth," Margaret asked reasonably, "then which of the partners has done the inheriting is more a matter of pure chance, wouldn't you say?"

"Humph," said her father.

Captain Iskansen stood again. "The gold vault door will be closed tonight for the last time until we dock," he said. "If any of you want to take one last look at our precious cargo—not as precious as the lives and fortunes of our passengers, but precious nonetheless—you have one more hour."

He paused for a sip of wine, and continued, "I will ask you all to be patient with us when we dock. As a final safety precaution the gold will be unloaded before the passengers debark. It will be quite early in the morning, and it should take no more than an hour and a half, so none of you should be inconvenienced. I hope and trust that you've all had a pleasant voyage. Well, barring that one unseemly incident, of course, as pleasant as we could make it for you. And I thank you all once again." He raised his glass, nodded his head, and sat down.

* * *

"There is going to be some people awaiting at the dock what is going to be most unhappy at the turn of events," the Artful Codger remarked into his pea soup. "They will consider themselves greatly inconvenienced."

"That's the truth," Cooley the Pup agreed. "It's funny how things turned out, ain't it?"

"Angelic Tim McAdams ain't exactly a philosophical bloke," the Codger said. "He's going to require a bit of explaining, and I'm glad

I ain't the one as is going to have to do it."

"Maybe you are the one," said the Pup. "I don't fancy that Mr. Sherlock Holmes, as he is now calling himself, is going to be any too eager to do it for himself."

"Do you suppose that Holmes is right?" the Codger asked. "About the Bank of England giving us a reward for helping save the gold?"

"He sounded like he meant it," said the Pup. "But I ain't counting on it till the guineas is clinking together in my pocket."

"Won't that be something?" marveled the Codger. "Why, it'll be almost like getting paid for honest work."

"Mind how you talk!" said the Pup. He pushed his chair back and stood up. "I want to go take one last look at the gold, which is as close as we're going to get."

The Codger rose. "I'll go with you," he said. "You know, it's a shame Holmes got that second bump on the head. If he was still Pin, he'd have a way for us to get at that gold."

"Maybe if we cosh him again..." suggested the Pup.

"It don't work like that," said the Codger.

"Pity," said the Pup.

* * *

The Empress of India steamed up the Thames and tied up at Queen's Dock at quarter to five the next morning, while the passengers and most of the city were still asleep. The two following ships, the cruiser H.M.S. *John of Gaunt* and the revenue cutter *Ajax*, which had kept the *Empress* in sight since she rounded Gibraltar, went their own ways, replaced by a pair of police boats, a company of the Household Guard, a squad of London constabulary, a bevy of Scotland Yard plainclothes men, and a pride of bowler-hatted special guards employed by the Bank of England, who were to oversee the transfer of the gold from the ship's vault to the two special armored wagons which were pulled up at dockside. The dock area was lit by gaslights and lanterns on posts, and two powerful electrical floodlights from the ship, and many of the men were carrying lanterns; but a cold, damp fog had settled in for the predawn hours and no object more than a few feet away could be clearly seen.

Inspector Giles Lestrade was in charge of the Scotland Yard contingent, and he had just finished placing his men when he heard his name called by someone standing in the open hatch to the cargo hold. "Inspector Lestrade, is that you? Come up here, please, you're needed!"

Lestrade swung his lantern around. He knew that voice. "Holmes?" He shone the light up toward the hatch. "What are you doing there? For that matter, what are you doing anywhere? Where have you been?"

"Later," shouted Holmes. "Come up here, please. Bring your men!"

Lestrade paused and contemplated the possibilities. Holmes wasn't supposed to be there. Holmes was missing, presumed dead. Still, perhaps—

"Well, Lestrade," Holmes bellowed from his perch in the cargo hatch. "Are you coming or aren't you coming? This is a matter of the utmost urgency; no time for you to ponder."

"Coming, Holmes," Lestrade called back. Holmes, if it was Holmes, was right, pondering could come later. And questioning. He gave two brief blasts on his police whistle and led his quartet of plainclothesmen up the ramp to the hatch.

It was indeed Holmes standing there. The same well-remembered arrogant posture, the same familiar overweening gesture as he beckoned them forward. "This way," the world's foremost consulting detective said, leading them into the ship and around a corridor.

"This had better not take too long," Lestrade said, huffing to keep up with Holmes's long strides. "We have the gold to look after. The unloading is due to begin any minute now."

Holmes stopped short halfway down the corridor, where a cluster of men in a variety of uniforms and mufti were standing by what looked like an open bank vault door. "The gold appears to have already been unloaded," Holmes said.

"How's that?" Lestrade halted and looked over the group in front of him: several army officers, a few ship's officers, and assorted civilians. They all glowered at him as he approached, as though he were responsible for something, although he had no idea what.

Holmes introduced him to a general, the ship's captain, and some people of lesser importance. Lestrade would have been greatly impressed had he time for such thoughts. He took a breath. "What do you mean, it's been unloaded? The armored wagons just arrived a few moments ago."

Holmes indicated the open vault door. "This is where the gold was," he told Lestrade. "A bit over two tons of the stuff. It was there last night. As you can see, it is no longer there."

Lestrade went over and peered through the door. There was an inner door of iron bars, which was still closed. Looking through the bars, Lestrade saw a room about twelve feet square and eight feet from floor to ceiling. The walls, floor, and ceiling of the room were made up of riveted iron plates. There was no apparent entrance to the room except the door through which Lestrade was now peering with interest. The room appeared to be empty, save for a few scraps of charred wood. "The vault?" Lestrade asked.

"Indeed," said Captain Iskansen.

"Two tons of gold?"

"A bit more, I fancy," said Holmes, "just a bit more."

"Gone?"

"Afraid so," said General St. Yves. "They were here yesterday. I saw them. Gold bars all boxed up in stacks of tidy boxes, six to a box."

"I imagine it took up much of the vault, this gold."

"It made a pile about so high in the center of the room," St. Yves said, holding his hand on a level with his chin.

"There was a space a foot and a half wide from the walls to allow walking around the, ah, pile," Captain Iskansen said.

"And it was here yesterday?"

"I closed the outer vault door at nine in the evening," Iskansen told him. "Twenty people—at least twenty—saw it there just before the door closed."

Sighing a long and wheezy sigh, Lestrade unbuttoned his inverness, reached into his suit-coat pocket, and retrieved his notebook and a stubby pencil. He examined the pencil with interest, and then gave the point a few swipes with the blade of a pocket knife laboriously produced from another pocket. "All right, then," he said, licking the tip of the pencil and opening the notebook to a fresh page, "I might have known it wouldn't be no ordinary kind of case, not with you here, Mr. Holmes."

Lestrade turned to General St. Yves. "Tell me about it."

The group of men around him took it in turn to explain how the gold had been kept and secured and guarded, from Calcutta to London, in constant view, until that very morning.

"These gentlemen and I came down here at precisely five A.M. to open the outer vault door and await the arrival of the representative of the Band of England," Captain Iskansen ended the story. "And we found"—he waved a hand at the empty vault room—"this."

Closing his notebook, Lestrade turned to Holmes. "I'm surprised that you're not in there at this moment, crawling around on your hands and knees, examining the cracks in the floor for bits of dust."

Holmes smiled. "The captain has not seen fit to open the inner door yet," he said. "When he does, I will avail myself of the opportunity to, as you say, crawl about the floor. Unless, of course, you have a solution to our conundrum."

"I can assure you," said Captain Iskansen, "that there are no hidden panels, trapdoors, or other concealed entrances to or exits from this vault room. Except for the doorway in which we stand, there is no way in or out of the vault."

"When was the last time that there inner door was opened?" asked Lestrade.

Captain Iskansen took an envelope embossed with wax seals from an inner pocket. "This has been in my safe since we left Calcutta," he said. "In it resides the only key to the inner vault door." He flicked it with his finger. "As you can see, the seal has not been broken."

Lestrade scratched his head. "It's beyond me," he confessed. "If what you say is so, then you'd best let Mr. Holmes into the room as soon as possible to crawl about and get the knees of his trousers dirty. There's nothing else for it, and I don't see how that can help. But then, I never see how Mr. Holmes solves his little problems until he explains them. And often not then."

Holmes smiled a tight little smile. "I can't say how the trick was accomplished yet," he said, "but would it surprise you to know that our old friend Professor Moriarty is aboard this ship?"

"Moriarty? Here? No!" exclaimed Lestrade, stretching the "No!" out into something like a cat's wail of surprise. "What the bejiggers is the professor doing here?"

"Returning from a very interesting visit to Calcutta," came Professor Moriarty's voice from down the corridor, "very profitable."

Lestrade turned to see the professor and a heavyset man who walked with a military bearing approaching. "I hear there's been an unfortunate occurrence in the gold vault," said Moriarty.

Holmes took two steps forward and thrust a jabbing finger in Moriarty's direction. "And just how did you know that, Professor?"

"Why, it's all over the ship," said Moriarty. "News like that can't be kept secret."

"Say," said General St. Yves, "I posted guards at the ends of the corridor with instructions to let no one pass. How did you get by the guards?"

Moriarty smiled grimly. "I told them that you wished to speak to me," he said. "Surely that's true, isn't it, Holmes? As soon as a crime happens anywhere on earth, Sherlock Holmes wants to talk to me about it."

"You've outdone yourself, Professor," Holmes said. "An impossible crime on a ship at sea, and you right there in the same ship at the same time. It's as though you're challenging me."

"Someone may be challenging you," Moriarty said, "but it isn't I. And I doubt whether the challenge was deliberate—no one, myself included, had any way to know you were on the ship until the attack. If it comes to that, *you* didn't know you were on the ship until—"

"What attack?" Lestrade asked, looking from one to the other.

"And just what was so profitable about your trip to Calcutta?" Holmes demanded.

Moriarty made motions with his hands as though he were piling small invisible boxes on top of larger invisible boxes in the air in front of him. "I have arranged for English translations of two ancient Hindi astronomical texts: the *Grahanayayadipaka* by Paramesvara and the *Yuktibhasa* by Jyesthadeva," he said. "Dr. Pitamaha of the Department of Astronomy at the University of Calcutta didn't have the funds to have it done. Now he does."

"I see," said Holmes. "So you're using this gold to support the Indian system of higher education."

"A worthwhile endeavor," Moriarty said. "But I didn't take the gold. My word on it."

Holmes looked sourly at Moriarty and then turned to Captain Iskansen. "I think you'd best unlock the inner door now," he said. "It's time for me to crawl about and get the knees of my trousers dirty." He patted his pockets and located a small magnifying glass. "While I'm at it, I would suggest, Lestrade, that you have the *Empress* searched thoroughly, top to bottom, stem to, ah, stern. Two tons of gold is hard to disguise."

"Where do you suggest I look, Holmes?" asked Lestrade.

"Ignore the obvious places," Holmes said. "Look in places that are so obscure that you don't see how the gold can be there, or look at what's in plain sight, and see if it isn't gold."

Lestrade opened his notebook. "How's that again, Mr. Holmes?"

"Never mind. Just do make a record of all the places you've looked. And post men around to see that no one moves anything large and bulky about until you've had a look at it. And see that nobody goes ashore."

"I don't know if I have that authority, Mr. Holmes."

"I do," said Captain Iskansen. "No one leaves the ship until you say so, Mr. Holmes."

"There are some special guards from the bank," Lestrade said. "I'll get them aboard to help."

"And keep an eye on him," Holmes said, taking off his jacket and pointing his long, sharp nose in Moriarty's direction.

TWENTY-NINE

A PRETTY TRICK

There is a tide in the affairs of men,
Which, taken at the flood, leads on to fortune;
Omitted, all the voyage of their life
Is bound in shallows and in miseries.
WILLIAM SHAKESPEARE

A twenty-one-pound four-ounce bar of gold is not very large, gold being one of the heaviest natural elements. It would not be difficult to think of any number of ingenious hiding places for one bar of gold. But two hundred and some of them in six-bar wooden crates, or even out of the crates, is another matter. They would make an awfully noticeable lump just about anywhere. And if you separate them and scatter the two hundred and some bars of gold in various hiding places aboard a ship, even a ship as large as *The Empress of India*, you'd think that a band of dedicated and trained searchers would unearth—or perhaps unship?—at least one of the missing bars.

None were found.

The search went on. Lestrade went down to the vault to share information—such as there was—with Holmes.

"Have you discovered anything?" Lestrade asked.

"Several suggestive facts," Holmes said, dusting off his knees and emerging from his two-hour investigation of the vault walls, floor, and ceiling. "Nothing conclusive."

"I'd appreciate your sharing your thoughts with me," said Lestrade, "inconclusive though they may be."

Holmes nodded. "There are holes in the walls," he said.

"Holes?" Lestrade rubbed his hands together. "Holes, indeed! Well, now—"

"Perfectly circular holes, nine of them, three in each of the side walls and three in the rear wall. Six feet off the ground. Slightly less than one inch in diameter."

"Large enough for someone to have slivered the gold bars and passed the slices through," Lestrade suggested.

"All in one night?" Holmes asked. "Besides, the holes lead to air pipes that feed up through the decks and end at a ventilator topside. I inspected the pipes from the outside. They are firmly painted in place, and the paint is at least a few months old."

"Air pipes?" Lestrade frowned. "Whatever for?"

"They serve a dual function, according to the ship's first officer. First they would supply air in the event that anyone got locked in the vault. And second, they would cause the room to flood if the ship sank."

"That's curious," said Lestrade. "Why would they want the room to flood?"

"Pressure," explained Holmes.

"How's that?"

"In the event of attempting to retrieve the gold—or whatever might be in the vault—from a sunken ship, the pressure of the water on the vault door would make it impossible to open unless it was equalized by the pressure within the vault. Or so the first officer explained it to me. In other words, the vault has to be equally flooded for the door to open."

"Ah!" said Lestrade, not understanding a word of the explanation. "So that explains the holes, through which, at any rate, the gold could not have been removed. And have you any other findings?"

Holmes shrugged. "Some burned bits of wood, perhaps twenty in all. None over six inches long or an inch wide. Most much smaller. Some gray dust of a particularly powdery consistency."

"And they relate to the crime?"

"They are anomalous, but I have no explanation for them as of yet. The task is to collect facts. When we have enough facts, we can make deductions."

"But not yet?"

"No, not yet. And you have made no discoveries?"

"The soldiers who were on guard last night report hearing a strange 'wooshing' noise shortly after midnight."

"A sound unfamiliar to them?"

"They had never heard it before."

"Anything else?"

"The lights stayed bright all night."

"The lights?"

Lestrade gestured. "These electrical lights in the hall. They, apparently, stayed bright the entire night."

"And that is unusual?"

"The guards report that the lights often fluctuate, brighter and dimmer, during the course of the night."

"But last night they didn't?"

"That's what they say."

Holmes rubbed the side of his nose. "Thank you, Lestrade," he said. "That is very interesting."

"Really, Holmes? What does it signify?"

"I don't know. I know little of the operation of electrical lighting—but I'll put a bit of money on the proposition that Professor James Moriarty knows all there is about electrical lighting—and a bit more than he's told us about the disappearance of the gold!"

Lestrade looked doubtful. "You've expressed that belief often before, Mr. Holmes, and been proved wrong."

"Or been outsmarted by a clever rogue!" Holmes interjected. "Well, we'll see what's what this time. I'll find that gold, Lestrade—see if I don't."

"I certainly hope so, Mr. Holmes," Lestrade told him. "So what would you have me do now?"

Holmes stared at the far wall for a minute, and then poked

Lestrade in the waistcoat with a sharp forefinger. "Keep a close watch on Professor James Moriarty," he said.

Lestrade sighed. "Very well, Mr. Holmes. Anything else?"

Holmes's finger went forth again. "Send one of your men to procure some professional divers," he said.

"How's that, Mr. Holmes?" Lestrade asked, retreating slightly from the probing finger.

"If the gold isn't on the ship, it has to be somewhere. When you have eliminated the impossible—divers!"

"You believe that the gold is no longer on the ship?"

"I believe no such thing—I did not conduct the search myself. If it comes to that, I will do so." Holmes did a series of baritsu warm-up exercises to relieve the tightness in his arms and legs from crawling around and peering into cracks and corners. "But as you have searched and you haven't found the gold, it is reasonable to assume that the gold bars are no longer aboard. There wasn't time between last night and this morning to melt them down and turn them into, oh, say, statues of an Indian goddess, but they might have been thrown overboard for later retrieval."

Lestrade nodded. "I see," he said. "But how did... whoever... get them out of the vault?"

"I haven't decided yet," Holmes said. "But get them out he did, clearly, as they are no longer here."

"The passengers are raising a fuss. They want to go ashore," Lestrade said.

"No doubt," said Holmes. "I suggest letting them debark. Make sure you have their names, and inspect their luggage."

"The customs people will do that," Lestrade said.

"Yes. Of course."

"What's that about Indian statues?" Lestrade asked.

"Professor Moriarty's midget friend is bringing a couple of crates of them back, presumably to sell in the sort of store that carries little Indian statues," Holmes explained. "Each of them should be examined with the thought that a gold bar might have been, ah, inserted into its interior. I don't really think you'll find anything, Moriarty is far too subtle for that, but we mustn't overlook the obvious."

"Have you any reason to believe that Professor Moriarty is involved?" Lestrade asked. "Beyond the fact that you always assume that he is?"

"My dear inspector..." Holmes took a breath and considered. "I often become convinced that Professor Moriarty is involved in some major crime, especially if it is difficult to solve, or even explain, because I know the sort of man he is, and the sort of challenge he likes. If you know of a man who, let's say, makes intricate and precise pocket watches and fits them into impossibly small square cases, and you find him standing next to such a watch, in such a case, the presumptive evidence is strong. I admit that I cannot accuse him of this particular crime because I have no proof that he was involved and only the vaguest notion as yet as to how it was carried out. But that very secrecy, the very impossibility of the crime, is one of the professor's hallmarks."

"I see," said Lestrade, a not-so-fine edge of sarcasm to his voice. "It couldn't have been done, therefore the professor did it."

Holmes chuckled. "Not up to my usual standards of logic, is it? I'm afraid Moriarty has that effect on me. Come, let us go upstairs and reason together." He put his around Lestrade's shoulder. "There is an answer to this conundrum, and perhaps we can find it."

* * *

"Well," said the Artful Codger, tightening the leather straps on his small steamer trunk, "a good time was had by all while it lasted. It's time to set foot back on good old terra-bloody-firma."

Cooley the Pup sat down on his bunk, his arms crossed firmly about his chest. "I ain't leaving."

"What do you mean, you ain't leaving? You've got to leave, don't you? I mean, we're there, we've arrived; we're back in bloody old London, ain't we?"

"And down there on the dock somewhere are bloody old Angelic Tim McAdams and the Twopenny Yob, ain't they? And they're going to want to know where the gold is at, ain't they? And what are we going to tell them?"

"We'll just tell him the truth."

"That Pin Dok Low turned out to be Sherlock Holmes?"

"Well, it's the truth."

"And a lot of help that will be. 'Where is the gold?' McAdams will ask."

"Well, we'll just tell him how we rescued it, and how we're going to get a reward. We'll split the reward with him, that should make him feel better about it."

"Oh, we will, will we?" Cooley the Pup stood up and leaned forward, his nose inches away from the Codger's nose.

"What's the matter? You unwilling to share with a pal?"

"A big pal with a nasty disposition and a tendency toward breaking bones? Naw, I'll share with him, all right. And just what is it I'm supposed to share?"

"The reward."

"And which reward would that be?"

The Codger started to answer, and then a horrified look crossed his face. "You don't think—"

Cooley the Pup nodded forcefully. "I do. I certainly do. They ain't got the gold now, what it has gone missing. And it stands to reason that they ain't going to pay any reward for it what they ain't got it, now, don't it?"

The Artful Codger grimaced. "Stands to reason," he agreed.

"You think the professor's got it?"

"Professor Moriarty?" The Codger thought about it. "Seems likely," he said.

"You think Sherlock Holmes will find it?"

The Codger pictured Angelic Tim McAdams waiting for them somewhere near the dock. "If he don't," he said, "I think we should turn right around and take the *Empress* back to Calcutta."

"I was thinking the same thing myself," said the Pup.

* * *

The Honorable Eustace Bergarot, governor of the Bank of England, leaned back in an overstuffed chair in the Owners' Lounge, one of the small suite of rooms reserved for any of the Board of Directors of Anglo-Asian Star steamship line who should happen to travel aboard the *Empress*. It was being used as the command center for the continuing investigation into the missing gold. Standing or sitting around the Honorable Bergarot were Holmes, General St. Yves and his daughter, Captain Iskansen, Moriarty, Colonel Moran, and Inspector Lestrade. It was now noon, and most of the passengers had left the ship, but the refitting for the return voyage was yet to begin.

"I've asked that everything be kept as it is until we determine what happened to the gold," Holmes explained.

Bergarot nodded. "Quite right," he said calmly, his hands wrapped over the golden lion that formed the handle of his ebon walking stick. "What did happen to the gold?"

Inspector Lestrade stepped forward. "If I might be permitted," he said.

"Certainly."

"Whoever did you out of your gold," Lestrade began, "and however it was accomplished—"

"I must correct you on one thing, young man," Bergarot interrupted. "Strictly speaking, it isn't my gold. I couldn't let that pass without commenting, so there would be no doubt."

"I meant, of course, the Bank of England's gold," Lestrade said.

"So did I, young man. Strictly speaking, it isn't the bank's gold that's missing. That is, the gold has never been turned over to an official of the bank, so the loss, if any, will have to be covered by the insurers of Anglo-Asian Star lines. Lloyd's of London, I assume, carries the policy."

"Lloyd's has the ship," affirmed Captain Iskansen, "but I believe the special cargo is self-insured."

Bergarot raised an eyebrow. "The board is carrying the whole indemnity? If so, this will put the company into receivership. No small group of private individuals can withstand such a loss."

Iskansen shrugged. "So I believe," he said. "Perhaps some of the individual members carry personal policies. At any rate, they're selling the firm to Green Star, from what I understand. For all I know, they already have."

Well," said Bergarot, "even though the bank suffers no loss if the gold is not recovered, we would, of course, prefer to have it safely in our hands. Word of this will get out, and I'm afraid the public might not make so fine a distinction as to who lost the gold. We cannot have public confidence in the bank shaken. We cannot." He turned to Holmes. "So I implore you, Mr. Holmes: Find my gold!"

"We have searched the ship," Holmes told him. "I'm beginning to think the gold was dropped overboard during the night, perhaps with a floating buoy to mark the spot. Steam launches are being sent back along the *Empress*'s path to see if they can spot such a thing."

"How did they—whoever they might be—get the gold out of the vault?" Bergarot asked.

"That is still to be determined," Holmes admitted. "It seems impossible, two tons of gold disappearing overnight, but there must be something I am not seeing."

"Perhaps," Moriarty suggested softly, "you're seeing more than is there."

Holmes wheeled. "Are you trying to hint as to how you did it?" he asked. "Or are you trying to further misdirect me?"

"Are you saying that this gentleman is the, ah, culprit?" Bergarot asked, with a wide-eyed glance over the top of his spectacles.

"Were I to do so directly," Holmes replied, "he could sue me for slander. I haven't a shred of proof. And yet those two large Scotland Yard men are standing behind him at my request, to assure that he doesn't disappear as the gold did, until this crime is solved. Even the professor will admit that this smacks of the sort of crime that he would delight in."

"I take no delight in crime, Mr. Holmes," Moriarty said. "You do me an injustice. More than that, it shows how little you understand me."

Holmes wheeled to face Moriarty. "Pray enlighten me," he said.

"What we are faced with here is a seemingly impossible crime," Moriarty said. "Something over two tons of gold disappearing from a closed vault overnight, with guards in the corridor the whole night. Is that a fair statement?"

"I admit how you accomplished it has me puzzled at the moment—" Holmes began.

"That's how it looks to us, Professor," Lestrade cut in.

"Then you must ask yourselves why the crime is impossible," Moriarty said. "It is foolish to make a crime appear impossible if it adds one scintilla of complexity, or one second of additional time, to the act—unless the criminal has a damn good reason."

"And had you?" asked Holmes.

Moriarty sighed a long-suffering sigh. "If I had wanted the gold," he said, "I would have let the Thuggees take it and then sunk their ship."

"Thuggees?" asked the Honorable Bergarot.

He was ignored. "You could have done that?" asked Captain Iskansen.

"Easily," Moriarty affirmed.

General St. Yves drew himself out of his soft chair and glowered at Moriarty. "They intended to kill everyone aboard *The Empress of India*," he said intently, his ears turning red at the thought. "You would have permitted—encouraged—that?"

"Of course not," Moriarty responded, angry in his turn. "What do all of you take me for? The Thuggees were much too occupied to attempt to sink the *Empress* or kill the passengers. Their only thought was to escape. If it could have been arranged for them to escape with the gold, they would have done so. But they wouldn't have lingered for any lesser reason. And before you berate me for having been willing to blow up their ship, are you not planning to hang the few prisoners you have?"

"How would you have retrieved the gold from the sunken ship?" Holmes asked. "The ocean must be half a mile deep out there."

"The latest diving bells are quite capable of such a depth," Moriarty told him. "And I have a few ideas for improvements in the design that I'd like to have an excuse to try out."

"But you didn't do it," said St. Yves.

"I never intended to," Moriarty told him. "I have trained my mind to explore all possibilities in any situation. I do it now without conscious thought or intent."

"I knew it, Professor," cried Margaret St. Yves. "You could never deliberately sink a ship, not with living people aboard. No truly ethical person could."

"I thank you for that," said Professor Moriarty.

"So," Holmes said, "the ideas for crimes come to you unbidden."

Moriarty considered. "Crimes, yes," he admitted. "But also ways of improving scientific instruments, philosophical theories of varying worth, snippets of doggerel verse—I make no claim to being a poet—dubious insights into historical facts, and sudden observations regarding the follies of the human race."

"Hmmph!" said Holmes.

"You do the same," Moriarty told him. "For all of your vaunted powers of ratiocination, your startling leaps of deduction are largely a result of the workings of what Dr. Freud calls the unconscious mind."

"Perhaps," said Holmes, "but my unconscious does not plot criminal activities."

"Really?" Moriarty asked. "What would your friend Dr. Pin Dok Low say about that?"

Holmes looked stricken. "I confess," he said, sitting down. "It must be that in some dark recess of my mind—"

Moriarty waved a negligent hand. "Try not to let it bother you, Holmes," he said. "In the nooks and crannies of the mind of each of us dispiriting thoughts gather. Or so Dr. Freud would have us believe."

The Honorable Bergarot looked from one to the other of them. "Perhaps," he suggested, lifting the cut-crystal glass, part of a set reserved for the use of the directors, and sipping the '17 San Tomás de las Aguas port, also reserved for the directors, with which it was filled, "we could return to the subject at hand."

"The missing gold," said Lestrade.

"Prescient of you, Inspector," agreed Bergarot.

"Holmes could tell you where it is," Moriarty said, leaning back in his chair and sipping at his own dram of fine port. "If he'd clear his mind of the presumption that I was involved in the crime, which, as is so often the case, is clouding his otherwise laudatory thought processes."

Bergarot looked over his spectacles at the professor. "You claim that you were not involved in the theft?" he asked.

"I do."

"But you know how it was done."

"I believe so," Moriarty said.

"Because you did it yourself?" Holmes suggested.

Moriarty shook his head. "Consider that if I had, I would not be standing here exchanging gibbets of wit with you. I would be long gone."

Holmes eyed him suspiciously.

A young lieutenant of the Lancers, in the full dress uniform that the British climate made comfortable once again, stepped into the room and saluted his general. "Sorry, sir," he said, "Major Sandiman requests that you return to the briefing room as soon as possible. There are questions about the debarking orders and, well, sir, everything seems to be turning into a muddle."

"Ah," said General St. Yves, pushing to his feet. "Good to be needed, I suppose. I'd better... if you gentlemen will excuse me..." He eyed the remaining port in his glass, and then downed it in one swallow and followed the lieutenant out of the room, pausing at the door to say, "Margaret, my love, if I'm not back shortly, our rooms at the Northumberland Arms should be awaiting us. I imagine you can make your way there without my assistance."

"I imagine so, Father," Margaret affirmed.

"Sorry to leave," the general said, eyeing his empty port glass with a sigh of regret. "Do send someone along to tell me how this all comes out—and where the bally gold is!" And he was out the door.

"Yes," Bergarot said, recapturing the group's attention. "The gold. Where is it?"

Captain Iskansen had jumped to his feet immediately after St. Yves, and now stood indecisively in the middle of the room. "My job," he said. "I am being horribly remiss. The debarking. The unloading of cargo. The reloading. I really shouldn't be here. I really mustn't stay." He put his hat firmly on his head and headed for the door. Pausing in his turn, he turned and said, "Keep me informed, will you?" and he was gone.

"If you do know where the gold is," Holmes told Moriarty, "do share the information with the rest of us, and we can all get on with our duties."

"I believe I can deduce its location from the information at hand," Moriarty said. "You could, too, Holmes, if you'd allow yourself to take cognizance of the obvious."

Bergarot stirred. "I believe you," he said. "It makes perfect sense to me. You know where the gold is because you didn't take it. Fine. Now share the information with the rest of us."

"Let us construct a syllogism," Moriarty said. "Not one of Lewis Carroll's sort, but a more complex structure."

"Ever the professor of mathematics, eh, Moriarty?" commented Holmes.

"Perhaps," replied the professor of mathematics. "First premise: we are faced with a seemingly impossible crime; the gold could not have been removed from the vault while it was locked and under guard, and in any case it could not have all been removed in the space of one night."

"That's true enough," grumbled Inspector Lestrade.

"Second premise: the gold was there yesterday."

"It was seen to be," Bergarot affirmed.

"Third premise: it is now gone; the vault is empty."

"Except for a few cinders, essentially so," Holmes agreed.

"Now we must reach for the conclusion. In doing so we will keep in mind the axiom that when the impossible is removed, whatever remains, however improbable, must be the truth."

Holmes glared at Moriarty. "I believe I have said something of the sort myself upon occasion."

"Yes," Moriarty agreed. "So, conclusion: since the gold could not have been removed from the vault last night, it *was* not removed from the vault last night."

Moriarty's declaration had a powerful effect on his listeners. Director Bergarot's mouth opened mutely. The lines in Holmes's face hardened; he disliked being made sport of. Lestrade guffawed. "You're not saying we've all been mesmerized, are you, Professor? The gold bars are still there, but we can't see them? Like one of those fantastical Professor Challenger stories from *The Strand Magazine*?"

"You have the horse in view, but you've placed him behind the cart, Inspector." Moriarty made a twisting motion with his hands. "Reverse that thought."

Holmes's face suddenly twisted in a spasm of thought, and then relaxed, and he slapped his hand down on the table in front of him. "Of course! It's obvious!" he said. But then his eyes narrowed and he thrust a bony crooked first finger up in warning: "But that still doesn't prove that you had nothing to do with it."

"If I did, why would I be telling you about it?" asked Moriarty.

"A clever ruse," said Holmes.

"Enabling you to retrieve the gold," expanded Moriarty.

"True," Holmes said. "True."

"What are you two talking about?" demanded Inspector Lestrade. "It isn't obvious to me. Where is the gold, if you suddenly know, and how did it get there?"

"It couldn't have been removed last night," Holmes said, "so it wasn't removed last night. It was removed earlier."

"Probably much earlier," Moriarty agreed. "And over a period of time."

"But," objected Margaret, "everyone saw it there. Dozens of people must have walked by that vault room every day, and the gold was there."

"Was it?" Moriarty asked. "What did they see?"

"Gold bars," Margaret said. "Stacks of them—in wooden boxes. I saw them myself. Didn't I?"

"It looked like gold, certainly. In a sense it was gold. What you saw was a *trompe-l'oeil*." Moriarty told her. "A cleverly done painting to fool the eye. The gold you saw was gold leaf."

She thought it over. "Well, if so, it certainly fooled my eyes."

Holmes got up and, with a slow, measured step, began walking around the table, his gaze toward some unseen distant horizon. "Our view was limited," he said thoughtfully. "No chance for much perspective." He continued walking, his forefinger pressed to his nose.

"And the bright electrical lights helped the illusion," Moriarty added. "They eliminated shadows. It was a sort of clever stage illusion."

"Stage illusion!" Margaret put her hand to her mouth. "The professor!"

"I agree," said Moriarty. "The professor."

"What professor?" asked Lestrade. "You? Are you admitting—"

"I actually saw him with paint on his sleeve once," Margaret said. "He said, if I remember correctly, that he was painting a prop."

"Well, he certainly was," Moriarty said.

"Professor Demartineu," Holmes mused, "and his friend Sutrow the magician."

The Honorable Bergarot swiveled in his chair to look at Holmes, who was passing behind him. "Magician?"

"I see it now," said Holmes. "The disappearing lady—the disappearing gold bars. Nothing but a clever illusion."

"An illusion?" Lestrade asked, lacing his hands behind his back and trying to look thoughtful. "Hmmm. An illusion. Go on, Holmes."

"The illusion was put in place, a *trompe-l'oeil* of the cases of gold. And behind this wood-and-canvas flat, the gold was removed. It could have begun the day we left Calcutta, and it was probably finished weeks ago."

"How was this done, from a locked and guarded vault room?" Bergarot asked.

"Why?" asked Margaret. "Why create a mystery—an impossible crime?"

"Ah," said Moriarty. "There's the crux, you see. The how and why are tied together. The illusion of an impossible crime, created because it had to be an impossible crime."

"I'm afraid I lost you when the impossible became possible," said the Honorable Bergarot. "Or was it the other way around?"

"If it wasn't an impossible crime, you see, then there would have been no mystery as to how it was done," Holmes said.

"And if there was no mystery as to how it was done," Moriarty continued, "there would have been no mystery as to who did it."

"So, in order to conceal the fact that the gold was being stolen—" Holmes began.

"He had to make it appear that the gold was still there," Moriarty said.

"Who had to—" began Bergarot.

Holmes stopped pacing and wheeled to face the table. "But it had to be removed early so that it could be concealed. That's obvious."

"Once you realize that, the rest follows," Moriarty said. "When the thread is picked up at any point, the skein unravels."

"The rest of what?" demanded the Honorable Bergarot.

"If I'm supposed to be arresting somebody," complained Lestrade, "I wish you'd tell me who. If I'm supposed to be recovering the gold, I wish you'd tell me where it is. I'll await the explanation as to how it got there for a later time."

"It becomes clear once you realize why the crime had to appear impossible," Holmes said.

"Elucidate," said the Honorable Bergarot.

"Assume that we had not been allowed to look through the gated inner door every day; that the vault door had been closed since we left Calcutta."

"Yes?"

"And the door was opened this morning, and the gold was gone. Who took it?"

"The captain had the only key," said Bergarot.

"Exactly!" said Holmes.

"But it was sealed in an envelope," Margaret protested.

"A heated thin blade under the wax," said Moriarty. "Opened in an instant, and none the wiser."

"Amazing!" said Bergarot. "So the only reason the gold was left on display every day was because it actually wasn't there."

"Sleight of mind, you might call it," said Moriarty. "If the gold was there until last night, then the captain couldn't have taken it because nobody could have. Turn it into an impossible crime, and the list of suspects is as large as your imagination will admit."

"But how did he get the gold out of the vault?" Lestrade asked. "And what did he do with it? We've searched the ship."

"Looking for gold bars?"

"Why, yes, of course."

"But if they weren't removed all at once last night, then there's no reason to assume that the gold is still in the shape of bars," Moriarty said. "Gold is gold, no matter how it's stretched, pummeled, or deformed."

"I'm getting all mixed up, the way you're telling it," said Lestrade. "I have no doubt that you're right: when Sherlock Holmes and Professor Moriarty agree on something, there's no point in arguing about it. But just what is it you're right about? What happened to the gold, and how did it happen?"

Holmes and Moriarty looked at each other. Moriarty gave a slight nod, and Holmes took a breath. "Any given detail might be wrong," he said, "but on the whole, it had to go like this: when Captain Iskansen decided to take the gold, he enlisted the aid of Professor Demartineu and Mamarum Sutrow, who devised the plan. Or perhaps they came to him, it cannot—"

"Yes, yes," said Lestrade. "One came to the other. And then?"

Holmes shrugged. "Iskansen supplied the key, Demartineu and Sutrow painted the false front, and the gold was removed."

"How?" asked the director of the Bank of England.

"In the evening, when Captain Iskansen came to close the vault door, there was always a small group of people with him," said Sherlock Holmes. "One of them presumably stayed behind in the vault overnight, and left with the group who opened the door the next morning."

"Like Mamarum the Great's trick with Lady Priscilla," Margaret suggested.

"Much like that, yes," Holmes agreed.

"But the room was completely empty when they opened the door this morning," Margaret said. "What happened to the *trompe-l'oeil* structure?"

"The guards reported hearing a strange whooshing noise in the night," Moriarty said. "Magicians use a material called flash paper that disappears in a whoosh of flame if a lit cigarette end is applied to it. The paper is put in an aqueous solution of nitric acid and then dried. It's how they make those wonderful flashes when something appears or disappears."

"The false front was made of flash paper?"

"Perhaps of something with a bit more structural integrity. Let us call it flash-cotton. And a short fuse was left burning so the structure would vanish with a flash in the middle of the night."

"And the gold?" asked Bergarot with single-minded interest. "What of the gold?"

Holmes looked at Moriarty for help. His ratiocination had not taken him that far yet.

"Melted down," said Moriarty. "A small carbon arc furnace powered from the electrical circuit."

"And how can you possibly know that?" asked Lestrade.

"It would explain the dimming of the lights," explained Moriarty.

"Melted into what shape?" pursued Bergarot.

"Square, I believe," Moriarty told him.

"Square?"

Moriarty nodded. "Sheets a little less than one foot square, and perhaps a quarter to a half inch thick."

Margaret gave a slight gasp. "The floor!" she said.

"You are a very quick young lady," Moriarty said approvingly.

"What floor?" asked Bergarot.

"The ballroom floor has been redone this trip," Margaret told him.

"In solid gold, is my guess," said Moriarty, "with a surface of oak."

"The workmen would have to know," Bergarot objected. "It would have to be a fairly large conspiracy."

"There's a lot of gold," said Moriarty.

They headed out to the ballroom as a group and Moriarty made the experiment, prying up one of the parquet squares. "Suspiciously heavy," he said. He turned it over.

"I'll be damned!" said Bergarot.

"I'll get Captain Iskansen," Lestrade said, clapping his bowler firmly on his head. "And those two magicians!"

"I doubt it," said Moriarty. "They're long gone, I fancy."

Holmes stood up. "Well, you have your gold," he said to Director Bergarot. "I think I'll go home now."

THIRTY

THE RETURN

Home is the sailor, home from the sea,
And the hunter home from the hill.
ROBERT LOUIS STEVENSON

FROM THE UNPUBLISHED JOURNAL OF JOHN H. WATSON, M.D.

Sherlock Holmes has returned!

Sherlock Holmes is the most exasperating man on the face of the earth.

I visited 221B yesterday, planning to look through some old case-books to refresh my memory concerning one of Holmes's early cases—involving the king of a small East European country and a tin of poisoned sardines—and there was a light on in the study window. I dashed upstairs, not knowing what to expect, and there he was—sitting in his confounded armchair in his wretched old red dressing gown, smoking his blasted pipe, with the latest copy of *The Strand Magazine* turned down on the table next to him, gazing out the window. He did have the courtesy to look up as I entered the room.

"Watson, old man," he said. "I knew it was you by the sound of your boots on the stairs. It's good to see you again!"

My knees sagged, and I clutched the door frame for support. I'm sure I came as close to fainting as I have ever done. "Holmes," I gasped, "is it really you?"

He laughed. "Yes, my dear friend, no false identity, no disguise. It is me in the all-too-mortal flesh."

"Dear friend?" I expostulated. "Dear friend? And you don't even have the courtesy—the kindness—to tell me you've returned?" I staggered over to a chair and sat down heavily.

Holmes jumped up, concern in his eyes, and crossed over to me. "Watson, I am so sorry," he said. "I did not realize the effect this might have on you. Here," he continued, turning to the highboard where reposed the tantalus and gasogene. "Let me fix you a brandy and soda. You'll feel much better after a brandy and soda."

He poured brandy and squirted soda water into two glasses and handed me one. "As to where I've been," he said, returning to his seat, "I'm afraid that is one adventure that will have to remain untold. As to what I've done, I can say that I've eliminated one of the world's greatest villains."

"Professor Moriarty," I gasped. "You finally succeeded in—"

"No, no." Holmes shook his head ruefully. "I'm afraid Professor Moriarty is still with us."

"Then who?"

"A man calling himself Dr. Pin Dok Low. Perhaps he was Chinese, perhaps not. He believed himself to be evil incarnate, and tried hard to make it so. I can honestly say that he will never be seen in this world again."

"Ah," I said. "Then some good has come out of your absence."

"Yes," he said, sighing. "Some good."

THIRTY-ONE

THE OLD LADY OF THREADNEEDLE STREET

It is a flaw
In happiness, to see beyond our bourn,–
It forces us in summer skies to mourn,
It spoils the singing of the nightingale.
JOHN KEATS

The ancient, well-marinated, oak-paneled office of the Honorable Eustace Bergarot, up on the third floor of the Bank of England, had just witnessed a rare ceremony: the Bank passing out money. The hoard of gold had been transferred to the vaults, and the directors had decided that, considering all the circumstances, it might be proper to reward some of those involved in preserving it.

"Riches beyond the dreams of avarice," Peter Collins said as he and Margaret left the room after the event. "Two hundred pounds."

"Truthfully, I did not expect any reward," Margaret told him.

"Nor did I," Peter agreed. "The Old Lady of Threadneedle Street is not known for her munificence. I shall practice no more equine dentistry." He put his hand on Margaret's arm, and she paused and turned to him. "I have an idea," he said lightly. "What do you say we combine our fortunes?"

"Really? And just how do you propose we do that?" she asked.

"Well, I thought, you know, ah–" He paused to gather his courage.

"If you were to see your way clear to marry me, don't you know, then we could, you know, that is..." His voice faded out.

"Are you proposing to me?" Margaret asked, surprised to note that her own voice was quavering slightly.

"I thought that's what I was doing," Peter told her. "But if you object or, you know, would rather not, why then I might very well have been speaking about something else. Fox hunting, perhaps. Although I must say I've never been overly fond of fox hunting; always seemed to see it from the fox's point of view, don't you know."

"You're burbling," Margaret said.

"Well, d-dash it, will you marry me or not?"

"For two hundred pounds?"

"Well, you know, if we put our rewards together, it would be four hundred."

"So we're to live on four hundred pounds and your income from the Indian police? Will we have to move back to India?"

"Well, no," Peter told her. "I've resigned my post. I think I'm going to be working for the Foreign Office, but I can't say just when I'll start, or what it will pay."

"Ah!" Margaret said. "Then are we to live on four hundred pounds?"

"I rather thought we'd use it for our honeymoon," Peter told her.

Margaret sighed very deeply. "You're not a very practical man," she said. "I think I'll have to keep the accounts when we're married."

Peter broke into a wide smile. "You will? Marry me, I mean."

"I suppose I'd better," she said. "I'll have a little money to—"

"Margaret, my dear," Peter interrupted, looking shocked. "You don't think I'd live off my wife's money, do you?"

"Men!" Margaret muttered.

"My father would never approve," he told her. "As I have an income of my own of twenty thousand a year, he would think it most unseemly were I to touch a penny of yours."

Margaret felt her eyebrows go up. "Twenty—"

"That's all, I'm afraid," Peter said. "My older brother George Linley Thomas, Viscount Hagsboke, will come into most of the estate. We can stay at the hall if you like, I have a suite of rooms, but

I rather think we'll take a flat in town, don't you?"

Margaret looked at him sternly. "This isn't more of your foolishness, is it?"

Peter shook his head. "No, I'm afraid it's mostly my great, great, great grandfather's foolishness. He was an admiral under Pellew. King George made him an earl, and he married an heiress. His descendants have enlarged the holdings, but it isn't really hard when you start with a large enough bundle."

Margaret stared at him for a long moment, and he looked embarrassed. "That doesn't bother you, does it? I mean, it doesn't make any difference, my having money?"

She shook her head. "I told my father I'd marry you rich or poor, and I guess I meant it."

"Oh, good," he said.

* * *

It was ten o'clock of a cool September morning when Mr. Maws, with the measured, stately tread of the true aristocratic gentleman's gentleman which he'd been practicing until it almost looked natural on his oversized frame, entered Professor Moriarty's study, a silver tray held up by the tips of the outstretched fingers of his left hand. "He's back," he said, lowering the tray so Moriarty could remove the calling card.

Moriarty took the card, looked at it, and snapped it between his fingers. "So he is," he said. "Show him in."

"That I will, sir," Mr. Maws said. "But don't you go haring off to India or noplace again. You get yourself into enough trouble right here in England to last a righteous man a lifetime or two."

"I appreciate your concern," Moriarty said. "But I fear no evil as long as I have your good right arm to protect me."

"But where was I when you was in mortal danger on that boat, I ask you? I can't do you much good if I'm butling in this here big house whilst you're off on a boat getting shot at, now, can I?" Mr. Maws flexed his broad shoulders. "I would have done them a bit of good if I'd been there, I tell you."

"And I missed you sorely," Moriarty told him. "Show Colonel Moran in, and then finish packing for our trip to the Moor. I want to try that new clockwork mechanism in the ten-inch refractor."

Mr. Maws nodded, and retreated. A minute later he ushered Colonel Moran into the room, sniffed, and left.

Moriarty waved Moran to a seat by his desk. "Back so soon?" he asked. "I didn't expect you for a couple of months yet."

"Little Pook wanted me to stay around a bit longer," Moran said. "He certainly did. But I had a hankering for Paris, so I left as soon as it wasn't downright insulting for me to get out. I plan to get me a suite at the Plaza and stay in Paris until I tire of it. And no man of my acquaintance has ever been known to tire of Paris. Any man who's tired of Paris is tired of life."

"If your interests are centered around gaming and the, ah, fair sex," Moriarty agreed, "that's certainly true."

"And the food," said the colonel. "Don't overlook the food. They don't know how to eat here in England. They chew, and they swallow, but they don't eat."

Moriarty laughed. "The cuisine won't go through your money quite as quickly," he said, "but I understand that enough rich food can ruin your liver."

"Perhaps, but what has my liver ever done for me?"

"And gaming and women can ruin both you and your digestion, leaving you unable to enjoy any of the three."

Moran raised an eyebrow. "My dear professor," he said. "Let me see if I understand this. You're warning me about indulging in these three most pleasurable vices because, if I do, eventually I won't be able to indulge in them any longer?"

Moriarty laughed again. "I guess that was one way to interpret what I was saying," he said. "Just ignore me and live your life as you please."

"Oh, I do—I will," Moran replied. "But in the meantime, I have something for you." He reached into his inner jacket pocket and tossed a large envelope across the desk to Moriarty.

The professor opened the envelope and withdrew a stack of Bank of England currency.

"Thousand-pound notes," Moran said, carefully picking just the right cigar from his silver case and rolling it between his palms. "There's twenty of them."

"Indeed?" asked Moriarty. "So the maharaja came through."

"Like a proper British gentleman," Moran said.

"I gathered that from your Parisian plans," Moriarty said, sliding a glass ashtray across the desk to Moran. "But it's nice to know I'm right."

"He said to me, 'I trust you kept your part of the bargain, and the Lady of Lamapoor was obtained without violence.'" Moran lit his cigar and puffed on it with a pleased expression on his face. "I told him as how she was surrounded by violence at the time, but it was not of our doing and we rescued her from it. He said as how he trusted me and would not ask for further details."

"It must be nice to be so trusted," Moriarty observed.

"Damn it to hell," said Moran. "If I'd known he wasn't going to check up on me, I would have just busted a few heads open to get the blasted Lady and not bothered telling him about it."

"You'd lie? Colonel, I am astounded!" Moriarty said.

"Yes, you are," said Moran.

"I, in turn, have something for you," Moriarty said. He opened a drawer in his desk and pulled out an engraved, embossed, sealed, and countersigned document. "It's an order on the Bank of England for five hundred pounds," he said, tossing it across the desk. "A reward for aiding in the safeguarding of their gold. How the directors arrived at the figure, I do not know. They weren't quite as munificent as Little Pook, but it will suffice."

"Indeed," Moran agreed. "And a like amount for you?"

"Twice that for me," said Moriarty.

Colonel Moran nodded. "That's a like amount," he agreed. "After all, you might say you saved the gold twice. Although, to tell you the truth, it did surprise me that you told the tale. Why not let Iskansen get away with his little scheme? It was no skin off our nose."

"It would have been," said Moriarty. "They were going to examine the statuettes."

"Ah!" said Moran. He tapped the ash from his cigar into the tray. "Did they ever find Iskansen?"

"He and the magicians have thoroughly disappeared. And not quite all the gold was recovered, so their larcenous striving was not entirely in vain."

"A well-planned endeavor deserves to be rewarded, I say," said Colonel Sebastian Moran. "And we've done quite well out of it ourselves."

"The directors were actually in quite a giving mood, all things considered," Moriarty said. "Holmes got a bonus on top of whatever he had been supposed to get for safeguarding the gold. Which, I suppose, in a backhanded way, he was doing even as Pin Dok Low. They awarded varying amounts to such of the Duke of Moncreith's Own Highland Lancers as were involved in the engagement, along with a stipend for the widows of the men who were killed. They even saw fit to include the Artful Codger and Cooley the Pup in their largesse; as well as a few hundred for Peter Collins," Moriarty said, "who will presumably be combining it with a similar amount given to the plucky Miss St. Yves. Collins and St. Yves are to be wed, I understand."

"A wonderful institution," Moran said, standing up and stubbing his cigar out on the large glass tray. "For those as are fond of institutions. I wish them both the pleasure of it."

"Indeed," said Professor James Moriarty.

"I'll be leaving for Paris almost immediately," Moran told him. "I can be reached through Cook's. If anything, ah, interesting crops up that's in my line, let me know."

"I shall," said Moriarty. "If you don't mind being dragged away from the City of Earthly Delights."

"Come, now," said Moran. "I do realize that there is more to life than gaming, dining, and wenching. I wouldn't want my skills, such as they are, to get rusty from disuse. Not entirely, at any rate. And associating with you is, if I may say so, a rare pleasure in its own right."

Moriarty chuckled. "I'll keep that in mind," he said.

Mr. Maws appeared in the office doorway with Colonel Moran's hat and coat. Moran shrugged into the coat and clapped the bowler firmly on his head. "Well, I'll be off, then," he said. "Ta, Professor. Or, as they say, *au revoir*."

"Goodbye, my friend," said Moriarty. "Take care."

"Oh, I shall, Professor," said Colonel Moran. "You can count on it." He started for the front door, and then paused and turned back. "I'm off to spend my nights in Paris," he said in a bemused voice, "and you're off to spend yours huddled in a greatcoat and woolen scarf peering through a bloody great telescope in the dank and dreary Moors." He shook his head. "And they say *you're* the genius!"

The sound of Moriarty's laughter followed Colonel Moran out onto Russell Square as he raised his stick to hail a passing hansom cab.

ABOUT THE AUTHOR

Michael Kurland is the author of more than thirty books, but is perhaps best known for his series of novels starring Professor Moriarty. The first volume, *The Infernal Device*, was nominated for an Edgar Award, and received stellar reviews, including this from Isaac Asimov: "Michael Kurland has made Moriarty more interesting than Doyle ever made Holmes." It was followed by *Death By Gaslight*, *The Great Game*, *The Empress of India* and *Who Thinks Evil*, published over a period of more than thirty years.

Kurland is also well known as a science fiction writer, and is the author of *The Unicorn Girl*, as well as the bestselling *Ten Little Wizards* and *A Study in Sorcery*, fair-play detective stories set in a world where magic works. He has edited several Sherlock Holmes anthologies and written non-fiction titles such as *How to Solve a Murder: The Forensic Handbook*. He lives in California.

THE PROFESSOR MORIARTY NOVELS
MICHAEL KURLAND

A sweeping and eloquent detective series featuring
Sherlock Holmes's nemesis, Professor James Moriarty.
Aided by an American journalist, Benjamin Barnett,
and his infamous network of informers, criminals and
'specialists', Moriarty reveals himself to be far more than
just "The Napoleon of Crime", working for both sides of
the law, but always for his own ends.

The Infernal Device
Death By Gaslight
The Great Game
The Empress of India
Who Thinks Evil

SHERLOCK HOLMES
The Will of the Dead

GEORGE MANN

A rich elderly man has fallen to his death, and his will is nowhere to be found. A tragic accident or something more sinister? The dead man's nephew comes to Baker Street to beg for Sherlock Holmes's help. Without the will he fears he will be left penniless, the entire inheritance passing to his cousin. But just as Holmes and Watson start their investigation, a mysterious new claimant to the estate appears. Does this prove that the old man was murdered? Meanwhile Inspector Charles Bainbridge is trying to solve the case of the "iron men", mechanical steam-powered giants carrying out daring jewellery robberies. But how do you stop a machine that feels no pain and needs no rest? He too may need to call on the expertise of Sherlock Holmes.

SHERLOCK HOLMES
The Spirit Box

GEORGE MANN

Summer, 1915. As Zeppelins rain death upon the rooftops of London, eminent members of society begin to behave erratically: a Member of Parliament throws himself naked into the Thames after giving a pro-German speech to the House; a senior military advisor suggests surrender before feeding himself to a tiger at London Zoo; a famed suffragette suddenly renounces the women's liberation movement and throws herself under a train.

SHERLOCK HOLMES
The Stuff of Nightmares

JAMES LOVEGROVE

A spate of bombings has hit London, causing untold damage and loss of life. Meanwhile a strangely garbed figure has been spied haunting the rooftops and grimy back alleys of the capital. Sherlock Holmes believes this strange masked man may hold the key to the attacks. He moves with the extraordinary agility of a latter-day Spring-Heeled Jack. He possesses weaponry and armour of unprecedented sophistication. He is known only by the name Baron Cauchemar, and he appears to be a scourge of crime and villainy. But is he all that he seems? Holmes and his faithful companion Dr Watson are about to embark on one of their strangest and most exhilarating adventures yet.

SHERLOCK HOLMES
Gods of War

JAMES LOVEGROVE

1913. The clouds of war are gathering. The world's great empires vie for supremacy. Europe is in turmoil, a powder keg awaiting a spark. A body is discovered on the shore below Beachy Head, just a mile from Sherlock Holmes's retirement cottage. The local police are satisfied that it's a suicide. The victim, a young man, recently suffered a disappointment in love, and Beachy Head is notorious as a place where the desperate and depressed leap to their deaths. But Holmes suspects murder. As he and Watson investigate, they uncover a conspiracy with shocking ramifications. There are some men, it seems, who not only actively welcome the idea of a world war but are seeking divine aid to make it a reality...

SHERLOCK HOLMES
The Army of Dr Moreau

GUY ADAMS

Dead bodies are found on the streets of London with wounds that can only be explained as the work of ferocious creatures not native to the city. Sherlock Holmes is visited by his brother, Mycroft, who is only too aware that the bodies are the calling card of Dr Moreau, a vivisectionist who was working for the British Government, following in the footsteps of Charles Darwin, before his experiments attracted negative attention and the work was halted. Mycroft believes that Moreau's experiments continue and he charges his brother with tracking the rogue scientist down before matters escalate any further.